"IT SEEMS LIKE I'VE SPENT THE PAST DECADE WAITING FOR YOU."

"Lord!" Venice breathed. "How can you say that to me? You don't even know me!"

"I know you like I know the rhythm of my heart."

"Who *are* you?"

A plunge in a mountain lake could not more effectively have robbed him of breath. *Venice didn't know who he was,* Noble realized. It was an odd sensation. As though all of his flesh was hardening into stone, while inside he was shattering into thousands of lethal, piercing shards.

She hadn't recognized him. But she'd allowed his touch. The touch of a sunburnt, rangy stranger . . .

Other **AVON ROMANCES**

DEVIL'S ANGEL *by Marlene Suson*
THE HEART AND THE HEATHER *by Nancy Richards-Akers*
MY LADY PIRATE *by Danelle Harmon*
NIGHT SONG *by Beverly Jenkins*
THE SAVAGE *by Nicole Jordan*
TEMPT A LADY *by Susan Weldon*
WILD FLOWER *by Donna Stephens*

Coming Soon

BELOVED DECEIVER *by Joan Van Nuys*
LAKOTA SURRENDER *by Karen Kay*

And Don't Miss These
ROMANTIC TREASURES
from Avon Books

LORD OF THUNDER *by Emma Merritt*
RUNAWAY BRIDE *by Deborah Gordon*
THIS FIERCE LOVING *by Judith E. French*

Anything for Love

Connie Brockway

AVON BOOKS ◆ NEW YORK

ANYTHING FOR LOVE is an original publication of Avon Books. This work has never before appeared in book form. This work is a novel. Any similarity to actual persons or events is purely coincidental.

AVON BOOKS
A division of
The Hearst Corporation
1350 Avenue of the Americas
New York, New York 10019

Copyright © 1994 by Constance Brockway
Inside cover author photo by Proex
Published by arrangement with the author
Library of Congress Catalog Card Number: 94-94325
ISBN: 0-380-77754-1

First Avon Books Printing: October 1994

AVON TRADEMARK REG. U.S. PAT. OFF. AND IN OTHER COUNTRIES, MARCA REGISTRADA, HECHO EN U.S.A.

Printed in the U.S.A.

RA 10 9 8 7 6 5 4 3 2 1

For Ruthie's girls,
My mother, Marcia,
And my aunts, Pat and Lois,
and
David and Rachel,
My love and my loveling

Prologue

Manhattan, 1862

It wasn't a slum ... quite. But the street was hard against the edges of the Lower East Side and tenements were stacked higher here. Smoke-blackened brick and wooden cliffs mounted up against the fume-dimmed sky. Down the concrete canyons a river of humanity streamed, eddied, and churned.

A man, his greasy palms rubbing over his huge belly in an obscenely comforting gesture, emerged from an alley. His red-rimmed eyes narrowed in his oily face as he watched a woman and a young girl of eleven or twelve pass by. Their clean, trim figures were out of place in the sea of dirty factory workers and ragged shop hands hurriedly slurping weak noontide tea beneath an even weaker autumn sun. The man's cruel gaze fixed with avid interest on the child. Casually, too casually, he matched his pace to hers, so intent on his quarry, he didn't notice the gangly teenaged boy who fell into step behind him.

Why should he? The boy, his head shorn, his clothes hanging from slender shoulders, could have been any one of thousands of immigrant brats. He was perhaps cleaner, his back straighter, but the wary, knowing expression on Noble

"Slats" McCaneaghy's old-young face was the same as those around him.

The girl and the woman turned into a less crowded side street. The fat man slipped behind a cart, his piggy eyes following their progress. Noble swore under his breath. He'd told Trevor Leiland time and again that the woman, Nan, wasn't fit to be a nursemaid to Venice, Leiland's only child. More and more often Nan returned here, where Leiland had originally found her and, with a characteristically grand gesture, taken her to Park Avenue, assuring her that a job would be her salvation. Noble knew better. Money couldn't buy freedom from an addiction and Nan was as confirmed an addict as Noble had ever seen.

When Noble had warned Leiland of it, Trevor had, with a tight smile and cold eyes, pointed out that Noble and his mother were prime examples of what his munificence could achieve. Three years ago, they had been little better than Nan. His mother, a newly immigrated Irish widow, had become Leiland's cook. And Noble, a streetwise brat, had been tutored right alongside Leiland's own daughter. Now nearly seventeen years old, Noble would soon begin studying at Yale . . . solely through Leiland's generosity.

Noble should have been grateful. He should have been down on his bloody knees. Instead, he was angry because of Venice, Trevor's vulnerable, unprotected little daughter. Because one day, one of Leiland's charity cases was going to get Venice hurt . . . or worse.

But it wasn't going to be today.

The fat man was flexing his arms. A few witless asses might have underestimated his strength, but Noble knew better. There was muscle enough beneath his thick, jiggling flesh. It would be easy for him to snatch Venice. She'd fetch a pretty penny in one of the higher-priced brothels. After the piggy man had sampled the wares, of course.

The thought made Noble ill. He'd known of twelve-year-old, even ten-year-old prostitutes, but they weren't ... children. Venice was. More innocent and sweet than anyone he'd ever known. And Noble, who'd never experienced a real childhood, wasn't going to let anyone destroy hers.

The man rubbed his beefy hands together, shouldering his way through the throngs of people: rag merchants pushing heaping carts, cigarette girls with nicotine-stained fingers and hard eyes, garment carriers, boiler tenders, pressmen, cash girls, and seamstresses. All singing the same song of need and hopelessness and desperation: "Buy from me, give to me, help me!"

Noble saw Venice pause in front of a battered storefront. Her dark head bent to study something behind the filmy glass display window. Nan, clearly bored, drifted further down the avenue, toward the gleaming wares on a vendor's jewelry cart. Noble could have gladly choked the stupid wench for abandoning Venice.

The fat man's thick, colorless lips stretched into a smile. Moving slowly, he waded through the rabble of human scavengers, his gaze fixed on Venice's petite figure. A few more steps and he'd be abreast of her. He shoved his hands into his pockets. One, Noble knew, would hold a rag for her mouth, the other a small lead-filled leather cudgel. He'd seen the trappings of this trade before. Quickly Noble slipped close beside him.

The man looked around, his gaze sliding complacently over Noble, as if certain he presented no threat. There was no one here who would try and stop him. There was no one here who was even going to care. All the faces were the same. Blank, numb, devoid of anything but hunger. Suddenly, the man made his move. Quickly, decisively, he surged forward, surprisingly light on his feet for someone so obese.

Noble was quicker.

He darted in front, blocking the man's way. His opponent stopped short, his protruding belly colliding into Noble. Noble stood his ground. The man frowned, deep lines scoring his oily forehead.

"Get outta here, ya friggin' gutter rat," he muttered, a note of confusion in his voice. Slum kids didn't defy those bigger than themselves. Not unless they wanted to meet their end kicked near to death by steel-toed boots in a back alley. Noble's interference unsettled him. *Good*, thought Noble. Standing toe-to-toe, their gazes met on an even level, though Noble was dwarfed by the man's massive girth. Noble didn't make any move to get out of the way.

"What d'youse want?" the man asked in a snarled whisper, obviously worried about alerting Venice, who was still studying the shop window a few yards away.

Still blocking the man's path with his lanky body, Noble jerked his head in her direction. With a calm he was far from feeling, he slowly shook his head, his eyes never leaving the man's face.

A vile curse issued from the man's contorted lips as he studied Noble, openly confounded by Noble's silent guardianship. He shifted on his feet, clearly uncertain what to do.

The obese man glanced at Venice. Once more, Noble shook his head. Words weren't necessary. The man already understood that if he tried to snatch Venice, Noble was going to try and stop him. Noble might not win, but he could fight like a junkyard dog. All slum brats could. And if the fat man tried to take Noble on first, Venice would still be alerted to her danger. Either way, he was going to lose and Noble was betting a lot of blood and bruises that the man would let the whole thing go. It was a bet Noble had made more than once on Venice's behalf. Usually, it was a bet he won.

Aiming a stream of viscous phlegm at Noble's scuffed boot, the man started to edge backward. Just before he'd turned completely, Noble heard Venice calling his name.

"Slats! What are you doing here?"

The fat man darted a glance back at Noble. Noble's eyes never wavered from his. If he'd turned his head when Venice had called, the man would have clubbed him with the "tickler."

Thwarted, the man shambled toward a recessed doorway. He stepped over crates and refuse choking the steps and disappeared into the dingy interior. Noble waited a full two minutes before deciding that the fat man had truly given up the hunt. From the corner of his eye he watched Venice approach. She laid her hand on his arm and looked up into his face, her piquant features filled with pleasure. Her mouth opened, but before she could speak, Noble cut her off.

"You're going home. Now."

The pleasure faded slowly from her eyes, replaced by hurt. Noble heard himself growl with frustration, feeling like a cur for destroying her delight. But, damn it, she'd better start learning to watch out for herself.

In a few months he'd be gone, leaving behind this squalid, hated city. He had dim memories of the emerald-clad mountains and sapphire skies of Ireland and he was going to find them again, or something like them. But he honestly didn't know if he could bring himself to leave Venice to her father's vainglorious preoccupation with saving the world, or the tender mercies of alcoholic nursemaids and licentious nannies. The thought of being unable to watch over her cut him like a knife. And it twisted his gut that nobody else seemed to give a damn whether or not she was safe.

"I don't know why the hell they let that woman drag you around down here."

"Nan doesn't drag me anywhere, Slats," Venice protested. "Please don't tell. It was entirely my idea. I begged." Tears filled her eyes.

Noble was having none of it. Even if Venice was too kindhearted, she was also far too overindulged. Half the problem with Leiland was that as soon as Venice started leaking tears, he allowed her anything. Anything as long as she didn't make a scene, didn't call attention. Anything but his time.

"It's true. I throw myself on your mercy," she said dramatically. "But . . . after hearing you once lived here . . . I just had to see what it was like."

"The bloody hell," Noble muttered. "I hope it has met all your lurid expectations. And now that your vulgar curiosity has been satisfied, you're going!"

Hurt and confusion made Venice's voice quaver. "It wasn't like that, Slats."

"Fine. Now we're going to find that . . . woman and get out of here. It isn't safe."

"All right. But I think you're overreacting. Nothing is going to happen. It's high noon. The streets are full of people." Her trusting, blissful, innocent smile made him feel immeasurably older than his seventeen years. "And you're here."

Noble grunted, took hold of her forearms, and spun her around. Gently, he shoved her ahead of him. "Go."

He didn't see the fat man slinking out of the

shadows, watching as they made their way along the thronged avenue. "And who the bloody hell do you think you are?" the fat man muttered under his breath. "Some sort of friggin' hero?"

Chapter 1

Denver, Colorado Territory
1872

The train's chief engineer stood on the number three platform of the Denver train depot, staring into the loveliest, saddest eyes he'd ever seen. Gray they were, like the wings of a mourning dove, soft as the mist stealing over the heather of his native Irish soil, and twice as heartrending.

The engineer sighed, resigned and enraptured. "Now, missy, don't ye cry. I'll do it. I'll make that extra run up from Denver to Salvage. I'll do it on me day off. Yer freight'll be delivered by midweek."

Like sunshine breaking through dark clouds, the young lady's eyes miraculously cleared. Delight glowed where only a second earlier there had been sorrow. She dashed the back of her hand across her damp cheeks.

"Oh, that's wonderful! I can't thank you enough, sir!" she exclaimed. "And while you're at it, might ye be doing me another teeny favor?" she continued. "Just a wee thing. Find me some champagne? I'm not sure this Salvage place has any."

Her lovely face was utterly radiant now. Remarkable recovery the little lady had made. The nagging suspicion that he'd been gulled crept into the engineer's mind. He narrowed his eyes on her.

8

She smiled back so brightly that he immediately dismissed the treacherous notion. The lass was a saint, she was. With a grin and a nod, the engineer hurried off to do the saint's bidding.

"Honey, you played him like a two-bit fish on a four-bit hook." A female voice, amused and awed, spoke from behind Venice Leiland.

Venice, caught rubbing her hands together in satisfaction, spun around, her dark hair flying about her shoulders. A woman in a green taffeta dress was regarding her from beneath an extravagant hat, the dyed wings of a hapless canary drooping over the brim. Her bleached hair, its color in no way outshone by the chromium yellow feathers above it, was curled on either side of a pretty, broad-cheeked face. Painted red lips were spread in an admiring grin.

Like an unrepentant kid, Venice's cheeks immediately dimpled. "Incorrigible, am I not?"

"I don't know nuthin' 'bout 'encouragin' ' but I'd wager you're a real lulu when you set your mind to it."

"Lulu?"

"Sure, honey. You know, a piece of work, hell on wheels, a real hayburner," the woman answered.

"Fascinating."

"I 'spect you could be that, too, if you'd a mind," the woman replied, sending a sharply assessing look up and down Venice's beautifully fitting jonquil-yellow dress.

"Miss Leiland?" A uniformed, becapped porter hurried over. "Is there anything at all I can do for you?"

"Are you really Venice Leiland? Trevor Leiland's kid?" the woman asked, something that might have been embarrassment entering her twanging drawl.

It was common knowledge that Trevor Leiland

owned half of New York City. More to the point, Trevor and his brother Milton were the principal trustees of the Leiland Foundation, the philanthropic organization that funded the Leiland-Hawkness Spur Line. The spur line that climbed seventy miles to the tiny town of Salvage, making it the most remote jumping-off point in the Rockies. Which made Salvage one hell of a profitable place to sell things. And Salvage just happened to be the site of the woman's new business, the Gold Dust Emporium.

The porter's gaze narrowed. Stepping in front of Venice, he shoved a finger under the other woman's nose. "Clear off, sister. Your sort ain't welcome here."

"Cayuse Katie is welcome everywhere!"

The porter took a threatening step forward.

"Ah, keep your shirt on, ya gandy dancing piece of buffalo wallow!" Katie huffed. Nonetheless, she adjusted the beribboned pelisse over her shoulders and kicked out her voluminous skirts, preparing to leave.

"What did you mean, 'keep your shirt on'? What's a 'gandy dancing piece of buffalo wallow?' " Venice asked.

Katie decided to humor the little lady. "Maybe I better introduce myself. Cayuse Katie Jones, ma'am. Native of the Rocky Mountains, owner of the Gold Dust Emporium, Salvage, Colorado Territory."

"You're a *native*? From Salvage?" Venice didn't wait for a reply. She placed both hands on Katie's shoulders and looked squarely into her surprised brown eyes. "Miss Jones, I have a great favor to ask."

The porter snorted. "I bet it ain't the usual 'favor' she gets asked."

Katie shot him a quelling glance. "Yeah?" she

prompted, turning her attention back to Venice. "What?"

"I came out here rather precipitously when the spur line employees wired to inform the foundation that my uncle hadn't been heard from in six months." Her worry for Milton's welfare, a worry that she had kept carefully under control, threatened to surface. She cleared her throat. "Not that this is particularly unusual, but Uncle Milton neglected to insure that the spur line payroll would be met during his absence. He handled all the finances for his expedition funds himself."

"Expedition?"

"Yes. My uncle is a paleontologist. That's what he's been doing in Salvage for the past seven years. Looking for fossils."

"Ah-huh." Katie was wearing a fixed expression of false interest with which Venice was all too familiar. She didn't elaborate. There was no reason to alarm anyone by revealing how close the foundation was to eliminating the funding for Milton's Rocky Mountain explorations. Even Uncle Milton was nearly ready to admit defeat and relocate his search for dinosaur bones. He'd written that he would spend a last season here, but unless he met with success, no more.

When Venice had read the letter from the spur line engineers, she'd realized that closing down the spur line would mean closing down Salvage. She'd been haunted by the conviction that the foundation was responsible for those people who depended on the spur line for their livelihood.

And then, Trevor had exiled her from New York, and Venice had formulated her plan—a plan that could benefit both Salvage and herself. Somehow she was going to find a way for this town to become fully self-sufficient.

In doing so, maybe she would garner some of her

father's respect. And if he respected her, he might be willing to allow her a say in the foundation's management. And *then* she could do something worthwhile with her life.

After their last disastrous interview, that possibility had seemed remote. Her father had all but accused her of purposely sabotaging his political aspirations. She was, he'd declared, just like her mother—a social disaster. Maybe, at one time she had done some outrageous things to get his attention, Venice conceded, but no more. She was a responsible and capable adult and she'd prove it. And Miss Cayuse Jones could help.

"You were saying?" prompted Katie.

"Miss Jones, I want to help Salvage. But to do so, I need to find out everything I can about the town. Its assets and debits. Its resources and lack thereof. I haven't had time to research the town's economic health. My father wanted me well away from New York during his campaign for a seat on New York's city council."

Katie's brow furrowed questioningly. Venice flushed.

"You see," she said, "the New York papers wrote these *stories* about my last African safari. They claimed I became a member of a cannibal tribe. Merely because I wore a certain artifact to a benefit ball." Venice stopped. Her lips trembled. "That necklace was *not* made of human bones!" she exclaimed. "They were baboon bones!"

Katie opened her mouth to reply, but Venice plunged ahead. "Within a month, I was a sensation. Unfortunately it isn't the first time stories had been written about me. But it was the straw that broke the proverbial camel's back. At the moment, my father can't *buy* a vote."

"I sorta doubt that," Katie said dryly.

"There is one thing, Miss Jones, that money cannot buy: the good opinion of the middle classes."

"Honey, don't I know it," Katie said feelingly. "But why are you telling me all this?"

"Why? Because I want you to feel sorry for me and grant me this favor," Venice answered ingenuously. "I have come out here hoping to put to rights the muddle in which my uncle has left the town. That's where you come in. I want you to tell me everything you know about Salvage. Everything."

"That's it? You just wanta talk?" Katie asked.

"Yes, talk and share my Pullman car, of course. Would you please consent to traveling the rest of the way to Salvage with me?"

Katie's grin in response to the porter's horrified gasp was instantaneous.

"Miss Leiland, please, you don't want to have the likes—" the porter stammered.

"Why, sure I will, Miss Leiland," Katie cut in.

"Wonderful! That is, if there is no Mr. Jones?"

"Oh, somewhere out there"—Katie motioned vaguely toward the north—"there is. But it ain't likely he's fool enough to show his face anywhere near me. That is, not if he 'spects to keep it whole," Katie said calmly, smiling at Venice's astonished expression. She didn't elaborate.

"Ahem. Yes. Indeed. My coach is just over here." Venice took Katie's arm, gently pulling her toward a Pullman car a few yards away. The porter leaped forward to open the brass-fitted door.

"And please, call me Venice, Miss Jones."

Katie lifted the hem of her green skirt and trod directly on the foot of the suddenly attentive porter, flashing him her own brand of dazzling smile as she swept past him into the coach. "Sure, Venice honey, anything you say."

* * *

The Salvage Ladies' Conviviality League—which included every decent woman in town, a grand total of nine—waited on the crowded, sagging depot platform. Like a line of soldiers awaiting inspection by an exacting commander, they stood grimly resolved to do their duty. Backs straight, eyes forward, they clutched their hand-tatted drawstring purses, cotton gloves hiding work-roughened hands, calico bonnets shielding noses from the intense mountain sun.

They were here to give Miss Venice Leiland the sort of reception a lady of her position demanded. After all, her family's philanthropic foundation supported the fragile artery on which Salvage's life depended, the Leiland-Hawkness Spur Line.

At the opposite end of the platform stood another group of women, in every respect as committed to conviviality as their sisters. Just a more tangible form of it.

Like a bizarre species of poultry, twenty-odd hurdy-gurdy gals roosted on the depot's fence rails in red satins and striped crepes, their hair twisted about like cunningly placed rats, their faces powdered and painted. They sounded like birds too, their constant clucking interspersed with an occasional shriek of raucous laughter. Most of them were there to see the lady who'd won the Gold Dust on a pair of aces: Katie Jones.

In between these two factions, spilling out into the streets behind the depot, stood the rest of Salvage, more or less. Three hundred and some men: miners, barflies, adventurers, outfitters, and prospectors. They milled uncertainly between the two groups of women, unwilling to align themselves too firmly with one or the other. Any perceived desertion and either bunch could make a man's life a living hell.

But damned if any man-jack of them was going

to miss the arrival of two of the most celebrated women in Salvage's short history: the new saloon owner, Cayuse Katie Jones, *and* Miss Venice Leiland who, the stories went, was wild as the wind, pretty as a mountain laurel, and smart as a whip.

It was the last metaphor that had Tim Gilpin, the *Salvage Clarion*'s editor, concerned. The problem was he *liked* living in Salvage.

Though it had been over a decade since Tim had heeded Greely's call and "gone west," he still maintained a few ties to the New York City newsroom where he'd apprenticed. He knew a great deal about the beautiful Miss Leiland, the most important being that Venice wasn't the flitterygibbet the newspapers loved to make her out to be.

Not only had she graduated magna cum laude from Vassar, but it was also rumored she'd administered the trusts for a few of the Leiland Foundation's smaller programs. Yup, even if no one else took the little lady's credentials seriously, Tim Gilpin did. He lifted a stubby, ink-stained finger and gnawed nervously at the nail.

He was in the process of starting on another fingernail when he heard his name being shouted. Standing on the balls of his feet, Tim craned his neck to see who'd hailed him. Anton and Harry Grundy, owners of the local mercantile, were lounging against the far wall, with big grins on their faces, a couple of ladybirds plastered against their respective sides.

"Timmy! Tim-im-mee!" hooted skinny, redhaired Harry, lifting a bottle and waving it around his head.

With a sigh, Tim elbowed his way through the crowd. He knew Harry would keep up that insistent hollering until Tim acknowledged him.

"Hello, Harry," Tim said. "Anton."

Anton, strong as a bull, half as smart, and twice as belligerent when drunk, squinted blearily from behind the buxom woman he held.

Neither of these two lads was especially long on brains, but because of their awe-inspiring sloth, it was hard to tell just how scarce of wits they really were. If they'd had any ambition at all, they would have been two of the wealthiest men in the territory. As it was, they were still plenty rich.

A few months after coming out West to seek their fortunes, they'd shown up on the porch of their uncle Zeb Grundy's mercantile. They were broke, drunk, and unrepentant. Zeb, who hadn't seen his only living relatives in years, took one look at his heirs, clutched his heart, and called for a pen. He was dead before he could change his will.

Four months later, the spur line opened. Within two years, Anton and Harry, the least likely to succeed couple of no-goods in the territory, were very rich men indeed.

"Which woman you come to get an eyeful of, Tim?" Harry asked with a wink and a leer.

"Son, you might just be looking at the end of the line when you fill your eyes with the likes of Miss Venice Leiland," Tim answered dolefully.

"What d'ya mean?" demanded Anton.

Tim clapped Anton on the back. "Wise up, Anton. The only reason Salvage exists at all is because for some reason a rich old man has decided something is waiting to be discovered in these mountains."

Harry smirked, drawing deeply on the bottle he lifted to his mouth. "He's been looking fer them ancient skeletons of his fer years now."

"Seven years. Seven years during which time Milton has been keeping open the spur line that supplies Salvage with the freight that makes this little town rich." Tim looked to see if his words were having any impact on the pair. Anton was blissfully slobbering over his liquor bottle and Harry was busily trying to peer down the front of his friend's dress.

Tim cleared his throat. "Now, his niece, Miss Venice Leiland, one of the Leiland Foundation's junior trustees, is arriving. It's time to ask yourself a question, lads. Do you think Milt's gonna find bones in them thar hills?"

" 'Course not," scoffed Anton. "Old Milty woulda found 'em by now if they'd been there to find."

"Exactly. Milt's already said he's pulling out next year unless he finds something worth sticking around for. Tell me, gentlemen, what do you think Miss Leiland is doing here?"

Anton and Harry stared blankly at him.

Tim sighed. "Let's put it this way. If you grub-staked a mine for seven years and finally went to see what the damned thing had got you and you found out the answer was a big fat nothing, what would you do?"

"Close down!" Anton and Harry yelled simultaneously, grinning hugely, certain they'd guessed the correct answer.

"Exactly." Tim took one look at their self-congratulatory smiles and shook his head, turning and walking back through the crowd.

The Grundy brothers' grins stayed in place for a full minute. They collapsed at roughly the same instant as comprehension slowly took root.

Harry pushed himself off the wall and grabbed Anton by the shirt collar, hauling him upright. "Come on, boy, we got plans to make."

"What kinda plans?" Anton asked.

"I don't know yet, but we better make 'em quick."

Katie settled back in the deep, tufted velvet settee and popped another candy into her mouth. For perhaps the hundredth time, she cast an appreciative glance around Venice's private coach. "I been in a couple of real fine houses in my day but this has 'em all beat." Venice smiled as she watched Katie's gaze tally up the red velvet curtains at the windows, the oriental carpets on the floor, the polished walnut sideboard by the wall, and the embroidered curtains hiding the bed at the far end.

"Nice. Real nice," she said.

"Thank you," Venice said politely.

"Yup, you got it all: money, looks, and brains. Lots of brains. Who'd a guessed that underneath that dainty little face was a natural born con artist."

"I beg your pardon?"

"I seen how you handled the engineer . . . and any other man what stumbles into your strike range. And you know what you're about, too. Last time you turned a man into a moon-faced idiot, you *winked* at me! Hell," Katie said, popping another chocolate into her mouth. "I oughta be paying for the honor of watching you in action. And I myself ain't no stranger to twisting men round my little finger!"

Venice nodded. "Mr. Jones."

"Him and others," Katie said vaguely.

"You and Mr. Jones had a fight?"

"Nope. No fight. You can't fight someone that ain't there. He and me, we just split up. Years ago."

"I'm sorry."

"Don't be. Shouldn't have got married to begin with. Oil and water, honey." She snorted derisively. "But that's what true love'll get you every time. How 'bout you? You married?"

"No. Not yet."

"Hey!" Katie straightened, flushing beneath her powder. "I'm sorry. You probably got some beau you're all googoo-eyed in love with."

Venice smiled and moved to a cherry vanity beside a window. "No. I'm not in love with anyone. My opinion of love is very similar to your own."

She lifted back the heavy embroidered drapes and gazed outside. "Tell me, Miss Jones, how can I gain the people's goodwill?"

Katie shrugged. "I don't know. I'd say build a church, but that seems a bit like suggesting the cat be let in the barn. I know! Throw a party. Everyone loves a party."

"I like parties, too."

"Sure," said Katie. "Make a big announcement. Be real 'howdy-boys' friendly."

"I can see why people choose to live here. It's lovely," Venice said, taking a last look at the panoramic view before seating herself in front of the vanity mirror and brushing her hair.

"Don't you have a maid or something to do that?" asked Katie.

"No. I had more than my share of maids when I was a child." Venice paused. "None of them stayed very long."

The old feeling of being left behind, like a piece of shabby clothing that was just too much trouble to bother packing, swelled inside Venice. With it rose unbidden the image of a thin lad with solemn brown eyes and a worried, angry expression. Even he'd left. Even after he'd promised not to. She gave her hair a vicious tug with the hairbrush, willing herself to let the past go.

The coach door swung open and the crowd at the Salvage train depot surged forward, eager to see the celebrated Miss Venice Leiland. But everyone stopped like befuddled sheep when two ladies instead of one descended the short flight of steps. There was no way to tell which one was Venice Leiland.

Both wore bright, feminine dresses. Both had on hats. The younger, brunette one was a bit more disheveled looking. Her inky locks fell in a tangle of tight ringlets down her back while the blonde woman's saucy curls tickled her round, ruddy cheeks. Both were pretty; the slight, pale-skinned gal perhaps more delicate, but the blonde was very womanly with soft curves and pink skin.

The blonde lady came down the steps first, leaving the darker one to stand at the top of the stairs. Miss Leiland would exit first, wouldn't she? The crowd milled uncertainly.

The small, dark-haired woman took a step forward. A hush fell over the mob. In a husky, rich voice she called out, "Howdy, Salvage! How would you like a party?"

Howdy? No further evidence was required. As one, the Salvage Ladies' Conviviality League swarmed forward to encompass the very lovely, very blonde "Miss Leiland."

Chapter 2

Two days later, Venice sat in the Pay Dirt Saloon, perched in front of a plate of coagulating, lard-fried eggs. Drumming her fingers on the table, she stared at Tim Gilpin.

"Your mother died when you were . . . ?" the editor asked.

"A child."

"And yet, even though your father is one of the country's most sought-after bachelors, your mother's memory has kept him from remar—"

"Mr. Gilpin," Venice said, cutting him off, "enough. I have answered nearly every one of your questions. I have done this fully cognizant that my words may not be printed in context, and will undoubtedly be altered to foster whatever ridiculous notion about me you wish to convey. I have been subjected to the press's tender mercies before. I have spoken to you as a favor and now I expect you to return it. Where are my uncle's records of the Leiland Foundation account?"

Tim squirmed. Once little Miss Vassar here got wind of how much cash her ditsy old uncle had wasted searching these God-forbidden mountains—not to mention all the freight that had been shipped up free of charge on the spur line—she'd be sure to pull her family's cash outta Salvage faster than a dog pulls his head outta a skunk's hole. And everyone in Salvage knew it.

"It isn't as if anyone has any desire to actively hinder your attempts to ascertain the Leiland Foundation's financial involvement in Salvage, Miss Leiland," he said reproachfully.

She braced her slender arms on the table, leaning even farther forward so that their noses were separated by a mere hand's width. "You'll excuse me if I evince something less than confidence in your assurances, Mr. Gilpin," she purred, "but since arriving in this *place* two days ago, I have been repeatedly *hindered*. First, I find my uncle's home occupied by a skunk who, at your sheriff's gentle eviction—I believe he threw some empty liquor bottles at it—left behind a decidedly olfactory memento, making the house completely uninhabitable. Next, when I seek lodging, I find that the dear, 'convivial' ladies of town haven't a single bed to spare and the only solution anyone can think of is to ship me back to Denver. Only the 'notorious' Miss Katie Jones is willing to provide me accommodations."

"She's got plenty of rooms," Tim muttered. "Or, leastwise, beds."

Venice ignored him. "And now, *now* Mr. Gilpin, I find not one soul—and here, Mr. Gilpin, I make an enormous leap of faith in ascribing souls to beings barely on a nodding acquaintance with soap—not one soul in town has the vaguest notion of where my uncle has gone, where his records are, or even where the Leiland account is held!"

The editor looked miserable but no closer to givings her information than before. Venice took a deep breath and modified her tactics. "Mr. Gilpin, I have never had such a hard time prying loose information." Venice smiled, tilting her head at the angle that usually made men respond to her as though she were some adorable lap dog in need of spoiling. From the next table, she heard something clatter to the floor.

She lowered her lids, fluttering her lashes. The person at the next table begged the Lord for mercy. The editor looked glassy-eyed.

Venice suddenly felt herself flush. Lately her own ridiculous posturing had grown more and more repugnant to her.

Deliberately closing her fist around the lapel of Tim's jacket, she pulled him forward, surprising herself with the strength her ire lent her. "Why is everyone being so *difficult*?" she exploded. "I've tried to be civil. I thought a er, *fandango*? would be a nice way to introduce myself. Only to find I am being boycotted by your Convivial Ladies for inviting 'undesirable elements' like Miss Cayuse Katie Jones to the party.

"Not that I care, Mr. Gilpin." She blinked her eyes dry. She refused to cry. "Not that I care," she repeated forcefully. "But it seems to me a prodigiously self-destructive thing to do. Though coming from a population of people who actually have chosen to live in this malodorous, festering hellhole, one can hardly be surprised."

"Honey," Tim whispered in an awed voice, "you've got a fancier line of patter than a French whore has underwear."

Venice's eyes grew round. Tim's hand shot up and clamped over his mouth. Above the broad gag of his palm, he stared mortified at Venice. For a full thirty seconds, they sat frozen. And then she laughed, a full-throated, infectious sound.

"I know," she admitted through her laughter. "It's a terrible habit. Happens every time I get upset. I just mouth the grandest damnations I can think of. Nothing but a spoiled brat having a tantrum. At least," she said, and her smile grew gentle, "that's what a boy I once knew claimed."

"I didn't mean it as a criticism," Tim hurried to assure her. "You have a lovely flair for editorial expression."

Venice laughed again. "I don't like newspapermen very much, Mr. Gilpin, so don't try buttering me up. I'm the one who'll do the buttering around here."

"Miss Leiland, I'd as soon have your salt as your butter."

"Humph!" she snorted, charmed in spite of herself.

"I'll quit my job, burn down the office, destroy the press. Just promise not to change the perfect prose propounding your pique. Don't edit one phrase, not one word."

"Amen!" said the masculine voice that had earlier entreated the Almighty. Venice swung her head around. A young man sat at the table next to them, his chin cupped in his hand, his eyes glazed over, and a beatific, lopsided grin spread across his freckled face.

"Did you say something, young man?" Venice asked.

"Yes'm. I said 'amen,'" the youth drawled unabashedly. With a dirt-rimmed thumb, he tipped his hat back on his head, revealing a scalp covered by pale hair as fine and short as a newborn kitten's pelt.

Memories of Slats, his head similarly shorn, flowed from Venice's memory. He'd looked something like this young man: gangly, loose-limbed, like a piece of taffy that had been pulled too thin—pale and taut.

"And just what were you saying 'amen' to, young Farley?" Tim asked indignantly.

"Whatever you was sayin', if'n what you was urgin' the lady here to do was to keep on talking. I didn't understand the half of it, ma'am, but I sure like listening to it. Anythin' that keeps that high-tone sauce rollin' outta that pretty mouth of yours gets my vote."

"Blaine Farley, are you getting fresh with Miss Leiland?" Tim demanded.

Blaine snapped bolt upright in his chair, as though face-kicked by a mule. "No, sir, I am not," he shot out. "I wouldn't offend Miss Leiland here for the mother lode. Swear to gawd, I wouldn't."

The boy's distress was so evident, Venice couldn't help taking pity on him. "And none was taken, Mr. Farley."

Clearly, she wasn't going to get any useful information from the editor. At least not today. She rose, brushing crumbs from her skirts. "I hope you will be able to come to my party . . . Mr. Farley."

The young man stumbled to his feet. Tim scrambled to get upright first.

"Good morning to both of you gentlemen," Venice said. Noting that Tim was attempting to shoulder Blaine aside and Blaine was making some sort of noise that sounded like a snarl, she quickly backed out the door.

Venice grabbed the hitching post in front of Grundy's Mercantile and clambered off the boardwalk, dropping a full twenty inches to the dust-choked street below. The clomp of sturdy boots drew her eyes up to three women marching determinedly toward her. They didn't pause, only nodded curtly as they passed.

None of the Convivial Ladies would have a thing to do with her. She'd tried to explain she hadn't been laughing at them, but at herself, for mistaking her for Katie. She wasn't so bold as to expect their friendship, but was a mutual regard too much to ask? She'd truly been looking forward to throwing a party for the careworn ladies and the hard-eyed men of this town. Until an anonymous note had arrived at the Gold Dust Emporium stating that proper ladies, no matter what their family's fortunes, did not consort with "women of ill-repute." The thought of that poorly worded missive still made her angry.

The Gold Dust Emporium, where she was heading, had the distinction of being the only bona-fide two-story building in town. The original owner, a homesick southern gentleman, had spent his last dram of gold wrapping the entire second floor with a Dixie-style verandah. Venice could see brilliantly dyed feather boas hanging like pennants from the upper railings and sequin-studded garments strewn over the peeling banisters, winking luridly in the brilliant morning light.

As she was about to cross the rut-scarred road, something flew past her ear. Absently, she swatted at it. Bugs were a given in any of the more unpleasant areas of the world—Calcutta, Cairo ... Salvage. The straw brim of her hat pitched forward over her eyes as one of the demons hurtled into its crown. "Bloody monster," muttered Venice, readjusting her bonnet. Something thunked solidly into her thickly padded bustle.

That was no bug.

She wheeled around, the motion dislodging a quarter-sized pebble from the folds of her dress, dropping it at her feet. Someone was pegging rocks at her! If it hadn't been for the bustle, she'd be wearing a bruise on her ... Eyes narrowing, Venice looked around for her assailant. There was nowhere to hide except behind the huge boulder that marked the northern boundary of the town. Resolutely, Venice stalked its perimeters.

No one was there, but her attention was caught by signs of recent digging. Obvious pickax marks formed a shallow pocket in the rock. Someone had filled in part of the indentation with a crude form of cement: What appeared to be—Venice leaned closer for a better look—a *bone* stuck out at odd angles from the moist mixture.

Tentatively, Venice extended her fingers toward what looked to be a tiny ribcage and then, as a precaution, drew on a leather glove. Gingerly, she tugged at the object. The mortar dropped in damp, gravelly clumps as she pulled the object free.

Venice shivered. The skeletal portions of two separate species lay in her hand. The body looked like some sort of rodent, but the head was definitely a bird's, possibly a crow's. What made it so revolting was that someone had fitted the bird's head onto the rodent's body, securing it with a twist of wire threaded through the base of the skull. The wire was all but invisible until you turned the gruesome thing over.

Somewhere in this town lurked some mighty disturbed children. Or perhaps, Venice thought, some perverse cult. The thought raised gooseflesh on her arms.

"Yuk!" She dropped the grizzly little body on the ground and hurried to the Gold Dust Emporium.

High above, their bellies pressed flat to the sheared-off top of the boulder, Anton and Harry Grundy watched the eastern gal drop their "fossil" like it was fresh dog crap and scoot off toward the Gold Dust.

"Well, what the hell do you think got into her?" asked Anton, rising to his knees as the saloon door slammed shut. "Do ya think she bought it?"

Harry's face twisted into an expression of contempt. He snatched the hat from his head and whacked his baby brother across the face with it.

"Jes' shut up, Anton!" he hissed, flopping over

onto his back and commencing to pick his nose. "I got more thinkin' to do."

"Hey, Venice," Katie mumbled morosely, dragging a straw broom across the floor.

"Miss Jones," Venice answered politely.

Katie tossed down the broom and wiped the sleeve of her kimono across her eyes, smearing last night's application of kohl into a muddy band. Plucking a soggy, half-spent cheroot from the sawdust-covered floor, she twirled it consideringly between her fingers, then reached into her pocket for a match and flicked her thumbnail across the head, setting it aflame. Inhaling, she caught Venice's expression of disgust and shrugged.

Venice's stomach, already primed on greasy eggs and the smell of stale smoke, rebelled. With a quavery smile, she edged past Katie and hurried upstairs to her room.

The last tenant's fragrance—an overpowering mixture of frangipani and lilacs—clung to the horsehair fainting couch and permeated the threadbare pile of the red velvet bed curtains. Venice's stomach lurched.

Pulling open the door to the second-story verandah, she scooted outside. She closed her eyes and took deep, even breaths. Better. Slowly, she opened her eyes. Immediately, she squinted. Facing west, the verandah was dark beneath its overhanging roof, slanting a long early-morning shadow into the field behind the Gold Dust.

The striped tents Venice had ordered for the party were scattered across the meadow. The eye-dazzling sunlight shimmered off their white canopies. A breeze found her, bringing with it the fragrance of the high, pine-rich mountains and ice-cold creeks.

So much beauty, thought Venice, her gaze trav-

eling from the carpet of sweet spring grasses to
the gleaming tops of snow-capped mountains. She
moved forward. So lovely and tranquil. If only
you didn't have to turn around and confront the
loud, stench-riddled, happily squalid sight of Salvage.

She was approaching the railing when she heard
the sound of splashing water. Stopping, she angled backward, moving deeper into the shadows.
She wasn't ready to be ogled by yet another slack-
jawed man. Despite her familiarity with such attention, Venice shied away from it.

The splashing continued and after a moment
Venice stood on tiptoe to catch a glimpse of whoever was gurgling, bubbling, and spluttering
down below. She slid a foot forward until she
could see the corner of a horse trough. Another
step forward and she could see a strong, tanned
hand holding on to the splintered wooden rim.
Half a tread, and she saw a powerful wrist followed by a long, bronzed forearm, tendons
stretched and delineated beneath the fine golden
skin. A stride and Venice stopped, as though she'd
just run full tilt into a blow to her stomach.

There, arms braced on either side of the trough,
just about to plunge his head once more into the
muddy, grass-flecked water, was the most extravagantly masculine *being* Venice had ever seen. Teak-
hued muscle banded the shallow bed of his spine,
rippling and flowing as he leaned his forearms on
the trough's rim. His pose stretched his faded
denim trousers low beneath his corrugated flanks,
revealing a contrasting strip of pale flesh, testify-
ing to a complexion varnished by years of intense
mountain sunlight. He straightened, shaking his
head. Long ropes of antique-gold-colored hair flew
out, scattering beads of water across his wide,

sloping shoulders. The air left Venice's lungs in a gentle whoosh.

He was a Greek Olympian, a satyr, a pagan deity, and a Christian saint all in one. Casually, he toweled off the glistening water trailing over his muscled chest, a chest as cleanly smooth as burnished metal, just as unyielding and twice as inviting. She'd read about attraction so intense, so spontaneous, as to be frightening. She'd dismissed the accounts as exaggerations. More the fool she. His magnetism was palpable.

The man twisted, looking for something on the ground, and Venice thumped feebly on her breastbone, hoping to induce her lungs to start working again. A tiny hiss of inhaled air had just managed to make its way past the constriction in her throat when the man turned back toward her. He flipped a chambray shirt over the hitching rail and began a leisurely, languorous, and—in Venice's opinion—absolutely carnal stretch.

Lifting his arms high above his head, he interlocked long, lean fingers, pushing upward, deliberately lengthening the ladder of sleek ribs on first one side and then the other. The tendons and sinews beneath his skin flexed and relaxed, dancing across the flat, washboard belly, rippling through the taut forearms.

There was no way such a physical ideal could contain a mind worthy of it, she thought. Please, don't ruin it by doing something stupid, Venice silently begged the man. Like talking.

She withstood the sensual onslaught for forty seconds before, with an audible gulp, she inhaled. The man's arms fell. Instantly, he dropped into a half-crouch, swiveling lightly on the balls of his feet, turning his face upward into the bright morning sun to scan the balcony.

His face was as beautiful as his body. Jaw,

cheek, and forehead were cleanly defined and perfectly proportioned. Because he was squinting directly into the morning sun, she couldn't make out the color of his eyes, but his brows were dark and his eyes were shadowed by what had to be thick lashes. His mouth was wide, firmly curved, his upper lid notched directly beneath his only physical imperfection, his nose. Though it was long and elegant, midway down from the high bridge it had been broken, and was now slightly askew. It didn't matter. His nose only accented the flawlessness of his other features.

"Someone up there?" the man asked.

Venice sighed, a soft sound of pure pleasure. His voice was as perfect as the rest of him, well modulated, a hint of intriguing raspiness coloring the deep timbre.

"Come on, out with you!" he demanded.

Venice tried to speak. An odd liquid sensation flooded her limbs. Her heart, thumping in erratic counterpoint to her breathing, didn't seem to be working properly. She wondered vaguely if she was having some sort of attack. All she could do was stare, beguiled and bewitched, at the provoked male beneath her.

With a sound of annoyance, the man wrenched the shirt from the rail and started to push an arm through a sleeve. Overwhelmed by the fear that he was going to cover all that wonderful sculptured flesh, Venice, without conscious volition, pursed her lips and let loose a low, clear, absolutely unmistakable whistle of appreciation.

The man's head snapped up. This time Venice caught the flash of amber-colored eyes as his gaze moved across the verandah, seeking her. An expression of puzzlement replaced his wariness. He punched his other arm through a sleeve. Venice sighed.

"Why do you want to go and do that for?" she said softly, not recognizing the low, throaty drawl as her own, certain she had lost her mind but unable to stop the words from coming. "You're so . . . so . . . *pretty* just as you are!"

The words arrested him in mid-motion. He stood still; not a nerve twitched. Slowly, captivatingly, a boyish smile spread across his face. A quiver of pure attraction nearly brought Venice to her knees. With a shrug, the man pulled the shirt off and casually tossed it over the rail. Looking up, he parted his lips. His straight teeth gleamed whitely.

"Lady," he drawled on a grin, "you ain't seen nothin' yet."

Chapter 3

The water in the trough, warmed by its few brief hours in the sun, had soothed Noble McCaneaghy's tired body, sluicing off the topmost layer of grime. But its balm hadn't even begun to compare to the one provided by the unseen woman on her shadowed balcony. No woman had ever whistled at Noble before. Winked, beckoned—if he was lucky—but never whistled.

It was a little unnerving to be the recipient of such a bold advance. For a second, the specter of his Irish Catholic mother stood stolidly aghast at such brazenness. Without much of a second thought, Noble banished her spirit back to Schenectady and her third, and hopefully last, husband.

Hell, Noble thought, grinning up at the dark form on the balcony, maybe I don't look as awful as I feel. The thought made his smile stretch wider. He had raced down out of the mountains determined to arrive back in Salvage in time to send his report on to Washington via the spur line. Now the throaty whispered approval of the unseen, fallen angel above him was going some way toward making up for that godawful trip.

The way he saw it he had two choices: stand here basking in the open admiration of a soiled dove with enough expertise in matters of masculine desirability to make any man's head swell with conceit, or drag his sorry rump around Salvage looking for a gallon of axle grease and a cake of lye to burn, blister, and delouse his hide. It really wasn't much of a choice at all and he made it the moment the woman called him pretty.

Noble knew she was a whore; after all, she was in a whorehouse. Yet, there was something so inexplicably ingenuous, and at the same time so unexpectedly sensual, about that simple whistle. And her voice, bless her heart, sounded as wholesome and unsophisticated as any girl sighing over her first crush.

What did it matter that it was all a show? She made him feel as young and guileless as Blaine Farley. And he hadn't felt that young in a long, long time.

What the hell, Noble thought, enjoying the game.

He lifted his right arm, making a fist. His biceps bulged creditably. Frowning in concentration, Noble clenched his fist tighter, willing the muscle to more impressive proportions. He was rewarded by a fluttery, utterly feminine gasp from above. One corner of his mouth lifted, a deep dimple scoring his lean cheek.

Throwing himself into the unaccustomed role, Noble raised his other arm and, taking a deep breath, pumped both arms simultaneously. His biceps swelled into hard, prominent ellipses. Noble, who'd never displayed himself like this before, took a covert glance at his arms. His dark brows rose in surprise. Not bad for a rangy, weather-beaten ex-soldier. He was even a mite impressed himself. Not bad at all. As if in agreement, the woman sighed again with satisfaction.

"You look just like a statue in a museum!"

What a crock, Noble thought, amused. Where had this kid come up with a line like that?

Chances were she wouldn't know a museum if she walked into one. But her voice was so convincingly awe-filled he couldn't help but smile.

"Sure, honey, a gol-durn Michelangelo, right?"

"Oh, yes!"

His swagger was short-lived. A sudden cramp drilled through the quivering muscle of his right arm. With a grimace, Noble dropped it, shaking the charley horse out as he searched his memory for more ways to amuse the little lady.

The only strong man Noble had ever seen had been a Romanian in a traveling medicine show. The bald-headed giant had gone through all sorts of contortions and displays of strength as the spielman toted the benefits of Kickapoo Indian Elixir of Manly Principles.

Noble wasn't about to start bending metal rods in his teeth, but he thought he could remember enough to keep his audience entertained. He clasped his hands in front of his chest and, praying that *something* would happen, pushed his palms together.

Something happened.

His pectoral muscles leaped into sharp, dramatic relief, corded veins throbbed into life, snaking in thick ropes over his upper torso. Up above him, the lady's sigh turned a moan.

Feeling the muscles in his back burn with his effort, Noble turned around, fervently hoping his back was worth looking at. Apparently it was.

"Oh my God, have mercy!" It was a whisper so rife with promise Noble's concern in keeping the lady entertained took an immediate and decidedly different bent.

"What do you say, darlin? Should we play a different sorta game?"

"Different?" she asked wonderingly. "You mean there's more?"

"Oh, I'm pretty sure I can come up with something."

"Then yes, I'd like that."

"Honey," Nobel chuckled. "I haven't any clue where you learned to sigh like that, but you could make a fortune on stage in Chicago."

"Oh, my! I assure you my appreciation for your physique is quite, quite real."

Physique? Appreciation? The kid must have gotten hold of a dictionary somewhere. Would probably add a couple bucks to her fee. Quite the little entrepreneur.

"Could you . . ." Her voice lowered seductively. "Do something more now?"

His grin broadened. "I can only try."

"Would you? Please?"

"Hell, honey, I'm the one who should be saying please. And, in answer to your question, yes," he said, surprising himself. Though he liked women as much as any man who'd spent too many years without regular feminine company, this would be the first time he ever paid for a bed companion.

The girls in the New York tenements had taught him early the sort of desperation that drove a woman to accept money for sex. He'd just never gotten over the notion that there ought to be more between a man and a woman than a layer of sweat and a ten-dollar bill.

But hell, he was tired and hot and, for a while, the girl on the balcony had made him forget that even though he'd nearly broken his neck getting to Salvage before the train left, the bill he'd been working to get Congress to pass might still be defeated. Maybe, if she was as pretty as her voice and as amenable as her sighs, maybe, just this once, he'd be willing to pay for the privilege of sweet, convenient oblivion.

Grabbing his shirt, Noble dragged his arms

through the sleeves. He didn't bother buttoning it. If things went the way he expected them to, he'd be taking it off in a few minutes anyway. With a grunt, he rolled an empty rain barrel under the overhanging balcony.

"Where'd you go?" the woman asked.

"Never you fret, honey, I'll be up directly," Noble said, pitching his tone seductively low, all traces of his Irish accent buried in a slow western cadence.

"Up?" It was a dreamy, unfocused query.

"Yes'm. Directly." With a catlike leap, Noble sprang on top of the upended barrel and reached up to grasp the bottom of the two balcony rails. He leaned back, testing his weight against the narrow pickets. They'd never hold. Instead he grabbed the overhanging floorboards.

"What are you doing?" she asked, clearly surprised.

"I'm coming up to show you the other things I can do. Like you asked."

"I did not ask!"

"Sure, hon," Noble muttered, concentrating on finding a handhold that wouldn't fill his palms with splinters.

"You can't come up!"

"Nuthin' to it, ma'am," Noble assured her.

"You can't!"

"Sure, I can." With a grunt, Noble hoisted himself eye level with the bottom of a soiled periwinkle blue hem. Periwinkle. He'd always been partial to that color. "See? You just go plump the pillows and I'll just swing on up—hey!"

He was in the act of tipping his head back to look up at her when the blue hem swished forward in a flurry of dirty lace and scruffy satin ribbons. A dull black boot shot out and, without a word of warning, stomped directly on his hand.

Yelping, he snatched his injured fingers away, catching his weight with his other hand. For a long moment he hung suspended by one arm, swinging six feet above the ground, flailing for a handhold and cursing a blue streak. Then he felt his fingers slipping. With a final, thunderous blasphemy, he fell, crashing into the rain barrel, his head ricocheting off the hard-packed dirt before finally coming to rest.

He lay sprawled there for a moment, flat on his back, watching the brilliant sun execute a mad fandango around the sky. Gingerly, he probed the corner of his mouth with his tongue, tasting the salty tang of blood. Overhead, a blurry figure swam. Long hair. She had long, dark hair.

"Are you all right?" she called anxiously.

She couldn't be serious.

"I just . . . I didn't want you . . . I never thought you would . . . you shouldn't have . . ." she sputtered.

She didn't *want* him?! He moaned and rolled over.

"I'm so sorry."

No. *He* was sorry!

"Say something!"

"Lady," Noble roared, lurching to his knees, "did you ever consider trying a simple no?!"

Above him, the door slammed shut.

Venice pressed her back to the door. From the lean, pantherish look of him, her hundred pounds wasn't going to be much of a barrier should the man decide to come in. The thought kicked Venice's already racing heart into a full gallop. She squeezed her eyes shut and listened to the man bellow at her. Against all reason, she found herself hoping he'd try climbing the balcony again, if only so she could watch the play of muscle in his long arms and chest.

She heard his voice—or rather his bellow—fade away and sighed. There. She'd done it again. Impetuously courted trouble and then been stupidly surprised when trouble climbed her balcony.

Her shoulders drooped. Her father was right. Given her well-documented reputation for impulsiveness, any decent, intelligent man would no more seek her company than that of a rabid baboon's. And there was no saying that the man who'd just stomped away was either decent *or* intelligent. And what matter if he was? He was as far removed from her world as those pine trees on top of the mountain were from New York City.

Before long, she would no doubt be married to one of the men her father had chosen, someone of her own social order, someone who would add prestige and profit to the Leiland Foundation. It was her duty to wed such a man. After all, as Trevor often reminded her, they both knew what disaster came of marrying out of one's class.

But she had hoped to become an asset to the foundation *before* she wed, so that she would have something of value to fill her life, something besides the tiresome round of teas and balls and luncheons that filled many a wealthy woman's calendar. If she didn't prove herself by the time she married, there would be no chance to do so afterward. Like her father, most husbands would take a dim view of her "administrative pretensions." Unless she had already proved her worth.

Unexpectedly, this latest "scandal" had bought her some time. Just before she left New York, Trevor had warned her that it would be months before any promising marital prospect would risk social suicide by courting her. And that meant she had months to prove her capabilities. She might have months, but she'd best begin now.

She pressed her ear against the door, afraid to peek out the window. He was gone, probably for good. Determinedly, she tucked the experience away, vowing not to waste any more time on useless speculation. But she couldn't help whispering, "If only . . ."

"Geez, McCaneaghy, you look like shit," Blaine Farley said cheerily as Noble hobbled into the Pay Dirt.

"Shut up, Farley." Noble said without rancor, easing himself into a chair across from the younger man. His mother's novenas had finally been answered, he thought. Why else would a prostitute have a sudden attack of conscience after going through all the trouble of getting his, er, interest up?

At least there'd been no witnesses to the debacle.

"Maybe you graybeards oughta take yourself a little con-ve-les-anse and leave this territory to us younger fellers," Blaine said. "I don't know why you're so damned set on making this here territory into some gi-gantic *park*. There's plenty of them back east just waitin' fer you and your picnic basket. The Rockies is a country made for explorers and adventurers, not bicycles. There's gold yet to be found up here and I aim to get my share."

"No one's found gold in these mountains in ten years, young fool. Gold's been played out." Noble tilted his chair back on two legs.

"What you been doin' up in the mountains this time, Noble? Geez. I thought you'd finished all that work fer the senators. Was you pressing daisies?"

Noble snorted.

"Come on, tell," Blaine demanded. "I'm interested. Really."

"Okay. I was counting the number of species in a particular quadrant so I could document a sample population. The men sponsoring the federal bill that's gonna create a national park out here needed some last-minute information."

"Gee, that sounds like fun."

Noble ignored Blaine's sarcasm. "Yeah. Until a couple bear cubs ripped into my gear and spread it all over the eastern range."

"I was wondering why you look like hell." Blaine laughed. "That why you're wearing that rattail shirt? They got *all* your gear?"

"Yup." Catching the eye of the big, buxom woman behind the counter, Noble shouted, "Bring me a cup of coffee—and make it real coffee, Sal, or I'll fudge you the entire bill, swear to God I will—a half-dozen fried eggs, some sort of meat you don't have to scrape the mold off, and a loaf of bread."

"Don't have no baked bread, got fry bread. Got nothing but elk jerky, ain't got no real coffee, and if'n you fleece me, I'll break your ugly Irish neck. So don't try sweet talkin' me, Noble McCaneaghy."

Blaine snickered. "You got a way with women, that's all there is to it, Noble. It's just an out-and-out gift."

"Aw, shut up, Farley." Noble's hand shot out, cuffing the boy's hat just hard enough to knock it from his head. Slowly, Noble leaned forward in his chair, staring at his young friend's close-shaven head. "Judas Priest, Blaine, you've been scalped!"

The boy's face turned bright red. "Not everyone wants hair so long you can hang yerself with it. Anyway, I had to. Turned up lousy."

Noble waggled his finger under Blaine's nose, *tsk*ing sanctimoniously. "I warned you about bawdy houses, Blaine. I distinctly recall warning you."

The boy's color deepened to a burning, raw crimson. Noble, conveniently ignoring the itch under his own arm, hooted with laughter. "Listen, son, if all you took away from that bed was a little extra company, you're doing pretty good."

Sal waddled by, slammed two steaming mugs on the table without stopping, and passed on.

"Noble." Blaine leaned forward. "I ain't never gonna go to one of them places again."

"Yeah?" Noble grimaced as the bitter brew scalded his throat. "Why? One of the girls giggle at the wrong time?" Noble had a fleeting dark thought of his unknown ladybird.

"Uh-uh."

Words fairly quivered on the kid's lips. Important words, if the way the boy's eyes were bulging was any indication. Noble was just about to prompt him when Sal made another pass by the table, sliding a huge platter of steaming, grease-soaked eggs and fried biscuits in front of him. It had been two days since the bear cubs had demolished his camp. He hadn't eaten since.

Grabbing a fork, Noble began methodically shoveling the oily, toothsome mess into his mouth. He spent a full ten minutes devouring food with single-minded intent before he remembered Blaine had been about to spill his guts.

He glanced up. Blaine was watching him in injured silence.

"Ah, yeah," Noble said, waving his fork encouragingly at Blaine. "You were about to tell me why you aren't going to go to any more whore houses."

Blaine took a deep breath. "I'm in love."

Oh. Again, thought Noble, popping the last scrap of bread into his mouth and fastidiously dusting crumbs from his fingers. Craning his neck, he searched the room for Sal.

"I really am in love."

Noble considered the empty plate in front of him for a few seconds. "Sal! What happened to that elk jerky?"

"Really, deeply in love."

"And it'd be real swell if someone could actually refill my mug with some of that stuff you jokingly call coffee."

"Aw, keep yer shirt on, McCaneaghy!" Sal's voice boomed from the back room. "I got other customers to see to."

"Yeah? Like who?" Noble hollered back. "There isn't anyone in here but Farley and me and if—"

"Noble, I said I'm in love!"

Noble frowned in irritation. "I heard you the first time, Blaine. I'm not deaf." He cupped his hand near his mouth and bellowed, "And a couple more eggs!" Turning his attention back to Blaine, he rested his elbows on the table and steepled his fingers in front of his lips, allotting Blaine his full attention. "Now, what's her name? Trixie? Jackrabbit Sue?"

"No, Noble, she ain't like that. She's a lady. A real, honest-to-God lady."

"Yeah, well, I'm happy for you, Blaine. Truly. Invite me to the nuptials and I'll stand up for you, but soon as I'm done here I gotta get that report over to the station. Do you know what time the train's leaving?"

The boy was staring at him with such patent incredulity that Noble laughed. "Aw, come on, Blaine. Every time I see you, you've fallen in love. Senorita Bianca, Jenny Price, Lola LaRue—"

"Ain't like that this time," Blaine answered sullenly.

"Great. You can tell me all about this paragon

later." The boy gave a deep, melodramatic sigh. Noble capitulated. "Okay, Blaine, you win. What's the little lady's name?"

Blaine cupped his chin and leaned forward, his gaze going all misty. "Miss Leiland. Miss Venice Leiland."

Noble had once been sucker-punched in the diaphragm. He'd been taken completely by surprise and, for a few awful seconds, the blow had utterly paralyzed him. His muscles had quivered but refused to obey his will. The air had rushed out of his lungs and he'd been unable to refill them. He'd felt absolutely powerless, vulnerable, and exposed . . . like he did now.

Venice. The memories were ten years old and they still hurt.

Chapter 4

"Venice is here, in Salvage?" The whispered words were drawn from his throat against his will.

"She shore is, every pretty inch of her."

"Where are they staying?"

"*They?*" Blaine asked, clearly puzzled.

"Venice and Trevor. Where are they?"

"I don't know no 'Trevor.' Miss Leiland—or Venice as you so overfamiliarlike calls her—come out here on her lonesome."

"Venice is here *alone?*"

Blaine bobbed his head in the affirmative.

Noble's mouth screwed up in disgust. What else should he have expected? He had read all the newspaper stories, a whole decade of them. At first, he'd looked forward to any mention of the pretty, impish child he'd felt so protective of. But later, after report had been heaped upon report, story had followed story, he'd read them as a way to remind himself of the corrosive powers of too much money and idle time. Her escapades spoke for themselves; Venice Leiland had become a thrill-seeking hoyden, a jaded adventuress.

It didn't matter. She had been out of his life for a long time.

Then why, when he'd heard the words 'on her lonesome,' had his stomach begun hurting in that vaguely familiar way?

"Aw, hell, Blaine."

"You should see her, Noble," Blaine breathed. "The fellers sits around just waiting to catch a glimpse of her. They trails after her whenever she sashays down the street—"

"*Sashays?* Dammit it to hell!" There it was. The knee-jerk reaction he'd always had regarding Venice. The thought of some guy hooting at her made all the muscles in his arm tense up, as if looking for something to slug.

"Um-hum." Blaine had cupped his chin in his palm and was staring out the window like a moonstruck calf. "Miss Leiland moves like a piece of down floating on a still lake."

Noble gritted his teeth.

"Miss Leiland has a voice like . . . like . . . well, I don't know what like, but it puts a body in mind of angels laughing."

"Blaine, you get over this infatuation right now," Noble told him. "That woman is about as close to being an angel as I am to being a saint. Boy, you couldn't afford to buy her handkerchief. You couldn't afford to buy the soap she has it washed in. No way. No how."

Blaine's brow furrowed into a thunderous scowl. "Noble, I knowed you're a lot stronger than me." Trepidation tinged Blaine's words as he stood up and stomped stiff-legged around the table. "You could lick me with one hand tied behind yer back." Noble stared in disbelief at the quivering young man standing over him. "But I wouldn't judge myself much of a man if I didn't do this!"

The boy's fist shot out, glancing off Noble's slack jaw and snapping his head back.

Noble bolted to his feet, upending the chair behind him, his hands clenched. In one stride, he had jerked the young man up onto his toes. Blaine met his gaze hotly, righteousness and fear warring in his pale, young eyes.

One look at Blaine's defiant face and Noble snatched his hands from the boy's collar and spun on his heels. Damn! Blaine thought he was some sort of knight in shining armor protecting his fair damsel.

"If you ever, *ever* hit me again, Blaine Farley, I'll bury you."

An audible whoosh of air proclaimed the kid's relief. "Didn't want to hit you, Noble," he said gruffly, "but a man can't have you gettin' over-familiar, bandying about a fine lady's name."

"Bandy about? Overfamiliar?" Noble sputtered. "Blaine Farley, you shavetail ass! When I was a boy, I *lived* with the Leilands. My mom was their cook. I wiped Venice Leiland's nose when she was too young to do it for herself. If I don't have cause to be 'familiar' with her, I don't know who does!"

"You *lived* with Miss Leiland? God in heaven," Blaine whispered reverently. "You really lived with Miss Leiland? What was she like? I bet she was a pretty kid."

"What was she like?" Noble asked, rubbing his sore jaw. "What the hell do you mean, 'What was she like?'! How about a 'Gee, Noble, I'm awful sorry I hit you in the face'?"

"Yeah, well, whatever," Blaine said dismissively. "But what was she like?"

"Into everything. Nosy, meddlesome, little speck of a thing, always asking questions and wondering how high was high." He couldn't help smiling at the memory of Venice's ten-year-old face covered with soot. She'd been trying to figure out how Saint Nick made it down the chimney. But that was then. A lifetime ago. "Forget it, Blaine. It's enough to say she caused as much trouble then as she's doing now."

"She ain't no trouble. She's the kindest, sweetest . . . she ain't a bit high and mighty. She's giving a party for the whole darn town. She'd ordered up a trainload of supplies for it, too. Already got tents set up on the field in case it rains."

"Venice is throwing a party? Why? Just what the hell is she doing here?"

"Well," Blaine said consideringly, "folks 'spect she's come to see if ole Milty found any of those bones he's always looking for and if he hasn't, she's gonna close down the spur line. She's going around asking fer all the spur line ledgers and her uncle's accounts and all sorts of stuff. Ain't had much luck getting any of it, though."

"How's that tie in with her throwing a party?"

"Guess she just feels bad about what she might have to do with the railroad. Closing it down and all. Ain't that nice?"

"That's just bloody grand." Apparently the Leiland penchant for buying approval hadn't stopped with Trevor.

"Where is she?"

"The Gold Dust."

Noble knew he couldn't have heard Blaine right. The boy pursed his lips, looking around guiltily, as though he'd personally escorted her to the saloon.

"Yup," Blaine said in response to Noble's silence. "The Gold Dust. See, there was this little misunderstandin' between Miss Leiland and some of the Convivial League."

"Yeah?" Why didn't this surprise him?

"Well, they kinda mistook Miss Leiland fer the new madam in town and when Miss Leiland tumbled to the ladies' mistake, she . . . ah, she laughed. Not that she was making fun of 'em," Blaine hurried to clarify.

"Let me get this straight. Venice comes to town and straight off gets mistaken for a prostitute. Instead of being offended, like a *normal decent* woman sure as hell would, she thinks it's funny. Next, she decides to throw the town a party to make up for closing down the spur line."

"Yup, only the Convivial Ladies ain't comin' 'cause Miss Leiland invited all the calico gals in town, too."

"Hell."

"Well, Noble," Blaine said reasonably, "she *is* renting rooms from the owner of the Gold Dust. She couldn't hardly do different."

"She's renting rooms at a whorehouse."

Blaine gulped. "It's only *kinda* a whorehouse. Cayuse Katie don't run the girls. They make their own arrangements."

Noble was trying to stay calm. He was trying to understand, but his jaw throbbed, his body itched, his ribs ached, and he wasn't looking forward to going to the Gold Dust.

Going to the Gold Dust?! He didn't want to go to the Gold Dust. But he was going to have to go there, wasn't he?

No.

He wasn't her guardian. He wasn't her anything!

Angrily, he dug in his pocket and pulled out a wadded paper bill, tossing it on the table.

"Why isn't she staying at her uncle's?"

"Skunk got in, stunk the place up real good. Which, Noble—I hate to mention it—but you've smelled a sight better yerself."

"I know!" thundered Noble, spinning on his heels. He stomped through the doorway. Hell and damnation! Who was he fooling? He'd learned long ago there was no use fighting this . . . this *compulsion* to take care of Venice.

"Where you going?"

"I am going to find Venice Leiland and get her

out of that whorehouse, out of Salvage, and out of my life!"

"Would you please tell Miss Venice Leiland there's someone here to see her, ma'am?" Noble asked the blonde woman on the other side of the bar.

"Cayuse Katie," the woman said, leaning one arm on the counter and placing a hand on her hip. She bent forward and the soft mounds of her breasts flowed against her beaded silk bodice.

"Katie," Noble said politely, "I gotta see Venice Leiland."

"Yeah, you and every other thing in pants, stud." She leaned further forward, threatening to spill over the top of her gown. "Though you're a sight more appealing than most of the hop toads that find their way in here." Reaching out, she ran a finger along his jaw.

Noble smiled and shook his head. "Tell her an old friend of the family's here to see her."

Frowning, Katie straightened, tugging at the straining seams of her dress. "You? A friend of the Leilands?" She snorted. "You ain't putting me on, are you? 'Cause if you are, Venice is just gonna politely tell you to go to hell. She's a lady, ya know." Pride fought with disappointment in the declaration.

"I'm not putting you on."

Katie reached under the bar and brought out a bottle of rye and a shot glass. "Well, have a drink while you wait. This ain't no social hall."

She turned and strolled the length of the bar to the staircase, jet beads bouncing on every round curve.

Unstopping the twist of cloth in the bottle neck, Noble poured himself two fingers of whiskey, staring into the huge mirror behind the bar. It re-

flected a sunburnt, wind-scoured man in faded
denims and a grimy, patched calico shirt. A man
who looked as anxious as a kid on his first day in
the army. Why the hell hadn't he gotten himself a
bath before coming here?

Behind him he heard the door to the saloon
open. He squinted into the mirror to see who'd entered and promptly closed his eyes.

A man stood just inside the threshold, leaning
nonchalantly on a silver-topped cane. He was
dressed in brown checked trousers and an expen-
sive-looking tweed sporting jacket. His gleaming
black hair echoed the macassar sheen of his luxu-
riant black mustache. Casually, he surveyed the
barroom, his gaze coming to rest on Noble. His
eyes widened.

"*Mick* Caneaghy," he said in a nasal Boston accent. "Why am I not surprised to find you here,
amongst the squalor?" He lifted his cane and
waved it around the room.

Noble turned around, studying the murky sediment on the bottom of his shotglass for a moment.
With a shrug he lifted the glass, quaffing the liquid noisily.

"I don't know, Thorny," he finally said. "Maybe
you was lookin' fer me?" He settled his elbows behind him on the counter.

" 'Maybe you was'? I see you've forgotten all
your elocution lessons. What a waste of a perfectly
good education. Yale's, that is." Cassius Thornton
Reed smiled.

Noble frowned, as though perplexed. "I don't
know 'bout that, Thorny," he said, his drawl exag-
gerated. "That Yale degree got me a job."

Cassius allowed himself a faint shudder. "Dear
man, you needn't have a college education to lead
gentlemen's expeditions. *Indians* do it all the time.

Oh, that's right. You're supposed to have done some sort of work for the Smithsonian."

Noble clamped one hand to his chest, his mouth dropping open in mock awe. "Thorny, you went to all the trouble to check up on li'l ole me? I didn't know you cared! I'm flattered right down to my toes!"

Cassius's lips pressed into a thin white line. "I merely heard of your employment in passing and it impressed me as any oddity might. Like you did at Yale. Irish upstart. All the professors gloating over you. But then, if you teach a dog to talk, who cares what it says?"

The only indication of Noble's anger was a blaze deep in his amber eyes, burning hotly, like the heart of a fire. He unhooked the heel of his left boot from the bar rail. Cassius took a step backward. Noble pushed himself off the bar counter. His lean length uncoiled in slow, pantherish strides, bringing him to within a foot of Cassius.

He stared at Cassius, held him captive with the mesmerizing intensity of his gaze. Slowly, he leaned forward. A fine sheen of moisture dotted Cassius's brow. A wicked curl twisted the corner of Noble's mouth. He leaned closer still. A tremor shivered through Cassius's stiff posture.

"Arf," Noble whispered.

Cassius stumbled back and Noble laughed.

"You are insufferable!" Cassius shouted. "A prime example of your base heritage."

Noble turned his back, returning to his half-finished drink at the bar.

"Where is the proprietor of this place?" Cassius demanded. "Owner! Barkeep!"

"Miss Jones is seeing to some of her . . . renters. She'll be down momentarily," a woman said.

In the mirror, Noble's gaze traveled past Cassius

up the reflected length of the stairs. His heart stopped. Venice stood at the top of the staircase.

She was black and white, shadow and light, against the dark velvet curtain of the unlit hallway. Her dress was made completely of cream-colored lace over dark gray silk, molding her body in a latticed sheath; her skin was nearly opalescent; her hair, a midnight cloud caught in a loose knot behind her slender throat; her eyes—God, her eyes were the same, an indescribable shade of dusk capturing light, like mercury. She had always been beautiful, delicate, a charcoal sketch of subtlety and nuance rather than a bold oil painting. The lovely little fledgling had matured into a glossy cliff swallow.

As she started down the steps, Noble forced himself to release his stranglehold on the shotglass. He took a deep breath.

"Why, this is a surprise. I certainly never expected to see you here . . ." Her voice was amused, sophisticated, cool. He tried to think of something to say, some way to return her greeting, something light, casual—". . . Mr. Reed."

Noble's gaze flew to the mirror. She stood on the last step, her hands held out in a welcoming gesture. Cassius, having managed to bury his anger, was claiming Venice's gloved hands in his own.

"What are you doing here?" she asked.

Noble had heard it enough times to recognize the welcoming smile in her voice. But his memories were of a piping soprano; this was a contralto, richer, deeper. A woman's voice. His belly muscles clenched tightly at the thought and he cursed himself roundly. What was he thinking? Venice was a kid he'd played nursemaid to, a little girl he'd loved like a sister. But his body mocked his thoughts. The sensations he was feeling were anything but fraternal.

"Doing here? Why, I am rescuing you from your inevitable *ennui*, dear lady." Noble found himself paying closer attention. He'd always assumed Cassius was like any number of his breed: vicious, spiteful, but ultimately harmless. But Cassius's quick change from anger to smooth equanimity had been too abrupt. It unsettled Noble because it suggested Cassius was deliberately hiding his true nature from Venice.

"Mutual friends told me about your decision to come west. Didn't surprise me, of course. If *mon pere* were making a bid at becoming the high muck-a-muck in New York these days, I'd want to leave, too. Crashing bore, having to kowtow to doddery old dames at those receptions."

"It wasn't entirely my decision." Venice sounded calm, but there was a subtle tightening of her voice. "Actually, I was sent away to ensure no more politically embarrassing stories were written about me. Seems I have become something of a liability."

"And what do you care a rap for what people think of you?" Cassius said. "Like to thumb your nose at them, I'd be willing to bet—and a deuced lovely little appendage it is, too."

Venice didn't respond to Cassius's cheek. She was perfectly tranquil. Noble wished he felt so composed. Any more of Cassius's overfamiliarity and he might have to teach him a few manners.

Swallowing the final drops of the whiskey in one short pull, Noble replaced the glass. He was wiping his lips with the back of his hand when he looked up. She was staring at him in the mirror. Her gray eyes were wide, her expression shocked. Their reflected gazes locked and held. She took a short step forward and stopped.

"Well, honey, you sure look a might better than the last time I saw you," he said to her reflection and was perversely pleased when her hands flew to her elaborate coiffure.

"You." It was a whisper.

"Yup. Me." He turned.

"I know what you must think," she stammered. "But really I'm not that type—"

"I don't really give a damn what you are or aren't." He was amazed to find he spoke the truth. Whatever she'd become, she'd been the one bright spot in the gray, dirty world of his youth. And he hadn't realized she'd left an empty place in him, until she returned to fill it.

Her face had grown pale. Drawn to her, he crossed the floor until he stood a foot away. She swayed forward, her lips parting slightly, but no words came out.

Noble smiled. She hadn't grown much taller in the past decade. She was still an elfin, fey creature, as easily crushed as a rose petal. She tilted her head back and he was caught in her silvery gaze.

"Where are my manners?" he teased, taking hold of her limp hand and raising it to his lips. He brushed a kiss against the smooth, cool skin and looked directly into her smoke-colored eyes. "Hello, darlin'." The old endearment slipped from his mouth. A faint, pink blush bloomed and died in the space of a moment on her cheeks.

He wasn't even aware he'd lifted his other hand until he saw his fingers hovering a scant inch above the soft, glistening tresses at her temple. He swallowed and feathered the silky mass away from the vulnerable skin. Like a half-feral kitten, she leaned tentatively into his light caress.

"How dare you touch her?"

Venice's eyes widened in alarm, her horrified

gaze riveted behind Noble's shoulder. "Mr. Reed! No!"

Noble dropped his hand, dragging his attention from Venice, and wheeled around.

Cassius was behind him, his cane held threateningly, his mustache quivering with indignation. "Insolent mongrel."

Noble took a step forward. "Back off, Reed," he rasped.

"Don't worry, Miss Leiland," Cassius said, cocking the hard polished cane higher overhead. "I'll teach this ruffian to respect a lady! After I'm done with him, he won't dare come near you again."

The heavy walking stick swung toward Noble. With a growl, he caught it in mid-descent. Ripping it from Cassius's grip, he flung it across the barroom. His arm shot back, his fist aiming for Cassius's chin.

Reed flinched and Noble's eyes narrowed. The jerk wasn't worth bruising his knuckles on. With an oath, Noble grabbed Reed's shoulder, spun him around, and shoved him in the same direction he'd flung the fool walking stick. Cassius stumbled into a chair, falling heavily to the floor.

His breath coming hard, Noble turned back to Venice. She was staring at him with wide eyes, an unreadable expression on her lovely face.

"I've already had a peck of trouble today, darlin'," Noble said softly. "I've been slugged, had my hand stomped on, and now I've nearly been caned by this ass, all on account of you. I hope you're worth it."

"I'm not. I mean, I *am*, but not in the way you mean. I really am not what you think I am," Venice said.

"Darling, you don't have to defend yourself to me. I thought all those newspaper stories I read about you would make a difference in how I feel, but they don't. I don't give a damn about them or what you think you are." Lord help him, it was the truth. "All I know is that you're here and it seems like I've spent the past decade waiting for you."

"Lord!" she breathed. "How can you say that to me? You don't even know me!"

She must mean he didn't know her anymore. She was wrong. "I know you like I know the rhythm of my heart."

"How?" She sounded oddly desperate as if she was hearing something she wanted to believe and yet was afraid of. "From some newspaper articles?"

"It's more than that, and you know it."

"Who *are* you?"

"What?"

"Who are you? Please."

A plunge in a mountain lake could not more effectively have robbed him of breath.

"That's the feller I told you about, the one said he was an old family friend," Katie said from the top of the steps.

Venice didn't know who he was, Noble realized. It was an odd sensation. As though all of his flesh was hardening into stone, while inside he was shattering into thousands of lethal, piercing shards. He kept his eyes on the crown of her head. He couldn't look into her eyes. It was all he could do to stand before her.

She hadn't recognized him. But she'd allowed his touch. The touch of a sunburnt, rangy stranger.

"Are you a friend of my uncle's?" she asked.

Twist your lips into a smile, boyo. "Yup. A friend of Milt's."

The answer seemed to relieve her, for a smile blossomed on her rose-tinted lips. She had always had a beautiful smile. It was fair dazzling now. He couldn't find an answering one for her. Not to save his soul.

The smile faltered.

"I seriously doubt that," sneered Cassius, who'd picked himself up and was leaning against the table, holding his side, as he avidly watched the interchange. Venice probably leaned into Cassius's touch, too, Noble thought. Fine. They deserved each other. Same class, same class of morals ... none.

Lord, and he had thought he knew her like the rhythm of his heart. Seemed there was still a bit of the die-hard romantic in him after all. This should purge him of the last of *those* tendencies.

"Leading a bunch of pack mules up a mountain hardly qualifies one as a 'friend,'" Cassius said. "Your uncle would never associate with common riffraff."

"Ain't nuthin' common about the type of riffraff he is," a voice averred loyally from behind Noble.

Christ. Just what he needed. A full-blown audience. "Go home, Blaine."

"Don't got one. Don't even got a room tonight. Evening, Miss Leiland," Blaine said, stopping before the object of his worship. "See my pal here found you. Must a been quite a surprise—"

"Shut up, Blaine. Now."

The cold imperative in Noble's voice brought Blaine up short. "But I thought, that is—"

"I mean it, Blaine. Not a word."

"I don't doubt your uncle would hire anyone available to lead him through the back country," Cassius was saying as though Blaine hadn't spoken. "From what I gather, he goes into some rather savage, uncharted territory. It only stands to reason he would need a ruffian to guide him."

"Hire?" asked Blaine, thoroughly confused.

"Yes, 'hire.' As in pay money to provide a service," Cassius said. "Family friend, indeed. Well, no matter."

"What do you mean, Mr. Reed?" Venice asked.

"Obviously your uncle has been regaling this chap with stories about you. Perhaps, knowing you were here, unescorted, Milton hired him to see to your safety. A bodyguard of sorts."

Venice looked askance at Noble, her expression troubled. "Milton doesn't even know I'm here."

"But if he did," Cassius went on, as though he hadn't heard Venice, "it was only because he didn't realize that someone of your own class would be here to see to your comfort." He shrugged. "Ergo, we no longer need him." He pointed at Noble.

With a twist of his lip, Noble returned to the bar counter and another two fingers of whiskey.

"But how could Uncle Milton know I was here?"

"Perhaps I am mistaken." Cassius shrugged dismissively. "What does it matter? All that need concern us is that I promise, dear lady, we'll have an exciting time."

Cassius's voice seemed unctuously suggestive to Noble. His hand trembled on the glass. Anger pulsed cold and bitter through his veins. *Unescorted. Exciting time.* Jaded, fast, and wanton.

Venice looked to where Noble leaned on one arm, his back against the bar, a splinter of wood he'd plucked from the scored surface rolling from side to side in his mouth. When he saw she was looking at him, he straightened.

"Sounds like you're gonna have a load of *fun*," Noble said. His words sounded bitter and their tone chased the blood from Venice's cheeks.

Noble spat the toothpick out and started from the barroom, pausing just long enough to hiss down at the bewildered-looking Blaine, "If you tell her who I am, they won't be able to find all the pieces of you."

"But *why?*"

"Even an Irish mongrel has a bit o' pride, Blaine, me boyo. Besides, she'll figure it out for herself soon enough."

Chapter 5

"**G**al, can you explain all that to me?" Katie asked as she trailed Venice into the rooms she was renting her. Wordlessly, Venice sank down on the edge of the bed.

Amber. The man's eyes were clear, light-catching amber, thought Venice. He was so beautiful and so ragged.

The man's words had been poetic, tender. He'd told her he knew her like his heart's rhythm. Then, seconds later, he'd dismissed her with a sneer. Why? From the moment their eyes had met in the mirror, there had been something so familiar about the man. It was unsettling. But then, she'd felt unsettled from the moment she'd first seen him at the watering trough.

"How come you went all white when you saw that long-haired feller?" Katie prodded. "And who was that other guy?"

Venice felt heat rise to her cheeks. "I thought he was angry with me."

"He who? The long-haired feller?"

Venice nodded. "I believe he mistook me for a woman of easy virtue and since I . . . er, disabused him of that notion, I thought he might be angry with me. But I don't think he recognized me."

"Now, why the hell would he think you were a calico gal? What do you mean recognize you? Is he blind?" Katie asked indignantly.

61

"Well, he might have some small justification for his misconception." Venice winced. "I whistled at him."

Katie's jaw dropped open. "Go on with ya. Never say it's true!"

The twinkle that had been noticeably absent in Venice's eyes for the past hour flickered back to life. "Yup."

"Here? How? Why? Ferget the why. I got eyes myself."

"I was on my balcony this morning and he was at the horse trough. Washing. Without a shirt on. And he started to put it on and I . . . I just whistled. I didn't mean to. And when he looked up, I called him pretty."

The stunned expression on Katie's face was too ludicrous to resist. Venice started to smile and then to giggle and finally gave way to full-blown laughter. After a second, Katie burst out laughing, too.

"Pretty? Hot damn." Katie dabbed at her eyes. "I've called good-looking hombres like that a lot of things, but pretty ain't never been one of 'em. What did he do?"

"He smiled," Venice said. "And then he did something that made all of his skeletal muscles manifest themselves in pronounced, lineal definition." She sighed. "It was wonderful."

"If you say so," Katie said doubtfully. "He really done it to you, hasn't he?" she added quietly.

Venice didn't deny it. "I don't even know him and yet I get the most incredible sensations when I look at him. He makes me feel all . . ." She stuttered to a halt, frustrated. She tried once more. "It's the most bizarre thing. My mouth goes dry, my skin itches, my fingertips, *everything*, starts tingling. I can't seem to catch my breath and it's almost frightening!"

"Just a darn minute, here. Honey, ain't you never been *hot* for a man before?" Katie asked.

Venice didn't know the vernacular, but Katie's meaning was perfectly clear. "Not like this."

"Chrissakes, honey, how old are you?"

"Twenty-two."

Katie vaulted to her feet and stood glowering down at Venice. "That's just out and out unnatural, that is!"

"I'm sorry."

The expression of abashment on Venice's face erased most of Katie's womanly outrage. "Ah, kid. You need a man. Bad. Luckily, you can do somethin' about it. And if'n I was you, I'd do it soon, less'n your body just sorta shrivels up 'fore it knows what it's missing."

"What do you suggest I do?" Venice asked, intrigued in spite of herself.

"Go back to New York, pick yoreself out one of them high-society beaus of yours, and get hitched."

Venice smiled wanly. "Like Cassius Thornton Reed?"

"That the other guy? The one in the nice duds? Sure, if that's what you want."

"Want? *Want* doesn't have much to do with marriage, does it?" She didn't wait for an answer. "I don't feel this way about Mr. Reed. I've never felt this way—at least to this extent—about anyone!"

"Shit. You get any notions about marrying that dirty range rider right out of your head."

"Marrying?" Venice repeated. "I said I found him extremely ... invigorating. I didn't say anything about marrying him."

"Yeah. Well, I did. High-class gals like you don't tumble into the sack with a guy less they has a gold band 'round their finger. And that would be one helluva mistake, even assuming you could get a footloose drifter like him to commit. Which, given your particular talents, I don't doubt you could."

"I know it would be a mistake," Venice said softly.

"Good," Katie replied. " 'Cause you'd just end up miserable. Like I was with that ne'er-do-well husband of mine, Josiah. You try breeding a horse and a donkey and you gets a mule . . . ugly, mean, and barren." A touch of ancient sadness colored her words, but after a snort of self-contempt she went on. "And once you get hitched, you can't get unhitched. Marriage is forever."

"There's always divorce."

"Worse than dying, to my mind. Nope," Katie said adamantly, "marriage is forever and *forever* is a long time to be paying for a tumble in the hay. You just stick to your own sort and you'll do fine."

"What am I supposed to do, Miss Jones?" Venice replied in a low voice. "There *aren't* any men of my sort. I'm as much an oddity in New York as I am in Salvage. At best, intelligent men consider me peculiar."

Her voice dropped sadly. "I am an oddity. I don't seem to be able to find much pleasure in the things most women do; parties, teas, musicales. I want to *see* things no one else has seen. I want to discover things; the source of the Nile, a new species of bird, the height of the largest Sequoia, the bones of a prehistoric animal."

"So? Do it. With your money, Venice, you could probably buy a new name for Niagara Falls."

"That's the problem," Venice said, frustrated because she couldn't make Katie understand. "The men my father introduces to me think a walk in Central Park is the ultimate adventure. Stocks, bonds, railroads are all they think of. Yes," she said, holding up her hand to stave off Katie's outburst, "I know; I have a duty. A duty to marry someone who will be an astute partner in the Leiland Foundation's management. There are charities and organizations and societies that rely on the foundation. I know all this."

Her hand dropped and she gave a nearly imperceptible sigh. "Believe me, Miss Jones, your well-intentioned lecture on marriage isn't necessary. No one knows better than I what disastrous consequences come of marrying for love. I just wish . . . well, what does it matter?" She shook her head and smiled wryly. "But he certainly was pretty, wasn't he?"

"Could someone hand me a cloth or something? I got soap in my eyes," Noble yelled from the storage room at the back of Grundy's Mercantile.

He leaned over the tub of water in which he was crouched, groping for a towel. Maybe nothing was going to wash away the feeling of inferiority the Leilands were so good at raising in him, but at least the Grundys weren't going to take advantage of him. He'd be damned if he was going to dry himself off with his own shirt.

"A towel!"

A sodden rag thwacked Noble in the back of the head. "Gee, thanks, Anton."

"Wasn't Anton, McCaneaghy."

Wiping the suds from his eyes, Noble squinted up at Tim Gilpin. "Gilpin. Shouldn't you be off telegraphing the East Coast stories about house-sized jackrabbits?"

Tim snorted. "Poetic license, McCaneaghy. That story paid for my new type set. 'Course, if you ever wanted to see *your* name in print, I could probably see clear to cutting you in on the correspondent's portion."

Noble rubbed a chunk of soap into his hair, working up a lather for the fourth time in order to wash off the thick layer of kerosene and axle grease he'd kept spread over his body for the past six hours. God, how he hated lice. Always had, ever since he'd lived in the tenements where lice and the attendant stigma of shaved heads had been inescapable. He'd spend a week in a vat of this noxious remedy, burning his skin and raising welts on his body, before he'd ever shave his head again.

"We could make a fortune, Noble. Wild Bill Hickok, Bill Cody, those boys have the right idea. Parlay a couple of adventures into a pile of money."

Noble got out of the tub, toweled dry, and pulled on clean underwear.

"Hell, boy!" Tim said. "Don't you know what a goldmine you are? Here's Wild Bill selling all sorts of balderdash to the eastern newspapers on the merit of a couple of long yanks of yeller hair and a mouth quicker than his reported aim with a pistol. Then, there's you. War veteran, Yale graduate, more real adventures than half the blowhards in print—*and* with long hair!—and you won't let me write down a word of it!"

Noble heaved the tub over to the back door of Grundy's Mercantile and tipped the oil-slicked water onto the ground. Crossing to the storage shelves, he began picking through untidy piles of ready-made clothing. "Since you're here, do me a favor." He leaned close to Tim. "Do I still smell like kerosene?"

Tim gave a cursory sniff. "Not too bad."

"Good." Noble picked out a white shirt and thrust his arms into the sleeves.

"Come on, McCaneaghy."

"Uh-uh," Noble said, pulling on a pair of jeans

and stuffing the shirttails into them. "Where the hell are Anton and Harry?"

"I don't know. They were in that shed out back when I came in, sawing something," Tim said in frustration. "I don't know what you have against making easy money."

"Just remember, Tim," Noble said, banging his boot heel down against the floor, "Milt subscribes to all those eastern papers. It might take them a while to get out here, and it might take me a while longer to get to them, but eventually we'll meet up. And if I ever read my name in any of them, I'll have your hide as a windbreak. Swear to God, I will."

"Fine. Give up a chance at fame and fortune. What do I care? It's not like I need you to write a story the New York papers will pick up. Not now. Not with a regulation, bona-fide, dyed-in-the-wool sensation staying right here in Salvage. Right at the Gold Dust Emporium." Tim polished his fingernails on his soiled vest. "A celebrity who's going to treat our little hamlet to a New York–style entertainment."

Noble hauled on his other boot and stood up.

"Prettiest sensation you ever saw," Tim prompted smugly.

Venice again. Noble dragged his wet hair to the back of his head in one fist and secured the tail with a leather thong. Without a word he pushed past Tim. Tomorrow he'd ship his records off to Washington, outfit himself, and take off for . . . for . . . away from her!

Cassius Thornton Reed straightened his jacket and picked up the expensive cheroot charring the dresser top. The woman lay sprawled on the bed in a tangle of sweat-scented sheets and blankets. Her large breasts were bare above the black and red corset, the sole piece of clothing she wore except for the fancifully spiked leather boots. She was asleep.

It hadn't been a very satisfactory coupling. Cassius had been too aware that Venice Leiland was renting rooms a few doors down the hall. No, not satisfactory. Still, he wasn't going to ruin his chances at the Leiland millions by indulging in his usual tastes. He'd probably been a fool to indulge himself at all, but on the way into the saloon, the whore had accosted him, grabbing his hand and rubbing it over her big, pliant breasts while squeezing him with nimble, eager fingers. He wasn't a man to deny himself pleasure.

Quietly, Cassius opened the door to the corridor and slipped outside. He paused, flicking the glowing cheroot at the spittoon near the top of the stairs. He'd always been partial to big, white breasts. Next time, he promised himself as he tiptoed past Venice's door and started down the steps, he was going to get his money's worth.

He didn't even notice the first spirals of smoke rising from the hall runner a foot in front of the spittoon.

Watching something black and shiny scuttle into the thin ticking of the mattress Sal had rented him decided Noble; the floor would be less crowded. He pulled off his boots and tugged his shirt free of the waistband. He kicked open his bedroll and spread himself on top of it. Clamping his hands behind his head, he stared up at the ceiling. It was well past midnight, but he'd be damned if he could sleep.

It was her fault. Her and her wide, gray eyes and her stilted little "Who are you?" Apparently she'd afforded him as much room in her memory as she had the butcher's dog. In other words, none. Noble flopped onto his side, ramming the wadded-up jacket he used for a pillow into a different configuration.

She'd dogged his footsteps for over three years, until he'd gone to Yale. She'd been his shadow. His *cluricaune.* Fey, spritish lassie.

Angrily, Noble heaved himself to a sitting position. Irish drivel. Restlessly, he paced to the room's small broken window, tearing off the piece of canvas someone had tacked across the opening.

With unseeing eyes, he stared down the road to the Gold Dust. He knew her type. Constantly craving something new, something different, something to sate jaded senses. Privileged beauties who devoured stimulation like dowagers ate chocolate, greedily hoarding thrills, no matter what the cost to themselves or others.

Young women like Adele.

Noble balled his hand into a fist against the window jamb. He hadn't thought of Adele in years. He added her resurrected image to the list of offenses he counted against Venice.

Adele Sumner. Black-haired, black-eyed society darling. Her long pale fingers pressed over his lips as they stood in the dimly lit back hall of the Leiland mansion. Her eyes darted nervously behind him to ensure no one saw her with the cook's son.

"Boy, you can come to my room later, after midnight. Mind you now, don't get caught or I'll scream you right into gaol."

He'd been seventeen and a randy young fool and he'd gone to her room. Well, he wasn't seventeen now, and he wouldn't *allow* himself to act the fool. He would see things as they were. No excuses, not even for Venice.

Beneath the light-stubbled swath of the Milky Way, his gaze traveled to the saloon where Venice slept. Thin tendrils of diaphanous fog embraced the second-floor verandah. Or was it something else? The sharp scent of burning wool reached Noble's nostrils at the same time that his bare feet hit the hard-packed ground beneath his window. He launched himself down the street, racing toward the Gold Dust.

Behind him, a fire alarm started clanging. Voices shouted out behind Noble as he sprinted the last hundred feet to the front door, tore it open, and vaulted up the stairs. The fumes hung in a dense shroud here, the acrid smell burning his nostrils, parching his throat.

"Fire!" a hysterical female voice screamed. Up ahead squeals of terror and muffled profanity erupted from behind the closed doors. A man burst from a room, hopping on one foot as he tried to drag on a boot. The frightened woman behind him stuffed belongings into a carpet bag as she stumbled into the hall.

There was no way to tell where the smoke was coming from. It drifted thickly in the narrow hallway. People were choking and coughing, men outside calling for pails. The woman with the carpet bag stumbled past him, her red eyes streaming tears. He grabbed her arm.

"Where's Venice Leiland?" he yelled. She twisted out of his grip.

"She's using Katie's room! Last door!" she yelled. His eyes stinging, Noble raced forward, squinting through the poisonous blanket.

At the end of the hall, he raised his fist and pounded on the paneled door. "Venice! Venice! You've got to come out!"

Unidentifiable phantom bodies lurched through the smoke, emerging from rooms, jostling and clawing in their panic to make it down the single, cramped stairway. Sobs were covered by angry demands and hoarse cries.

"Venice!" Noble grabbed the door handle and yanked it savagely. It was locked.

He stepped away, planted his back against the wall opposite the door, gritted his teeth, and kicked. Wood splintered. He kicked again. The door burst open.

Venice stood pressed against the door leading to the balcony. The light from a guttering hurricane lamp flickered over the folds of her white nightgown, gilding her features. Her eyes were wide and stricken.

"I was going out there." She lifted a shaking finger toward the verandah. Her shadow parodied her movements on the wall behind her. Noble slammed the door shut, picked up a blanket, and jammed it at the base of the door to keep the poisonous smoke at bay.

In three steps, he was before her. Another step, and she was in his arms, pressing her face to his chest. He held her fiercely, tightly, then effortlessly lifted her in his arms. She was safe. His relief was a physical sensation.

Katie's voice rose, loud and imperative above the commotion outside. "It's out! Do you hear me? Just smoke left! Some asshole set the carpet on fire, but it's out now! Don't kill yerselves stampedin'! Stay in yore room and open the windows!"

The tension ebbed from Noble's arms. "Did you hear?" he asked Venice, his mouth skimming the glistening black tresses that spilled over her shoulders.

"Yes," she murmured.

"You won't be able to spend the rest of the night here. As soon as we can, we'll get you over to the Pay Dirt. You can have my room there."

"Thank you." Her voice was a faint sigh. The feel of her lips moving against his throat, combined with the abrupt release of tension, was wreaking havoc on his body.

The skinny little girl had become a womanly armful. Hard on the heels of that thought came self-disgust. Gingerly, Noble lowered her to the ground. *Disgusting old goat. Here the poor girl is shaking like a leaf and all you can think about is kissing her senseless.*

Brusquely, Noble set Venice at arm's length and, determined to be reassuring, patted her gently on the shoulder. Not a good idea. She was warm beneath the thin cambric nightgown. Now that the danger was over, he was remembering with disturbing clarity every detail of her body against his: the weight and movement of breasts freed from bindings, her softness pressed to his hardness, the curve of her waist, the jut of her hip bone low on his belly.

Seemingly of their own volition his fingers curled over her upper arm, pulling her closer. She came willingly, bending toward him, graceful and yielding and comely. Her eyes, as soft and dangerous as the smoke, met his expectantly. Slowly, incrementally, he lowered his head. Wonder and welcome touched her lips with the promise of a smile.

Then he was touching her mouth with his own. Petal soft and warmly pliant beneath his. Her breath was as sweet-tasting as nectar. With a groan, Noble sipped the exhalation from her lips, afraid to ask more of the kiss, unable to help himself.

He released her arms to keep from dragging her closer to him. His traitorous hands slid to the silk-textured column of her throat, measuring its length, pausing on the fluttering pulse beneath her skin before lifting his palms and cupping her delicately formed head. He winnowed his fingers through the downy soft hair on the nape of her neck, smoothed the curls from her temples, his lips never leaving hers.

They could burn me for a witch, Venice thought wildly. She had conjured him here. She must have. For reality could never so faithfully adhere to fantasy.

She should be appalled by his boldness, frightened by his unexpected embrace. But his touch was so gossamer light, so undemanding. She could only stay, held by the awesome gentleness of his touch, the perfect, quivering control he exercised.

His warm breath sluiced over her mouth. The firm curve of his lips gently polished her own. His long, strong fingers played over her features with the delicacy and dedication of a blind artist.

Her heart thudded in her breast. Her body, awakened suddenly to an unsuspected universe of pleasure, urged her forward, demanding more. She gave in to the need to touch him in turn, to feel his body, his face. Carefully, she stroked his lean, dark cheek. His lashes slashed down on his cheeks as he closed his amber eyes. He turned his head, rubbing the side of his face against her palm.

His long, tangled hair coiled on his throat, antique gold strands gleaming against brown skin as rich as autumn oaks. She hesitated only a second before bracketing his beard-roughened jaw between both hands.

Instantly, his arms came about her. He stroked to her waist, arching her into him, with his other hand tilting her face to his. She would have fallen, but his arms held her fast, locked against his powerful male body bending over her.

His mouth left hers, finding the arch of her

neck. He rubbed his lips along her throat, tasting the flesh with exquisite care.

Wet, hot, and dangerous. She quivered in response to his sensual assault, her palms reading the thirsty motion of his open mouth.

With a groan, he lifted his head, his golden gaze burning down at her. His chest heaved beneath the worn shirt. Heat and hardness, brute strength and poignant tenderness assailed her senses. She clung to him, light-headed and breathless.

He gritted his teeth suddenly, wrenching his gaze away, releasing her from the molten heat holding her captive. Passion was an addiction, an instantly acquired one, and Venice's long-denied body ached for sensations just learned. She moved her hands down the strong pillar of his neck, following the broad slope of his shoulders, and finally drew him back down to her. He resisted. His body tightened.

In confusion, Venice searched his face.

He was staring at the bed where she'd heaped her dresses, preparing to throw them from the balcony. When his eyes returned to hers, they were shuttered. He straightened, hauling her upright, grasping her wrists and dragging them down to her sides.

"It was you," he said, "You're the woman in the blue dress." His golden eyes gleamed; the moonlight washed over his clean, angular features. They were set in a fierce, familiar expression. And suddenly she knew.

"Slats McCaneaghy," she breathed.

Chapter 6

So, she remembers, Noble thought. Well, at least she's still capable of being embarrassed.

He dropped her hands as though they were scalded by the same heat that flamed her cheeks. He stepped back, disgusted because a part of him didn't care that she'd teased him from her balcony with no thought to the possible consequences. A part of him just wanted to feel her pressed against him once more.

It made him so angry that he swore. Venice gave a little gasp. Damn, if he didn't have to stifle the impulse to apologize—apologize to *her*—for being less than a gentleman! God, where was his sense of humor?

"Slats. This is wonderful! Where have—"

"It was you on that balcony, wasn't it?" he demanded again, refusing to believe in her radiant welcome. He wouldn't be duped by her again.

"Yes," she said. "But where have—"

She was a white-faced, bold little piece of goods.

"And you hadn't any idea who I was." He didn't even try to sort out why it mattered so much that she hadn't recognized him. Why should she? He was the cook's brat.

"No. I would never have recognized you at first glance," she said, smiling.

" 'First glance'?" Noble echoed dryly. "Honey, that was more than glancing you were doing."

75

She blushed. He could see the pink stain even in the flickering light of the oil lamp. "I couldn't see you clearly."

"Ha! I got the distinct impression you saw everything just fine," Noble said. "What was wrong, honey? You get bored waiting to close down the spur line? Needed a little diversion?"

"*Diversion?*" her voice rose. "Just what do you think I am?"

God, she sounded indignant. Then again, she'd sounded indignant when she was ten and explaining how she hadn't been spying on him and the parlor maid in the gazebo. Seemed like Venice had graduated from spectator sports to active participation.

But he wasn't a sport.

"You're just another thrill-seeking society hussy."

"How dare you?" Her voice was low and furious.

"I'll tell you how. Answer me this—if you're capable of honesty—what were you doing on that balcony? Trying a little experiment? Didn't you just want to see if the mountain tramp was as easy to get all worked up as one of your New York boyfriends? Wal, let me warn you, darlin', I'm no one's experiment."

Picking up her periwinkle dress, he crumpled the fragile fabric. She was a born heartbreaker. He was glad he had missed watching her turn into another Adele, sneaking off with the cook's son to discover if *they* did it better.

He was *glad* Trevor had barred him from the Leiland mansion . . . and Venice.

"Experiment?" she exploded, quivering. "What inconceivable temerity, you insufferable piece of . . . of . . . gandy prancing buffalo swallow!"

His mouth gaped. "Where the hell did you learn that?"

"That is none of your business."

"Yeah, right. And I can't begin to tell you how glad I am about that."

She made some sort of strangled noise and shook the black coils of her hair. The movement drew his eyes to the sway of her unbound breasts beneath the pristine white nightgown. His body clenched in immediate response. He fought back the desire he felt building.

"Just what the hell are you doing in Salvage, anyway?" he asked furiously. "Flirting with strangers, alienating every decent woman in town, and nearly getting yourself killed in a fire?"

"I don't appear to be dead. But given a few more minutes with you, one of us may yet succumb," she returned just as furiously.

"You can't take care of yourself any better now than you could ten years ago," he spat in disgust.

"I beg to differ. I've *had* to learn to take care of myself. And since we're demanding explanations ... where did *you* disappear to ten years ago? And why didn't you tell me who you were downstairs earlier? Were you afraid of me ... or ashamed of yourself?"

What an act. Had she cared so little for him that she hadn't even inquired about where he'd gone after he'd been banished from the Leiland's mansion? It was a new hurt. On top of all the old ones.

"Ten years ago I was drafted into the union army, sweetheart."

"Oh, God. I didn't—"

"Course," he broke in, "you might not have realized there was a war going on, being all wrapped up in cotton batting on Park Avenue like you were." He didn't care that he was being unfair.

"Why, you presumptuous, sanctimonious, insufferable . . . scarecrow!"

"*Scarecrow?* Wal, I'm real sorry, honey, that I'm not all greased up and slicked out like that society eel you have slithering around your ankles."

"Are you, by some chance, referring to Mr. Reed?"

"Yeah." Noble thrust out his chin. "I am."

Her silver eyes disappeared between thick black lashes. "At least Mr. Reed has a sense of commitment. At least *he* cares enough to honor his promises."

"What the hell is that supposed to mean?"

"I'll tell you what I mean! You promised you'd always, *always*, be my friend and then you left, disappeared without a word, not one word, in ten years!" She had taken a step closer and Noble found he'd backed up.

"What were you going to do if I showed up on your doorstep, Venice? Offer me a job as your stable boy?" he asked sarcastically.

"I can't believe you think our friendship meant so li—" She stopped herself, apparently thinking better of her words, and cast a deliberately disparaging look over his half-buttoned shirt, ill-fitting jeans, and bare feet. "It might have been a step up!"

He pulled himself straight. "You," he pronounced, "have become a snob."

"And *you* have become a bully!" She had to tip her head back to look him in the face. She glared at him.

"I am not bullying you!" Noble thundered.

"You are so! You sweep in here without so much as a by-your-leave, kiss me, and then start shouting at me because I didn't recognize you!"

"That is not why—"

"How *could* I have recognized you! You're six

inches taller, sixty pounds heavier, and—" she reached up and grabbed his ponytail, "—you have *hair!*" She gave it a sharp yank.

"Ouch!"

She put her hands on her hips. "And, I might point out, *you* didn't recognize *me* either!"

He had begun to feel a bit sheepish, uncomfortably aware that her accusations were justified. But the reminder of her wanton behavior rekindled his righteous indignation.

"I would have recognized you if you hadn't been hiding in the shadows, whispering throaty come-ons to me."

A muscle jumped in her cheek. "Well," she said stiffly, "I may have acted impetuously in whistling at your ridiculous masculine posturing earlier today, but I certainly wasn't whistling out the window a few minutes ago."

"Ridiculous masculine—!" Noble sputtered. "You seemed to like it all right when you were sighing from your balcony. In fact I thought you were gonna throw yourself off the damn—"

"You *awful* man! The way you're acting, one would suppose I'd set this dratted place on fire myself, just to lure you out of whatever hole you've spent the night in, for the extremely dubious pleasure of being slobbered on by you!"

"Slobbered?" He'd had enough. "Lady, if I hadn't seen that damned dress, I'd have you on your backside with your skirt up around your ears right now. And we *both* know it!"

A lady would have succumbed to a fit of the vapors at such raw language. Apparently Venice was no lady.

She took a step closer, her nose an inch from his chest, and the belligerent thrust of her delicate jaw matched his own. "You'd *like* to think so," she said defiantly.

Nah-uh. Not this time. He'd call her bluff. He speared his fingers through her thick, sleek hair, roughly pulling her closer, cradling the back of her head.

Her eyes widened in surprise and she placed her hands on his chest, her fingertips just grazing his naked skin above the unfastened opening. She pushed ineffectually at him. He smiled, an evil smile of intent, and forced her nearer. He stared into her moonlit eyes a second before lowering his mouth over hers.

She tasted like a man's most erotic dream. His tongue slid between her lips touching the rough silk texture of her own. He had meant to frighten her, but the force and intensity of his passionate response to her confounded him. He tore his mouth away.

Without a backward glance, he spun on his bare heels and ripped the blanket from beneath the door jamb. He flung it aside, cursing profusely as he left.

Venice raked trembling fingers through her hair. She wasn't afraid. Despite the danger radiating from his long, tensile body, Noble McCaneaghy hadn't frightened her.

She'd spent years mourning his loss, wondering when he would come back, and more years wondering what had happened to him. Now she knew.

He wasn't "Slats" any longer. That pale, scrawny, skin-headed boy had become a hard, bronzed panther of a man. Only his golden eyes were still familiar.

She picked up the periwinkle dress from the floor and amended that appraisal. His dictatorial, bull-headed disapproval of her actions was familiar, too.

If he felt so sure that she had become a seasoned hussy, then why had he kissed her so . . . hungrily?

She planted her fists on her hips, the movement drawing her attention to the matronly folds of thick, virginal white cambric. No holy sister in a cloistered order wore a more blameless gown. Her sense of remorse faded as her sense of injury grew.

So, she had whistled at him, displayed a minor degree of aesthetic appreciation. So what? And if she were guilty of using her feminine charms—flirting, she believed he'd called it—to ease her way in the world, what of it?

It was a male-dominated world and women—even rich, privileged women such as herself—had been given a completely unsatisfactory arsenal with which to compete. A woman would have to be a fool or a saint not to use every weapon at her disposal. Venice didn't claim to be either.

She stomped over to the bed, retrieved her dressing gown, and gave it a violent snap to shake the smoke fumes loose. Wrenching open the door to the armoire, Venice flung the gown inside. As she did so, Katie appeared in the doorway, a garishly embroidered kerchief held over her nose. The concern drained from her eyes when she saw Venice.

"Hey, was that McCaneaghy leaving your room?" Katie's voice, muffled behind the cloth, was alive with interest. "Boy, do you work fast! Honey, you got a future here, should your daddy ever lose his money and—"

"It wasn't like that," Venice said. "Mr. McCaneaghy is not at all what I expected."

"Better?" Katie asked in an awed voice.

"No. I mean, I didn't have the opportunity to ... I mean I don't want to know if ... oh, damn and blast!"

"Wal, fine, Venice, whatever you say."

"Nothing happened! *Nothing!*"

"Calm down, honey. Rome wasn't built in a day . . . you'll get him."

"I repeat: I don't want him."

It was a lie. Judging by the way Katie's lids narrowed in patent disbelief above the handkerchief, she knew it, too.

One little fact stood like a wall between Venice and her anger: Noble's kiss.

It wasn't her first kiss, but it might as well have been. When she'd used the word "slobber" to goad him, she'd used a word her other suitors had inspired. There had been nothing in the least "slobbery" about Noble's mouth on hers, his tongue . . .

Oh, Lord.

It had been as wonderful, as magical, as marvelous and beautiful and exhilarating as anything she'd ever experienced.

And it had come from a man who'd broken her heart once already.

Bright, late morning sun streamed in through the window. Pressing the heels of his hands against his eyes, Noble groaned. It felt as though someone had emptied a bucket of sand devils behind his lids. But he deserved his discomfort. He'd been so busy storming around in high dudgeon last night, he'd forgotten he'd originally offered Venice his room. So much for chivalry.

Maybe it was all for the best. He wouldn't have trusted himself to be alone with her for two minutes, let alone the ten it would have taken to escort her over from the Gold Dust. Plus, he'd have had to camp outside the door, separated from her and the promise of her lush lips by a scant few feet. Even in the mind-clearing light of full day, it still seemed too much to ask of a mortal man.

Naw, Venice had been just fine. By all ac-

counts—and he had asked around after getting
back last night—Venice had that blonde saloon
owner fretting over her like a mother hen.

More important, she had money, lots of it. And
Leiland money, particularly in Salvage, could buy
anything, including a room.

Still, anxiety for her was churning his stomach.
Wearily, Noble accepted his fate. He'd never be
comfortable until he actually saw for himself that
she was all right.

Fetching his shaving gear from the saddlebag,
Noble whipped up suds in the mug. He lathered
his face and peered into the mirror. He didn't
much like what he saw.

Venice must think he was certifiable. What had
he been thinking of, yelling at her like that? *Thinking?* That was the problem. Ever since he'd heard
Venice was here, he'd given up the habit of conscious thought. He didn't do a whole lot more
than react these days. Charging into her room,
grabbing her, kissing her, and then all but calling
her a trollop before stomping away.

What was it to him if she'd grown up to be like
Adele?

The razor slipped in Noble's hand and a dot of
blood blossomed amidst the thick, white lather. He
swore. As soon as he saw her, he was going to
apologize. Even if it killed him.

Katie blew froth from the mug of beer, topped it
off, and slid it down to one of her few paying customers. Surreptitiously, she sliced off a wad of
chewing tobacco and dropped it into the keg. It
gave the weak brew a bit more kick for the dollar.
Lord knew, she needed every cent she could eke
out of this place. Here it was, almost eleven
o'clock, and all she'd sold was a couple of beers
and a half dozen cups of coffee.

She looked over the interior of the Gold Dust Emporium. Oh, it was filled all right; plenty of men sat at the tables, lounged at the counter, and leaned against the walls, all as quiet as sinners on baptism day, their grizzled faces turning with nauseatin' regularity toward the top of the staircase.

It was disgusting. The fools gawked at Venice like she was a two-headed calf. And now, the jackasses had taken to sitting around, hoping to impress Miz Leiland with their virtuous sobriety, all so she'd smile at 'em and maybe dance with 'em at tomorrow's shindig.

Well, shit, this weren't no church social hall. This was a saloon!

Katie slapped a wet rag down on the counter. First and foremost, Cayuse Katie Jones was a businesswoman. Alien considerations like friendship aside, one fact stood out like a mud hen in a flock of snow geese: Venice Leiland was bad for business.

Worst of all, it shouldn't oughta be that way! Venice attracted more men than Reverend Niss's notorious revival meetings. There had to be some way to turn a profit from her presence here.

A door on the second floor opened and every head in the room snapped to attention. Peggy, auburn ringlets bouncing along with everything else, sashayed into sight. A groan of disappointment rose from the men.

"Wal, excuse me!" Peggy said, mortally offended. "But seems to me like I was good enough fer more 'an a few of you just last week."

The men ignored her. Peggy's face turned a magnificent shade of red. Twitching her tail, she stalked back the way she'd come.

Much more of this, thought Katie, and the girls will be finding other places to board. There was only one thing for it, Katie thought with a sigh. She needed to push Venice off the pedestal all these pipe-dreamin' fools had put her on.

And the best way to do that, for everyone concerned, was to get Venice bedded.

Once Venice was *one* fella's concern, these jerkwater would-be beaus could come drown their sorrows right here at the Gold Dust! And that one feller should be Noble McCaneaghy.

It was a plum good idea. The revelation that Venice was a twenty-two-year-old virgin still unsettled Katie. And while she was absolutely convinced that Venice should choose a groom from New York's upper crust, maybe, while she had the chance, Venice *should* have a taste of plain old animal. And Noble McCaneaghy was one fine-looking animal.

The angry swirling of Katie's rag lost speed, slowing to big, measured circles.

McCaneaghy had raced clear from the other side of town on seeing a little smoke and then shot straight up to Venice's room, ignoring everything in his path till he'd made certain she was safe. That was interesting. Real interesting.

Poor little Venice, thought Katie pityingly. That man had her so balled up inside, she didn't know whether to laugh or cry. Whatever McCaneaghy had said or done up in that room had only whet the kid's appetite.

Katie smiled. She was a good gambler. One of the territory's best. All she had to do was stand back and watch and see which way the cards fell before she sat in on the game. She would find a way to cash in on Venice Leiland and turn the Gold Dust into a profitable venture. And the one who was going to ante up was Noble McCaneaghy.

Chapter 7

By the time Venice's feet touched the cold floorboards the next morning, her anger had burned itself out, leaving a few facts amongst the ashes.

Her childhood knight had become a ragged nomad. The soup kitchens and homes that had been funded by the Leiland Foundation were filled with men like Noble; men who'd seen too much.

She knew from reading newspapers that many war veterans were adrift in the territories, seeking to lose themselves in the harsh, unforgiving landscape. It couldn't be more obvious that Noble had become one of them, she thought, remembering the torn clothes he'd been wearing yesterday. And there hadn't been a horse to keep him company at that water trough. He probably couldn't afford one.

She pulled on a russet- and green-striped dress, worked the small, bone buttons through their hooks, and adjusted her fashionable collapsible bustle. As she arranged a large, silk-flower-bedecked bonnet on her head, her thoughts wandered back to nine years before.

After Noble had gone, it had taken her months to screw up the courage and ask her father what had happened to him. She still remembered making the long trip up the marble stairway to her father's inner sanctum, the fourth-floor library.

His chill expression on seeing her at the door had grown rigid when he had heard her question. He'd motioned her to take a seat on the far side of the huge walnut desk that dominated the hushed, gaslit room.

Noble, he'd explained in a grave voice, had forfeited his sponsorship to Yale and disappeared. Apparently, her father had continued, he hadn't the strength of character necessary to meet the demands placed upon him. Noble had been a failed experiment and now he was best forgotten. Doubtless he would end an unproductive and purposeless life in circumstances similar to the one Trevor had found him in.

It was the last mention her father had ever made of Noble McCaneaghy.

Venice stared down at her hands, surprised to find she'd twisted the fringed end of her silk shawl into a tangled knot.

No wonder Noble had reacted so strongly to seeing her. He was *embarrassed.* And Noble had ever been a proud lad. If she saw him again, she'd do what she could for him. He'd been her friend. She owed him more than she could ever repay.

She left the room and started down the hallway. She might *not* see Noble again. He might already have gone, drifting toward some vague future, a shadow slipping from her life. Well, she thought sadly, what more could she expect.

Besides, she abjured herself, she should be worrying about Salvage's future, not her own past. At least in Salvage she might make a difference.

At the top of the staircase she stopped and peeked around the corner. Sure enough, *they* were waiting.

Doesn't anyone in Salvage have a job? she wondered, taking a deep breath and starting down the stairs. Everyplace she went seemed to be crowded with men picking their teeth, their noses, or their fingernails.

She stepped off the last riser and the men turned toward her. Several stumbled to their feet. Those wearing hats swept them from their heads, crushing them against their chests as she passed. It was a little unnerving. She smiled tentatively. Mumbled "ma'ams" met her overture.

"Hey, Venice," Katie called from the opposite side of the room. With a sense of relief, Venice headed toward her. The men fell back, parting like the Red Sea.

"Good morning, Miss Jones," Venice said. "Have you been able to ascertain the identity of the owner of the local bank? I do not wish to indulge in paranoia, but I begin to suspect a conspiracy is afoot. Not only has the bank been closed since I arrived, but no one can tell me who actually works there."

Katie frowned over a thick piece of twine she was securing to the brass rail at the end of the bar. "Someone's gotta know something." She handed Venice the end of the rope. "Tie this to the leg of that chair, will ya?"

"Certainly," Venice said, uncertain what Katie was up to but glad to be of service. "Do you think the postal service might have any information?"

"Don't know, hon. Now, where is that . . . ?" Katie muttered, rummaging beneath the counter.

Venice finished tying a sturdy square knot. Seeing Katie's preoccupation, she decided not to pester her with any more questions. She sidled past the men, nodding and smiling her way to the door and out into the bright spring sunshine.

Her plan had seemed so simple. She would interview the owners of the larger businesses in Salvage and determine to what extent they relied on the spur line. Then she would assess the town's resources and, finally, develop a plan for their self-sufficiency.

And if she were successful, her father would have to take note. He'd have to admit she had an aptitude for something other than scandal.

But first, she needed the townspeople's help. And, by heavens, she was going to get it. With that thought, Venice forged across the dust-laden street, making for Grundy's Mercantile.

The second she stepped inside, her nostrils were assailed by the pungent odor of rancid bacon. Two men, one she recognized as the cook over at the Pay Dirt and the other unfamiliar, were haggling over a greenish side of pork lying on the counter. No shopkeeper was present to mediate the proceedings.

The men paused long enough to offer her gap-toothed grins before returning to their argument. Venice walked along the shelf-lined walls. Grundy's was well—if untidily—stocked with all manner of supplies: candle molds, feather beds, chamber pots, spades, holsters, tents, and stakes. Barrels of beans, molasses, flour, rice, and sugar stood open to the elements—and the local insect population. A few grains of brown rice in one barrel started to move of their own volition.

At the back of the store a length of canvas was hung across an open doorway. Voices floated from beyond it.

"Dammit, Anton," a reedy voice piped, "if'n you'd jes hold the damn thing, it'd set up fine."

"It's too heavy," another voice insisted. "Yore gonna have ta bolt it."

"Oh, yeah," the first voice returned sarcastically, "that's gonna look real natural now, ain't it?"

Venice peered around the curtain into what seemed to be a storage room. Tall shelves, piled with heaps of mismatched goods, obstructed her view. "Excuse me," she called.

A sharp-featured, red-haired man popped up from behind a massive workbench. His eyes widened and a sickly smile creased his pockmarked cheeks.

"Miz Leiland! Anton! Look who come callin'!" He seemed to kick something—or someone. A blurted oath confirmed Venice's suspicions. A blocky, thunderously scowling face rose from behind the same workbench, towering over the red-headed man.

"Shi-it, Harry! Why'd you kick me? I knowd who this is fer . . ." The behemoth's little eyes followed the other man's riveted gaze. His small, round mouth formed an *oh* of surprise.

Venice smiled. "Might one of you gentlemen be the proprietor of this establishment?"

"Yup." Both men gulped simultaneously.

"Then you are Misters Grundy?"

The redhead shouldered past the giant, scrambling to a halt in front of her. He started to hold out his hand and then, as an afterthought, wiped the palm on his pant leg and offered it to her again. She shook it.

"Harry Grundy, Miz Leiland." He jerked his head back toward the giant who was still open-mouthed and mute. "That's Anton."

"Delighted."

"Yup. Well . . ." Without a word of warning, Harry grabbed Venice's elbow and spun her around, yanking her out of the storage room. "Now, what kin I do fer you, ma'am?"

"Ah, I was wondering if I might have a few moments of your time," she said as Harry reached behind her and jerked the canvas back over the doorway. "My family finances the foundation that maintains the Leiland-Hawkness Spur Line."

Harry bobbed his head in understanding. Venice continued. "The spur line's raison d'être has been my uncle's archaeological expeditions. But as my uncle has failed to find anything of scientific significance in his seven years here, he will be moving on next season. Thus the spur line's original function ceases to exist."

Harry's eyes looked a bit glazed over.

"Do you understand?" she asked gently.

"Nah-uh."

"The spur line may close down," she said.

"Oh."

"I am hoping to find something on which to anchor Salvage's future. Some resource, some distinction—"

Harry gave short, understanding jerks of his head. "How long we got?"

"Excuse me?"

"How long we got before you close down the spur line?"

"*I* am not—"

"It's okay, Miz Leiland. We understand. Salvage has gotta make the grade, pure and simple."

"But I don't have any inten—"

"But jes' counta Milt didn't find nuthin' don't mean there ain't anythin' sci-en-tific here to discover."

"I understand your feelings, Mr. Grundy. But my uncle is a trained paleontologist. If there were any fossils around here, he would have found them," she said.

"Don't be too sure!"

She looked up, startled. Anton's big, rough features floated, bizarrely disembodied, above the canvas curtain leading to the storage room.

"This mountain's just about bustin' its seams with real live ark-te-facts . . ." Anton said.

Harry glared at his brother. The giant's voice petered out.

Harry turned his attention back to Venice. "Mebbe I can help you, Miz Leiland."

"I'd appreciate any help I can get," she replied eagerly. Finally here was someone willing to tell her something. "Do you know where the bank owner—"

Harry cut in as smoothly as if Venice hadn't opened her mouth. "Ain't surprising you missed some of the rare things we got around here. You ain't even been in our fair city a week yet."

Venice felt her lips twitch. *Fair city.* "That's only too true."

"Has you even been to the Ringo Clements camp?"

"No."

"Gotta see that. It's where Ringo Clements up and ate his partner, Matthew Morris, back in the winter of '53. Didn't know he was only three miles out of Salvage or he probably wouldn'ta done it. Now there's a regular tourist attraction."

"I'm sure." Venice pressed a hand to her stomach.

"People'll line up to get a look-see. Sorta exciting." Harry winked at Venice. "I heard you like a little excitement yerself."

The word "excitement" acted like a red flag to Venice. She hated that word. She hated reading it, she hated hearing it, she hated its use in any connection with herself. And she especially hated this ... *person* thinking she would find Wingo Clemens's disgusting and unnatural dining habits in any way "exciting." She'd had enough.

"Thank you for your help," Venice said with chill formality before sweeping from the room. "Good day."

"Excitement, indeed!" she muttered furiously,

tears of frustration stinging her eyes as she stomped out the door and straight into a rock-hard male chest.

She hit him with enough force to produce an audible *woof* from him and knock her off balance and into the street. She staggered a second until her boot heel caught in her hem and tripped her. She landed on her bottom in the dust, her fashionable collapsible bustle collapsing beneath her. Her huge, elegant bonnet tipped over her eyes, blinding her.

"Damnation!" she ground out.

The next instance someone caught her beneath the elbows and lifted her effortlessly to her feet. The same someone gingerly lifted the brim of her hat and peered at her, scowling. Noble McCaneaghy. Of course.

"Where are you hurt?" he asked worriedly.

Only by an enormous strength of will did she manage not to rub her behind.

"I'm not." She blinked up into his golden eyes, waiting warily for him to resume the verbal battle they'd started last night. He didn't.

"Why are you crying, then?" he demanded.

"I'm not crying," she answered, surprised. "I'm ... I'm mad!"

He released the breath in a whoosh of what she was sure was relief. There was no way she was mistaking it, she realized. He was still worrying about her, even after all these years. The thought produced an unexpected flush of pleasure in her.

Almost as much pleasure as the feeling of his fingers, solid and strong, still wrapped lightly about her forearms.

"Shoulda known," he said. "Even as a kid, you never cried when you were hurt, only when you didn't get your way."

She lifted an imperious eyebrow. "I got over *that* years ago."

"Sure." He grinned. His very eyes seemed to smile. She'd almost forgotten that smile, the way it invited a person—no, the way it invited *her*—to join. It was still too tempting to resist. She smiled back.

"Okay. Maybe I still backslide now and then," she conceded.

His smile stretched broader and he released her arms. After a fractional hesitation, he started brushing the dust from her sleeves.

"So, why are you mad, Venice?" he asked, his hands working impersonally on her sleeves, lifting her bonnet from her head and blowing the dirt off. "Tell me."

For some reason it didn't seem odd that she was standing in the middle of a dirty street in a squalid town high in the mountains while Noble McCaneaghy—a man who until last night she hadn't seen in ten years—dusted her off as casually as a nanny would her charge. And it didn't seem in the least strange that she wanted to confide in him. She always had.

"It's this town," she said. "I want to help these people, but I can't do anything for them if everyone remains determined to keep me in the dark."

"I'm not sure I understand."

"No one will tell me where Uncle Milton keeps his ledgers, or his account books, or anything."

"Maybe they don't know."

"Not know?" she asked incredulously. "Noble, a rough estimate says that three-quarters of the townspeople ship their supplies up on that spur line. Someone, somewhere, has got to have an invoice for *some* of that freight."

"Oh."

"How long do they think I'm going to sit

around waiting for the foundation ledgers? Do they think I'm just going to get tired and leave?"

"Maybe," Noble mumbled, replacing her hat, standing back and scowling at it a second before readjusting the angle.

She put her hands on her hips and tapped her foot. "But you know what peeves me the most?"

"I'd say you were a mite more than peeved."

"You're right. You know what *angers* me the most? That these people think I'm so *stupid* that I'll just go away if they don't cooperate. If I really want answers, all I have to do is send one wire to the spur line office in Denver and the train stops running today."

Noble dropped to his knees in front of her and caught her tapping foot. The laces had come undone. Deftly he began retying them. "Sounds like a typical Leiland tactic," he said, his voice growing tight.

"They aren't my tactics, Noble," she said softly, her anger playing out as she noticed the way the sun glinted off his bowed head. A tingle started where his broad hands brushed the silk-clad skin above her boot.

"Aren't they?" he murmured. He'd finished relacing her boot and for just a second his fingers lingered on her calf, a touch so near a caress that the breath caught in her lungs. He must have heard. He turned his head, looking up at her from where he knelt. His thick gleaming hair fell across most of his face. All she could see were his eyes, dark, intent.

With something that sounded like a muffled curse, he bolted upright. "Listen," he said, "I don't live in Salvage. I just wander through now and then."

He was backing away, putting even more emotional distance between them. She took a step forward.

"Maybe you could help me, Noble."

"I doubt it. I don't even know why you're so concerned about this town."

"This town is the foundation's responsibility. The foundation saw to that when it allowed the people to use the spur line for seven years."

"You oughta talk to some of these other folks, not me. They know more about—"

"But they don't know *me*. You do."

"Do I?" The question was quiet.

"Yes. Please, Noble? Just talk to me?"

That stopped him. He looked around, like a trapped animal, his eyes finally coming back to her.

"Sure. Why not?" He sounded resigned. "What's one conversation? Sure. I can do that."

She smiled and was amazed when he seemed to flinch. Maybe he was still sore from falling off her balcony.

"I was gonna go eat breakfast at the Pay Dirt."

"Wonderful. I, ah, I have to go back to my room." She wasn't going to tell him she had to go get some money. He'd insist he pay for her meal and she'd already surmised that Noble McCaneaghy didn't have a dime to spare. "I'll meet you there."

"Okay," he said. He turned around and started off toward the end of the street, muttering, "A conversation. Probably won't take too long. What's a little talk between old acquaintances?"

Apparently Noble, too, felt badly about last night. They'd once been the best of friends. Unwilling to analyze the pleasure that thought gave her, Venice clambered back up onto the walkway and hurried back toward the Gold Dust. A few men called to her, doffing crushed and stained hats as she passed, as gallant as any wealthy gentlemen. They might not be particularly clean, but they were the proudest dirty people Venice had ever met.

The thought brought her to a full stop. Salvage attracted a different sort of people; people uncomfortable with rules and regulations—and soap— flourished here.

They must be nigh on desperate to keep their peculiar paradise alive.

Small wonder they saw her as the enemy. And, she thoughtfully allowed, she'd given them every reason to, rushing in, demanding ledgers and inventories like any accountant before he closed the door on a business.

But she would prove she wasn't uncaring or unsympathetic . . . to Salvage and Noble.

She was so deeply engrossed in her thoughts that she didn't notice Tim Gilpin until she was beside him. He was nailing handbills on a front wall.

"Why, Miss Leiland!" Tim said happily. "I heard you had a spot of excitement last night."

There was that word again. "You're not going to write that I set the confounded place on fire in order to indulge my purportedly warped need for adventure, are you?" Venice asked suspiciously.

Tim chuckled. "Good heavens, I wouldn't consider doing such a thing."

Venice relaxed. "What are these?" She pointed to the flyers in his hand.

Tim fidgeted, kicking a pebble around with his toe. "Well, I have to earn enough to keep the newspaper afloat," he said, "and if someone pays me to run off a few handbills and nail them up around town, I can't afford to let easy money slip through my fingers. I have to—"

Impatiently, Venice sidestepped the editor and read the advertisement:

SINNERS!

FLORITA DEVORES, THERESA MERRY TERRY AITKENS,

AND

MADEMOISELLE "FIFI" LA PALMA

WILL SPEAK, IN DETAIL, ON THE SUBJECT OF THEIR

FALL FROM GRACE, TRANSGRESSIONS, MULTITUDINOUS

SINS, DEPRAVITIES AND ADDICTIONS

TONIGHT!!!! 8:00 SHARP.

DONATIONS TAKEN AT PAY DIRT SALOON

BY REVEREND CARL NISS.

SALVATION ALSO DISCUSSED.

Venice frowned, perplexed. "A revival meeting?"

"Yeah," Tim mumbled.

"You know, I've never been to a revival meeting—"

"You don't want to go to this meeting, Miss Leiland."

Venice shrugged. "I expect I'll pass. I don't go out much in the evenings. Regardless of what the press thinks." She smiled at him teasingly. "I'll be seeing you at tomorrow evening's party?"

"Yes, ma'am. You can count on it, Miss Leiland."

She had nearly reached the end of the boardwalk when she heard her voice being called.

"Miz Leiland!"

She turned. Her polite smile froze on her face. The Salvage Ladies' Conviviality League was approaching. There were six of them, marching.

Courage, she told herself. "Ladies?"

A pretty girl, her upturned nose dusted with freckles, stepped hesitantly forward.

"Er, Miz Leiland," the girl said, "my name is Suzanne Gates, ma'am. The Salvage Ladies' Conviviality League has made me, ah, *asked* me to, that is, most of the guild—"

"All of the guild 'cept Agnes Dupre!" a voice averred loudly from behind the stammering girl.

"All the guild," Suzanne continued, her voice gaining volume and certainty, " 'cept Agnes Dupre, what penned that note to you in the first place, *without* checkin' with us other league members, wants to apologize fer that note."

The ladies behind the girl nodded vigorously in agreement.

"You do?" asked Venice in amazement.

"Yup. We does. And we know this is forward and all, but we'd be real grateful if you would sorta let us reconsider your kind invite to that party yer givin' tomorrow night, so we could come."

"Realize it ain't very well done of us," another woman said, stepping forward. "But we sorta got roped into taking a stand before we even knew it. Agnes jes' kinda took fer granted none of us would want to, well, you know."

Venice's pleasure dimmed. "All of the ladies of Salvage are invited. And I do mean *all*. Including any ... boarders at the saloons in town."

"Yes'm," Suzanne Gates said, clearly abashed. "We understand. We won't cause no one no reason to take offense. Sake's alive, ma'am, we ain't been to a party, a real party, *never!* Not a one of us plans to waste time actin' all hoity-toity when we could be dancin'."

Venice allowed her delight to take firmer hold. "Well, I'd be delighted to have the Convivial Ladies accept my invitation."

The five other ladies stepped forward. "Now that that's settled, what can we do to help?"

"Do?" Venice asked. She had taken care of most of the arrangements before her arrival. The next spur line run would be carrying supplies for the party.

"Yeah, do," a big raw-boned girl said. "What can we bring? I got a couple of crocks of bread n' butter pickles I saved from last summer."

"I got a good couple gallons of buttermilk," another woman said. "I kin get at least forty, fifty dozen biscuits outta that."

"Me and my sisters can make a mess of pies," someone else chimed in.

Overwhelmed by the offers, Venice threw up her hands, laughing. "Whatever you ladies would be so gracious to offer, I would be only too happy to receive."

"Sakes, no one's gonna get any biscuits if I stand here all day!"

In a flurry of excitement, the ladies scurried off, happily bemoaning the time they didn't have and the things they had to do. Within five minutes, only Suzanne Gates was left, gazing wistfully at Venice.

"Is there anything else?" Venice asked gently.

"No." The girl blushed prettily. "I was jes' admiring yer dress. It sure is pretty."

Venice looked down at the shimmering, gemcolored skirts. Her gaze traveled to Suzanne's worn, sun-bleached calico.

"Would you, would you like to bor—" Venice stuttered to a stop. She didn't want to offend the young Miss Gates. How did one make such an offer? *Should* one make such an offer?

"Could I?" Suzanne exclaimed, bouncing up and down on her toes. "I would rightly *love* to borrow one of yer dresses, Miz Leiland. If I could wear one of yer gowns, that skinny Blaine Farley would stop twitchin' my hair like it was still in pigtails!"

"Miss Gates," she said, "you come to my room at the Gold Dust Emporium tomorrow evening at seven o'clock and we'll deck you out in the loveliest gown in my wardrobe. If Blaine Farley twitches your pigtail after that, he isn't worthy of the title male."

Suzanne blushed and beamed. Venice gave her a conspiratorial wink and turned her gently, pushing her forward. "Go on, now. And remember, seven o'clock."

"Yes, ma'am!" the girl promised and quickly scooted off. Venice smiled after her retreating figure, fairly dancing over the plank boards. It must be wonderful to have a special man who made you feel so special, so aware, so . . .

She pushed the treacherous notion away and with it Noble McCaneaghy's golden-eyed image.

Chapter 8

Noble didn't have to look up to tell Venice Leiland had just entered the room. Only the odd, rich, and deucedly pretty Venice Leiland would invoke absolute and concentrated silence.

Noble placed his knife and fork down on either side of the plate. He kept his gaze fixed on the slabs of half-charred meat and steaming potatoes. She'd taken so long, he'd begun to hope she had decided not to join him.

That little scene outside had shaken him. He'd reacted automatically, out of long-forgotten habit. And it had seemed so harmless: straightening her hat, dusting her off, tying her boot . . .

That was his mistake. He'd touched her slender calf and felt the silken warm texture of her, even through that damned stocking, and gone as hot and hard as a randy sixteen-year-old. He'd looked up into those mist-colored eyes of hers and felt as though he were drowning.

She scared the hell out of him.

The chair beside him scraped the rough floor planks and a russet-striped skirt switched against his denim-clad leg.

"Noble?" She sounded a tad hesitant.

There was nothing to do but get this over with. He looked up. Every man in the room had turned his avid interest toward the table where Noble and Venice sat. Maybe he should just rent the damn

102

stage over at the Empress Theater and sell tickets. "Eat, you pack of hairy, skin-shanked, flea-ridden sons of bitches!" Noble barked.

The men hurriedly returned their attention to their food, but their eyes kept sliding back toward Venice. Not that he could blame them, Noble thought when he finally allowed himself the pleasure of looking at her. She was every man's dream of womanhood.

Fine resolutions you make, boyo. Here you are not only staring at her like she's a tender yearling and you're a starved wolf, but you're ready to leap over the table and haul her back into your arms.

"I'm sorry," Noble mumbled.

"Excuse me?" she said.

"I'm sorry for—" Noble looked around. Every head in the room was tilted in their direction. He lowered his voice. "I'm sorry for my less than chivalrous behavior last evening. It seems in my relief in finding you safe, I transgressed certain common laws of decency."

Venice was staring at him, wide-eyed. Such perfectly gray eyes, such curling black lashes. Mentally, Noble shook himself and hurried on. "I assure you it shan't happen again."

"What happened to your accent?"

Accent? For a moment, Noble was confused. "I went to college. Remember? You ought to remember; your daddy paid for most of it."

That was not strictly true. Trevor had paid for the year before he was drafted into the Union Army. When he came back, his own sweaty manual labor had paid for his degree.

"But as your friend Cassius Reed will tell you, you can't whitewash a piece of no-account trash. I'm no more 'college' than you are 'Colorado.' Just amuses me sometimes to remember the good ol' days."

Damn it. Some apology. Her lovely face had paled.

"You don't know what I am, or am not, Noble," she said. "You weren't there, remember? As a matter of fact, I've been in the Rocky Mountains several times in the past years. I spent two months with Uncle Milton in the dunes area south of here."

"You're kidding."

"No, I'm not. I've spent a season on the Amazon, too. I . . . I've seen so many fascinating things. I just hope I get the opportunity to see more someday."

She sounded so wistful. She noticed his expression and smiled. "You needn't look so shocked," she said. "You might recall that I never did particularly like living in the city."

"That's true." He leaned back in his chair, relaxing slightly. "You were always begging me to take you camping in Central Park."

She smiled. "And you never would. I suppose no one would let you."

He chuckled. "Reason I never took you was that I hadn't the first notion how to set up a tent."

Her eyes sparkled. "You're kidding."

He held up one hand. "It's true. Think of it, Venice. I was a sixteen-year-old kid from the Lower East Side. How was I supposed to know how to camp?"

"But you always said that before your father went to fight in the Crimean War your family lived on a little farm in northern Ireland."

"True. But I was four, Venice. We immigrated the year after my father died. I didn't do a whole lot of camping before we came to America."

"Why didn't you tell me?"

"And fall off that pedestal you had me on?" He

snorted. "Hardly likely. I rather liked being idolized."

She laughed. "Charlatan!"

"Yeah. Well, adulation was sort of addictive."

"Humph."

"You worshiped the ground I walked on."

Somewhere in the past ten years she'd acquired a dimple. It was the most damnably provocative thing he'd ever seen. He wondered how many other men thought so too. "But by now you've probably had lots more experience as the adored rather than the adorer," he said.

Her smile lost some of its brilliance.

"I'm sorry," he said, feeling like a louse. "I didn't mean that the way it sounded."

"I, too, am sorry," she said softly.

He cocked his head, bewildered.

"I'm sorry if my behavior yesterday led you to believe I was a . . . well, you know."

He didn't help her. Couldn't help her.

"My appreciation for your appearance," she said with a gulp, "was spontaneous. I have never done anything like that before. You can rest assured, any future impulses shall be acted on only after due consideration."

The speech came tumbling out in a rush. Noble snorted in response to the breathless self-indictment.

"I seriously doubt the Venice Leiland I knew could ever hold off doing something till she'd given it 'due consideration.' "

"Too true, Noble. Maybe I better stick to making promises I can keep." She bit her lip. "I'm sorry, I didn't mean to belabor the point."

It took him a second to realize that she was referring to the promise he'd broken ten years ago. For the first time, he realized just how much of a betrayal his leaving must have seemed to her.

Of course, she didn't know all the circumstances. He was certain of that. His lips flattened.

She reached across the table, laying her hand over his. It seemed so ingenuous, so natural, but the electricity shooting up his arm, tingling his flesh at the merest contact with her . . . well, there wasn't anything innocent about *that!*

"We'll just forget last night, shall we?" she suggested.

Yeah. Sure, Noble thought. Forget the feel of you high against my chest. Of your mouth opening beneath—He withdrew his hand from her touch. Her satiny skin blanched even further.

She thought he disliked her touch! That was a laugh. He wanted to sweep her out of the chair and carry her to his room and . . . *please God, make her say something, anything to keep my thoughts from their present course.*

Her eyelids fluttered and a sad smile bowed the perfect curve of her lip.

"What have you been doing, Noble?" she asked, trying for a bright tone.

"This. That. Mostly exploration."

"Exploration." She nodded encouragingly. "That sounds fascinating."

He frowned. Something wasn't quite right about her attitude. "It has its moments."

"And how have you been, Noble?" she asked quietly.

"Great," he said. "Wonderful. Couldn't be better."

"I'm happy to hear that."

She didn't believe him! Doubt lurked in her artificial smile, in that too-sincere tone.

What did she think? That if a man didn't end up like her father, playing ruler of the world from a Park Avenue mansion, he was a failure?

"I . . . ah . . ."

Noble stared at her in amazement. She was acting as nervous as a cat crossing a creek.

"I wonder. Hmmm." She furrowed her brow in mock consternation. "Noble, I have a problem."

He snapped to attention.

"What?"

"Oh, nothing too trying, but something you might be able to help me with. You see, it's important that I talk to my uncle if I'm to be able to do anything for this town."

"Why is Salvage so important to you, Venice?"

"I told you."

"And that's all?" he asked suspiciously. "You feel responsible?"

"The truth?"

"Yes."

"I have plenty of money, Noble, but I don't have the respect of the foundation's board of trustees. It doesn't matter to me what the popular press prints about me, but those stories have undermined my credibility. Particularly with my father—"

"So you're still trying to prove yourself to Trevor?" Noble interrupted, unwilling to hear any more. Each word drove home just how far apart they'd grown.

"You don't understand."

"Sure, I do," he said. "Take a two-bit town and see if you can make it measure up." Sorta like taking a slum brat and seeing if you can teach him Greek and Latin.

She nodded. "You can help me," she continued. "No one in Salvage is going to let me find my uncle's accounts, so I'll have to find my uncle. You were just saying that you are familiar with these mountains." She took a deep breath. "I would like to hire you to guide me to him. I will, of course, compensate you well for taking up your valuable time—"

Noble felt his mouth start to gape. Venice held up a hand as though to stop him from interrupting. She needn't have worried. He couldn't have uttered a word. He felt pole-axed.

"I will open an account for you and you can charge whatever you need to my name." Her tone softened. "Please avail yourself of the opportunity to purchase some new shirts."

She was offering him charity! He glared at her. High-handed, imperious little do-gooder!

She hurried on. "To be applied against your fee, of course."

He choked. No words came out. He tried again. "Is that supposed to be a balm to my pride?"

She stared at him.

"Listen, Venice, I don't need your charity, your work, or your goodwill. And I sure as hell don't have any desire to help you win your daddy's blessing."

"I didn't mean to offend you."

"Well, you did! I am not some two-bit saddle tramp. 'Exploration' was *not* a euphemism for kicking around the mountains!" he shouted.

"It wasn't?"

Her surprise spurred his indignation. "No!"

"I'm sorry. I misunderstood." She didn't sound sorry. She sounded pleased! "But you don't have to get so upset. From the way you dress, I'd supposed that you were a bit down on your luck."

"I am *not* upset."

"Your pride is bruised. I understand," she said in those same compassionate tones.

"My pride is *not* bruised!"

"Really. I know what it's like to have people assume the worst about you."

"I bet you do."

"What did you say?" The impartiality had dropped from her tone. Good.

"Tim says you got kicked out of New York. So you decided that while you were on vacation you might as well play savior to a two-bit stinkhole and a two-bit drifter? Is that about the size of it?"

"I was not kicked out of New York!"

"Ha! Why don't you just take the next train back? You can be sitting at Delmonico's with some fool drooling over your hand by Saturday night."

"Oh!" Venice said, and this time Noble could hear his own offended dignity echoed in her increasingly strident voice. "This is important to me!"

She was *shouting* at him.

He waved his hand at her, gesturing for her to keep her voice down. Every eye in the room was on them. Noble gritted his teeth, trying to make it look as though he was smiling. *Brat.*

This is ridiculous, Venice thought as she glared down at the hard, determined features of her would-be guide. She was allowing this *man* to upset her. And, despite her memories of him as an Irish lad, Noble was now a man, just like any other man. And Venice knew quite well how to deal with *them.*

She wasn't sure she believed there was a purpose to his wanderings in these mountains, but she did know that regardless, he could still use some money. She owed Noble a debt for their friendship and she was going to repay it with or without his cooperation.

In no more time than it took to form the thought, Venice filled her eyes with tears. They overflowed her lower lids, slipping slowly onto her lashes. Not many, just two or three wet trails. Just enough to impress upon him how very sad his pig-headed, obstinate, unwarranted behavior was making her. Just enough to make him do what she wanted.

She willed a tremor to her lips. Reaching out her hand, she recovered Noble's fingers. She gazed deeply into his eyes, paused a second for added impact, and then whispered in a tremulous voice, "Can't we help each other? Please?"

He snorted.

There was no other word for it. A blatant snort and then a sound that might have been a choked laugh. It couldn't be, she thought. Men had many reactions to her tears, but laughter wasn't one of them.

She turned her trembling lips into quivering ones. A flood of tears escaped her eyes. She took a deep, deep breath, consciously swelling her chest in a sigh. She even threw in a ladylike sob.

"Please!" she begged.

Noble didn't want to laugh. He really didn't. But his sense of the absurd, so notably absent during the past twenty-four hours, was making an unheralded and not particularly well-timed comeback.

Venice had always been able to cry at will. Once, she'd even made money off the parlor maid's kids, betting she could get a river flowing inside thirty seconds. She'd won.

Practice had, indeed, made perfect. Since he hadn't fallen flat on his face the minute she started leaking tears, offering to do anything she wanted shy of self-mutilation, she redoubled her efforts. And she didn't look all that appealing.

The dewy-eyed effect was ruined by the thunderous scowl she couldn't hide. Her nose was getting red. And her lips, a moment ago so soft and tremulous, were wobbling. She was blubbering. Hell, she looked funny.

He laughed. Full-blown hilarity that once started,

was impossible to stop. Venice looked stunned. Her mouth was hanging open and her eyes were almost popping from her head and—

Someone's hand swung him around. The wind erupted from his lungs in a painful whoosh as a fist drove into Noble's belly. Another blow landed in his kidneys and lights of pain exploded in front of his eyes.

"You insufferable cad!" Cassius drew back his hand for another punch.

Still doubled up from the blow to his gut, Noble blocked it just in time.

Hell! he thought as he struggled backward, buying time to get his lungs working again. He was getting damned tired of being hit every time he spent more than a minute with Venice Leiland.

"What are you doing?" Venice cried, grabbing for Cassius's arm and missing.

"This swine made you cry. No man in my presence will cause a lady tears and have the deed go unavenged!"

"Stop it! Stop!" Venice yelled.

"You pompous, asinine piece of bear scat!" Noble straightened, the air finally back in his lungs. This time he wasn't going to be fobbed off by any flinching, squinting, or shaking on Cassius's part. He was going to beat the shit out of the bastard.

Noble drew back his arm, cocking his wrist. Suddenly, Venice was between them, throwing a hand against each of their chests, trying to push them apart. Noble swore, pulling his punch up short, barely missing Venice's cheek.

He'd almost hit her.

The muscles of his upper arms began to tremble. The eviscerating, overwhelming impotence spread rapidly through his body to his chest, his belly, his thighs.

He'd almost hit Venice. He was going to either throw up or buckle to the floor.

"Coward," sneered Cassius. "Look at him shaking. And well he ought, Miss Leiland. Only a craven makes a woman cry."

"You hit him! You struck him with your fists!" Venice exclaimed.

"As I shall thrash any bounder who makes a defenseless woman weep!" Cassius declared stoutly.

"Well, he didn't really make me . . ." Venice trailed off into incoherence.

Thank God, she didn't appear to realize just how close she'd come to getting hit. Noble forced the image away, concentrating instead on Cassius.

"I didn't what?" Noble asked Venice, silently promising Cassius a future encounter. One *without* Venice in attendance.

"Miss Leiland doesn't have to explain anything to you, you cur!"

"That's right!" Venice wheeled around, glaring at Cassius. She looked like an elegant Siamese cat facing off with a coyote. "And I needn't explain to *you*, either. I didn't say anything to you the other night about your audacity in following me out here all the way from New York, but now I feel I must. You don't have the right to interfere in my life. Not yet."

"But I thought—"

"I don't care what you thought!"

Not yet? What the hell did that mean? Noble wondered jealously. What liberties had she allowed this smirking rodent to make him so confident of their relationship? Noble's fists clenched at his sides.

Venice was trying to gather her composure. "I do not mean to seem like an ungrateful churl. Thank you, Mr. Reed, for your concern, misplaced though it is. Mr. McCaneaghy did not do anything untoward. Your interference was unnecessary."

"As you wish, Miss Leiland. But all things considered, you can't mean to continue this mad notion and stay in this backwater hole. We could go to Paris or Lon—"

"Yes, I do. But then, mad notions are rather a strength of mine."

Cassius stared at Venice for another moment before shooting a glare at Noble. "Lucky you have a champion, McCaneaghy. Some people are simply attracted to charity works."

If Noble could have trusted his legs, he would have beaten the living hell out of the man. Venice, however, seemed unaffected by Cassius's taunts. Her smile was as sweet as it was dismissive.

"Never fear, m'dear," Cassius assured her. "I will be staying within calling distance for the duration. Regardless of your protests, I could never bring myself to leaving you to the mercy of these ... yahoos." Cassius jerked forward into a bow before marching through the door.

Noble flopped down in his chair. He didn't trust himself to any but the most elementary movements. His mouth was still dry. Venice's eyes narrowed on him.

"Don't worry, darlin'. This particular *yahoo* is lighting out of here as soon as he can!" he said.

She didn't deign to answer. She just left.

"High-handed, domineering, overbearing, misbegotten son-of—argh!" Venice stomped into the Gold Dust.

It was dim inside. For some reason Katie had pasted cheap brown paper over the windows. The ever-present crowd of silent men was lined around the room.

Katie breezed forth from behind the bar. "You musta been talking to McCaneaghy."

"And why would you assume that?" Venice demanded.

"Jes' a wild guess, hon." Taking hold of Venice's hand, Katie pulled her along.

"Well, you're right," Venice said, stumbling after Katie. "I *was* talking to him. I was offering him a job. A means to recover his pride, help me, and earn some honest money. And you know what he said?"

"Nah-uh. You haven't eaten yet, have you, Venice?" Katie stopped beside a table laid with a checked cloth.

"He refused! He all but told me to get out of town!"

Pulling out a chair, Katie shoved Venice gently down and pushed her to the table. The last was executed a little too forcefully, the edge of the table catching Venice square in the ribs. "Ow!"

"Sorry." Katie snapped open a big, square napkin. "What was you sayin', now? You offered McCaneaghy a job? Shoot, honey, he's already got one. Works for some outfit back East. Smith's and Son or somethin'. And what do you mean yore leaving town?" She stepped behind Venice and wrapped the napkin around her neck, tying the ends.

"He does?" Katie must be referring to the Smithsonian. A trill of pleasure that Noble really was doing explorations underscored her indignation. She wasn't going to be sidetracked. "I am *not* leaving! No one is sending me away from anywhere again!"

Katie lit the wicks of a pair of mismatched candles.

"But I know where I'd like to send that thick-skinned, long-haired . . ." Venice muttered darkly.

"How's about a nice cup of tea and maybe a cheese biscuit for your lunch?" Katie asked.

"I'm sorry, Miss Jones, I wasn't attending properly," Venice said, reaching behind her neck and fumbling at the napkin's knot. "I don't care for any lunch, thank you."

Katie swatted Venice's hands away. Venice looked up in surprise.

"Sure, you do," Katie insisted.

"Really, I'm not in the least hungry and—"

"If she ain't gonna et, I want my two bucks back!" a masculine voice said.

"Me, too!" another man called.

"An' me!"

"Yeah, Katie, we didn't pay two bucks to gnaw on a couple of rock-hard biscuits."

"Shut up a minute, there! I'm just gettin' her settled," Katie bellowed over Venice's head.

With dawning awareness, Venice turned in her chair, looking around her. She was seated in the center of the room, in an area roped off by the very twine she had helped to tie earlier. Men crowded up against the cordon. Many wore old, outdated day coats—sentimental reminders of past lives—atop dusty overalls and sweat-stained calico bib shirts. Most had knotted gaily colored kerchiefs and bow ties around their necks. Several had slicked their unwashed hair with shoe black.

One man, buck teeth displayed in a grin that was nearly as prominent as his Adam's apple, kindly directed Venice's attention to a piece of cardboard suspended above her head. She read: DINE WITH MISS VENICE LEILAND! $2

In utter mortification, she lowered her face toward the plate in front of her and whispered urgently from the side of her mouth, "Miss Jones! How *could* you?"

"Well," Katie said defensively, "I was just thinking how's it was such a waste. You being here and all these mangy skunks always hanging around, never spendin' more'n a dime."

Venice made herself smile as she said through her teeth, "But to charge a *fee* for these men to watch me eat! It's ... it's ..."

"It's business," Katie said. "And business ain't been so good since you took up residence. A gal's gotta eat. And I always did have a right healthy appetite."

She pulled out a chair, dragged it close to Venice's, and sat down. "All these lovesick prairie dawgs is so busy tryin' to impress you with what gentlemen they are, they ain't orderin' drinks. Half the gals that rent rooms from me are thinkin' about finding other lodgin' counta the men don't want to come, er, 'callin',' with you down the hall. Darn it, Venice, this seems to me like a harmless enough sorta way to make a buck."

"But to put me on display!" Venice protested. "Surely, you must have known you needed only to ask and I would gladly, happily, give you any money you wanted!"

In wonder, Venice watched Katie squirm in her seat. The blonde saloon owner fidgeted with the cutlery and made odd, gruff little clearing sounds in her throat. She refused to meet Venice's eyes.

"Well?" Venice prompted.

"I know this is sorta pre-sum, er, pushy, but I ain't never had too many friends. Ain't never felt the need fer 'em, leastways ones of my own gender, if you catch my meanin'." Katie smiled. Venice smiled back, a genuine smile this time, and Katie relaxed.

"Well, I figure you and I are 'bout as close to bein' girlfriends as I'm ever likely to get." Katie waved down Venice's would-be interjection. "Like I said, I don't know much about bein' a friend, but one thing I know for absolute sure is you don't never ask friends fer money. Not ever—shut up, now, Venice, honey—no matter how rich they are. It jes' kinda would stop bein' friendly like then."

Katie considered her a friend. There had been few opportunities in Venice's life for friendships and she very much appreciated what Katie was offering.

This, however, wasn't the time or the place, and Venice wasn't the sort of woman who made syrupy confessions as, she suspected, neither was Katie.

But there were other ways to acknowledge Katie's friendship. Lifting her chin, Venice surveyed the roomful of waiting men. Summoning up every ounce of her charm, she turned her most potent smile on the group. Sighs of pleasure whistled through the room.

"Gentlemen," Venice called out gaily, "please take down that rope and pull your chairs nearer so that our dinner together might be a more intimate occasion."

With a roar of delight, the men complied.

It was after midnight, but Cassius knew he wouldn't be getting to sleep for some time. He was hot and heavy and uncomfortable, like every man who attended Reverend Niss's revival. Damn! The things Fifi LaPalma had "confessed" to the huge crowd of men were even more lurid than his own fertile imagination could conjure. And Fifi had described them explicitly.

He was going to have to find a woman. It shouldn't be too hard.

Apparently, all the whores in town made "donations" to Niss in order to stand outside the saloon, ostensibly to "hear the word." They disappeared with the men as soon as the performance broke up and earned more in that one night than most did in a month. If they didn't pay up, several of the "brothers" who traveled with Niss saw to it that their evil influence was removed from the immediate vicinity.

Cassius had almost skipped Niss's performance, sure McCaneaghy would be there. A careful review of the room had shown he wasn't. Cassius had always assumed McCaneaghy had maintained his repulsively spotless reputation at Yale by running to mongrel bitches, not being able to afford the pedigreed courtesans most of Yale's student elite enjoyed. But maybe Noble was a bloodless eunuch. Or maybe he was just getting a little something from someone else. Like Venice Leiland.

The thought infuriated Cassius. She couldn't be lying beneath the likes of him. But Cassius had seen the alacrity with which she'd sprung to McCaneaghy's defense this afternoon.

For months in New York, Cassius had chased after Venice Leiland, indulging her every whim. He'd even borrowed money in order to follow her out here, sure she'd be impressed by his devotion and adventurous spirit, as well as thankful for his urbane company.

Instead, he'd found her fawning over the rough, uncouth Noble McCaneaghy. Well, Cassius swore, he was going to turn the situation back to his advantage. Somehow, the Leiland fortune would be at his disposal. He just had to figure out how.

Chapter 9

Noble was gone. Venice had watched him leave hours ago, as the dawn sky filled with mauve-colored clouds. She'd thought the promise of money, and maybe even some leftover fondness for her, would be able to keep him here. But she'd been wrong.

Well, it wasn't going to do her any good standing around feeling as though she'd been abandoned by her dearest friend. He was a complete stranger to her now. A stranger with the smile of a saint, the touch of the devil, and the visage of a Celtic deity, but a stranger nonetheless.

She made herself smile at young Blaine Farley. He looked as awful as she felt. "Are you all right, Mr. Farley?" she asked. Blaine nodded, his bloodshot eyes glazing over slightly with the movement of his head.

"Jes' fine, ma'am." His tone didn't convince her. "Where'd you want this trestle?" He pointed at the big plank table he'd dragged out of Herman's Funeral Parlor and Barber Shop.

"If you're certain you're up to it, you can place it over there," Venice said, pointing toward a grassy area nearby.

Wordlessly, Blaine set about dragging the table toward where other men were setting up various tents, booths, and kiosks.

She looked around her. The meadow behind the

Gold Dust had been transformed. Striped tents flanked a central area where dozens of tables were set up. Men were busily stringing hundreds of the colorful Chinese lanterns Harry Grundy had found moldering in a corner of the storeroom.

One of the saloon girls was helping another tote an enormous basket of potatoes toward a kettle suspended from a tripod. For some reason, the "calico gals" of Salvage were in amazingly good moods and in rare charity with one another. They scurried about, their striped corsets, filmy wrappers, and vividly colored dresses flashing here and there as they prepared food for hundreds.

With so many people working so hard to make the party a success, Venice would be damned if she'd let thoughts of Noble McCaneaghy interfere with her social duties. She had some charming to do and by God, she was going to do it! It was just fatigue that made her eyes feel so gritty and watery, she told herself.

Yesterday's encounter between Cassius and Noble still haunted her. She had never before realized just how sheltered her life had been. For the first time she had seen one man strike another in anger.

She could still hear the awful, dull thwack of Cassius's fist hitting solid flesh and Noble's gasp of pain. But far more shocking than the actual blows had been Noble's reaction. He had acted as though such fights were a common, everyday occurrence.

Now, finally, Venice had evidence for what her father had always declared; Noble lived by a code she was only dimly aware of. That knowledge unnerved her.

How could she be attracted to a man who was so completely alien to her? And she definitely was attracted. There was no denying the frission of excitement he invoked with his slow drawl and his lightning-laced touch. Perhaps it was just as well he was gone.

But it didn't feel that way.

"Miz Leiland!" Tim Gilpin hailed her as he jogged up, his florid face shiny with perspiration. "Your shipment is in!"

"It is?"

"Yes, ma'am! It just arrived. Five boxes with your name plastered all over the sides," Tim said, leaning over and bracing his meaty hands on his thighs as he puffed. "I had some of the boys set 'em out back of the loading platform. What's wrong, Miss Leiland? You don't look very happy."

"Oh, I'm sorry Mr. Gilpin. Of course, I'm delighted with the news," Venice said. "I just wish Mr. McCaneaghy were here to enjoy the party."

"Why?" Tim scowled.

She was too distracted to take offense at his belligerent tone. "Mr. McCaneaghy and I knew each other back East."

"Oh?"

She didn't elaborate.

"Small world," Tim grumbled. "Well, Noble isn't gone. I just saw him down at the station, not ten minutes ago."

A swift, potent tingle of pleasure rushed through Venice. "You did?"

"Yeah."

"That's wonderful! Oh, this is grand news, Mr. Gilpin."

"From the way you're grinning, I'd say it was a far cry better than grand," Tim said slowly.

Venice laughed. "Oh, dear me, sir! This is most, most felicitous!" Venice grabbed hold of Tim's hands. "Thank you!"

"Congratulations," Tim said dryly.

"Mr. Farley!" shouted Venice. Blaine looked up from the pleated paper skirt he was nailing to a nearby table. "Mr. Farley, would you be so kind as to do me a service?"

He snapped to attention. "Anythin' you want, I'll git, Miz Leiland. You want money, I'll become a millionaire. You want water from the ocean, I'm off this minute. You want snow from the North Pole, I'm—"

"Nothing so taxing, Mr. Farley," she said. "Please, ask some of the men to go down to the station to pick up the goods I've had shipped up for the party." She paused. "But wait a while, please."

"You got it, ma'am."

Venice knelt in the center of the railway station platform, the crowbar she'd finagled from the station attendant in hand. Four of the five boxes addressed to her had been opened, their contents carefully inspected and returned to their crates.

Noble, one shoulder braced against the wall in studied nonchalance, poked through the nearest open crate with his toe. Wine bottles. A whole crate full. He looked over at Venice. She must have felt his gaze for she looked up, bestowing another dazzling smile on him. Noble pressed his lips tightly together, trying not to answer her siren's call.

After yesterday, he'd needed time to think, so he'd wandered up and taken some last-minute measurements of a creek north of town. He'd returned to the train station to ship this last bit of data back East and was just about to leave when Venice had come sailing in.

He'd braced himself to face yesterday's termagant, but instead she'd been all winsome smiles. She was unpredictable, and it was driving him loco. He couldn't figure it. Yesterday Venice had been ready to skin him . . . and he couldn't really blame her. But laughing at her manufactured tears had allowed him a few minutes of blessed reprieve from the potent attraction he felt toward her.

His threat to leave Salvage had never been more than bravado, or wishful thinking. He wouldn't trust anyone to watch over Venice. Anyone, that is, except himself. Certainly not Cassius Reed.

Though God knows they certainly suited each other. They were from the same class, the same background. They probably had the same friends. Yeah, old Cassius might be an ass, but he was definitely a better mate for Venice than—

Better *mate?* Where the hell had that word come from? Noble thought. He spat out the wood splinter he'd been rolling around in his mouth and scowled furiously. *You get your head on straight here, boyo. Venice Leiland isn't for the likes of you. Never was, never will be.*

Unwillingly his gaze slid to where she knelt. There were smudges on her white shirtwaist. Her skirts were a pile of lace petticoats, ruched hem, and silk ruffles around her slender calves. Forcing the iron crowbar twixt the lid and lip of the last crate, she pried it open.

A pile of cedar wood curls filled the box. Venice frowned.

"I don't remember ordering anything that would need to be packed in wood shavings," she murmured. "In fact, I don't remember ordering a fifth box at all." She leaned over, tilting her head to read the label. "That's my name, though. Odd."

She straightened and dished handfuls of wood onto the floor. More followed, and more, until she sat amidst a large pile of shavings. The fragrant cedar entangled in her hair, caught in the nap of her skirt, and clung to her bodice. She looked too damn appealing.

With a snort of self-contempt, he turned and

walked to the doorway, his hand clamping above the door frame. He stared, unseeing, into the street. He could hear her behind him. The aroma of wood mixed with whatever perfume she was wearing: fresh mountain glen and purchased sensuality. The two scents should have warred with each other but didn't. Instead, the combined fragrance was powerful, alluring, quixotic, and arresting. Like her.

"Oh, God!" Venice gasped in a low voice. Noble's head snapped around. She had sunk back on the floor, her hands pressed to her chest. Instantly, he was beside her, pulling her up, enfolding her in his arms.

She clung to him, burying her face against his shoulder.

"What's wrong? Venice, what is it?"

"In the crate."

Still holding her pressed to his side, he released one arm from around her and bent forward, rummaging amongst the wood shavings. Something cool, smooth, and hard curved beneath his fingers. Impatiently, he brushed more wood away. White bones gleamed in close-fitting half-spirals. A skeletal rib cage.

With his free hand, Noble reached down and tugged. Half a skeleton appeared. Curiously, Noble pulled the rest of it up. With a sound of disgust, he dropped it back into the crate.

Someone had bolted an antelope's horn to the skull of what looked like a coyote or a bush fox. There was something grisly, something singularly unpleasant, in the idea of putting together mismatched parts of dead animals. It was more than unnatural; it was gruesome.

Venice made an unintelligible sound, burrowing her face against his throat.

"Why are you holdin' on to Miz Leiland like that?" Blaine Farley demanded.

Noble swore.

Blaine Farley stood in the doorway, indignation and jealousy burning in his eyes.

Hot-headed young fool, thought Noble. Half-heartedly, he started to pull Venice's arms from around his shoulders. She wouldn't let go and Noble, never having been able to deny Venice anything, found to his utter self-loathing that he wasn't about to start now. He settled his own arms firmly around her back and pressed her closer still, glowering at the red-faced boy quivering with outrage in the doorway.

"If you even *lift* your hands, I'm gonna kill you, Blaine," Noble promised.

"Step away from her!" Blaine demanded. As if in answer, Venice's arms tightened around Noble.

"Listen, Blaine," Noble said, determined to keep his patience, "someone sent Miss Leiland some sort of thing. It scared her. That's all."

Blaine's stance lost some of its belligerence. What had the crazy kid been thinking? That Noble was going to take advantage of the situation? Not that he wasn't capable of it, he jeered at himself, but in a railway station? Come on, he had a little more decorum than that.

Noble's voice cracked like a whip in the quiet room. "That is the last time I ever explain anything regarding Venice Leiland and myself to anyone. Next time someone decides to play knight errant, I'll see he earns the title. I'll flamin' fry him! Is that clear?"

The boy gulped. "I'm sorry, Noble. But I come in and see you and her and I—"

"Is that clear?"

"Yes, sir."

"Good. Now, get out of here and find that

worthless station attendant and ask him who delivered this crate and when. Do it. Now!" Without another sound, Blaine scooted out of the station.

"What is it, darlin'?" Noble asked, stroking the silky tendrils falling across her forehead. "Why does this hoax bother you so much?"

She looked up at him. Silver-eyed Mab. Black-haired, white-skinned changeling.

"It happened before. A few days ago. Someone buried a mouse with a bird's skull wired to it and then pitched pebbles at me to lead me to it. I thought children might be responsible, but there aren't many children in Salvage. And where would a child find the wherewithal to bolt something like this together?"

"Not everyone who'd think something like this is funny is a child," Noble said. "I know you, Venice. You might not like it, but a couple mismatched animal parts aren't enough to scare you. Not the kid who used to beg her Uncle Milton for snakeskins and deer skulls."

She didn't say a word, just laid her head against his throat.

"Venice, honey. Tell me."

She nodded. "It's stupid, really."

"Honey, I am as familiar with stupid as a priest is with catechism."

She laughed softly, the air escaping her lips caressing his throat. His arms tightened around her.

"Promise not to laugh?" she asked.

"No," he said solemnly.

"You were a merciless boy, Noble McCaneaghy, and you've become a merciless man."

"Just an honest one. Talk."

"Last winter, I was in the Amazon. A tribe of local hunters approached the camp. One of their children was very ill and they'd heard we had potent medicines. All we really had was some laudanum, which we gladly shared. Apparently, it enabled the boy to get some much-needed sleep. Nature did the rest."

"Yes?" Noble prompted.

"Their medicine man proclaimed me a great magician. Noble, I didn't even administer the laudanum. It was our guide. Unfortunately the guide was a local man. Since *I*, however, was safely on my way out of the area, never to return, I presented no threat to the medicine man's authority." Venice's tone was sardonic.

"For saving the boy's life or, as I suspect, more for leaving, he gave me a necklace made of the tiny knuckle bones of a baboon."

"Interesting taste in jewelry, Venice."

"Oh, I never intended to wear it. I just didn't want to be rude and not accept it. But this spring, I was invited to an adventurers' ball. On a lark, I wore the necklace."

"I see you outgrew your impulsiveness along with crying when you didn't get your way," he teased gently.

He felt her lips form a smile against his throat.

"No one told me the press had been invited." The chill in Venice's voice proclaimed how she felt about this oversight. "The next morning the newspapers, *all* of the newspapers, printed stories about 'Venice's Headhunters Give Her Chain of Human Bones.' Trash. Pure, unmitigated trash. Unfortunately, a religious sect believed it. They decided I was a godless pagan. Since then, they've sent me things, as a reminder of my depravity."

"*Your* depravity?"

"Yes. It would be laughable if the things they sent weren't so ghastly."

If he hadn't been holding her he wouldn't have noticed the tiny tremor that shook her. "In what way?"

"Ugly things. This"—she pointed at the skeleton—"brought it all back."

Noble could just about guess what some of those ugly things were. A history of horror remained unvoiced behind her simple account.

"And Trevor? Where was he when you were being hounded?"

Surprise registered in Venice's voice. "What could he have done? We tried, and were successful, in keeping the incidents involving this sect from the press. Father was on the first leg of his campaign. If the press had gotten word of those ... things, the results would have been disastrous for his political career."

Had she been afraid whenever a package arrived? Noble wondered. Had anyone been there to hold her? To tell her not to worry? Had anyone even bothered to keep the damned packages away from her?

"*His* career?" Noble demanded angrily. "What about you, Venice?"

She pulled slightly away from him, amazement in her expression. Her shaking had subsided. The color was returning slowly to her face. Still, she made no move to step further away from him.

He nearly groaned. What was he supposed to do with her, looking at him like that? With her breath, sweet and warm, fanning his chin? Was he supposed to be a gentleman and release her? Hell, he'd never pretended to be a gentleman. He wasn't going to start now. Most especially not now.

"I don't think it can be the same people," he murmured.

"No." She sounded a bit breathless. "I don't either. It has to be someone else playing a joke. It just took me by surprise."

"Everyone in Salvage knows Milton is looking

for bones," he said. "Someone's getting a good laugh out of this. Someone with a distorted sense of humor."

"You always did know the right thing to say."

"No, I didn't. I didn't know what to say before I left, so I didn't say anything."

She reached up and touched his cheek, a feather-light stroke. "Before that. Before you left. You were always my Galahad."

"Maybe once. Maybe to the little girl you used to be. It's easy being a knight in shining armor to a kid. Especially a lonely little kid like you were."

"I wasn't lonely. Not when you were around."

What the hell was he doing? He tried to pull back, but he just didn't have the strength of will. Her body was firm and warm and molded to his own.

"I'm no Galahad, Venice." His words were a warning.

"No. But then, I'm no Guinevere."

"More like Morgana," he whispered.

"Wasn't she the witch?" Her fingertips danced along his jaw. Hunger erupted in him at her touch.

"Aye. A witch. She besotted that poor English ass Arthur until he couldn't see straight."

"What do you see, Noble?" She tilted her head back. Each breath she drew lifted her breasts, pushing them softly against his chest. Each exhalation took away that sweet contact. Breathe in. Out. A long heartbeat and he was lost in her eyes, luminous, lovely.

Should he taste her? *Aye, taste her.*

"I can't see a bloody thing," he murmured and lowered his head.

"Wal now, what have we here?"

Grinding his teeth in frustration, Noble wheeled around, pulling Venice behind him.

Harry Grundy sauntered into the station house,

looking as pleased as a toad in a sinkhole, his pale eyes lighting on the crates littering the floor.

"What do you want?" Noble's voice sounded harsh to his own ears, but Harry didn't appear to notice anything amiss.

"Afternoon, Miz Leiland," Harry said, doffing his oversized top hat before clamping it firmly down over his ears. "Jes' come to find out if'n you'll be needing them supplies you mentioned. Looks like yore stuff got here, though." Grundy wandered around the crates, peering curiously into each box.

"Yes, they're for the party, Mr. Grundy," Venice said shyly as she stepped forward to Noble's side.

She was hastily resecuring the loose strands of her hair into a tight, severe arrangement on the nape of her neck. Noble wanted to pull it free, to see it rippling in sinuous coils down her back. He wanted . . . He made himself stop. That was the problem: he *wanted*.

"Ah-hem." Harry halted before the crate containing the horned coyote skeleton. He bent over and let out a long, low whistle of appreciation. "Wow! That sure is some sorta fossil, ma'am! Where'd you ever discover such a rare, wondrous thang as that?"

"I didn't," Venice said tightly. "Someone sent it to me."

"Really?" Harry's eyes widened. "Who'd ever give away a precious, sci-intific thang like that? Wonder where they done found somethin' like that?" He chewed his lower lip.

Noble looked over at Venice, certain she would share his amusement, but she was watching Harry Grundy as intensely as Harry was staring at the coyote bones.

"What do *you* think, Mr. Grundy?" Noble heard the suspicion in her voice. Could Harry Grundy be her sardonic, black-humored practical joker? Noble didn't think so. Cow pies on the school marm's chair were probably the pinnacle of Harry Grundy's comedic endeavors.

"Me?" asked Harry. Without pausing to ponder his answer, he blurted out, "I think it come from around here, ma'am. I think some sci-intific-minded in-di-vidula done sent it to you as an example of all the wonderful fossils jes' waitin' to be discovered in these here Sawatch mountains."

"Wonderful fossils?" Venice asked in astonishment. "This *thing?*"

"Sure," Harry countered, his tone as mystified as Venice's.

Noble felt his mouth start to twitch. Obviously, Harry Grundy viewed the coyote skeleton as a great discovery. Just as obviously, Venice couldn't quite believe anyone ambulating on two legs could be stupid enough to mistake the grotesque skeleton for a fossil. Venice hadn't reckoned on the Grundys.

For a full moment, Venice and Harry stared at each other. Finally, it must have dawned on Harry that he'd been made a fool by someone's idea of a practical joke. A frown slackened his lips and his skin rivaled his hair for brilliance. He kicked mightily at the crate containing the coyote skeleton.

"What a stupid waste of time!" he spat, and, giving the box one last vicious kick, he turned and stomped from the rail station.

Venice, a laugh bubbling in her voice, said, "For one minute I thought Harry Grundy might be my prankster."

Noble returned her smile. *Smiling with Venice. This was dangerous. Made a man want—there it was again.* Clearing his throat, Noble stepped backward, groping for the door. The uncomfortable suspicion that he was running away stuck in his mind.

"Where the hell did that Blaine get to?" he mumbled. "I'll just see if I can find out who sent this crate. If I do, I'll let you know." He stepped backward through the door. Her fragrance followed him.

"Noble?"

"Yeah?"

"Thank you."

He shifted uncomfortably. "No problem."

"And Noble?"

"Yeah?" Christ. Any longer alone with her and they were going to be right back where they were before Harry Grundy walked in. And what the bloody hell good was that going to do either of them? None. Venice wasn't for him. Could never be for him.

"Won't you come to the party tonight?"

"Ah, I don't know."

"Please?"

"Maybe."

Damn, but she had a wonderful smile.

He'd better remind himself at every opportunity that Venice Leiland thought of him as another charity case to sponsor. And he'd better remind himself that Venice Leiland was a shameless flirt who'd whistled at him. That she was a woman with an oily Lothario trailing after her and a reputation to make a mother weep.

But even if he reminded himself of all this till doomsday, he still wouldn't believe it.

Chapter 10

"If I didn't respect your horse sense, I'd be real worried about you right now, Venice," Katie said.

"Worried? Whatever for?" Venice asked.

Katie gathered a fistful of dark hair and started shoving hairpins into the elaborate coiffure she was building on top of Venice's head. "The way you look at McCaneaghy puts me in mind of a wolf watching a lamb," Katie said. "You all but lick your lips, gal."

Venice felt her face burn. "I most certainly do not—"

"Yes, you most certainly do," Katie interrupted. "Ain't nuthin' wrong with it, long as you keep your sights clear. McCaneaghy might be an interesting night, but he ain't no future."

"I really don't—"

"I 'spect that Cassius is more the sorta feller you oughta be checking the teeth on."

Venice knew she shouldn't encourage Katie's incredible outburst, but she couldn't help herself. "Check his teeth?"

"Yeah. You know. Like you check a horse's teeth to see if it's gonna go the long haul. I'm talking about marriage, Venice."

Venice felt her back stiffen. She didn't want to marry Cassius Reed and she certainly didn't want to discuss him. "For someone who hasn't seen her

133

husband in seven years, you certainly have some rather emphatic opinions on that hallowed estate," Venice said tartly.

Katie grunted and thrust the last hairpin into place. She came around to Venice's side and sat on the edge of the bed next to her. "Listen, Venice. Marrying Josiah Jones was the biggest mistake I ever made."

"Why did you marry him, then?" Venice asked.

" 'Cause he had me all worked up just the way McCaneaghy has you in a lather. He was a trapper. He brought his furs down out of the mountains to this bit of a town where I was dancing. Lord, was he a sight! Tall and big and . . ." Katie sighed.

"It sounds like you loved him very much," Venice said.

Katie blinked in surprise. "I loved his *body* very much. Don't you go mixing up the two like I did!"

"There had to have been more to it than that," Venice insisted.

"Well, I'll allow he knew how to have a good time." Katie's tone was caustic.

"What happened?"

Katie lifted her hands. "We got married, spent two weeks in bed, and then he dragged me up to this little poke-ass shanty clinging to some god-awful rock in the middle of nowhere and left. The bastard."

Venice had never heard Katie sound so dispassionate.

"Said he was going to run his traps. I spent five months living on beans and hardtack and jerky. He never did come back."

"My heavens!" Venice exclaimed. "Did he die?"

"Josiah? Don't you believe it, honey. Mink and beaver got all trapped out so he moved farther north, or west, or who the hell cares? Lucky for me some trappers came by in the spring. Seems they were accustomed to using Josiah's shack as a way station." Her lips flattened into a thin line. "They even had a message from him. He was sorry. That's all. Sorry."

"What did you do?"

"They took me down to town and I took the first stage out. Ended up here and there and wherever."

"How sad," Venice said.

"Sad?" Katie didn't even consider the word. "What woulda been *sad* is if I hadn't woke up to the fact that I was just plain in-fat-u-ated with a broad back and a ... well, never you mind. 'Nuff to say that what *I* learned, *you* oughta take to heart: a cat don't go pining after cougar."

Venice was silent, staring at her hands.

"You understand what I'm saying, Venice?" Katie asked gently.

"Oh, yes." Venice said softly. "I've heard it many, many times before. 'Wealth like ours precludes any vague romantic notions, Venice. We have a duty. The foundation's philanthropic pursuits are more important than our personal whims.' "

"I didn't say that."

"I know. It's the second part of the speech."

Katie scowled. "It's just better to stick to your own kind, is all."

"Wasn't anything about your marriage worth the risk? Do you still ... dislike your husband?"

Katie sank back, her face set in cold, hard lines. "Dislike is too tame a word, honey. I despise him."

Venice bit her lip.

Katie reached over and took her hand, giving it a little squeeze. "But that don't mean you can't enjoy some of the more, ah, earthly pleasures before you do hitch up with one of your own sort. If you want I can—"

A knock interrupted Katie's proposal and Venice's shoulders slumped in relief.

"Miz Leiland?" a young male voice called from the other side of the door. "It's me, Blaine Farley."

"Yes?"

"Noble McCaneaghy says you're to come down to Grundy's pronto. There's a couple Utes there what got a letter what got to do with your uncle."

Venice jumped up. "I'll be right there!" she called, grabbing a shawl. "What does the note say? Is he all right?" she asked, scooting out the door past Blaine.

"I don't rightly know, ma'am," he said, hurrying to catch up with her as she half ran down the stairs, out of the saloon, and into the street. "Never learnt to read. Got the impression he was fine. The Utes wouldn't come down like this just to announce some feller was dead."

Blaine leapt ahead of her onto the porch of the mercantile and held out his hand. "Only reason they'd come was if'n someone paid 'em to come and that someone would have to be alive." He hauled her up and, with a debonair flourish, kicked open the door.

Though Noble was farthest away, she saw him first. It was as though every one of her senses had been anticipating him. Everything else faded into insignificance when he was around. She turned, hoping she wasn't making a spectacle of herself with her open stare.

She needn't have worried. He wasn't paying any attention to her. He was slouched against a table, his hat tipped back on his head, speaking in an unfamiliar language to a pair of Indians.

The first Indian was tall. His nose was beaky, his close-set eyes intelligent and thoughtful in his dark copper face. The shorter of the pair seemed more relaxed. His broad face and wide mouth looked as though they were fashioned for laughter.

Noble glanced up. His eyes warmed with welcome and Venice's heart beat a staccato path to her throat. His gaze lingered before fixing on something behind her.

It was as if someone had shut a door. His expression froze.

"My dear!" Venice whirled toward the sound of the panting voice behind her. Cassius stood just inside the doorway, a hand clutched to his side as he tried to catch his breath.

"I saw you ... running in here ... and concerned lest something be ... endangering you ... I hurried after you." He limped forward.

Endangered by what? Venice wondered. Had Cassius thought she was here to do battle with the Grundy's rice barrel?

She found herself staring at him critically. *This* was the sort of man—possibly *the* man—her father expected her to marry. This overdressed, wheezing ...

Venice bit down on her aversion.

Cassius was exactly the sort of man she *should* marry: wealthy, shrewd, and business-minded. She would never be more than moderately fond of him. If he left her it would never hurt like when her mother had left or like Josiah's abandonment had hurt Katie or like Noble's ... She pushed the thought away.

Cassius was perfectly suitable. She should be pleased he was interested enough to have followed her out West. Instead, she was annoyed because he was standing between her and Noble.

"Blaine said these gentlemen had news of my uncle, Noble," she said.

Wordlessly, Noble pushed himself upright and crossed the room. One corner of his mouth curled as he looked Cassius over at the same time that he handed her a piece of paper.

Grundy Mercantile
Salvage, Colorado Territories
June 3, 1872

Mssrs. Grundy,
Enclosed please find banknotes in excess of four hundred dollars, U.S. currency. These moneys are for the purchase of the enclosed supply list and any pack animals necessary to transport. Please fill this order as quickly as possible and release it to my representatives Trees-Too-High and Crooked Hand to convey to my camp.

Also, it occurs to me that my extended absence might be causing concern amongst my colleagues or possibly the Leiland Foundation. Please reassure any inquirers that I am in perfect health and the best of spirits and inform them that by the end of this season I hope to return with exceptional news.

Sincerely,
Milton Xavier Leiland

"Oh, thank God he's all right!"

"Didn't know you were that worried," Noble said, frowning.

"I . . . I wasn't. It's just that I'm happy he hasn't met with some . . . unexpected difficulty. I really wasn't *worried*, per se."

"You don't have to pretend, Venice," Noble said softly. "It's okay to care about your uncle."

"She doesn't need *you* to tell her that," Cassius said.

"That's right. She doesn't need me at all, does she?" Noble returned in a curiously flat voice.

Venice scanned the note again, then looked up into Noble's carefully bland face. "Do you suppose . . . ?"

"I don't suppose anything," Noble muttered, his eyes still fastened on Cassius.

"Well," Venice said to herself, "there's only one thing for it. I'll have to go up there myself."

"You can't!" three male voices exclaimed in unison. Blaine, embarrassed by his sudden outburst, turned a rich crimson. Cassius's mustache quivered with indignation, and Noble bolted upright, his dark brows lowering over his golden eyes.

"Excuse me, gentlemen," Venice said, "but I *can*. I shall simply accompany Uncle Milton's cargo to his camp."

"Now, Miz Leiland . . ." Blaine began.

"How can you even suggest an unchaperoned trip?" Cassius demanded.

"Of all the fool notions I have ever heard, *this* has got to be the most idiotic. If you haven't a single care for yourself *or* your reputation, fine. But you can't—I repeat, Venice—you *cannot* ask these men to haul your skinny rump up to Milton's camp."

Skinny rump?!

"And why not?" she demanded. "I've been on safari before!"

"Dammit. This isn't a chaperoned picnic in an exotic locale. There isn't going to be anyone fixing you tea and crumpets every afternoon. No cots with linen sheets."

"I know that! I can . . ." She glanced at Blaine. "I can gruff it out."

"Ah, that's 'tough it out,' Miz Leiland," Blaine suggested respectfully.

"Whatever! I can gruff it *and* tough it out!"

"Listen, Venice. This isn't just a matter of whether or not you can put up with dirt under your fingernails. Think!"

She glowered at Noble.

"It's a four-day trip! If any white man in the territory got wind of the fact that these men," he gestured to where the Utes were calmly standing, "were taking a white woman up into the mountains—alone—they'd be as good as dead."

Noble's words cleared her thoughts, like a plunge into an icy bath. He was right, of course. But the possibility that her uncle had found something that would allow this dirty, squalid, and perversely endearing little community to survive and—she admitted—the idea that she might be the one to orchestrate it, had momentarily bedazzled her.

Noble was watching her closely.

She lifted her chin and spoke with quiet dignity. "You are correct. It was thoughtless of me. But I will still, somehow, make the journey to my uncle's camp."

Crooked Hand watched the interplay between McCaneaghy and the skinny little woman. With all the whites nattering at once, it was hard to comprehend their conversation. That was one of the many problems his people, the Utes, had communicating with these interlopers. They were overwhelmingly rude, constantly talking over one another, like squawking ravens. Only by carefully listening had he been able to unravel their conversation. Apparently the woman wanted them to take her to Mil-Ton and the men did not like the idea.

The idea wasn't intelligent enough to warrant dislike.

"Why do you turn your back on this woman,

when it is clear you have a care for her, McCaneaghy?" Trees-Too-High asked curiously.

Noble made a gesture of frustration. In his halting Ute, he said, "She . . . she not my tribe. What
I want makes no matter. She needs go with some
man to her father's brother's camp."

Only good manners kept Crooked Hand from
cringing. McCaneaghy had meant to honor the Ute
nation by learning their tongue, but he was completely inept at the rich subtleties of the language.

"You go with her," Crooked Hand said.

Noble shook his head. "Woman belongs to this
other man's camp. She should not with me be."

Crooked Hand frowned, trying to understand.
" 'Be' with you? You mean she should not lie with
you?"

"No!" Noble nearly shouted.

Crooked Hand thoughtfully tugged on his ear,
trying to make sense of this. "Why?" he finally
asked.

"Because I cannot keep her!"

The other whites had finally stopped their inces-
sant chattering and were looking at them.

"The other man," Crooked Hand said, "he could
keep her?"

"Yes!" Noble bit out the word and with it he
seemed to surrender the fierceness from his long
body. "Yes."

"What is he saying, Noble?" the boy asked.

Crooked Hand sighed. It was better to speak in
English anyway. It sounded cramped and ugly no
matter who spoke it.

"Okay, then. One of these men take the woman
to Mil-Ton's camp," he said in English.

The woman's eyes—gray, like a gosling's down—
widened. She took a step toward Noble. Crooked
Hand could see the pleading in her. McCaneaghy
answered as if she voiced a need, his body bending

toward her before halting. Crooked Hand could feel him fighting her unvoiced request.

He was going to lose. The woman's power over him was too strong. Crooked Hand could see it as clearly as the scar on a lightning-marked pine. McCaneaghy did not stand a chance.

Suddenly, the other white man—the older man with the hair under his nose—barked out, "If you want to journey to your uncle's encampment, Miss Leiland, I will of course be honored if you would accept my company. I am sure these ... people will guide us," he said.

The woman looked around. Her cool eyes, which were so hot when she looked at McCaneaghy, flickered uncertainly between the two older white men.

"I'll take you up to yore uncle's camp, Miz Leiland!" the boy said. "I'll make sure you're all tucked in at night and no big, bad bears comes prowling around."

"Stuff it, Blaine," McCaneaghy said.

"I mean it, Noble. I'd be proud as he—as kin be to escort Miz Leiland!"

"Looks like you got yourself a pair of gallants to choose from, Venice." McCaneaghy's tone was wry and the woman turned the color of ripe juniper berries.

"We will take this white woman and her chosen companion for a fee," Trees-Too-High declared. "Tomorrow morning, before sun rises."

"A fee?" asked the woman.

"Yes," Trees-Too-High said. "One hundred dollars."

"That's absurd!" sputtered the man, Cassius.

"Leaves me out," mumbled the boy, scratching his head.

"I will, of course, be willing to pay the guide fee

and any additional costs for whoever accompanies me." The woman's gaze touched McCaneaghy. "As Noble has pointed out, I cannot ask these men to take me alone."

Crooked Hand could see the muscles jump in McCaneaghy's cheek.

"No, madame," said the hairy man. "I cannot allow you to spend your money when I alone shall reap the benefits of your delightful company."

"*I* sure can't ask you to pay my way, ma'am," the boy said apologetically. "My mama would have my ears on a plate if'n I so much as thought of it."

"Looks like Cassius here is the only one who can afford you," McCaneaghy said. "As it should be. You'll be better off with someone who knows what fork to use. Never know when you might need to pop open an oyster shell."

"There's a thread of sense in McCaneaghy's drivel. Please be assured, I'll see to your . . . comfort."

Something in the man Cassius's tone made McCaneaghy bolt one step forward. He stopped suddenly, the tension in the air nearly palatable.

The Cassius man ignored him. "We'll make an adventure of it, shall we?" he asked the woman.

"I . . . well . . ." Her gaze darted pleadingly toward Noble, who was fiercely studying the floorboards. "I guess, I mean . . . that is, thank you, Mr. Reed. I'd appreciate your company," she finished unhappily.

"It's settled then!" Cassius exclaimed. "We'll have a smashing time. Doing the explorer stint and all."

"For God's sake!" Noble strode to the door. "When you decide when you're going to commence this 'adventure,' tell me. I got some things

I've been meaning to send up to Milt." He slammed the door behind him.

The woman spent two heartbeats watching the closed door, her expression sad. Disgusted, Crooked Hand touched Trees-Too-High's arm, signaling for them to leave. He'd spent more than enough time in the whites' company for one day.

As the hostess, it was Venice's duty to begin the party by welcoming her guests. Her mind, however, kept slipping back to Noble.

"Honey?" Venice heard Katie say next to her.

"Yes?"

"There's nearly four hundred people milling about here waiting for a signal from you to commence partyin'. This is yer chance to say somethin' bout you bein' in Salvage and what fer. Tell 'em somethin' nice, Venice," Katie urged in a gentle voice. "These folks have lived and worked in this no-count town for years and they're afraid yore gonna make it so they have to leave. The ladies especially."

"The ladies?"

"Yeah. The Convivial Ladies." Katie motioned toward the women clustered together near the outer edges of the crowd. Their sunburnt faces were alight with interest, wreathed in smiles.

"They're good women who've left homes back East to make a life out here. They're the kind of women who turn territories into states. That's why they're here, honey. To make Salvage a permanent kinda place. A place to raise kids and build houses. And they're willin' to work hard. Damn hard. But they need to know they haven't set roots on rocky ground. You tell 'em, Venice. And don't use no five-buck words!"

Venice stared at Katie. Who'd have thought Katie would be spouting Biblical allusions and so eloquently championing a group of women who normally wouldn't so much as raise a hand in greeting to her? Venice nodded and Katie started clearing the center of one of the trestle tables.

Lifting her skirts, Venice stepped up onto the seat.

"Any particular reason you wants to be standing on this table, Miz Leiland?" one of the men asked politely.

"Ah, yes. I wanted to talk to the people a minute."

"You want I should get this herd to listen to you, Miz Leiland?"

"That would be very kind, indeed, sir."

"Frank Fields, ma'am," the man said. "We had lunch together over at the Gold Dust the other day." Still smiling, he reached inside his thick wool coat, withdrew a pistol, and held it high above his head. "I'd plug my ears if'n I was you, miss."

Just in time, Venice stuck her fingers in her ears. The pistol report shot across the field, reverberating off the walls of the surrounding mountains.

"Listen up!" shouted the man.

Venice looked down at the expectant, wary faces turning toward her. With the right words, she could be a hero tonight. She could fair make these people like her. And she wanted that. Very much.

"Hello! I am Venice Leiland."

"Shoot, honey, we knows who you are!" someone yelled. The general noise level rose as people started laughing and calling to her.

"All right. You know who I am. And you think you know why I'm here. But you're *wrong!*" Conversation dwindled to a trickle. A few people murmured uncomfortably.

"I am *not* here to close down the spur line!"

Someone whooped and another hollered "Hooray." The crowd started buzzing again. Hastily, Venice held up her hand for silence.

"Eight years ago, my uncle approached the Leiland Foundation and asked them to sponsor his search for prehistoric fossils in the Colorado Territory. That request was honored. That funding has been responsible for the supply line running from the East to Denver and up here. In other words, the Leiland-Hawkness Spur Line."

"We know that!"

"So?" someone called out.

"*So*, my uncle has spent seven years exploring these mountains for ..." She looked around. *No big words.* "... old bones. Without success. When my uncle left earlier this year neglecting to payroll the spur line, the Denver office contacted the foundation. The situation was reviewed and the recommendation made that any further funding of expeditions in this territory be terminated ... along with the spur line."

Unhappy murmurs rose from the crowd.

"Listen. Please! I didn't come here to personally close down the spur line, like you all seem to fear. If I had, it would be closed by now."

"Then why'd you want all them papers and ledgers and stuff?" a man hollered.

"Because I wanted to determine if Salvage could survive *without* the spur line."

"Hell, Miz Leiland, the spur line *is* Salvage." The mob buzzed concurrence.

"I know that now!" Venice called back.

The people around her shifted.

"I came to Salvage to see if there weren't something we could do to persuade the foundation that Salvage merited the sponsorship of the Leiland Foundation all by itself."

"I thought you come to Salvage 'cause your daddy kicked you outta New York."

Venice stared out into the crowd and laughed. These people were never going to allow a person to dissemble.

"Fair enough!" she called, still laughing. "I *was* exiled. But I didn't have to go to Salvage! And I *have* come to help you. But I believe that the necessity for my intervention is now in question."

"Say what?"

"It appears Salvage might not need my help. If what my uncle's note suggests is indeed true, the Leiland-Hawkness Spur Line will make the Salvage run for many years to come. Listen." In a loud, clear voice that carried over the silent crowd, she read her uncle's note.

"What's it mean?" asked an excited voice near her.

"I *believe* my uncle has found what he's looking for. In other words, there are bones in them thar mountains!"

The cheers started in front and swelled back through the crowd, hoarse with relief and happiness. Hats soared into the sky, borne on the stiffening evening breeze. Men and women clapped each other on the back.

Venice beamed at the happy, laughing mob. "Salvage! Let's have a party!" she called.

No further encouragement was necessary. A fiddle sang to life and a horn called back in gay harmony. A skirt flashed and suddenly the people of Salvage were dancing.

Venice was stepping down from the table when Tim Gilpin placed a hand at her elbow and lifted her to the ground. He alone of three hundred some men didn't look very happy.

"Mr. Gilpin?"

"Miss Leiland. What if you're wrong?" he blurted out in a gruff voice. "What if your uncle hasn't found any fossils?"

Venice met his worried look steadily. "Then I'm afraid we're back where we started," she said quietly. "Don't worry, Mr. Gilpin. In the larger world my uncle is a renowned paleontologist." She put a hand on Tim's arm. "Tonight, at least, don't worry."

She angled past him, nearly colliding with the Grundy brothers.

"Well, shit. I guess this means our job ain't done yet," she heard one of them say. She hadn't gone another fifteen feet before she was dancing in the arms of an enthusiastic miner. Within five minutes, she'd forgotten all about the Grundys' "job."

Chapter 11

"Cayuse Katie Jones somewhere around?" Anton Grundy asked Noble as he peered into the darkened barroom.

Lord, what a moose, thought Noble. Aloud he said, "Haven't seen her for a while, Anton."

"Crap." Anton blinked down at the burlap bag he held in one enormous paw and then toward the party going on in the field around him. "Well, give 'er this when she come. Tell 'er she owes me *two* dollars. I ain't gonna stand 'round waitin' on her while everyone elst drinks up all Miz Leiland's fancy likker." He waved his hand in the direction of the meadow.

Venice's shindig was in full swing. Probably not a moment too soon, either. Unless Noble missed his guess, the string of clear days the territory had enjoyed was about to come to an abrupt end.

It was getting darker by the minute. Late afternoon clouds, shredded on the jagged peaks of the surrounding mountains, had disappeared beneath a slow rolling bank of sulfur-tinted thunderheads. Sudden gusts of wind danced the Chinese lanterns on their wires and rustled the paper skirts nailed to the tables.

"Sure will," Noble said when he realized Anton was waiting for him to answer.

Anton tossed the sack on the porch. "That's *two* bucks. Tell her." He turned, lumbering off into the crowd, muttering, "Them things is hard to catch . . ."

"You're welcome," Noble said, lifting his mug after Anton's retreating bulk. He leaned against the makeshift bar Katie had set up on the Gold Dust's back porch, feeling a little tipsy and not at all unappreciative of that fact. The bar was nothing more than a plank set across a couple of rain barrels and hung with a tablecloth. Nailed to the front was a sheet of paper that read FREE BOOZE.

Except for Noble, there wasn't anyone taking up the generous offer. He understood the lack of interest. The bitter burn of the cheap whiskey clung to the inside of his mouth.

Noble grimaced down at his tin mug. As far as he could tell, everyone was making sure every last drop of champagne Venice had shipped up was finished well before the storm broke—everyone except him.

He took another swig just as Katie rounded the corner in time to see the look of revulsion on his face. Gamely, Noble tried to hide his loathing.

"Ah, Anton Grundy was just here," he said. "He left that sack for you."

Katie's eyes widened and she darted over, scooping up the bag. She wheeled to face Noble.

"Said you owed him two bucks."

"Two bucks!" Katie's voice rose.

Noble shrugged. "That's what he said."

"Two bucks for—for a—" She glanced down at the bag. "Moth-eaten bolt of calico?"

"Whatever," Noble said disinterestedly. Katie grinned. "What's with the free liquor?" Noble lifted a brow questioningly.

Katie leaned over the bar, glancing in both directions before confiding in a low voice, "That Frenchie stuff ain't gonna last another fifteen minutes. Once that's gone, folks are gonna remember about good, old Katie giving away free liquor and come running. Only when they hit the porch they're gonna discover it ain't free any more, and I'm gonna make a killing." She slapped her hand, palm down, on the plank.

Admiration made Noble smile. "You're quite a savvy businesswoman, Miss Jones."

"Cayuse Katie, hon," Katie said gruffly and glanced down at the bag in her hand as though just remembering it. She straightened. "I gotta put this away," she said, opening the back door and slipping inside.

"Not that I don't like the company, mind you, but why ain't you at the party?" Her voice floated back to him from the darkened barroom. "Everyone's havin' a grand time of it. Dang, I fergot to lock up the office. Be right back." Her voice trailed off.

Noble shot another rancorous glance at the party going on around him. Everyone *was* having a fine old time.

There was wine, music, and food, an overabundance of food. The Convivial Ladies, not to be outdone by the soiled doves fluttering around their own cookfires, had obviously prepared to launch a counteroffensive. They had met the barrage of stews, meats, and vegetables with a volley of baked goods: fruit pies, raisin-studded turnovers, ginger cakes, buttery rolls, and flaky biscuits.

Most of the men, however, were more interested in finding a female to drape their arms around than in eating. Toward this end someone had dragged the piano out of Mrs. Gates's front parlor and Mrs. Gates herself was pounding away on it while her husband displayed an unsuspected talent for sawing on a fiddle, and the Pay Dirt's Mexican chef coaxed pulsating, vibrant notes from a battered horn.

Everyone seemed to be dancing. And no one danced more often, or more tirelessly, or more gaily, than Venice Leiland.

She'd made a fine recovery from her little fright at the railroad station, Noble thought sourly.

He had watched her give her little speech to Salvage, officially opening the party. She had sounded concerned and sincere, as if the Leiland Foundation would do everything in its power to keep the spur line running.

But the cold, hard reality was that the existence of the spur line depended on just one thing—Milton's finding prehistoric fossils.

Noble's hand, braced on the porch column, tightened into a fist. There weren't any "terrible lizard" bones here. He'd spent five years out here, scouring the mountains and the valleys and the washes, and he'd never seen anything that resembled a dinosaur bone. Neither had Milton. But that didn't matter to Venice. She'd say whatever these folks wanted to hear. Anything for love.

Noble stared at the cloudy brew settling to the bottom of his mug. He was tiptoeing along the fine edge of infatuation himself and he knew it. It was stupid, it was futile, and it could only mean a whole world of hurt. And Venice Leiland already accounted for more than her share of hurt in his history.

All evening he tried not to watch Venice, but he might as well have avoided watching a lightning bug at midnight. She was wearing a scarlet skirt with deep, ruffled tiers, the heavy flounces belling out in rippling swirls as she twirled. Her blouse was a simple white smock like those worn by most Mexican women. Nothing special, until Venice put it on, cinching it at the waist with a bright twist of satin. Then it became something else. Something that ought to be outlawed.

The thin cotton dipped low over her breasts, clinging to the soft swells. Each time she bent, the fabric seemed on the verge of falling off her shoulders. What the hell was she doing in that get-up, anyway? Was this supposed to be her way of blending in with the locals?

Smiling humorlessly, Noble groped under the cloth covering the bar, pulling out a whiskey bottle and pouring himself another finger or so, his gaze drawn once more to Venice.

It wasn't just the way she looked, like some exotic species of bird. It was everything—her smile, her voice, the way she laughingly agreed to yet another leering man's demand for yet another dance, the way her eyes sparked with amusement when the idiots plied her with enough nonsense to fertilize Kansas.

Abruptly, Noble wondered if *he* amused her. He didn't much like the thought.

Bringing one man at a time to his knees must seem pretty tame stuff to a coquette of her accomplishments. Hell, why not bring a whole *town* of men to their knees? Now there was a challenge, Noble thought bitterly.

Yeah, and you'd be just about the first to break your kneecaps, you'd drop to 'em so fast, a wicked voice inside him jeered. Who do you think you're fooling? Every opportunity you get, every excuse, you use it to touch her. Because you want her as badly as . . .

He tipped his head back, pouring the raw alcohol down his throat in one huge gulp, drowning the voice. His head swam. Damned cheap rotgut.

"I'd go easy on that if I was you." The woman—Kitty? Katie?—was watching him with concern.

Why couldn't Venice have eyes like hers? A nice shade of blue, like a sky or something. Why'd

Venice have to have eyes like green woodsmoke? Soft and deep and warm.

"Not to worry, ma'am." Noble brought two fingers to his forehead in a polite salute. "I acquired quite a head for whiskey during the war."

"Mister, I can't tell you how many ex-soldiers have told me the same thing," Katie said. "You ain't been settin' here drinkin' this whiskey all afternoon, have ya?"

"Not all afternoon, ma'am. Just the last few hours." Noble straightened indignantly. He might be a little off balance, but he wasn't that foxed!

Cassius Reed came up from behind them. "The Irish are by nature predisposed to certain weaknesses. Alcohol is but one of them."

Venice had danced with *him*, too, thought Noble. And she was going to be traveling with *him*. Alone except for the Utes, laughing with *him* ... smiling at *him*. Because *he*, as Noble had gone to pains to point out to Crooked Hand this afternoon, could afford to keep her. Well, fine. She belonged with *him*, didn't she?

"What'll you have, Mr. Reed?" Katie asked. "How's about a nice stiff bourbon? Drinks on the house."

"Fine. Just don't try and foist some of your watered-down cider off on me."

"This has plenty of kick to it, mister," Katie promised, handing him a shotglass.

"Cheers, madame," Cassius snickered, taking the glass and tipping it in Katie's direction. He drained it in one long pull before returning it to Katie with a curt, "Again."

Wordlessly, Katie complied. Cassius turned his attention to Noble. "You look all out of sorts, McCaneaghy. What's the matter? Smithsonian finally realize they're wasting their money on you?"

"Everything's just fine, Reed," Noble said, managing to pull a smile from some hidden reserve. He wanted to slug the guy. Venice would probably end up marrying this ass, and the hell of it was he'd all but handed her to him on a silver platter.

"How 'bout you, Thorny? Oh, that's right. You sorta gambled away most of your inheritance, didn't you?"

Cassius's face went blank.

Noble stroked a thumb down his cheek, considering Cassius carefully. "You know, when I saw you out here, all togged out in those nice new clothes and toting that nice fancy luggage, I sort of thought you'd found a new cash cow. But now I don't think so. Nope. I don't think you have much money at all."

"I'll recoup my losses, McCaneaghy," Reed said smoothly. "Maybe even here. This territory is just one big pie and everyone back East wants a piece. I could bring down an entire mountain with the new hydraulic systems, and do it for pennies. Find gold or silver or whatever treasures they hide."

He was just the type of man who'd do it, too. The thought made Noble's jaw ache. Cassius was just one of a thousand like-minded, greedy developers. What were millenniums of nature's careful artistry to those cigar-smoking men in Park Avenue club rooms? Nothing.

A sudden, sickening notion occurred to Noble. "You know, Reed, I'll bet you haven't had much luck getting those investors. Is that why you chased Venice Leiland out here?"

Cassius didn't answer. There was something ominous about his uncharacteristic silence.

"You didn't follow her here just so she would have someone of her own class to play cribbage with. Ain't your style," Noble continued thoughtfully. "You've never been concerned about anyone but yourself. I wonder if Venice knows about the Reed family fortune. Or should I say *mis*-fortune?"

Reed's thin control broke. "Celtic peasant! Just because you managed to gamble your beggarly pence into a few dollars doesn't make you any more palatable! You just stay away from Venice Leiland. Do you hear me? Or I'll thrash you within an inch of your life."

Suddenly, Noble was tired of this game. Tired of Cassius and his blind arrogance and his pathetic threats.

"Did you hear me, McCaneaghy?"

"Yeah," Noble said, studying the sunset and the mountains and the ugly little town of Salvage. "I heard you. But my back isn't turned and it isn't going be turned so you'll just have to wait for another day—or night—to make good on your threat."

He heard Cassius sputter with rage but didn't bother lifting his eyes from the mug he held until he heard the man stomp off.

"You gonna sit here and let that shavetail mule scare you off?" Katie demanded, her hands on her hips.

"Scare me off what?"

"He told you to stay away from Venice! You gonna stand for that?"

Noble shrugged. "She's not my concern."

"The hell she ain't. I've seen how you two look at each other. Makes a blacksmith's forge seem cool."

Noble twisted uncomfortably. "You got one helluva imagination."

"You're a bloody fool, Noble McCaneaghy." Katie shook her head in disgust. "Of all the men in this territory she could set her fancy on, Venice Leiland—the prettiest, finest piece of womanhood I ever met—sets it on you. And you just sit here, moping in the dark while she dances with every—"

"And just what the hell am I supposed to do about it?" Noble burst out angrily. "Venice Leiland might as well be the Queen of Sheba for all the good it'll do me."

"Pig-headed, ornery . . . she *likes* you!"

Somewhere, deep inside, he realized that if he weren't half-lit he wouldn't be shouting his anguish for all of Salvage to hear. Unfortunately, he *was* half-lit. "Bloody hell! What am I supposed to do?" he repeated. "Follow her around like some stray hound begging for a pat?"

"Nope," Katie said, suddenly smiling like a cat in front of a bowl of cream.

"Then what the hell do you want from me? Want me to set myself up so the next time she walks out of my life I can—"

"Remember when you and I used to dance in the conservatory?"

Damn it all! He'd always had a sixth sense where Venice was concerned. Why now, of all times, did it have to fail him? He spun around so quickly that his head swam and he had to grab hold of the bar to keep from falling.

"Remember?" Venice repeated.

Her eyes were shining, her hair piled in gleaming waves atop her head, exposing the graceful, vulnerable length of her neck. She arched a brow. "Do you remember how to dance?"

"Nope."

"Oh, fer Chrissake," Katie sputtered and, with a disgusted snort, left.

"I'm not surprised," Venice said saucily.

"What do you mean?"

"Judging from your impaired ability to stand upright, I'd say you were inebriated."

"You got that right."

She narrowed her fine eyes on him. "Well, small wonder you can't dance. You can't even *walk.*"

"I can walk just fine. I got drinking down to an art form."

"Oh, Noble. Is that how things are for you?"

Distress was evident in her expression. Distress and . . . concern? He couldn't stand to have her concerned about his immortal soul.

"Don't get your fur up, Venice. I just meant that I know to the drop how much whiskey it takes to get me drunk. Learned it somewhere south of Missionary Ridge."

"I don't understand."

"I got a bit beat up in the war. Ended up in a field hospital. They used whiskey to take the edge off my . . . discomfort. As of yet, I haven't had nearly enough."

He didn't tell her the rest. That they'd used whiskey because there was no laudanum or morphine. He didn't want to watch her concern become pity. He really did not think he could stand her pity.

She released her breath. He got the distinct impression his answer had relieved her. Her next words confirmed it. "Good," she breathed. "I mean, I've been to the homes for the ex-soldiers." She lowered her eyes. "I'm glad you haven't succumbed to any addictions."

"You've visited veterans?"

"Yes. You needn't sound so incredulous." That got her dander up. "The Leiland Foundation endows several Soldiers' Relief Funds. I even administered one."

What else had she done in the past decade? He was about to ask, but she had already returned to her original topic.

"Still, it's a pity to find that you haven't any excuse for not dancing other than that you haven't the rudimentary athleticism necessary."

Now *his* dander was up.

"What'da ya mean?" Noble demanded.

"You were never any good at it, anyway. No sense of rhythm. Bad timing. Tin ear."

"Hey! I wasn't the one who was always stomping all over her partner's feet. I've been around horses and mules and oxen for the past ten years and I haven't ever had feet near as black and blue as the summer you taught me how to dance."

She sniffed haughtily. "I haven't heard anyone complaining tonight."

"These men are too well-mannered, or too oblivious, to complain."

"Ha! I have gotten much, much better."

"We'll just see, shall we?" He held out his hand, the uncomfortable notion he'd been adroitly maneuvered tickling his dignity. He ignored it.

She stepped forward and took his proffered hand. Trying desperately to see this as a challenge rather than an opportunity to hold her, Noble tugged her after him to the edge of the churning, swirling dancers. He set his hand on her waist and she placed her hand on his shoulder, burning him with sensation, even through his shirt.

"Ready?" he asked, his voice gruff.

"Yes." She looked happy and eager and just a trifle shy. He relaxed and with a smile swept her out into the crowd as the Pay Dirt's cook began to play a savage-sweet Spanish melody.

She was graceful and fluid and elegantly formed and she had, indeed, become a wonderful dancer. Thank God Katie's whiskey had loosened his inhibitions or he would surely be tromping all over her. As it was, when he misstepped he simply caught her light form against him rather than stumble into her. She didn't seem to mind. She laughed. A pretty sound. A beautiful sound.

"Do you give up?"

"Yes," he said solemnly.

"Then I *have* improved?" she asked pertly.

"That too."

"You aren't half bad yourself."

"Ha. I just pick you up and fling you around."

"Yes, but not every man here 'flings' as rhythmically as you do."

He laughed and she joined him, tightening her hand on his shoulder as he twirled her one more time, lifting her high against his chest before dipping down with the last strains of the haunting Spanish tune. He ended bent over her body.

The candles in the fluttering Chinese lanterns spread flickering light and shadow across her cheeks and softly parted lips, over her throat and the gentle swell of her breasts. He felt awash in sensation, trembling on the cusp of something dangerous and mysterious and far more addictive than mere alcohol.

He drew her upward.

She'd linked her hands around his neck to steady herself. He picked her up in his arms and strode out of the crowd, away from the dancing candlelights and into the shadow-cloaked night beyond the circle of laughter and gaiety and safety.

Wordlessly he released her, let her warm, womanly body slide down his own hard, shivering length. She swallowed. He could just see the movement in her throat. The cloud-burdened night sky was a fathomless darkness above them, the deepening twilight affording scant light.

"Noble . . ."

"Shh." His breath labored in his chest. "I won't do anything."

"You won't?" He wanted to believe he heard regret in her hushed reply.

"I just want a minute. Just a minute to hold you without sharing you."

"I don't understand." She hadn't made any move to retreat from him. She sounded breathless and confused and a little drunk herself.

"I don't either." He reached up and touched her cheek, skated his fingertips along the delicate line of her chin, brushed them across the incredible soft swell of her lips. "I just want to be with you."

"But you can be with me." He could barely make out her face now; the evening shadows had nearly enveloped them. But he heard the confusion in her voice. "You can accompany me to my uncle's camp."

His hand dropped. "And take Cassius's place?"

She was silent.

"Instead of Cassius?" he insisted.

He barely made out her tiny nod.

"For how long?" He'd almost forgotten, God help him, almost forgotten that she didn't belong here. Didn't belong with him.

"Take his place for how long? A week? Two weeks? No thanks, honey. I never hire on for piecework."

Suddenly he had to get away from her. He thought to leave her standing in the dark, but the darkness seemed to follow him instead.

Chapter 12

Venice stalked the perimeters of the party. Her hem switched angrily around her ankles, creating a trail of dust that marked her progress. She had had enough of Noble McCaneaghy's on-again, off-again responses, one minute kissing her, the next pushing her away.

When she'd been a lonely little girl, Noble had been a godsend. But the way she felt right now, he might as well have come straight from the fires of hell. And she wanted to send him straight back.

It was her own fault. She'd *expected* he would take her to his uncle, she'd *expected* he'd want to be with her, she'd *expected* they'd pick up the friendship that had been left hanging ten years ago. She twisted her fingers in her skirt, her childlike sense of betrayal still fresh and raw. You'd think she'd have learned not to expect things from people by now. Still, he had no right to treat her so callously.

"I brought you some champagne, Miz Leiland," Blaine said, trotting toward her, champagne sloshing in his haste. "Guess I finally beat Noble to the punch."

Venice gasped. "You didn't hit Noble, did you?"

"Hit Noble?" Blaine parroted, wide-eyed. "Mrs. Farley didn't raise no fools, Miss Leiland."

"Excuse me?"

"I'm never gettin' into a fist fight with Noble

McCaneaghy. They say he's faster with a right hook than most men are with a gun."

"Then what did you mean that you beat his punches?"

Blaine smiled in sudden understanding. "I meant I got here before he did."

Venice shot a swift glance over to where Noble's broad back had disappeared into the crowd.

"Yeah," Blaine continued, "the way he grabbed that liquor bottle from Miss Katie's hand, I thought fer sure he was hurrying to get you a refreshment. So, I thought to myself, 'Miss Leiland's taste probably runs more to champagne than rot-gut.' So I hightailed it over here with this." He grinned triumphantly.

"Very perceptive of you," Venice said, accepting the glass he thrust at her and taking a sip.

"Yeah ... well." Blaine nudged the dirt with the toe of his boot, obviously casting about for some topic of conversation. "I ... I guess you was real surprised when you figured out that Noble was your cook's kid."

"Cook's kid? Is that what he told you?" Venice asked. "He didn't tell you we were friends?"

"Ah, no. He just said his ma used to work for your daddy and he had to, ah, wipe your nose."

Had to?! So that was all she'd meant to him. A snotty-nosed brat he'd had to keep an eye on. That was probably why he was so loath to take her to her uncle. He didn't want to resume old responsibilities.

"Quite right," she said, lifting the glass to her lips and tossing down the champagne. "And that's all he said?"

Blaine shrugged. "Said it would be a lot more comfortable for him if you was still a kid."

She smiled humorlessly. "It would be for me, too."

Oh, yes, there was something new between them all right, she thought sardonically. Something that set her pulse racing and made it hard to breathe. She derived a perverse pleasure in knowing this new aspect of their relationship chafed him, too.

She'd expected Noble to ask her to dance. She'd looked forward to it. And when they had danced, it had been fun. But afterward . . .

She fanned herself with a folded piece of paper. After the dance he had simply scooped her up into his arms, his jaw set, and walked with her into the shadows. His intractableness should have been intimidating, the hunger in his gaze frightening . . . but instead it had been exciting.

And then he'd left.

"I guess I ain't much for small talk," Venice heard Blaine say and pulled her attention back to the young man. His voice was morose and he was still making diagrams in the dust with his toe.

"Not at all, Mr. Farley. I am purely in love with your accent."

"You are?" He brightened. "Well, that's right nice. I . . . ah . . . I sure . . . um . . ." His face fell. Clearly her praise had tongue-tied the lad. "Well sh—, er, shoot."

"Maybe there is something else we could do?" she prompted him gently, noting that the lively polka the band was playing was one of her favorites.

The relief on Blaine's face was laughable. He cleared his throat. "I'd be right honored if you'd consent to lettin' me have another dance, Miss Leiland."

With one last glance toward the vacant porch, Venice bobbed a curtsey. "I'd be delighted, Mr. Farley."

Beaming with delight, Blaine grabbed Venice

around the waist and, jerking her off her feet, spun her around. Her chignon slipped and her hair uncoiled, spilling down her back. She laughed. Whatever Blaine lacked in expertise, he made up for in enthusiasm.

Another man claimed Blaine's place as soon as the polka ended, giving Venice no chance to recapture her wayward tresses before being whirled away. Another man took his place and another his. Dance after dance unfolded with partner after partner.

Venice loved it. She loved the underlying thrum of distant thunder counterpointed by human laughter. She loved the muted colors of the flickering Chinese lanterns bobbing on their wires and the scents of roasting meat and spiced wine, cinnamon, and cloves. Everyone was happy. Everyone except Noble, and she refused to think about him.

Why, even the chill bite of the approaching night air couldn't cool the warmth in her cheeks after so many dances. Venice shook her head at the bearded man beside her and graciously declined his request for a second dance.

"Some gal's been lookin' for you," Katie said, appearing at Venice's side. "Said you were gonna lend her some dress or something. I sent her to your room."

"Suzanne Gates. Heavens! It's nearly eight!" Venice gasped. "I've been having such a lovely time, I forgot all about her. All these nice gentlemen, so flatteringly attentive, so pleasant, so respectful. Not one an ill-mannered, obstinate lout. Not one!"

"What's wrong, Venice?" Katie asked.

"Wrong? Why nothing! I'm having a lovely time. How could I have a better time? I couldn't!"

"Come on, honey. I seen McCaneaghy holding up the porch at the Gold Dust."

"Why should I care? Honestly, Miss Jones, I don't know what you're talking about. Haven't I just said I'm having a splendid—"

"Yeah, honey, you did." Katie grabbed hold of Venice's arm and led her off.

True to Katie's word, Noble was leaning against a column. He averted his eyes the minute she stepped up onto the porch. Hot with mortification, she bit her lip, trying to stop it from quivering. Last time she'd cried, Noble had laughed. She wasn't going to give him another opportunity.

Snapping her chin up, Venice swished imperiously past him, her red skirts slapping against his legs. He stepped back but in the process his spur snagged the deep, laced ruffle on her hem. She tried to jerk her skirts loose and heard the unmistakable sound of ripping fabric. She glared up at him.

Damn him. Arrogant, amused, and far, far too masculine. Disgustingly so. His long, tawny hair gleamed in the light escaping from the porch windows. He looked tall and lithe and dangerous. His teeth flashed in an insolent grin.

"Sorry . . . ma'am." With the smooth, economical grace she'd come to associate with him, Noble leaned over and pulled the material free of his spur. He straightened. Lord help her, he had nearly golden eyes, laughing eyes. She recoiled haughtily from his amusement—and promptly recaught her hem in his spur. She stumbled, starting to fall.

He was there to catch her. Strong hands gripped her bare upper arms, pressing into her skin. She drew in a deep breath, heat and tobacco and whiskey. Heady stuff. She looked up to see if he felt it, too—the heavy lure of body seeking body, female seeking male.

His smile faded. He looked unhappy. Well, far

be it from Venice Leiland to impose her presence on someone who didn't want her around.

With a curt nod, she sailed into the Gold Dust, leaving him there.

"My, you certainly were nice to him," Katie said, trailing behind. "I thought you fancied McCaneaghy. You used to know him, didn't you? Blaine said his ma worked for you."

"Yes, I did know him. A long time ago. But our friendship appears to . . . that is, Mr. McCaneaghy now seems to find me objectionable."

"What a piece of sh—"

"I don't wish to inflict myself on anyone who finds me objectionable. I have my pride."

Katie stopped outside the room, looking Venice up and down. "Are all society gals like you?" she finally asked.

"I haven't a clue," Venice answered. "Why?"

" 'Cause if they are, it's a wonder there's any kids born in New York at all," she said, opening Venice's door and pushing her inside. "Go on, get in there and don't worry about McCaneaghy. Katie's got it covered."

Still shaking her head, Katie closed the door.

Suzanne Gates, hands demurely clasped in her lap, sat straight-backed on the bed. The minute she saw Venice she leapt to her feet.

"The blonde woman said it would be okay if I waited for you, ma'am," she said.

"I'm sorry I'm so late. Something distracted me," Venice said. "Now for that gown . . ."

Noble inhaled deeply, trying to gauge the effects of the whiskey. Not too bad. The hell of it was, he couldn't quite figure out what he was intoxicated on, cheap whisky or expensive sins. Either one was sure to do mortal damage.

The back door swung open and Katie stepped

outside. She put her hands on her hips and looked up at the black clouds heaping on top of the mountains. "Nice night," she said.

"Yeah," Noble answered, following her gaze. If you're partial to hail. What the hell was the woman up to? He squinted up at the blackness and immediately felt his balance threatened. He touched a hand to his head, willing the world to stop spinning. "Well, I better get moving if—"

"No!" She grabbed his arm and clung. He stared at her in astonishment. She managed to approximate a smile. She released her grip on him and casually dusted his sleeve. "Night's young yet. Think it might rain?"

"Might."

"Might what?" Blaine asked, approaching them, two cups of hard cider in his hands. Idiot, thought Noble. If Venice drank all the stuff Blaine had been toting after her all night, she'd be ready to float.

"Rain," Noble and Katie said in unison.

Blaine gave them a look that clearly questioned their sanity. Noble and Katie continued to stare up at the sky. "Yeah, seeing how them's storm clouds, I 'spect you might be right. Anyone seen Miz Leiland?" Blaine asked.

Pathetic, lovesick pup, thought Noble. Blaine had been trailing after Venice all afternoon. It was amazing her nose wasn't purple from banging it into the fool every time she turned around.

"Upstairs," Katie said.

"Oh," Blaine replied, disappointed. He sighed, leaning against the porch rail. "Guess I kin wait. Hell, I'd wait till Ezekiel blows his horn if I thought Miz Leiland would—"

"Oh, for God's sake," Noble spat. He snatched one of the cups from Blaine's hand and drained it in one long, satisfying draught. If he had to witness every man—including the young idiot in

front of him—make an ass out of himself over
Venice Leiland, at least he didn't have to do it anywhere near sober. Blaine started to protest. The
look Noble shot him made him think twice.

Noble was just about to grab the second cup of
cider when a sudden, high-pitched scream broke
from a second-story window.

"Sakes alive! That was Venice! Mercy!" Katie
clasped her hands dramatically to her chest.
"Someone's gotta save her!"

It didn't sound like Venice to Noble, but his
body's reaction was instantaneous. Diving for
the back door, he shot through it and raced for
the stairs. A hand on the banister and he vaulted
over the railing, landing halfway up the staircase,
still moving. He reached for Venice's door, crashing it open so hard that it bounced against the
wall. He entered the room half-crouched in anticipation of violence.

He blinked. A young girl in petticoats and a
chemise stood on the middle of the bed. A yellow
dress was crushed to her waist. Her eyes were
huge in her freckled face. She was stuttering, terrified.

Venice was pressed against the wall next to an
open armoire.

"It's all right. I don't think it's dangerous, Suzanne," she was saying. Her voice held a questioning quaver. Her eyes were riveted on a huge
king snake napping on the floor of the armoire.

Even though Noble knew this particular species of snake was harmless, he could appreciate
how intimidating one this large could be. Particularly if you thought it might be poisonous. Particularly if you were afraid of snakes like Venice
had always been. His jaw clenched. He'd like to
find whoever had done this to her.

The snake lifted its head and lazily uncoiled a

third of its length. Venice gasped and the girl on the bed shrieked again.

Suddenly, Blaine crowded in behind Noble. "What the hell's going on?"

The girl on the bed took one look at Blaine, glanced fearfully at the snake, and promptly launched herself at the boy. The impact of her body hitting his was audible.

Noble watched the expressions on Blaine's face change in rapid-fire order. He was painfully easy to read.

For half a minute, Blaine stared at Venice. It took another few seconds for him to realize that Venice didn't even know he was in the room. She was too busy watching the snake. After that, it took Blaine about a second more to recognize that fate had conspired to place an armful of half-naked, warm, and willing female flesh in his embrace. His grin as he tightened his hold on the girl was nearly idiotic with delight.

"Get me outta here, Blaine," the girl pleaded.

He needed no further prompting. Making soft clucking sounds, he scooted the girl out the door and off for further comforting.

Venice looked up at Noble.

"I'm ... I'm afraid of snakes." The admission was obviously painful.

"I remember."

"It was in the closet. It was there when I opened it."

"Amazin' where those damned things'll git to," Noble drawled, trying to make light of the situation even though he hated the fact that someone had purposefully frightened Venice. Fury pulsed through his body.

"No, Noble. Someone put it there." A touch of anger colored her own fear now. "My practical joker?"

"I'd guess so." Striding across the room, he grabbed the sleepy snake behind the head and, stalking to the window, dropped it outside.

"Was it poisonous?" she asked.

"Nah," Noble said shortly.

She sighed her relief, clearly embarrassed by her fear, which made him angrier. Hadn't Trevor even allowed Venice to be afraid?

"Judging by how slowly it was moving, I suspect it had just eaten," he said. "Wasn't in an aggressive mood at all. Someone just wanted to scare you, Venice, not hurt you."

"Still, I admit I'm glad to be leaving Salvage tomorrow. Maybe whoever it is will tire of their pranks by the time I return." She smiled.

She was leaving tomorrow with Cassius, Noble remembered. There just wasn't enough liquor in Salvage to keep that thought at bay.

"Don't you think?" she prompted.

"Maybe."

She was too damn beautiful. His gaze traveled hungrily over her, committing to memory everything from her small, naked feet to her narrow waist up to the creamy white skin exposed by the dipping neckline, where the feminine flesh trembled with each fear-laden breath she drew.

Fear? He looked up into her eyes. There was no fear there now. Just a dark, intoxicating awareness. And a pull as physical as anything he'd ever felt. His gaze feasted on her. Her smooth cheeks; her tender throat; her lush, parted lips; her long, tangled curls. He frowned. When had she let her hair down? *Who'd* let it down?

Cassius?

"You'd better hang up your dancing shoes sometime before dawn if you're planning on going with the Utes, lady. They won't wait on you just because you indulged a whim to try and bedazzle every single hick in this town."

She stared at him.

He couldn't help himself. He wanted her to protest, to deny the thinly veiled accusations. "I'd have thought you'd care for more of a challenge, Venice. Or are you content with any victory?"

She pulled back as though he'd struck her. Then a light ignited in her dark eyes. "But I haven't danced nearly enough."

"What?" He snorted, goaded by his imagination, seeing her held by dozens of men, hundreds of arms, none of them his. Seeing her disappear into shadowy corners with them, seeing them bend over her ...

"You mean there's a man in Salvage who hasn't had his arms around you at least twice?"

It sounded dirty, even to his own ears.

She didn't even blink. She didn't so much as hiss a denial. Instead, she placed her hand on her ribs and slowly, deliberately, smoothed her palm downward over the thin, loose material, pulling it tight across her breasts. She stared into his eyes, never breaking contact, and glided slowly toward him. The roll of her hips was a flagrant invitation.

She stopped a hand breadth away, tilting her head back. Her hair fell down her shoulders like black satin streamers. Her eyes were cold, glimmering gems, arctic ice. Noble's fingers curled into fists, his nails biting through the thick callouses on his palms.

"Why, yes. I think there are a few men left," she purred, exaggerating the careful enunciation, the slow mouthing of each word a kiss on the air. "Like you. Won't you dance with me again, McCaneaghy? Won't you put your arms around me one more time?"

"What happened to 'Noble'?"

She shrugged. The movement caused the loose cotton to slip from her breasts, briefly exposing the shadowed valley between them. His blood thrummed dully in his ears. He had never wanted anything quite as much as he wanted to touch Venice Leiland at that moment.

"You don't give me any respect, why should I give you any?" she whispered.

He didn't trust himself to speak. She put a hand on his chest. His heart pounded in response. For the life of him, even though he knew this was as much playacting as her tears had been, he couldn't make himself smile, let alone come up with some hard, sophisticated response as one of her New York suitors would have. Oh no, the Irish slum brat could only wait, transfixed like the greenest of boys, awaiting her whim like a panting stable lad.

"What about it, McCaneaghy? One more dance?"

Her other hand joined the first, both palms flat over his heart. She must be able to read his desire in the heaving of his chest.

If he gave in to this mad impulse and took her mouth, here, now, how would he compare to her New York beaus? And how many were there to be compared to? God, he wished he didn't feel so fog-headed!

He stared at her long, elegant fingers splayed across his flesh. He watched her hands ride the deep rise and fall of his own harsh breathing.

"Aye," he rasped. "I'm flattered by the invitation."

"Don't be. You know how we *fast* New York girls are. Anything for a kick. You're on to me, Noble McCaneaghy. But you always were a perceptive lad." Her voice was sarcastic and bittersweet, low and hypnotic. "I just gobble up men for breakfast. How about it, McCaneaghy? Want to be eaten alive?" she purred.

It took all his effort to make his voice flat and disinterested. "I'll just have to decline the honor, Miss Leiland."

"What's wrong? Aren't I pretty enough?" She read something in his tense stillness, something she mocked. Her lips tipped in a scornful smile, moist and succulent and pink. "Just like I thought. Hypocrite."

With an undisguised moue of disdain, she jerked her chin up and started past him.

She was right. He was a hypocrite and the knowledge was too much.

His arm shot out and snaked around her waist, dragging her body hard up against his. And then he was kissing her, feeding on her lips with all the hunger and passion and need he'd failed to bury beneath common sense and self-preservation.

There was nothing gentle about his possession. He bruised her with his desire, forced his way between her lips, and lathed the sleek warmth of her inner cheeks with his tongue. She whimpered, clinging to his neck for support. His head spun with darkening passion and his hands trailed down her neck, stroking the silken skin on her shoulders and moving to cup her breasts.

He moaned, kneading the lush mounds through the damnable cotton, feeling the tips of her unbound breasts go turgid with his manipulation. He tore his mouth from hers, bending and catching her behind the knees, lifting her high against his chest so he could wet her throat with his tongue, taste her skin, suckle her breasts fiercely, hungrily through the thin cloth.

She gasped.

It was a small sound.

But it was enough. With a low curse, he came to

his senses, understood how close he stood to the brink of taking whatever he could bully, beg, or steal from her.

He let her go, dropping her legs and lowering her to the ground. She clutched at his arms, steadying herself.

"God, you're pretty," he allowed in a tight voice. "Pretty enough to tear the heart clean out of a man and serve it up for your amusement. The only question is, whose chest are you lookin' to rip open . . . ma'am? My own poor self? Sorry. I can't oblige."

He stepped back. She would never know how much that one step—breaking the sweet agony of her mocking touch—cost him. Her hands dropped.

"Like I said, you'd best be ready to leave at daybreak. I'll meet you outside the Gold Dust at five o'clock. I have something for you to deliver to Milton."

She stared at him, her expression unreadable. For the life of him he couldn't resist one last touch. He tilted her chin, forcing her to look up at him. Her eyes were shuttered, wary. Good, he told himself, and trailed his finger along her cheek.

"And no more New York society games. Or next time, I'll play to the bloody end."

Chapter 13

"This town stinks and I am getting wet standing here," Trees-Too-Tall told Venice. He waited for her reply from atop his pony. Venice, standing on the boardwalk outside the Gold dust, blinked up at him through the fine mist. She didn't know what to say.

"We will wait inside the trees." Trees-too-Tall pointed to one of the trail heads leading out of the valley. "Reed must come soon or we will leave without him."

"He'll be here," Venice promised, hoping she was right. Trees-Too-High kicked his pony forward.

"Aren't you going to take the pack animals?" she asked.

"McCaneaghy wants to put somethin' on 'em," he said, moving past her. "You and Reed bring 'em."

McCaneaghy wants, thought Venice bitterly. So what? She slung her satchel up behind her mule's saddle. The animal stood patiently, enduring the steady beat of cold rain. It looked as miserable as she felt. She tugged her wide-brimmed felt hat lower over her forehead and twisted her woolen scarf tighter around her neck. Her mood mirrored the black, boiling sky overhead.

Angrily, she dashed tears from her cheeks, glad the rain masked her sorrow, even if it was five-thirty in the morning and only a bedraggled yellow hound was there to witness it. There wasn't another soul on the streets, just a few carts, abandoned at some point last night, axle-deep in mud. What yesterday had been dust and hard-baked ruts was now knee-deep, reddish brown ooze.

The capricious wind turned suddenly, spitting chill sleet into Venice's face. Shivering, she turned her back to it, as she vowed to turn her back on Noble McCaneaghy.

He was convinced she was a . . . a wanton!

She had to admit, she had certainly acted the role last night. She had learned the meaning of desire, had responded to Noble's heat and passion with an answering hunger. She shivered as she thought of his mouth on her breast and immediately renounced her body's treacherous reaction.

Angry with herself, she blew on her hands, rubbing them briskly together. Another gust of wind stung her cheeks. Cassius had better get here soon.

And where was Noble? This morning, when she had come downstairs, she had found Tim Gilpin sitting at the bar in front of a long line of upended shotglasses. He'd said Noble would be arriving with the packages he wanted brought up to Milton.

That had been twenty minutes ago.

"Well, get on the mule."

Venice whirled around. Noble stood behind her, towering over her, his face shadowed by the brim of his battered Stetson. The whites of his eyes caught what little light there was in the pre-dawn gloom, making them seem to gleam with a feral light. A long, oiled canvas coat, the back slit open, flapped around the tops of his scarred, mud-dabbed cavalry boots. His collar was pulled up, obscuring most of his face.

He looked ominous standing there, the rain

beading on his broad shoulders, his face a shaded impression of hard planes and sharp angles, his amber eyes aglow. He stretched out a gloved hand. Instinctively, Venice jumped back. She could see a brief flash of white teeth and then he was reaching past her, ensuring the saddle roll was secure.

"You ever been on a mule, Venice?" he drawled.

"Plenty of times," she answered haughtily. "I am conversant with all things mulish."

His eyes narrowed and she was certain she saw the twitch of a quickly restrained smile. "Sure it wasn't just a real ugly horse?"

"Yes, McCaneaghy. I'm sure."

"Good." Without a word of warning, Noble placed his big hands on either side of her waist and hoisted her into the saddle.

"That was unnecessary." She wanted to sound icy with contempt. She suspected she sounded breathless. "I wasn't ready to mount yet."

"That supposed to make me laugh?" The humor was gone from his voice as though it had never been.

"What do you mean?" She scowled down at him.

"Don't play dumb, Venice."

"I assure you I am not *playing* anything. I was warned, remember?" she answered frostily.

He peered up at her, his expression unconvinced. "Look," she said, "I won't even begin to try and guess what you're referring to, but since your poor opinion of me couldn't be more apparent, I think I can safely assume that you believe I have made a lewd, racy, or immoral quip. So, since I wouldn't want to disillusion you, yes . . . you're supposed to laugh."

His posture subtly relaxed. "Ha."

"And I reiterate; I was not yet prepared to get up on this mule!"

"I'm dreadfully sorry, Miss Leiland." Noble tilted his head back. "Haven't all the men you danced with been by to say their fare-thee-wells yet?"

The devil spoke: Venice listened.

"Oh, my, Noble!" She trilled a little laugh. "The men heard everything—and I do mean everything—they wanted to hear last night. Anything I added now would be redundant."

His damnable gold eyes went flat and cold. His dark brows dipped over his eyes in a scowl. Wordlessly, he grabbed hold of her ankle. Venice squeaked. Noble smiled.

He lifted her leg over his shoulder, releasing her ankle so her leg rested against his back as he checked her stirrup length. Her awareness was instant, intense, and scandalous. She felt exposed, vulnerable, and weak with her knee notched over him like this. She could feel the big muscles of his shoulder bunch beneath her thigh as he silently worked the leather cinch. If she slid off the saddle, she'd be straddling him. Venice gulped. Noble snapped the buckle in place. He dipped his shoulder and her leg slid down and off his arm.

"Check the other stirrup." His voice sounded strangled. She stared at him. She was breathing too fast.

"You know how?" he barked.

"Yes, I do. I will." Trying to catch her breath, Venice leaned over, hoping Noble wouldn't notice her response to him. Damn! Of all the men in the world this one alone had to have the power to affect her so viscerally.

Noble, however, seemed too busy to pay her much attention. Muttering savagely, he lifted a heavy-looking crate to the back of a mule. He threw a rope over the box and wrenched it taut.

"You've *got* to be kidding!" a female voice intoned. Venice looked up.

Katie stood in the open doorway, her fluffy blonde hair sticking out in oddly becoming puffs about her sleepy face. She blinked blearily at them. "First, that Suzanne What-ever-the-hell-her-name-is is giggling with that scrawny Farley kid on my front porch 'til midnight—and her brother playing chaperone from the side alley didn't help business none, let me tell you. Then that dumb-ass editor mooning around the bar all night. Now, you two looking angry as May hornets and here it ain't even, it ain't even—Chrissakes, what time is it, anyway?"

"Six," Noble said, pulling a slip knot tighter.

"Six! Chrissakes. What? The mountain ain't gonna be there if you leave after breakfast? Geez," she grumbled. "I need my sleep. I gotta big day ahead of me."

"Big day?" asked Venice.

"Yeah. What with you leaving town, I expect all your beaus will be drowning their sorrows. And I expect they'll be doin' that drowning at my bar." The thought cheered her considerably. She rubbed her hands together with satisfaction. "Big day ahead. Yup. Big day."

"I'm sorry if I woke you, Miss Jones," Venice said. "I was waiting for Mr. Reed. And Mr. McCaneaghy. He wants to ship something up to my uncle." She eyed Noble accusingly. "What is it you wished to send?" she asked sweetly. "A copy of my dance card?"

"What?"

"Well, with your interesting preoccupation with the number and frequency of my dance partners last night, I felt sure you were keeping a running tally."

He grunted.

"You mean my Uncle Milton hasn't hired you to play the part of dutch uncle in his absence?"

"Nope." There was a grudging note of amusement in his voice.

"Good. Because you aren't very good at it."

"Lady, you aren't telling me anything I don't already know."

"So, what *are* you sending him?"

"Fossils. Nah, not the type your uncle's looking for, Venice. No dinosaurs. But I'm sure you know that. Just seashells. I promised Milton I'd send him any fossils I couldn't recognize. Been doing it for years."

"How long is it gonna take Venice and that Reed feller to get to her uncle's camp, Mr. McCaneaghy?" Katie asked.

"Crooked Hand says four or five days." He snapped the words out. "Plenty of time for a nice adventure."

Venice felt her back go rigid. "Oh ... an adventure can occur in one day, Mr. McCaneaghy. Or one night. You should have stuck around last night."

The rope Noble had been pulling snapped. He swore. The bronze hue of his skin deepened.

Good, thought Venice.

"What'd ya mean?" Katie asked. "McCaneaghy here was camped out under the balcony last night."

Venice's eyes grew wide. "You were. You mean you were playing *nanny* all night?" she demanded angrily.

"Don't give yourself so much credit. I didn't want to contend with the lice at the Pay Dirt and the Gold Dust is the only place in town with a balcony to keep the rain off. Nuthin' more to it than that."

Katie's gaze darted back and forth between the two of them. "I shoulda known," she muttered under her breath. "But it woulda worked with two normal people! Like that Blaine Farley. All that boy needed was to *see* a petticoat—" she grumbled to a halt. "Hellfire!"

As Venice and Noble glared at each other, Cassius emerged from around the corner of the Gold Dust perched astride a weary-looking mule. He was rigged out in a short, caped tweed jacket and wool trousers. A tan bowler with a dented crown was perched at jaunty angle on his macassar-slicked hair.

"Good morning, Miss Leiland." He touched the brim of his hat. "I say, where are the Indian fellows?"

"Good morning—" Venice darted a quick glance at Noble's grim profile and made herself smile, "—Cassius. Our guides are waiting for us at the trail head."

Cassius beamed. "Ah, good. We're ready to leave . . . Venice?" Her name slid unpleasantly off his tongue, like oil on still water.

With an unintelligible growl, Noble vaulted atop the boardwalk and slammed open the door to the saloon, disappearing inside. She stared after him. The doorway framed empty darkness.

Good-bye. Her heart seemed to be beating too slowly. She couldn't seem to tear her gaze from the place where he'd been. She would probably never see him again.

"Er . . . Venice?" Cassius repeated.

"Yes." *Good-bye.* "Yes. I'm ready to leave."

Cassius cracked the mule on the rump with his furled umbrella, moving the placid animal up beside Venice's. "Shall we, then?"

"Wait!" Tim Gilpin emerged from the Gold Dust. With one beefy hand he rubbed his head, standing his rumpled hair on end. "You take care, now," he said gruffly to Venice. "There are things in these mountains that can take anyone, no matter how capable, clean by surprise."

He walked out from beneath the protective overhang of the porch, heedless of the icy rain soaking his grizzled locks. He leaned a hand on Venice's pommel, capturing her gloved hand in his and squeezing gently. "Be careful, Miss Leiland."

Venice smiled down at him. Cassius snorted. "I assure you, sir, Miss Leiland will be more than adequately provided for."

He kicked his mule past the editor and, without a backward glance, started down the road. Withdrawing his hand, Tim narrowed his eyes on Cassius's plodding figure and, with careful deliberation, spat a stream of chaw-stained spittle after him.

"Thank you for your concern, Mr. Gilpin." Venice turned to Katie. "And thank you for your kindness, Miss Jones." She tried to keep from peering into the dark bar.

"Shoot, ain't nothing," Katie answered. "And don't you worry. I ain't never seen a feller got a worse case of the itch than that one." She jerked her head toward the Gold Dust's door. "You wait and see."

"Oh," Venice said, striving for a bright tone. "I somehow believe Mr. McCaneaghy and I have seen quite the last of each other. And I'm just as certain he's delighted about that."

"Honey," Katie said slowly, "about that stuff I told you about Josiah and me—"

"Our meeting up again after all these years was an accident. It should never have happened."

"Damn it, Venice. Listen to me. Maybe I was

wrong. Josiah never looked at me the way McCaneaghy looks at you. Maybe there is such a thing as true—"

Venice didn't need anyone fanning dead hopes to life. It hurt too much. "I have to go. Please, tell Mr. McCaneaghy I—Tell him he was wrong about me." She somehow found a smile. "He suspects I put that snake in the armoire myself."

"Oh, yeah—well, about that snake, I hate to admit it but I—"

"I'm sorry, Katie, I have to go." She nudged her mule forward. "And, please, tell him good-bye."

"Be careful!" Katie called, backing under the overhang and pulling her shawl tighter about herself.

"I will," Venice promised.

"Good luck!" Tim yelled.

Katie and Tim stood beneath the porch for ten minutes, watching Venice and Reed make their way slowly out of town and disappear among the pine trees. Katie sighed.

They were just about to go back inside when the door burst open and McCaneaghy strode out, his eyes sparkling dangerously and his mouth set tighter than bark to a tree.

"Which way?" he asked Tim.

"Well, that didn't take long," Tim said, looking grimly amused.

McCaneaghy rounded on Tim, his long, hard length tense. His voice was low, deliberate. "Look, Tim, if it starts really raining, their trail can be wiped out in a matter of minutes and with Trees-Too-High leading 'em, I wouldn't have a chance in hell of knowing which way they went. Utes don't follow the same trails as whites. Now, *which way?*"

Tim met McCaneaghy's burning gaze and pointed toward where Venice and Reed had entered the pines.

"Thanks," McCaneaghy bit out. "I'll be taking your horse."

"You just take care of Miss Leiland, Noble," Tim said gruffly.

"Yeah," Noble said, reaching into his coat and fastening the inside tabs around his thighs.

"I mean it."

"Sure." Noble flipped the coat shut and pulled his Stetson lower over his brow.

"If anything happens to her, I'll hold you responsible for—"

"If anything happens to her, I'll be where a lecture from you ain't gonna do any earthly good, Tim," Noble bit out between clenched teeth.

He impaled the stocky editor with a hard glare. Tim met his gaze. Unspoken words stretched between them. Finally, Tim broke the staring match with a curt nod. Without another word, Noble leapt from the boardwalk and headed for the stable.

"You mean he's going after her?" Katie asked, wide-eyes with confusion.

"Yup. Told me so when he came into the bar. He's going to trail them to make sure nothing happens. He isn't all that happy about it, though."

"I'll be damned! But if he ain't so happy about it, how come he's doin' it?"

Tim, still watching Noble striding up the mud-choked street, shook his head. "I don't think he can help himself."

The import of Tim's statement took about ten seconds to penetrate Katie's usually sharp mind. When it did, a huge smile spread across her face. She threw back her head and let out an enormous whoop of delight.

A shouting match between the new saloon owner and one of the whores woke Harry Grundy from a sound sleep. Cat fights, though common enough, were rare this early in the morning. Especially after a fandango like last night's, following hard on the heels of Preacher Niss's revival. Harry rose to his knees and peered out the window, his mud-colored eyes marking Noble McCaneaghy's progress.

"Well, the jigs about up on that one, boy," Harry muttered, flopping back on a bare mattress and staring moodily at the ceiling. The army blanket separating the Grundy brothers' respective sides of the room rustled.

"You hear me, Anton?"

"Yeah." A belch punctuated the remark. "I told you she was gonna see them bolts and wires."

"Shut up. How's I to know she was so all-fired clever?

"Think she's clever enough to figure out there ain't nuthin' in these mountains but a bunch of played-out mines and rock?" Anton asked.

"Yup."

"Think she'll close down the spur line?"

"Yup."

"That means no more free freight shipments."

"Wal now, that's right bright of you, Anton."

There was no word from the other side of the blanket. Anton's brain musta just up and quit trying to wrestle with that notion, thought Harry.

"If we ain't got no spur line, we ain't got no way to get stuff up here and that means we ain't got nothin' fer no one to buy."

"Yup."

"What are we gonna do?"

Harry didn't have an answer. He rolled onto his stomach, scratched his rump, and peered out the window again. Noble was gone.

"We'll end up going back to Dubuque!" Anton bellowed tragically.

Harry's eyes glazed over. Dubuque. No liquor on Sundays, women holding their noses if you didn't wash every month, little kids throwing spitballs at you. Dubuque meant giving up every wondrous aspect of the marvelous life Harry and Anton lived.

Had lived for seven years, ever since Uncle Zeb keeled over dead, right here on the front step of the Grundy Mercantile. Big, ugly old Uncle Zeb.

Harry could almost see the dear old fart lying there. He'd been stiff as a board by noon, a funny look cemented on his ancient face for all eternity. It was like he'd been hanging on for years, just waiting on Anton and him to appear in order to die blissfullike.

Old, dead Zeb. Old . . . dead . . . man.

Whooping with joy, Harry Grundy sprang from his bed and tore back the blanket. He wasn't going to give up Salvage and the mercantile and whores in velvet and all this other heaven-bestowed munificence. Not without a fight!

"Ain't you got no privacy at all 'round here?" Fifi LaPalma grumbled from the other side of Anton's massive bulk.

Harry ignored her. "I got it, Anton. I know'd what to do!"

Chapter 14

"**D**idn't anyone else think to bring an additional deck of cards?" Cassius demanded.

"No." Venice sighed. They'd been traveling for three days now, and each one had seemed longer than the last. Because of her companion, Cassius Reed.

"This will never do, never," he fumed.

Venice closed her eyes and counted to ten. If she had to put up with too many more of Cassius's petty complaints, she would end up killing him. Maybe she should just drown him in that vat of macassar oil he'd insisted on bringing for his hair.

"If you hadn't left the cards outside your tent last night, the wind wouldn't have blown them away," she said reasonably. "If you'd like, I can make—"

"First no proper bed linen, now this!" Cassius broke in, rifling through a mule's pack. "How, might I ask, are we to entertain ourselves in this dreary place?"

"Dreary?" Venice asked incredulously. "It's magical! Don't you think it's beautiful?"

"Beautiful? A dripping forest and a bunch of mountains?" He sniffed. "If I want to ponder the panoramic splendor of a mountainscape, I'd much rather do it from the comfort of a nice club chair in front of a painting than from a mule's back in a rainstorm."

"But you wouldn't be part of the magnificence then. You'd just be a . . . a spectator."

"Thank God," Cassius replied irritably, going on to the next mule's pack. "I'd go mindless with boredom were I forced to be part of this 'magnificence' for any length of time. And speaking of boredom, how are we supposed to occupy ourselves for the rest of the day?"

"If you are looking for something to do, you might help set up camp," Venice suggested.

"Set up camp?" Cassius echoed in disbelief. "That's what these bounders are being paid to do." He flincked his hand toward Tree-Too-High and Crooked Hand.

"They're busy trying to get a fire going."

"And not a moment too soon. I declare, I am quite chilled. No fire, bloody drippy forests all around, and no decent food." He snapped the flap down on the pack without bothering to reorganize the mess he'd made. "And nothing of value in here either. Nothing at all but some books."

He said the word as though it were a disease. "And this excavating equipment. I can't believe a man as wealthy as your uncle would not include some civilized accouterments amongst his supply list."

Venice started refolding the pack, still bemused that Cassius thought all this splendor "boring."

"Hmm," Cassius was murmuring as he sauntered toward Noble's crate. "I wonder what McCaneaghy has in here?"

"He said it's some fossilized shells for my uncle," Venice replied.

Cassius rapped his knuckles against the wood. The crate sounded hollow.

"I'll wager there's something other than rocks in here."

"Mr. McCaneaghy said he promised my uncle

he would send up any fossils he couldn't identify.
I'm sure that's all it is."

Cassius's gaze slid toward the other men. "Your
uncle probably requested a ... *libation*." He
mouthed the word, again jerking his head toward
the Indians. "That has to be it."

"I don't think so. Mr. McCaneaghy said—"

" 'McCaneaghy said'!" Cassius sputtered in exasperation. "My dear woman, you must learn that
you can't trust the likes of him. He's little better
than a savage himself, living outdoors like he
does."

"Then I must have 'savage' tendencies myself. I
like it here."

"Yes. Yes. Very nice for a holiday," Cassius said
dismissively. "But that's not what I meant. I meant
that McCaneaghy is not our sort."

"*Our* sort?"

"Noble McCaneaghy is nothing but an Irish
thug from the New York slums."

She'd had enough. "And just what would you
know about Mr. McCaneaghy, Mr. Reed?"

Cassius's face took on a smug mien. "I know all
about him. He was at Yale the same time I was."

"He was?"

"For a while, yes," Cassius said haughtily. He
sneered. "I know what you're thinking. What
would an Irish immigrant be doing at Yale? It
makes a rather droll story."

He leaned forward. A gossipy note underlined
his usual smooth tones. His eyes gleamed with the
special, distinct delight of someone about to share
a hurtful secret. Venice recoiled. His avidity was
repulsive.

"Noble McCaneaghy was a charity case. Some
rich man's social experiment. I would have
guessed he was probably the man's by-blow but
from the atrocious accent he had when he first

came to college, it was only too obvious he was right off the boat."

Is this the bigotry that Noble had had to endure at college? she wondered. Is this why he had left New York?

"This man paid McCaneaghy's way—his clothes, his apartment, his vices . . . everything! The tuition was the least of the expenditures!" Cassius leaned further forward. "Wait. It gets better."

"I don't want to hear anymore," she said severely.

He went on as though she hadn't spoken. "When McCaneaghy didn't live up to expectation, his mentor had him drafted into the army."

"Drafted?" Venice asked. Her breath caught in her throat. "No!"

"Yes. What else do you do with something that becomes a potential political liability?"

"You don't know any of this," she said urgently, not wanting to believe it was true, already knowing that it was.

Cassius finally realized his words were not having their desired effect. He sniffed as though offended by her disbelief. "I heard it firsthand from a clerk in the college assessor's office. No one was supposed to know, not even McCaneaghy . . . but McCaneaghy's unknown benefactor cut him off without a dime. He had McCaneaghy's name sent to the conscription officers."

The blood rushed from Venice's cheeks. Her father couldn't have been capable of a betrayal of this magnitude, could he? "A lie!"

"No." Cassius pronounced the word with savage satisfaction. "True. Verifiable. His benefactor *did* cut him off and gave his name to the draft."

His face took on a sly, suggestive expression. "Fairly excessive measures to get rid of a failed experiment, weren't they? I have often asked myself why would he do something so extreme, unless he and McCaneaghy had an 'extreme' relationship?"

Venice gasped.

"Oh, come now," Cassius said blandly. "It was just a thought. You're a worldly woman, Venice. You haven't been raised in a convent."

"You don't know anything!" Venice's hands clenched and unclenched at her side. "You and your *friends!* Vicious-minded little boys huddling in your rooms, giggling over your sordid suppositions! Haven't you a single shred of decency?"

Realizing he had gone too far, Cassius stepped back before Venice's verbal onslaught and blinked in rapid succession.

"I am sorry to have burnt your tender ears," he muttered.

"You haven't burnt my ears, you pompous ass!" Venice spat. "I am merely disgusted with myself for not realizing just how vile you are. I should have *begged* Noble to guide me before agreeing to your company!"

"Begged *Noble?*" Cassius sputtered. "I see you were more impressed with his manly attributes than I'd thought! How long has this been going on?"

Venice glared at him. "Fourteen years!"

"What?"

"Next time you spread filthy rumors, Mr. Reed, you'd best be sure of all the facts. Noble McCaneaghy lived with us when he was a boy. My *father* was his unknown benefactor."

Cassius stared, his mouth dropping open. Venice didn't wait for a reply. She swung around and stalked away.

"You're sure this is an accurate map?" Cassius whispered, squinting at the crude drawing by the glow of the dying campfire.

The Indian nodded. "Mil-Ton's camp is half day on this trail."

"And it's easy to follow? This trail, I mean?"

The Indians exchanged dubious glances. Damn their insolence! They stood there with water dripping down their oily locks, staining their filthy buckskin shirts, and had the temerity to judge him. *Him!*

"If you cannot follow this, it is better that we stay," the short Indian said. "The white woman is Mil-Ton's family and—"

"You will not stay!" Cassius nearly shouted. A twig snapped behind him and he jerked around, searching the rain-veiled shadows on the edge of the firelight. Nothing. His gaze darted to Venice's tent. No movement. She was still asleep.

"You will not stay!" he repeated in a furious whisper. "I paid you twenty-five American dollars! Ten for this pitiful excuse of a map and fifteen to leave with Milton's junk before morning. And you're going to keep to your part of the bargain!"

The tall, wooden-faced bastard just stood, gazing off into the rain. It was the short, thick-set Indian that was vacillating.

"The woman. She is yours?" he asked.

Who'd have thought that he, Cassius Thornton Reed, should ever stoop to persuading an Indian to do *anything?* Cassius bit at his nail and thought. Extreme circumstances called for extreme measures.

"Look, she's a wealthy society woman. *My* society. She wants to be alone with me. She is just too shy to tell you herself."

The short Indian didn't look convinced. "Why, if she is yours, does she watch McCaneaghy with such hot eyes?"

Cassius swore under his breath. He should have

known. Any fool—even these savages—could see
the way Venice panted after that Irish bastard like
a bitch in heat. He struggled to control his temper.

"Believe me, what Venice wanted from McCaneaghy she could get in five minutes. But when everything's said and done, I'm the one she'll end up
marrying. Listen, this is no concern of yours. You
don't want any trouble. Don't get involved. Just
take the money and leave."

The short Indian exchanged doubtful looks with
the taller one. The taller one shrugged. "It is as
McCaneaghy says. The woman is not of McCaneaghy's people. We'll go to Mil-Ton's camp and
bring him his stuff. We will tell him where his
brother's child is."

"You do that." By then, Cassius thought, it will
be too late for old Milton to do anything to save
his niece's already far-from-spotless reputation.

Without another word the Indians disappeared
into the surrounding forest, as silently as the rain
falling from the sky, leaving Cassius bent over,
studying the map.

It looked as if there was a stream a quarter mile
from here. If he led Venice there, they could get
"lost" for a couple of days and he'd still have a
good idea where they were. She didn't ever need
to know that they were never farther than five
miles from Milton's camp.

By then he was sure to have recovered her good
opinion of him. He scowled. How was he to have
known Leiland had been McCaneaghy's anonymous benefactor?

As for her father throwing McCaneaghy to the
draft office, that much was true. Venice had
looked laughably shocked by that bit of information. Cassius smiled bitterly. It was amazing Venice didn't realize what her father was capable of.

He shuddered at the thought. The consequences

should Trevor Leiland ever hear that Cassius had hinted about his having an unnatural relationship with McCaneaghy made Cassius's stomach churn. Leiland would crush him.

He had to make sure Leiland never heard. By getting rid of these savages, he had two days in which to play the hero for Venice. He could do it. After all, just three days ago she'd called him "Cassius."

And if she didn't come around by the time their "honeymoon" ended? Why then, he'd have no choice but to explain to her father the circumstances of their unchaperoned trip, intimating, of course, that the newspapers might be made privy to the unfortunate story.

Trevor was singularly ambitious. Considering the upcoming elections, he would make sure that Venice accepted Cassius's marriage proposal. All of New York society knew that Venice Leiland would do anything for her father's approval.

A gust of wind rippled the map in his hand and spat sleet into his face. Folding the map, he tucked it into the inside pocket of his jacket and headed back for his tent. This just might work out better than he'd hoped.

"Don't despair, dear Venice, *I* shall deliver you from this wilderness!" Cassius said, throwing his arm out in a grand, sweeping arc. He had been making such ridiculous, theatrical gestures and issuing inflated assurances all morning.

Venice's eyes narrowed. He was altogether too happy at having been deserted by their guides.

"You're sure you haven't any idea why Trees-Too-High and Crooked Hand left?"

Cassius turned in the saddle, a puzzled frown on his face. "Trees-Too—? Oh! The savages. Who can say, m'dear? Most likely," he continued in that infuriatingly artful tone, "having absconded with their ill-gotten gain they are even now riding into yet another of these mountain's festering toss pots, seeking to barter your uncle's equipment for 'firewater,' as I believe it is colloquially known."

Venice didn't bother hiding her disgust.

Cassius blinked in offense. "Primitives like those are ruled by their impulses, dear lady. They are not like us. Certainly not to be trusted."

"*I* trusted them."

"I know," Cassius returned sadly. "And look what it got you. I shudder—absolutely shudder—to think what horrors might have befallen you were I not here to ensure your welfare."

Nothing, Venice was quite sure, nearly as horrible as having to endure another hour of Cassius's company.

She tugged the brim of her hat lower over her ears and squinted up at the sky. Icy droplets stung her face. Clouds the color of new bruises churned on a lead-colored canvas. Just last night, Crooked Hand had said a bad storm was brewing in the west and had warned her that they should not travel today.

For Trees-Too-High and Crooked Hand to just up and leave in the middle of a rainstorm in the dead of night didn't make sense. And yet, that's exactly what had happened.

She'd stalked to the sputtering campfire this morning, determined to ignore Cassius. But he had greeted her with a grave demeanor and the unfathomable information that their guides—and their pack mules—had disappeared while they slept.

Misreading her bewilderment, Cassius had haughtily assured her that they were well rid of the "bounders." He was adept at reading the landscape. They need only ride south to find a stream that they could follow.

He hadn't listened to her ensuing protest. Instead, he'd pulled down the tents, cramming all their equipment into two enormous canvas bags and throwing them onto his long-suffering mule. Then, he'd trotted off, heading into the woods.

With all of her belongings on Cassius's mule, Venice had had no choice but to follow—which she had been doing for hours.

"See?" Cassius called, pointing ahead. Venice squinted through the rain.

He had halted his mule at the head of a clearly defined trail. It plummeted to the floor of a narrow valley, to a rushing stream sixty feet below them. From her vantage, she could see that the stream entered the valley through a rift in the canyon wall a mile upstream. A quarter-mile downstream it disappeared around the bend of the deepening gorge.

"I told you not to worry, m'dear. *I* am here. *I* will protect you." Cassius touched his index finger to his nose. "How fortunate for you that you have a capable man on whom to rely. A woman needs a man to support her, don't you think? A captain to guide her through life's little squalls. A patient teacher willing to instruct her. A noble mentor whom she can revere . . ." His voiced lowered suggestively. "A lover?"

She made a choking sound.

"Don't worry. I am a sophisticated man. I am able to overlook your little infatuation with that Irish upstart. I am certain that having indulged your—sense of adventure shall we say?—you will be more appreciative of a man of your own class."

He didn't wait to hear the growl erupting deep from Venice's throat. He flipped back around and swatted his mule on the rump, sending the unbalanced creature staggering down the incline.

Venice didn't follow him. She couldn't. Her rage upon hearing of her father's treatment of Noble had become numbing anguish.

No wonder Noble had never come back to the Park Avenue address. Now his attitude, the hot and cold, the pull and push, made sense. Trevor had betrayed him, and now Noble found himself attracted to his betrayer's daughter.

Trevor Leiland, knight-errant of the lower classes, Venice thought bitterly. She wouldn't have blamed Noble if he hated all the Leilands! And she could certainly understand this distrust of them. He would be a fool not to be suspicious of her.

In the quick-witted youth, Trevor had seen an opportunity to impress New York society. He'd planned to present the son of his immigrant cook as a superlative result of his social reform programs. Someone like Noble, taught to speak and dress and read, could help realize Trevor's political aspirations.

Trevor had used Noble like a performing circus animal.

Then, apparently, Noble had done something that made her father angry. So angry—or was it threatened?—that he'd arranged to have Noble drafted.

The thought of her father's treachery hurt, but it didn't surprise her, which hurt even more. Venice had always suspected what her father was capable of. Now, she knew.

She pressed her mouth into a hard, resolved line. Trevor owed her some information. And this time he wouldn't be dealing with a twelve-year-old girl so desperate for his affection that she could choke back her doubts and questions.

"Yoo-hoo!" Cassius's call shook her from her preoccupation.

She looked around. Cassius was completely lost to sight. He was probably still babbling to the air about the uses a man could be to a woman. She kneed her mule forward and peered over the edge of the trail. Cassius was bouncing along thirty yards ahead of her and twenty feet below, muttering . . . more like rumbling.

Venice frowned. That sound wasn't Cassius.

The rumbling grew louder, turning from a dull, hammering drone into a roar. Her mule fidgeted and shivered. Suddenly, she realized it was not the mule that was shivering, it was the ground.

She stared down at the stream, her gaze following the bubbling ribbon of water to the jagged chasm upstream. There, through the stinging veil of rain, she saw a huge wall of churning, gray water pouring from the fissure, lashing high up the sides of the narrow valley, careening down on them in a thundering din.

Flash flood!

"Cassius!" she shouted. "Come back!"

Cassius, pausing next to a tall, ancient pine, was oblivious to his danger. He twisted about, calling, "Can't hear you, m'dear! Bloody rain makin' an ungodly racket!"

She motioned frantically with her arms. "Come back! Hurry!"

She could see the flood clearly now, devouring trees and spitting them out as it boiled forth. Cassius's mule must have sensed its danger, for suddenly it reared back, bucking Cassius from its back.

With a shrill, trumpeting bray the mule tore back up the trail. It galloped past Venice as she struggled to control her own panicking mount.

"Climb the tree, Cassius!" she screamed at the top of her lungs.

"Wha—?" Cassius asked dazedly, pulling himself to his knees.

"The tree! There's a *flood! Climb!*"

Comprehension poured into Cassius's blank face. He leaped upright, grabbing for the branches of the pine and scrambling into its lower boughs. Hands and feet clawing the bark from the trunk, he scrabbled and scratched his way higher.

Then the river was upon him.

It thundered and bellowed, making the ground shudder, booming and echoing as it swept along the narrow defile. Water, hitting the rocks with incredible force, shot hundreds of feet into the air, showering Venice with blinding spray. Huge trees, their thick trunks bobbing like apples in a wash basin, struck the sides of the canyon and shattered like kindling under the impact. Below her, boulders tore free from the ravine walls, scraping the very rock of the mountain from the ancient water bed.

As quickly as it had approached, the head of the flood swept past her, racing down the mountainside like a runaway train. It left behind a surging river that covered the valley floor, cresting some thirty feet up the chasm walls.

Venice looked to where she had last seen Cassius. Somehow the ancient pine still stood threequarters covered by the newly created river. It was listing badly. Cassius clung a mere eight feet out of the water, his arms and legs wrapped in a death grip around the slender top. His eyes were squeezed shut and his mouth was moving soundlessly.

Venice's relief was short-lived. Abruptly, the tree pitched a few feet closer to the river. Cassius's eyes flew open.

"Get me off of here!"

Frantically, Venice looked around. Every piece of equipment, every article of clothing, everything that might help them, including rope, was in the pack on Cassius's runaway mule.

Chapter 15

Noble loosened his pony's reins, and cupping his raw hands together, blew into them. He was cold and he was wet. His stomach had begun growling an hour ago and his back was cramped from bending in the saddle all morning, studying the ground for signs of Venice's party.

The fog, filtering amongst sentinel pines and coating everything it touched in a glistening sheath, complicated matters. Because of the way sound carried, he'd hung back, letting Venice get a good three miles ahead so she wouldn't hear him and realize he'd followed her.

He might have given in to the idiot compulsion that had driven him from the Gold Dust and sent him chasing, unprepared and ill-supplied, into the mountains after her, but she sure as hell wasn't going to know it! He still had a small shred of self-respect left, dammit.

And if he got within visual range he might have to watch her with Cassius Reed. He didn't know whether he could stomach watching Venice flirt with him.

It didn't seem to matter that he knew Venice would end up marrying Cassius or someone just like him, that she *should* marry someone just like him. After all, Cassius Reed would make Venice a perfect mate.

A silver spoon was buried as deeply in his pink

little maw as it was in Venice's. His bloodlines were equally blue. He'd been all but bred to decorate Park Avenue clubrooms and Newport beach cottages with his suave presence.

Noble's mouth flattened.

No. Better to follow well out of range of eye and ear.

He would straggle along after them until they reached Milton's camp and then, once he saw for himself that Venice was safely delivered to her uncle, it would be "Adios Miss Leiland!" And, for his heart's sake, he hoped it was the last time he ever laid eyes on her.

In all other areas of his life, he was a deliberate, even-tempered, objective man. But when it came to Venice Leiland he became a blithering idiot certain that the woman lived under the constant threat of imminent danger, and that *he* was the only one who could protect her from it.

And he'd thought *Trevor* was mentally unbalanced!

Noble pulled a piece of jerky from an inside pocket and wiped the lint off of it, the image of Venice the morning she'd left Salvage haunting his thoughts. She'd looked as fresh and silky as new-skimmed cream. With that outsized coat enveloping her, and her booted feet dangling out of the stirrups, and that red cap pulled over her ears, she could almost be mistaken for a lad.

Except for the utterly feminine feel of her waist beneath his palms when he had lifted her into the saddle, and the womanly modeling of her thigh pressed intimately against his back, and the hot rush of sweet breath touching his mouth as she'd breathed, "Yes. I do. I will."

He was still gnawing the rain-washed jerky when he entered their abandoned campsite. Casually, he leaned out of the saddle and started looking for their sign.

His eyes narrowed as he read the ground. The back of his neck prickled with alarm.

Two groups had left the camp, in two separate directions. The Utes on their unshod ponies had left well before daybreak, leading the pack mules directly west, higher up into the mountains. The other two had broken camp maybe three-quarters of an hour ago. They had gone in a southerly direction.

He headed south. After a few miles, his unease turned to flat-out worry. The two ahead of him were tracing the natural slope of the mountain's shoulder, wending their way downhill. At this rate, sooner or later they were going to stumble onto a stream bed. Stream beds, just after the spring melt and particularly in the midst of a heavy rain, were notoriously dangerous highways for flash floods. He couldn't believe anyone would be foolish enough not to stay away from low ground and out of narrow places, but that's exactly what they were doing.

Heedless of the treacherous footing, he kicked his pony into a canter. At the same time, the air about him burgeoned with a low hum. The dull roar grew louder and louder. Noble pulled his pony to a halt and listened.

A mule broke from the trees ahead of him. It galloped straight at him, ears laid flat and foam flying from its mouth. Suddenly, the canvas bag flaying its wind-bloated sides broke free, strewing its content along the path. The panicked mule's eye rolled in terror. Braying, it lunged forward and bolted past Noble, disappearing into the rain-lashed trees, leaving behind scattered clothes and equipment. A pink dress, a lace—

Noble tore his hat from his head and dug his

heels into his pony's flanks, racing in the direction
the mule had come from. Fear choked him as he
bent low over the gelding's neck, whipping its
rump with his hat, spurring it into headlong flight.
The pony scrambled and slipped, tearing through
the pines, neck stretched straight out, mouth open,
sucking air.

His deviled mount tore into a sharp corner and
slipped on the slick, wet shale, falling sideways on
its haunches. Noble stuck like a burr. Standing in
the stirrups, he dragged the pony's head up,
shouting into its ears. The horse lurched to its feet
and plunged on, goaded by rain and voice and
heel.

Another corner, a quarter-mile of ice-glazed
granite, and he saw her.

She was on her knees at the edge of a gorge.
Her hair was plastered to her shoulders. Her great
coat snapped out, buffeted by the wind. Below
her, floodwaters half-filled the chasm. And
damned if it didn't look like she was climbing
right into it!

"Venice!" he yelled.

The din was horrendous. She couldn't hear him.
He was almost even with her now. He swung
from the racing pony, pulling back on the bit,
bringing it skittering to a halt. He hit the ground,
lost his footing, and fell to his knees. Air exploded
from his lungs. He pushed himself up, his arms
trembling, and stumbled to his feet.

It was okay. It was all right. *Venice was safe.*

He stood, eyes closed, head thrown back. The
heat behind his eyes turned into tears of relief,
mingling with the cold rain streaming down his
cheeks.

"Venice!"

She turned. There was no surprise in her eyes,
just an overwhelming gladness. An instant of rec-

ognition and she was racing across the slippery
rock. Another instant, and she was in his arms. He
caught her in mid flight, lifting her from the
ground, crushing her to him, reverently stroking
the black curls from her pale brow, touching her
chilled cheeks with his fingertips, staring into her
silver eyes.

He loved her. It didn't matter if she was Trevor
Leiland's child and as beyond his reach as the
moon. He loved her. He always had.

He closed his eyes. Loving Venice didn't make
her any more attainable. He could never say the
words. But he could no longer deny it to himself.

"Thank God!" he murmured reverently, tucking
her delicate frame against him. Wet wool, cool
fine-grained skin, sweet breath—God, if he'd lost
her!

"Noble!" she sobbed, twisting in his embrace.
"You've got to help him!"

"Him?"

"Cassius! He's stranded on a tree! You have to
help him. Quick! The tree is going to be torn loose
any minute!"

She pushed herself away from him. Bracing her
fist on his chest, she pleaded, "You have to!"

He didn't, of course. He could walk away right
now, dragging Venice with him, and no one would
hold him accountable. Even if he stayed, a mere
second or two delay and Cassius would—

He released his hold on her. She grabbed his
hand, tugging him forward.

"Wait." Noble strode over to where his pony
stood, head down, sides heaving. He unhooked a
thick coil of rope from his saddlebag and, leading
the pony, followed Venice to the trail head.

Immediately below him and a short distance
out, he spied Cassius. He was perched on the
branch of a heavily listing pine tree, marooned fif-

teen feet out in the middle of a boiling river. His feet dangled a scant yard above the swift current beneath him. He looked up, wild-eyed, and spotted Noble. He looked desperate enough to do anything to survive—even plead for an Irishman's aid.

"McCaneaghy! You have to save me!" The tree shuddered as something in the stream struck the submerged trunk. Cassius screamed, "Save me! Goddammit! You have to! You—" His voice broke on a sob.

"Listen, Reed!" Noble shouted, uncoiling the lariat and tugging the pony closer. "I'm going to throw you a rope! You grab it and pull yourself to the edge here!"

He tied one end to the saddle horn and looped the remainder in his hand. Slowly he started swinging the coil over his head.

"You ready, Reed?" he shouted.

"No!" Reed whimpered.

"What?"

"I can't! I can't let go! I'll fall in! And I can't swim!"

"Dammit!" Noble exploded.

"Cassius, you *have* to catch the rope!" Venice shouted. "There isn't any other way! Try!"

Cassius sobbed, squeezed his eyes shut and nodded. "I'll try."

"On the count of three," Noble shouted. "One. Two. Three—" Noble pitched the rope. It shot out, uncoiling in the stiffening wind, streaming parallel to the shore. It settled on the current a good five feet shy of the tree.

"Hell!" Noble swore under his breath. "It isn't going to work!"

Venice touched his arm. "What's wrong? Why won't it work?"

"The wind's too strong, the rain is too heavy,

and there's not enough weight on the end of the line," he answered, hauling the rope back up.

"What can we do?"

Without answering, Noble untied the rope from the saddle horn and looked around.

Ten yards up from where they stood, a huge sheared-off boulder jutted like a shelf over the river. Wordlessly, Noble crossed over the top of the boulder, Venice picking her way after him. He looked down. He might as well have been on a diving platform.

Quickly, he knotted the rope around the trunk of a gnarled bristle-cone pine clinging to the very edge of the boulder. He passed the other end around his waist and through his legs, hitching himself into the makeshift harness.

"What are you—?" Venice started. She turned the shade of fine bone china, even her lips leaching of color. "Noble, you can't! Please! It's too dangerous!"

"Honey—" His gaze met hers. "There isn't any other way and there isn't any time." He brushed a stray tendril of hair from her jaw. "Listen. I'm going to swing over to that tree. Once I get there, I'm going to tie the tope around Reed. Then we're going to swing back. But I gotta go *now*. Before it's too late."

She nodded. He handed her his knife.

"You might have to cut the rope from around Reed."

He leaned back against the rope, testing his weight against the tree. Its ancient moorings held.

He climbed as far out on the shelf as he could and then, taking a deep breath, jumped. He plummeted toward the current and then the rope caught and he was swinging through the air, arcing toward Cassius.

He crashed into the pine tree. Needles and twigs

scraped his face and he was held by the boughs for a heartbeat before his momentum started dragging him back. Cursing, he clutched handfuls of sticky, needle-studded branches.

He found a foothold and pulled himself upright. The tree suddenly shifted beneath his added weight.

"You're gonna get us killed, you stupid Mick!" Cassius screamed from his perch a few feet away.

"Shut up, Reed, or I'll leave you here!" Noble snarled, untying the rope from around him and carefully creeping over to where Cassius clung to the tree trunk. He grabbed Cassius by the back of the jacket and jerked him away from the trunk, ignoring the other man's sputtering protests.

He looped the rope under Cassius's arms and cinched it tight. "Stand up," he ordered.

In answer, Cassius scooted closer to the trunk, rewrapping his arms around it.

"Stand up! We're gonna swing back to the side. But you gotta stand up so I can grab hold of the rope, too."

"I don't think I can," whimpered Cassius.

"Listen, you son of a—" A huge shudder shook the tree. Without any further warning, the tree spun loose of its precarious footing, and, caught by the hungry, surging current, whirled into the racing stream.

With a shriek, Cassius was torn free of the trunk. Frantically, Noble grabbed for him, catching Cassius around the legs.

Grappling madly, he felt himself sliding to the other man's knees. His arm muscles ached under the strain. He clutched fistfuls of fabric, trying desperately to keep from slipping further. Suddenly, impossibly, he felt Cassius start to kick his legs. With stunned disbelief he felt his grip fail, his arms kicked away. He heard Cassius cry, "You're hurting me! Get off!"

He fell.

The icy water seized him, dragging him beneath its boiling surface. Frozen blackness closed around him. The churning river tumbled over him, pitching him head over heels, spinning him against rocks, trees, and debris. He crashed against a boulder, tumbling wildly beneath the current.

Heat and pain erupted in his chest and throat. Dazed and disoriented, he was unable to tell the top from the bottom. His lungs burned and cold, dirty water filled his mouth and nose. He was drowning.

Suddenly, his feet scraped against something solid. He thrust against it. Praying he drove from the bottom upward toward the surface, he fought the water's inexorable grip.

He burst into air, gasping and choking, bobbing in the current like a child's bath toy. He was exhausted, not an ounce of fight left in him. His coat and boots dragged like stones on his body. His side was pierced by a numbing splinter of pain and he couldn't cough the water from his lungs.

The shore, impossibly close and yet hopelessly far away, disappeared and reappeared from his clouding vision as he flailed in the river's pull. He was never going to make it.

And then, far away, he heard Venice.

"Noble! No-ble!"

Terror and fear filled her voice. She might be in danger. She might need him.

He started to swim.

"Get up!" Venice shouted.

"Uh-uh. Gotta . . . rest," Cassius panted. He lay on his side, curled into a ball.

She bit her lip hard, holding back the hysteria that threatened. She left him on the ground and circled Noble's pony. Her rising panic was eclipsing her ability to think, to act. And she desperately needed to do both.

She rummaged through Noble's saddlebag looking for something, *anything*, to help her. Her hand closed around an unfamiliar outline; a pair of short cylinders fastened together in the middle. She pulled them out and immediately recognized them as binoculars. They might help.

"We need to hurry! Noble's out there. He might be injured! We have to find him before nightfall."

"Find *McCaneaghy?*" Cassius choked, rising to his knees.

"Come on, let's move." Venice slung the binocular strap over her shoulders.

"I fear—" Cassius took a deep breath, composing his features in a grave expression. "I fear that your Irish friend is, to be quite blunt, dead."

Venice's face expressed thunderous denial. "No," she said. "Noble is *not* dead. And we are going to find him."

"But—"

"I've wasted enough time listening to you," she said as she hurriedly untied and recoiled Noble's rope. "Now, understand this; we are not leaving until we find Noble."

Cassius's face drained of color. The slut *had* slept with McCaneaghy. She was packing the rope into Noble's saddlebags, her back to him, obviously having made her pronouncement, expecting him to fall over his feet in his haste to comply.

"Your lover is dead!"

She didn't respond, just swung up into the saddle and kicked the pony to within a few feet of him. She looked down at him, her expression implacable. "*Mr.* Reed, if, after this is over, you come near me again, I shall personally see to it that you are blacklisted from every New York drawing room for the rest of your miserable life!"

"What?" Cassius froze, horrified. "You don't mean that! We know the same people! We belong to the same *clubs!* You can't do this!" he screamed, grabbing for her. "You're crazy. Unbalanced!"

Venice's boot shot out, catching Cassius square in the chest and dumping him on his rump on the ground.

"Crazy?" She spat the word. "Maybe. But not stupid, Mr. Reed! The Utes disappear and you, who'd have trouble finding your way out of Central Park without a compass, suddenly know exactly where we are. You planned this all along! You risked our lives to get me alone with you."

The pony, catching the mood of its rider, danced dangerously near Cassius's outstretched legs. He jerked them out of the way.

"Now get moving!"

"No." Cassius stumbled to his feet, dusting himself off. His tone was sullen. "McCaneaghy is dead, I tell you. It's a waste of time."

"He's not dead. And we're not leaving until we find him!" She leaned over and with the speed of an uncoiling bullwhip, snatched his cravat, pulling him up onto his toes, the choking grip tipping him off balance.

"You're going to look for him!" she spat. "I'll start down here. You follow the ridge up top. We've wasted enough time!" She gave his neck cloth a savage yank. "Do you hear me?"

Choking, Cassius nodded.

Venice dropped Cassius's neck cloth. "Start moving!"

She spurred the pony down near the edge of the racing water and disappeared.

She deserves to be left out here alone, Cassius told himself. At the top of the gorge, he pulled the mule to a halt. Panting, he cast another glance back over his shoulder. She deserves it for spreading her legs for the likes of him.

He *had* to leave her. He had no choice.

Still, the memory of Venice's determined expression gnawed at Cassius. What if she got lucky? What if she made it out of these godforsaken mountains alive?

He'd never be able to show his face in society again. He might as well be dead.

Maybe he'd better do as she said and look around for McCaneaghy. Immediately, he dismissed the notion. They'd *both* likely die, in that case. No, the woman had made a stupid decision and now she would have to live—or die—with the consequences. He owed it to the world to survive.

She'd left him no choice. No choice at all.

Cassius tore a branch off a nearby tree. Cranking the mule's head around, he thwacked it on the rump. The mule bolted up the trail into the trees.

To the west, the sun found a tear in the thick clouds overhead. Purple thunderheads were mounting over the snowcapped peaks. It looked like one hell of a storm was brewing.

Cassius grinned. He couldn't help himself. No matter how competent Venice Leiland was, or how lucky, Cassius knew she wasn't going to be competent, or lucky, enough.

Chapter 16

In half an hour there wouldn't be enough light left to see, even with the binoculars. Wiping dust off the lenses, Venice raised them to her eyes again, sweeping the focus back and forth. She'd been over this section three times now with the same results. Nothing.

She jumped off the rock she'd been standing atop and looked up, studying the mountains to her east. The churning blanket of clouds above had occasional breaks in it, enough so that a deep rose-colored sunset glistened above the distant peaks. If necessary, there might be something of a moon to search by tonight.

Luck had been with her. The brunt of the storm had passed a few hours earlier, saving its fury for the more easterly range. In the far distance, she could see the veil of black rain coursing from the sky.

She fervently hoped Cassius was under that deluge. Within an hour of beginning her search, it had become obvious he'd run off. The coward!

She turned up the collar of her jacket. Even though the wind had died down, it was getting cooler with dusk approaching. Tonight, it would get cold. Very cold.

Her jaw muscles knotted with determination. She would simply have to find Noble before then. She wasn't going to give up and she refused to believe he was dead. She climbed over the rock-studded shore to where she'd tethered the pony.

All her life she'd endured a succession of people leaving her: her mother, her uncle, nannies, governesses ... Noble. She had gotten used to it, finally becoming so tired of mourning the losses that she had made herself stop caring.

Not this time.

She was going to find him. She was finished blindly accepting that whatever happened in her life was out of her control.

She swung back into the saddle and pulled the pony's head up, moving him down to the edge of the fast-moving river. It was clogged with debris: trees and branches, mud and leaves and sticks flowed swiftly by, hitting submerged log jams and spinning, or piling up on top of each other and creating eddies in the muddy current.

An occasional small corpse spun past her: a marmot, some rabbits, even a hapless mule deer. Each time she had to choke down the panic and yawning hopelessness that teased the edges of her resolve.

With an oath, she kicked her pony up into the trackless rocks, scrambling higher. She dismounted once more, tying the reins to a fallen aspen, and clambered up a steep rock outcrop for a better view of the river.

The far shoreline was dissolving into deepening dusk.

What would she do if she spotted Noble across the hundred-yard span of churning water? She ignored the treacherous thought as she slid off the jagged boulder, tearing her nails as she tried to slow her descent and scraping her arms in the thicket of brambles at its base.

Leaving the pony plucking at the thin spring grasses, she started picking her way once more through litter strewn along the newly formed banks. Twice her ankles got caught and twisted in the slippery, uneven footing. Twice again she stumbled, banging her shins and her knees. She got up, ignoring the fatigue that sank its teeth deep into her muscles.

She returned to the pony and mounted once more, forcing the reluctant animal onto a narrow deer trail near the river.

Half an hour later, her hands and feet were aching with cold and damp. Her wind-scoured cheeks were burnt raw and her shirt beneath the thick wool jacket was soaked with sweat. The sun, a brilliant orange globe impaled for a brief moment on a jagged peak, disappeared beneath the horizon.

Fresh tears traced muddy tracks down her cheeks and she dug the heels of her hands into their sockets, trying to clear her vision. She fumbled to strike a match and light the lantern she'd found amongst Noble's gear. Tiredly, she twisted her tangled mat of hair up and shoved it beneath her hat. She picked up the lantern and held it aloft.

The water looked like a black snake uncoiling with lethal power ar her feet. Above, the first stars glinted from between scuttling clouds.

She was exhausted. Every step was a lead-weighted labor. Her mouth was dry and her eyes stung from squinting into the sunset and straining to see a familiar form in the river's detritus. She didn't stop to rest. Rest might make the crucial difference between Noble's life and death.

She went on. An hour more. Two.

The sun had long since given up all claim on the day and a pale quarter moon offered only fitful illumination. Her feet, encased in cold, wet leather boots, had grown numb and she stumbled more and more often as the minutes ticked by.

Her eyes swam with strain-induced tears. Her throat felt swollen and parched, and her arms shook when she struggled to lift the heavy binoculars to her eyes. Deep within she knew she couldn't go on much longer. "No," she said in answer to the hopelessness threatening her. "No."

She forced high the trembling arm grasping the lantern and peered into the gloom. The light swept past a dark form tangled in the shadows of a huge log jam. She heard a sound above the din of the water surging into the impromptu dam. A groan. She wheeled.

"Noble!" she cried. "Where are you?"

Another moan and she found him. He was just out of the water, lying on his side. One arm was twisted beneath him, the other groping for leverage as he tried to push himself up. In a trice, she was off the pony, kneeling beside him.

Moonlight leached his long hair of color and cast a sickly pall over his face. Moving behind him, she carefully wrapped her arms around him. Linking her hands on his chest, she pulled him up, cradling him against her. He made an agonized sound deep in his throat. She answered with a sob. Slowly, she shifted him, laying him on his back.

"Noble?"

He didn't answer; his breathing was shallow.

She ran to collect the canteen and a few other supplies from his saddlebag: a blanket, a cotton shirt, and a flask of whiskey. She settled the blanket over him. Gently, she moved his head into her lap and started tearing the shirt into long strips, her worried gaze never leaving him.

He was shivering, his teeth chattering uncontrollably. Bending close, she dabbed at the dark blood smeared across his forehead. His eyelids fluttered open and he stared at her, his gaze unfocused.

"Well," he finally breathed. "I guess I'm not dead."

She managed a quavery smile. "Why is that?"

" 'Cause you're way too dirty to be an angel, and way too worried lookin' to be a demon."

She couldn't hold back her sob of relief.

"Venice, lass," he finally murmured, "dinna cry, love. Dinna weep."

Lord, she had always loved the soft timbre of his Irish accent. She'd thought she would never hear it again, had thought that time and circumstances had robbed him forever of those rich, lilting tones. For some reason that he should call her "lass" now, here . . . made her cry.

She leaned her forehead against his, sparing a moment to stem the flow of her tears.

She took a deep breath, hushing him. Then, carefully, she wound a strip of his ruined shirt gingerly around his head. Deftly, she examined his limbs. When she probed his left side, his eyes rolled back into his head and he fainted.

She bit her lip, making herself attend the problem at hand, tightly strapping his side as quickly as she could while he was not conscious to feel the pain.

When she was finished, she sat back on her heels and frowned. He hadn't come around yet. Worriedly, she felt his forehead. Cool. She frowned. No, *cold*. And soaked through to the bone.

He was freezing, even under the thick blanket. His lips were drawn back and he was trembling.

Somehow she had to get him warm. She looked around. They couldn't stay down here, near the river, where the wind swept over the frigid water.

If they were caught in another rainstorm, the river might climb another twenty feet up the canyon walls.

She had to get Noble out of here. Helplessly, she cast about, searching for some way to lift him onto the pony. She would never be able to get him into the saddle. There was only one way.

"Noble," she said.

He didn't move.

"Noble," she shouted near his ear. "You have to wake up. You have to help me. We have to get you on the pony."

He stirred restlessly. "Help you," he muttered.

"Yes. We have to get you up on your pony."

Gently, she tapped his cheeks with her fingertips. His right hand shot out, grabbing her wrist in a bone-crunching grip. His eyes blazed up at her. She gasped and tried to pull away. Confusion replaced the enmity in his gaze.

"Venice?" His grip loosened and fell away.

"Yes, Noble." She rubbed distractedly at her wrist. "You have to get up."

It took him a few seconds to answer, as though he needed time to make sense of her question. "Okay."

His big body had begun shaking again, the paroxysms wracking him. Fresh tears sprang to Venice's eyes. With an abrupt effort, Noble pushed himself upright and sat panting, his head falling forward onto his chest.

"Good," she said. "That's good, Noble."

Hooking her shoulder beneath his arm, she wrapped her arm around his back, trying to avoid his ribs. She squatted on her boot heels beside him. "Now, on the count of three you're going to stand up and get on that horse."

"Yes, ma'am. And it's a pony ... ma'am." The

slightest touch of humor colored the gasped words.

It was too much.

"Oh, God, don't! Don't be all heroic. Don't!"

"Don't cry, Venice." His blue-tinted lips twisted into a pitying smile.

"I'm not crying! Now, get up! On the count of three. One ... two ... three!" She strained beneath his weight, grimaced, and heaved. At the same time, Noble struggled to rise.

Sweat beaded Noble's face. She grabbed hold of the arm he had wrapped around her neck and pushed upward. He made it to his knees. Red-faced with the effort of supporting his weight, she panted, "Just ... a second ... while we ... catch ... our breath." She gulped for air. "Now, almost there—Up!" He lurched to his feet and she pivoted, using his momentum to impel him toward the pony standing quietly a few feet away. He fell, careening into the saddle. A sound of pain grated from between his clenched teeth.

"Don't faint!" Venice hollered into his ear, grabbing for the reins so she could keep the pony from walking away while Noble was still leaning unbalanced against its side.

"I'm not gonna faint," Noble muttered in disgust as he groped for the pommel.

"Good. Can you get up?"

He eyed the saddle. "Nope."

Venice hadn't gotten him all the way up only to be defeated by the four feet between the ground and the pony's back.

"Sorry," he said. He leaned his forehead against the leather seat. He was far too pale. The bandage near his temple had bloomed with a black stain. "I'm real sorry, Venice."

"Don't you dare be sorry!" Tears blinded her and she covered her eyes. She hadn't cried so much in a decade. "Yes, you will get up on that saddle!"

She jerked her hands away from her face. "Listen. Hold on to the saddle horn, Noble McCaneaghy, 'cause we're going to get over to that rock over there, even if I have to tie you to the pommel and drag you."

He squinted his eyes, peering at the boulder she was pointing to.

"Bloodthirsty wench," he mumbled.

"You don't know the half of it, mister," she said tightly, grasping him around the waist with one hand and holding the reins with the other.

She clucked softly to the pony. Pricking his ears, the animal started slowly forward, Noble's feet scuffling at its side, sometimes walking, sometimes being dragged.

Once at the boulder, Venice pulled, pushed, and goaded Noble into taking the single step up to the top of the rock. White-faced and trembling, he silently climbed up, swaying slightly when he finally made it to the top. Tying the reins to the pommel, Venice clambered up behind the saddle, sitting on the pony's rump, praying the animal wouldn't take exception to the unaccustomed feel of her there. It didn't. Leaning way over, Venice grasped the waistband of Noble's jeans.

"Come on, Noble. Just get your foot in the stirrup."

He fumbled for a minute before the toe of his boot caught. With a hiss of pain, he heaved himself up. Venice pulled. For a second he stood in the stirrup and then his long leg was over the saddle horn and he dropped into the saddle like a sack of flour. He slouched there, mouth open, panting for breath.

"You did it!" Venice said, patting him encouragingly on the back.

He shuddered and his head slumped forward, and Venice had the horrible impression that he was no longer conscious. Touching her heels gingerly to the pony's flanks, she clutched Noble to her, scooting forward into the saddle until the cantle bit into her stomach. Tightly bracketing his long legs with her own, she pressed his broad back to her chest, worried he would fall from the saddle.

"Lass." His voice was faint. "Ya mustn't take advantage of me in me weakened condition."

She bit back a burble of laughter. It felt too much like hysteria. The notion, unbidden and tantalizing, teased her; they were going to make it.

"Noble?"

He didn't answer. He must have slipped into a semiconscious state again. The pony walked tiredly onto the stony, moon-washed trail. After a second, Venice buried her face against Noble's jacket and, overwhelmed with relief, sobbed her heart out.

Moaning, Noble turned. Heavy hands held him down, his left side hurt like hell, and he was suffocating. He was hot, sweaty. Which was odd since one of the last things he remembered thinking was that he would never be warm again. He opened one eye. He was in a tent, under a pile of blankets.

Venice.

He shot up, ignoring the rip of pain in his left side. He flung the blankets off and started to rise when he saw the pale strips of cotton wrapped around his chest. He sank back on his elbows, his memory returning. Venice had had something to do with that bandage and if she could take the time to bandage him, that meant she must be all right.

He glanced down. He was naked except for his

still-damp union suit, and someone had peeled that back to his waist. Someone had cleaned his cuts. A neat job they'd made of it, too.

Venice again. He vaguely recalled her tear-stained face, remembered telling her not to cry. An impression of hands shoving, pulling, and hauling him swam through pain-dimmed memories.

Somehow she must have found help. They weren't that far from her uncle's camp. She must have made her way there.

Moving gingerly, Noble crawled to the tent flap and poked his head out. He shivered. It was early. The tent had been pitched along a sheer wall, near a copse of young aspen. Both the flat rockface and white paper bark of the trees were washed with morning's apricot glow.

Nearby a fire crackled in a neat stone ring, crisp curls of smoke drifting up through the trees. A kettle sat on the grate, the delicious aroma of coffee wafting toward him.

No one was in sight. Wondering where everybody could be, Noble straightened and immediately winced. Biting back an oath, he limped over to where his shirt and jeans hung from the lower branches of a young aspen. One look at his blood-stained shirt convinced him it was past its usefulness. He settled for wrapping a blanket around his shoulders and pulling on his stiff jeans—an exertion that left him pale and panting. Finally, walking stiffly, he made his way toward the fire . . . and the coffee.

Pouring himself a cup, he looked around. His hobbled pony was munching grass, its tail twitching away the occasional fly. It was the only animal in sight. With a dawning disbelief, Noble stared about the campsite.

No other tents. Just the one he'd crawled from. No packs. No gear. Nothing.

It hit him.

Venice had found him, bandaged him, and somehow gotten him here, *all by herself*. The enormity of the task struck him as did a sudden gut-twisting fear: *Where was she now?*

He wheeled around and the abrupt movement left him doubled over, gasping for breath.

"You're awake."

He looked up. Venice stood just beyond the tent, a water bucket in her hand. Her black hair was wild about her shoulders. Her jacket hung open, revealing a dingy white shirt, stained russet with dried blood. Mauve shadows encircled her dark eyes. There was a waxy, drawn look to her delicate features. She looked a decade older than her twenty-two years. And she had never looked more beautiful to him.

"You're okay, then?" she asked softly. Even from this distance, Noble could see the light catch her incredible silver eyes. He was a fool. His love for Venice was nothing more than an Irish lad's moon-gazing dream. But Lord, to have her *care* so much that she would risk her life for him ... It was almost enough to make a man believe in the impossible.

"You'll be okay?" she repeated, as though she would not be satisfied until she'd heard a confirmation from his own lips.

"Yes. Where's Reed?"

Her eyes narrowed and he saw the subtle tensing of a muscle along her delicate jawline.

"Mr. Reed has probably reached Salvage by now."

"What?"

"He took the mule and went ... for help." Her last words sounded doubtful.

"But why—"

"I don't know anything more," she said in a

voice that made it clear she didn't want to answer any more questions about Reed. Fine. He felt woozy enough.

"Okay," he said.

She nodded, setting down the bucket and turning away.

"Venice."

She stopped. He went to her, moving gingerly, and touched her shoulder lightly.

"What you did for me . . . I . . . no one's ever—" He fumbled to a stop.

She was watching him, her expression unreadable.

"Thank you," he said quietly.

She blinked. "You're . . . welcome. I'm . . . I'm going to get some water. You had best rest." She started walking away but paused a second and bestowed a smile on him before leaving.

He stood like a pole-axed steer, staring after her as she disappeared into the pines.

God help the men of the world, and most especially Noble McCaneaghy. Because when she smiled like that it made him doubt whether he'd ever find enough strength of will to keep away from her. And he *had* to keep away from her.

Because with a woman like Venice, once would never be enough. Not one kiss, not one dance, not one night. He could live with what he'd had with her so far; he could walk away and get on with his life. But what if they spent a night together?

There'd be nothing on earth that would keep him from her side.

What sort of future could he offer her, a woman used to everything?

He heard a faint lilting tune and cocked his ear toward the sound. Venice was whistling, a bright, off-key melody. A second later, she reappeared from the aspen stand, swinging the bucket.

When she saw him—exactly where she'd left him—a teasing smile lit her tired face. "Too sore to sit? Need a little help?"

He shook his head. She came up to him and, only half in jest, offered her arm. She looked infinitely appealing in her ragged clothes, with twigs in her ebony tresses. Too appealing. He grunted at her chivalrous offer and walked stiff-backed to the fire, easing himself down onto a flat-topped rock.

He watched her carefully hook the bucket onto a makeshift spit over the fire.

"Wherever did you learn to do all this?" Noble asked.

"Oh, I'm no ends resourceful. I have unplumbed depths." Her voice was a purr, and there was a challenging gleam in her eyes.

Noble nearly fell off the rock.

She dimpled ingenuously and went back to stirring the embers beneath the bucket.

"I . . . I . . ." God Almighty, what was he supposed to say to *that?* 'Cause if that was an invitation—and his body certainly seemed to want to take it that way since he was now as tight and tense as an elk in rut!—he'd best throw himself in the damn freezing river again.

"No kidding, Venice." Damn it, he sounded like Reverend Niss, both sanctimonious and leering. "I mean it. Where'd you learn to make camp?"

"No kidding?" she asked, sounding disappointed. "Okay. No kidding. I spent a couple of summers as a kid with Uncle Milton."

"You did? Here? 'Cause I've run into Milton any number of times in these mountains over the last few years and he never mentioned you were with him."

"No. Not in the recent past. When I was younger, a kid. He shepherded me around some of his archaeological sites. Egypt, Greece . . . Mexico."

"You couldn't have been more than—fourteen? fifteen?" Noble asked.

"Oh, don't sound like that."

"Like what?"

"Like you want to charge in and save me from my wicked uncle." He felt his cheeks flame and she laughed. "Not that I don't appreciate your knight-in-shining-armor impulses," she said, and her voice dropped, became gruff. "I do. I know you came after me because you were concerned for my welfare. I more than appreciate that fact, Noble. No one else has ever cared about me the way you do."

He didn't even try to deny it. "Yeah, well," he finally said dismissively, "looks like you're the one who did most of the saving. You were going to tell me why Milt dragged you around the world."

"Oh, yes. Mustn't let anyone thank us, must we?" she said in a gently mocking tone. "All right. I won't tease anymore. I believe the reason Uncle Milton dragged me about was that he thought I needed something to occupy my time."

"And digging in the Sudan was the answer?" Noble asked incredulously. "Couldn't you have taken up watercolors?"

"Oh, I loved it!" She laughed. "I've always loved it. Traveling about in unnamed forests, finding rivers no one has ever seen, identifying orchids. My father could never understand where I'd inherited my nomadic tendencies."

"I bet he didn't."

Venice apparently didn't hear the painful tightening of his tone.

"As for digging at Uncle Milton's site . . . I was most certainly never trusted with a spade. I was his chief bottle-washer. He told me I had a

definite future as a camp chef. I was, as you can
well imagine, no *ends* flattered."

"I had no idea," he said admiringly.

"It was after you left." The words were simple.
The accusation that had been in the same words
the first day she'd recognized him had vanished.
Why? he wondered. Why now, when they were
alone, did she abandon the anger that might have
provided some distance between them?

She had lowered her eyes and was twisting her
hands together in her lap, a shy smile on her lips.

"Venice, I'm sorry about everything."

She didn't say a word.

"I acted like a prime ass back there in Salvage.
And I haven't any excuse 'cept one; I was jealous."

Her gaze shot up. "You were?"

He laughed. She looked so damn incredulous.
"What, Venice?" he asked without thinking. "You
just can't believe I might be jealous of the
thought of another man touching you? I know I
haven't the right to feel that way, but when does
'right' have anything to do with my feelings for
you?"

He'd said too much. She was staring at him,
wonder and something else alive in her expression.

Where the hell did he think this conversation
was going? He was sore, aching, and growing
weaker by the minute, alone in the middle of nowhere with the woman he loved. A woman he
would never let himself have. He was amazed at
his own self-restraint.

Awkwardly, he pushed himself upright. "You
know, I think I'd better get some rest after all," he
mumbled.

She was beside him in a trice, linking her arm
around his waist. Thank God the pain ripping

through his side served to offset the tantalizing sensation of her arm pressing against him.

"Of course," she said. "Lean on me."

He did.

Chapter 17

"...Or to see 'Mr. Seward's Folly.' Now *that* would be fun!" Venice said, her chin cupped in her hand as she stared into the flames.

Noble, who'd risen from his nap long since and was now sitting by the campfire, chewing the fry bread she'd made, stared at her. "You're serious."

"I most certainly am."

"I don't know any other woman who, when asked what she would most like to do in the world, would answer 'Go to Alaska . . . for *fun*.' " He shook his head.

"That's my answer and it's not going to change no matter how much you sneer," Venice returned saucily.

"I'm not sneering. Just skeptical. What do you know about Alaska? They say there are mosquitoes up there so large they can bleed a man dry in ten minutes."

Venice shrugged. "So, I'll go in the autumn after they've all died."

"Autumn? Alaska doesn't have autumn. They have 'lots of ice' and 'a little less ice.' "

She chuckled. "You explorer types love to exaggerate—to ensure you keep all the interesting places for yourselves."

"Ever hear of something called frostbite, Venice?" Noble stretched his legs out, apparently enjoying their verbal sparring.

"Coward."

" 'Scuse me?"

Venice snorted. "Letting a little thing like ice keep you from an adventure like that."

He studied his hands, his brow furrowed. "Adventures can get you in trouble, Venice," he said and she smiled at his bowed head, the soft fall of his long hair caught at the nape of his neck by a leather thong.

He loved her, she realized.

Oh, maybe not the fairy tale, ever-after sort of love. That didn't exist. He loved her enough to be jealous of her; loved her enough to want to touch her, kiss her, hold her; loved her enough to follow her into the mountains so that he could make sure she was safe.

It was more than she'd ever had . . . or hoped for.

"Adventures are dangerous only if you don't have a knight in shining armor standing by," she said softly. "Once more, thank you for coming up after me, Noble."

His gaze skittered away from hers and to her surprise he blushed. "Wasn't any big deal," he mumbled. "And it sure wasn't like I had any choice."

She tilted her head inquiringly.

"Oh, come on, Venice. Ever since you were in pigtails I've had this need—some less-than-kind folks might call it a mental aberration—to make sure you're okay. Doesn't look like a decade's cured it."

She laughed. "Fortunately for me."

"You woulda been fine if Trees-Too-High and Crooked Hand had stayed." His amber eyes glittered. "I haven't any idea why they took off like that, but I intend to find out."

"I'm sure they had their reasons." It would be

pointless to tell him of her suspicions regarding Cassius. Noble's face had turned a dull, brick red already. Knowing how he already felt about Cassius, she thought he might use any excuse to punish the treacherous blackguard after they returned to Salvage. And she didn't want him getting into trouble on that . . . person's account.

"Still—" Noble glanced around. "You look like you could manage well enough without me. So, except for nearly getting myself drowned and obliging you to risk your life finding me, my tagging along didn't really accomplish much." Self-recrimination was rife in his voice.

"On the contrary," Venice said. "You saved Mr. Reed's life."

He scowled. "Like I said, didn't accomplish much."

"Noble—"

"Saving Reed's hide was that important to you?" he asked gruffly.

"Any—"

"No need to answer. That's the way it should be. You're both from the same city, know the same kind of people, share what your father calls 'social strata.' 'Course it's important to you. I know yesterday you didn't want to talk about him—"

"I was going to say," Venice broke in calmly, "that I would have felt the same about anyone's life. And I still don't want to talk about Cassius Reed. Now or ever. We might share a similar address and have accounts at the same bank, but in no other manner, shape, or form are we the same."

"But I thought you and he had an understanding."

"No. We never have, nor will we."

He smiled, a big, radiant grin. "Oh."

For some reason that piece of information seemed to restore his appetite. He reached for another piece of fry bread and dipped it liberally into the tin of beans warming on a flat stone near the fire. She'd found that tin and a few hunks of dried beef among the small, loose sacks of flour, coffee, and dried apples at the bottom of his pack. Noble must have been in a hurry when he packed. There was little lard, no salt, and no sugar.

It was going to be interesting seeing how long she could make their supplies last. Or how long she would need to. At the rate Noble was devouring food, they'd be out of supplies by sunset tomorrow. She should be worried.

"So, what I want to know is why Alaska?" Noble asked, washing down yet another piece of bread with a mouthful of scalding coffee.

She arched a brow at him. " 'Cause it's there and I haven't seen it and"—she dimpled triumphantly—"neither have you."

He launched into an immediate rejoinder, which she countered right away, both of them relishing the verbal sparring.

And suddenly tomorrow just didn't seem to matter.

Having stowed the rest of the cooking gear away and watered the pony, Venice dusted her hands on her pants legs. "I'm going to have a look at your side," she said in what she hoped was a no-nonsense tone.

"It's fine."

"We'll make sure of that."

Noble made a disgusted sound. "It's a scrape. It's not even bleeding anymore. You're making too much of it, Venice."

"It's a failing of mine. Indulge me."

"As if I haven't already—"

Venice didn't wait to hear any more. Without another word she strode toward the tent.

She'd been trying to get a look at the wound on Noble's side all day, and all day Noble had been putting her off. But she'd noticed that as dusk approached, he'd moved more and more slowly. The fact that he'd let her water the pony by herself told her a lot about how he was feeling.

Wrenching back the tent flap, she collected the whiskey flask and what was left of the shirt she'd sacrificed for bandages. Muttering under her breath, she marched back to where Noble stood.

"Take off your shirt."

"That's not a nice way for a lady to talk."

"I am not going to be embarrassed, browbeaten, or coerced from my intent," she said stiffly. "You can proposition me, swear at me, beg me, or threaten me . . . I'm not moving until I see your side.

Noble's jaw grew mulish.

"What's wrong, McCaneaghy?" she asked, sidling up to him. "I've seen your bare chest more than once in the past week. Seems to me you weren't so modest standing at the trough out back of the Gold Dust—"

"Okay! Okay!" he said, turning scarlet. "If you're so hot to see my weather-beaten hide, far be it from me to say no."

Without another word, he unbuttoned his shirt, shrugging out of the heavy chambray and whipping it from his arms. His eyes locked with hers in a battle of wills.

Lord, he was beautiful, standing there hard-flanked and pantherish, his shirt scrunched up in his fist, his amber eyes flashing.

"Turn around," she said.

"Geez. I should have realized you'd turn out to be a nag."

"You are so transparent, Noble McCaneaghy," she said. "I'm disillusioned. I've always thought of you as a tough, rugged man, but you're just afraid this is gonna hurt."

"You found me out," Noble replied, grinning.

She pursed her lips in frustration. "I want to have a look at those cuts, make sure they haven't turned septic. So, turn around!"

He complied, grumbling until a thought occurred to him.

"Say, does this mean you're going to *touch* me?" he asked, arching a dark brow.

"Well, it'll be a trifle difficult to attend you if I don't touch you, won't it?"

Nodding happily, Noble tossed his shirt to the ground and spun about. Lifting his left arm, he advanced slowly on her.

Venice took a step back. His smile grew broader. Another step brought him closer still. There was a predatory, stalking quality to his movements and in the silky, effortless slide of muscle beneath tight, smooth skin. Anxiously, she skittered backward until, with a soft whoosh, she collided against the tree behind her.

Immediately, she felt trapped, hemmed in by his size. The trunk at her back was a wall. The long arms reaching past her to brace on the lower branches on either side of her formed her prison.

His body cast a shadow over hers. He smelled of coffee, sun-heated skin, and the fascinatingly male scent that was uniquely Noble's.

"So? Tend me, lass," he whispered wickedly.

"Don't use that brogue on me," Venice said. Her voice betrayed her, breathless and anxious.

With his lips so disturbingly near her own came unbidden memories: of his mouth opening over hers, of his tongue thrust deeply into her mouth, hungrily searching hers, warm, wet . . .

She wanted to feel his lips tug on her breasts again, wanted to arch into his body and feel him lift her high against his hard length. She wanted all the intense, nerve-rich feelings he alone had awakened in her slumbering body . . . and heart.

But he was injured. The thought caused her hands to drop and made her take a tiny step backward.

She looked up, aware her breath had gone ragged. He was staring at her, his golden eyes intent.

"This might hurt," she whispered.

"Without a doubt," he said solemnly.

Gingerly plucking at the plaster sticking to his raw wounds, Venice bit her lip while carefully peeling them off the cuts. Noble didn't even appear to notice; he was studying her hair, her eyes, her lips.

"Why?" he asked suddenly.

"Why what?" She scrutinized the healthy pink ridges of the jagged cut. It wasn't oozing or gaping. He was disgustingly hearty.

"You used to like my accent, try to copy it."

"Aye, and I grew verra good at it, if I do say so meself," she said. "A regular daughter of the green."

His smile faded. "Not quite."

"I'm sorry," she said in confusion. "I wasn't mocking you."

"I know. I'd almost forgotten just how far New York is from County Cork."

She didn't understand. She frowned, dabbing whiskey on some of the deeper gashes, her betraying fingers lingering on their task, feathering gently over the firm, resilient flesh beneath their tips. She heard him inhale sharply and swear.

She tore a fresh length of cloth from Noble's ruined shirt.

"Venice, we have to talk." All the sweet teasing was gone from his voice, leaving raw emotion.

Reaching behind to refasten the binding around his ribs, Venice let her fingers skim over the coarse, raised welt of a dreadful scar.

Her hands dropped as though burned.

"What?" Noble asked immediately, head raised alertly, moving closer, sheltering her.

"That scar. The one on your back."

"Yeah? I would have thought you saw it when you cleaned my cuts the other night—"

"It was dark then. I couldn't see much of anything."

"Oh."

"That's all you have to say, 'Oh'?"

"Well," Noble tilted his head, openly bewildered. "What about that scar?"

"It's horrible!"

His expression grew flat, distant. "I'm sorry if it offends you," he said stiffly.

"Offends me? You're damn right it offends me. You were hurt!"

He smiled. "Oh."

" 'Oh,' again?! Where did you get it?" she demanded angrily.

"That old thing? Bayonet. In the war," he said. "Terrible wound. Lots of blood. Just awful." If it had been so terrible, why was he looking so smug?

"You could have been killed." Her voice, no more than a whisper, broke.

Without a word, Noble looped his arm around her waist and pulled her gently to him. "I'm sorry I teased you."

How could she ever have considered his embrace a prison? It was a haven. His big body was protective, comforting. Cupping her chin with long fingers, he tilted her face up toward his.

"It happened a long time ago," he said.

As though she didn't need to know to the very

date when it had happened, didn't need to know exactly how many days he'd lain on his—bed? Cot? Or on the bare, cold ground? How close had he been to dying?

She wanted to cry. If he'd died, who would have told her? Would she have had to hear about it from a stranger long after the fact, as she'd heard of her own mother's death?

"Venice."

She splayed her hand against his chest and for an instant allowed his warmth to penetrate her palm and shoot sensual heat up her arm. He was so vital, so *alive*.

"Venice," he said, speaking gently. "It was eight years ago. You're acting like it happened last night. It isn't a big deal."

To him, it was eight years ago. She hadn't had the benefit of all that time to get used to the idea of his near death. She'd been robbed of that time by her father. Her father . . . Noble's enemy.

"How many times have you come close to being killed?"

"What?"

"Can you respond to a simple query without resorting to monosyllabic grunts? I asked how many times you've courted death."

"Gee, I don't know." His feigned innocence was ruined by his big, fat grin.

"You're an idiot, Noble McCaneaghy, to be running around the wilderness skirting danger and flirting with death. For God's sake, man, have you no care for yourself?" she demanded furiously. "You, you, *adventurer!*"

"Aye, darlin'," he said, "just like you."

Noble couldn't help but bask in her concern. She looked like a pampered Siamese cat gone feral, fiercely elegant in spite of its tattered appearance.

"Yeah, well—" she allowed, her matted black

hair falling over one eye. She puffed at it but it slipped right back over her brow. Noble thought it looked damned provocative.

But then, this whole day had been damned provocative. From the heated debate they'd had this morning on whether or not two cents an acre was too much to pay for that giant ice floe to the north of Canada called Alaska, to laughing with her over Grundy's antics, to the touch of her cool fingers sliding across his overheated skin, it had all been too damned provocative.

And now she was angry at him. For getting bayoneted eight years ago.

Suddenly she clapped her hands on her hips, as though coming to a decision.

"I don't want to lose you. I won't be robbed of any more time. Not even by you."

"Pardon?"

She drew nearer. He could see the rise and fall of her breasts beneath the soft, torn flannel shirt. The neckline gaped open and there was a smudge of dirt just below her collarbone. She leaned forward and the thick, cool satin of her hair swept across his chest. He closed his eyes. She smelled like pine needles and rich, springtime earth.

Lord, how he wanted to make love to her; to bury his face against her throat and feel her arch against him. He wanted to catch her laughter in his mouth and smile against the velvety softness of her skin. He wanted to watch her, taste her, touch her . . .

But he didn't want just one night. And he couldn't ask for more.

"Venice," he said, trying to do the right thing. "We're still the same friends we were ten years ago."

"Ten years ago?" She tilted her head as though

listening to a far-off voice. "We were more than friends. You were my hero, Slats."

He felt the corners of his mouth tug up at the nickname.

"A godsend."

"Yeah," he said sardonically. "A regular Saint George."

"You were," she insisted. "And such a proud lad. I remember how the other servants' kids used to torment you for not kowtowing to them. You were the outsider. Like me. Maybe that's why we became such good friends."

"Maybe," he allowed with a tender smile.

"How many times did the butler's son and his cronies trap you in the carriage house, Noble?" she asked, remembered pity filling her dove-gray eyes. "Why *did* they shave your head?"

"To mark me." At her look of bewilderment he clarified. "To remind me I was a slummer."

"How many times did they do that?"

Noble shrugged. "Enough."

"I used to cry when I saw your poor, raw scalp." Venice's voice had become harsh, angry. "Is that why you finally started shaving it yourself, Noble? To rob your tormentors of that pleasure?"

She was right, that was why he'd taken a razor to his scalp. He didn't see her point though, so he stood silently.

"I think that made them angriest of all. That and your innate dignity, your scorn. It infuriated them. I remember once, after they'd caught you alone and your nose was bloody, I was going to tell but you made me swear not to say a word to anyone about what they'd done to you."

Noble gave her a crooked smile. "You kept a secret fair well, lass."

"Yes," she whispered. "But you don't know what my silence cost me. I should have done something. I can't keep silent again at your request."

"What do you mean?"

"I mean, it's too late to pretend that I'm a little girl and you're a fierce, gangly lad. And I don't want to."

He put his hands on her shoulders, looking down into her questioning eyes.

He'd never been able to accept less than what he wanted. And there was no way in heaven or hell he could make love to Venice and not want her to spend her life with him. He wanted that now. But it stood against all reason and all common sense.

Her father, a man she'd spent her life trying to impress, would cut her off like a gangrenous limb. Her friends would disown her. A few days ago he'd told Blaine that he couldn't afford Venice Leiland. Well, neither could Noble McCaneaghy.

He looked up into her dove-soft eyes. She was regarding him steadily.

"Come on," she said. He saw her black pupils dilate, felt the soft beat of her breath across his mouth. She reached down. Capturing his fingers in her much smaller hand, she gave a little tug. "Time for bed."

Chapter 18

Though it drizzled most of the next day, just before dusk, the sun broke through the clouds. Noble, however, was in no mood to admire the splendid sunset.

Instead, he'd spent the last half hour worrying about nightfall and how he was going to find the strength of will to keep away from Venice. Particularly since it had become clear that Venice did not want him to keep away. On the contrary—unless he missed his guess and had gone completely mad—she'd been trying to seduce him all day.

"If it had kept raining, I wouldn't have been able to find enough dry wood to feed a fire until dark," Venice said suddenly. He wheeled around at the sound of her voice, and stepped backward, putting the campfire safely between them.

"You can always use birch or aspen bark," he said.

"Oh, I can think of other ways to keep warm." She flashed him a provocative smile. With a deep sense of frustration, Noble felt his ears grow hot.

It was just like every conversation they'd had since she'd pulled him to his feet last night and led him toward his tent.

Fool that he was, he'd spent every foot-dragging moment on that short journey trying to rally enough willpower to resist Venice Leiland, and

then been paradoxically furious when he hadn't
needed it.

She'd seen him to the tent, ushered him in, and
left. He'd had the sinking feeling she was laughing
as she flipped the canvas flap down and disappeared.

Now, with each moment spent cloistered in
these mountains with her, he felt something suspiciously like desperation building inside him. As he
stood staring at her, all he could think to say was,
"Cut it out, Venice."

She laughed, deliciously amused. "Oh, Noble,
who'd have thought you'd turn into a prude?"

"I'm not one of your overbred New York lap
dogs, Venice. I don't do tricks," he warned her in
what he hoped was a dangerous growl.

But what had worked in her bedroom at the
Gold Dust wasn't working here. She just raised
both elegant brows in surprise and said, "Oh, Noble, you don't give yourself enough credit. That
trick of turning bright red is quite entertaining."

"Spoiled brat," he said.

"Better than a spoil sport," she countered. "And
if you spend any more time scuffing the toe of
your boot in the dirt and drawling, 'Shucks,
ma'am,' I'll accuse you of plagiarizing one of Mr.
Wild Bill Hickock's novels."

"Wild Bill—!" he sputtered. He snapped his
mouth shut, collecting his temper before saying
with as much dignity as he could muster, "I have
never said 'Aw, shucks' in my life. And I sure as
heck aren't going to call you, 'ma'am.' "

"Really?" She sidled from the other side of the
fire, swaying to within a few feet of him. "Wanta
make a bet?"

She winked. He ran.

Not literally, but from the way he stumbled back
and swung his head around, looking for some-

thing, anything, to divert his attention, it may as well have been running. And they both knew it.

He stomped to the tent and began digging through his saddlebag looking for his big jack-knife. Finding it, he flipped the blade open and closed, trying to decide what to do. He needed some work to vent a little physical frustration on.

He could cut some pine boughs for bedding. Better than hard ground. Yeah, a soft, fragrant bed . . .

Angrily, he shook off the seductive image. Stomping through the aspen copse to a stand of young lodgepole pines, he attacked the trees.

He worked for fifteen minutes, hacking away at blameless boughs sheathed in soft spring needles, only once peeking surreptitiously over his shoulder to see what she was doing.

Having already watered the pony, built a fire, and hung their damp overcoats near it to dry, she was wrapping the rabbit he'd managed to snare in wild leek leaves before cooking it. Her skill with camp craft was impressive. Everything about her was impressive.

He just wished she wasn't always so . . . *near*. Always within arm's reach, all the damn time. He knew she went out of her way to stand close to him. She *had* to know it was driving him crazy.

Why the hell couldn't she just shout her questions from the opposite side of that damn fire? Why did she have to swing her hips to within a few yards of him, just to talk? Why did they have to *talk* at all?!

Didn't she realize that keeping a safe distance between them was for her own good? Why the hell couldn't she appreciate that he was torturing himself in his efforts to do right by her?

He stood there, his arms filled with pine boughs, staring into the trees. Suddenly, he could feel her behind him. She must be fair breathing down his neck. This, at least, had to stop. He wheeled around, preparing to turn her ears red with the set-down he was about to deliver.

She was twenty feet away. Her quiet gaze rested on him.

"What?!" he demanded. God help him, he could hear the panic in his own voice.

"Nothing, I was just watching you."

"Why?"

"I was just thinking to myself that you don't seem the worse for wear after surviving that trip down the river. You're very strong," she said, taking a step closer.

He refused to step back. She came closer. Fifteen feet, ten, five. He shuffled where he stood. Her eyes brimmed with amusement.

"No, I'm not strong."

"Oh, yes, you are. Wonderfully strong and . . . fit," she said. "Everyone in Salvage agrees. Blaine Farley is quite in awe of you."

It wasn't a step back, he told himself. Not really. It was more like a sidestep. "Blaine would be in awe of a one-legged mule skinner if he thought the man had ever held a gun. He's just a kid."

"But *you're* not. Really, Noble. You're too modest. You have a beautiful—"

"Go to bed!"

"Excuse me?"

"I said that as soon as we've eaten, I'm going to bed."

"The rabbit won't be done for quite a while. Maybe we could just talk?" She sounded almost wistful.

"It's been a long day. And probably more of the same to follow. I haven't any idea how long before we find Milton, or he finds us. You can sit around here thinking about how strong your various male acquaintances are, but I'm going to ... to chop some firewood." Snatching up an ax, he plunged into the woods.

Venice stared after him for a full minute before finally giving way to laughter. Ever since she had begun to suspect that she, Venice Leiland—all five feet, two inches of her—could chase away big, strong Noble McCaneaghy with a few innocent—okay, not so innocent—words, she'd been unable to resist testing her theory.

She sobered as she watched him disappear into the copse. She loved Noble. She'd loved him for as long as she could remember. And she might have lost him in that river.

Lord, she was tired of being left behind. Tired of being afraid to get too close. Tired of letting other people's decisions dictate her life.

She knew there wasn't any future for them. Even if Noble could somehow forgive her father for his betrayal, she knew too well what happened to "love matches."

But there was *now*.

She wasn't going to spend the rest of her life regretting what might have been. She was going to hoard as many memories as she could of their time together.

He was trying so hard to be ... *noble*. She simply wasn't going to stand for it.

As she wondered how to hasten Noble's capitulation, Venice checked the rabbit meat. Gingerly she plucked the leaf package from the hot ashes near the edge of the fire and stripped back the leaves. A luscious, oniony aroma was released in a fragrant steam. Venice's stomach growled in response. She tested the meat with her finger and sighed. Perfect.

Fetching a bucket, she made her way to where a trickle of water flowed down the rock face. After filling the bucket, she returned to find Noble stacking what looked like an entire tree's worth of firewood.

He *was* magnificent. For a moment, she just stood admiring him, his size, his strength, the clean broad expanse of his shoulders bunching and slipping beneath his thin chambray shirt. Suddenly, his back went rigid. He jolted upright as though brushed by an electric shock. It was uncanny the way he seemed to be able to feel her gaze. Spinning on his heels, he glowered at her.

"What?" he said in exasperation. Venice couldn't tell who he was exasperated with. "What? What? What?!"

"Dinner's ready. I'll just make some coffee and we can enjoy our meal."

Noble watched as she started toward the fire, the heavy bucket banging against her legs. The water sloshed over the side, soaking her boots. Before he realized what he was doing, he leaped forward, taking the bucket from her.

"Thank you," she murmured.

"You want this on the fire?" he mumbled.

Nodding, Venice sat down and began picking the rabbit meat up from its leafy bed. It was hot. Startled, she dropped the meat and stuck her finger in her mouth, sucking on the tip. "Ouch," she muttered. Her little frown turned into an expression of pleasure as she tasted the savory juice. Her tongue flicked out to lick her other fingers.

"Mmm," she said appreciatively. "Good."

Noble didn't respond.

Venice looked up. Instantly she was transfixed by a fire hotter than the one that had burned her. Noble's unguarded gaze devoured her. His golden eyes gleamed in his dark, tanned face. He was motionless, yet tension, so tightly coiled as to be nearly palpable, radiated from his body.

The bawdy comment she was about to make died on her lips. Some instinct warned her not to toy with him. Not now.

"Would you put some coffee in the pot?" *Coward!* she abjured herself.

"Coffee?" Noble asked, shaking himself out of his trance.

"Please."

He reached into the bag beside him and dumped a handful of crushed beans into the kettle. Working efficiently, Venice divided the rabbit meat between two tin plates. Apologetically, she portioned out the last soggy piece of hardtack and handed Noble his meal.

For a few minutes, they ate in strained silence. Finally Venice peeked over at Noble. He was scowling fiercely at his plate, mechanically shoving food into his mouth. This was ridiculous. They were two civilized, reasonably intelligent people. They could talk.

"Ah." She cleared her throat. He looked up. Lord, he had the most beautiful, frightening eyes. She cleared her throat again and hurried on. "Blaine told me you did some sort of surveying work up here. And Katie mentioned the Smithsonian. And you mentioned you were doing explorations here."

"Yeah. Is there a question coming?"

"Well, I was just wondering"—she paused and caught her hands between her knees—"why here?"

Noble took a deep breath.

So, he thought, they were going to play polite chitchat. They were going to sit here as though he was some dilapidated old granddad at a church social, not a man so heavy and taut with desire he was close to leaping at her from across the bloody fire and tasting for himself the oil still slicking her luscious, inviting lips.

All right, then. He could do this.

Maybe.

"After the war, I went back to Yale and picked up a degree. I didn't know what to do with it, though, and I hung about the East Coast trying to decide. I was pretty tired of people by that time. Wars can make a man so he is unfit company for anyone but himself."

Venice bent forward in concern, and he smiled at her. "Nah. It's okay, Venice. I—what would you say? Got better? Came out of it? Anyway, I was in the cavalry in the war and while I was kicking my heels around New York, I ran into a former commander. One thing led to another and ended with the army offering me a promotion if I rejoined. I didn't have anything better to do, so I agreed. I was assigned out here, to Lieutenant Wheeler's party. I remember thinking it might be an interesting job." He smiled in recollection.

"Lieutenant Wheeler?"

"Yeah. We charted a good portion of the mountains, assayed, collected . . . even took a photographer with us. It was an interesting job. I grew to appreciate this land," he said quietly.

He grew to *love* the mountains, Venice thought, watching the fervent expression on Noble's face as he spoke.

"After my stint with the army was over, I started working for some men who wanted to make sure that these mountains were never lost."

"How can you lose a mountain?" Venice asked.

"Oh, you can. You can hurt the earth, Venice. You can hurt it bad enough so it can't heal."

She weighed his words carefully, her hands on her knees, her back straight. He had to give her this: she listened.

"And how," she finally said, "do you recommend we keep from doing that?"

"By safeguarding them. By understanding what we're doing out here before we allow men to rush in here with hydraulics and dynamite and dams."

"And that's what you've been doing? Trying to protect the mountains?"

Noble leaned back. "There's only one way to protect something from greed, Venice. You make laws. And that means politicians and that, my dear, means money. The people who need to pay attention to what we're trying to do out here pay attention to money. Right now, there's a bill drifting around in Congress that would turn the area north of here into a gigantic national park." He snorted. "If I can only convince a few more congressmen to see the advantages of such a plan. With a few more hard, cold facts and a lot more hard, cold cash, the bill should see its way clear to the president."

The water was boiling in the pot. Venice stood up, her expression thoughtful as she caught the handle with a hooked branch and lifted it from the fire.

"I might be able to . . . help," she suggested hesitantly.

The sense of empathy they had been enjoying dissipated like morning mist. Great, thought Noble, the Leiland Foundation to the rescue. Sorta like sending the dragon to rescue the maiden.

"You mean Trevor?" Noble snorted. "I hate to tell you this, Venice, but the people who oppose this proposed park all crawled from your dear daddy's rear pocket. The last thing in the world Trevor would want is *you* offering *me* his help."

"I didn't mean his help. I meant—"

"No," he broke in, unable to hide his bitterness, "I take that back. There's one thing he'd want less and that's for you to be here—or anywhere else in the world—with me."

For a moment he'd forgotten.

"No, Noble. I meant *I* might be able to help. I know how you feel about my father."

"I doubt that."

"I know why you didn't come back to the Park Avenue house."

He stopped, motionless. "Trevor told you?"

She shook her head. "Cassius Reed told me."

He relaxed. No matter what Reed knew—or thought he knew—he had no idea of the whole story. No one but he and Trevor knew that. "Yeah?"

"Yeah." She answered. "I'm ashamed to say I never—I believed it when my father said you left without saying a word, without explaining. Oh, Noble, I'm so sorry!"

"Forget it. You were right. I didn't say good-bye. But then, I couldn't."

"I understand. I'm surprised you still speak to me after what he did. It's no wonder you never wrote or sent word or . . . anything."

Noble frowned. "Just what did Cassius tell you?"

"He said . . . he said that my father stopped paying your tuition and had your name . . ." she paused, the words obviously hard to say, " . . . had your name sent to the draft office."

"And you think *that's* why I never came back to say good-bye? Because I was *mad?*"

She nodded. "Yes."

"Venice," he said sadly, "there was more to it than that. Your father told me that if I placed one foot on the sidewalk outside your house, he'd set the doorman on me."

"He threatened to have you beaten?" Pain and bewilderment were clear in her tone. He'd felt the same emotions nearly ten years ago. "Why?"

Noble didn't want to tell her. Even after all this

time, the thought of that final conversation still
made him feel dirty, as ugly and lascivious as the
street scum Trevor had accused him of being.

"Why, Noble?" she begged.

"Venice, let it go. It was ten years ago."

"Let it go?" she asked wildly. "Noble, for ten
years I've thought you made a promise to me as
casually as you would promise a puppy a walk,
and that you just as carelessly broke it. For ten
years, I've thought you abandoned me, without a
single thought. For ten years I've tried not to
care."

He held out a hand, wanting to touch her, to
ease her pain. She ignored him, the words tumbling out. "Three days ago, I found out that wasn't
the case. That my father drove you away. I need to
know . . . *why?*"

She had a right to know, though that wouldn't
make the telling any easier. He fixed his gaze beyond her, so that he wouldn't have to see her face
as he described the sordid meeting.

"The same day your father cut off my financing,
I received a notice from the draft office, telling me
to report. I knew who was responsible. I took the
train to New York and pounded on your back
door, demanding an interview. I kept it up until
the servants let me in.

"Your father met me in the hallway. I remember
the maids tittering in the rooms they were clean-
ing and the footman standing by the front door.
Trevor wouldn't even let me in a room. We spoke
there, in full sight and hearing of the staff, him
checking his timepiece and me quivering with
rage."

"Oh, Noble—"

"It was quite simple, as he explained it. The *experiment* wasn't turning out like he'd hoped. My
politics were too liberal, my interests not at all in

keeping with his plans. He was calling an end to the entire *debacle*."

Noble looked at her. Her eyes were filled with pity. " 'I've made a mistake,' he said. 'You are no longer welcome here.' And then, he said, 'And don't seek to curry my favor through your relationship with my daughter. It isn't seemly, the way you and she ... You're nearly a man, for God's sake! She's just a little girl.' "

Venice's hand flew to her mouth. He knew how she felt. A feeling of nausea, a phantom of that decade-old sensation curled in the pit of his stomach.

"I swear, Venice," he said urgently, "I never felt anything but brotherly affection for you. There was nothing vile about our friendship."

"I know."

"God, I hated him. I left, Venice. I didn't write, I didn't try to see you, because I didn't want to know if your father was poisoning you against me. I didn't want to imagine you being suspicious of every word I penned. I didn't want to wonder if you were examining my affection for something unnatural."

Venice's head was bowed. He had to lean forward to hear her words. "He told me you left because you weren't able to accept the responsibilities of college."

He shrugged.

"I believed him," she confessed. "Forgive me."

He lifted her hand to his mouth, feathered a kiss over the pulse fluttering in her wrist. "Well, I didn't believe him. More fool me."

"I don't understand."

"Ten years ago, I might not have loved you like a man does a woman, Venice," he murmured against her skin, his mouth a soft caress. "But maybe Trevor had a crystal ball, after all. Because

I surely love you now. And I would give anything for your love in return."

She lifted her hand to the golden head bowed before her.

He shivered at her touch, releasing her hand and rising to his feet. "But I'll never hurt you," he said sadly, and left her before she could reply.

Chapter 19

Venice awoke in the pitch-black tent. The blanket had bunched beneath her and the soft, fragrant bed she'd laid down on had turned lumpy and prickly. She wondered if Noble, after insisting he would sleep by the fire, was faring any better. Easing onto her stomach, she drew back the canvas flap and peered outside.

A fairy tale world met her startled gaze. Over the course of the past few hours, every cloud had been chased from the sky by a soft Chinook wind. Now, so close it looked as though she merely had to stretch out her hand to touch it, a velvety indigo heaven, encrusted with a million sparkling gems, spread above the mountains.

A crescent moon, hanging on the cusp of a rocky spire, added its light to that of the myriad stars, cloaking the earth in a pale, ethereal luscence. Each blade of grass, each frond, each rock seemed touched by phosphorescence, creating a phantom dreamscape in the strange twilight world.

Like a sleepwalker, Venice left the tent, moving into the night. She saw Noble, wrapped in a blanket and moonlight, standing beyond the fire, quiescent and magnificent, his handsome face turned to the sky. She went to his side. Without moving his head, he reached out and enveloped her hand in his much larger one.

"Watch," he whispered, his eyes riveted on the heavens.

With a sense of enchantment, she followed his gaze. A star suddenly broke free of the celestial tapestry and streaked toward earth, a brief dazzling shimmer of light trailing its descent. She caught her breath. "What is it?"

"Asteroid. Wait," he cautioned, and as he spoke another star, and then another, tore loose from the black night and dashed in fiery brilliance across the sky. In awe, she watched the spectacle as hundreds of points of light dazzled and sputtered and danced across the firmament.

They stood silently, hand in hand, watching the performance, as each minute more and more shooting stars ended their lives in the magnificent display.

"You always reminded me of a star," Noble finally murmured, so quietly that Venice was certain he spoke to himself. "As far out of my reach as any burning sun."

There was no bitterness to his tone, and his expression, bathed in the eerie light, was relaxed.

He smiled, a tender smile of recollection. "Not that I can't appreciate a star. I remember the first time I met you. You, in all that stiff lace and shiny satin and bows and curls . . . I didn't own a pair of decent boots and my britches were so patched you couldn't have told their original color.

"Not that it mattered to you. Even as a child, you were a rare, comely lass, sweet and generous and burning with curiosity. You were completely unaware of the bad in people, of the depths to which desperate people could sink."

He turned to look at her and his smile grew gentler. "But what do stars know about abysses? They are made for heights and that's as it should be. That's where they should stay ... safely in their heavens."

"Not all stars stay in the sky," Venice said. "Like those." She gestured toward the sky.

"True. Some fall to earth. They die in the descent." He started to pull his hand free from hers, but she clung to him.

He shook his head sadly. Gripping her shoulder with his free hand, he bent close to hers. His face was set, determined. "I'm no fool, for all my foolish dreams."

"I'm no star, Noble."

"Yes, you are." His tone was implacable. She tried another tack.

"If I remember right, falling stars are drawn to the solid ground. If I have to be your star, you have to be my earth, safe and strong and constant."

He chuckled. "Oh, I'm earthly all right."

"I mean it, Noble," she said seriously. "What's between us—it's irresistible."

"When a star falls, it leaves a great, black crater. I'd like my heart whole. Now go back to bed. The show's over."

His tone was dismissive and his hand dropped from her shoulder. He started to turn and suddenly Venice knew that if she let him go now, she'd regret it for the rest of her life.

"I love you, Noble," she said.

He stopped. His back was to her and she could see his broad shoulders slump, ever so slightly, as though he'd just been dealt a blow. She went to him.

"Every other man I've ever known has made me feel like an oddity. You make me feel ... complete in myself. How can I help but love you? You've been my friend, my confidante ... even after you left, I whispered secrets to your specter!"

She touched his arm. His muscles tightened beneath her palm. She exhaled, silently pleading for him to do something, say something before her courage abandoned her.

She smoothed her hand up his arm and across his shoulders. The muscles jumped to taut life beneath her touch. Under his thin cotton shirt, his body was warm.

"Don't." His tone was tight.

She steeled her nerve and brought her hand around the rigid ladder of his ribs to the hard flat plane of his belly. He held himself as stiff as fire-tempered steel.

When she fumbled with the buttons on his shirt, his breathing grew labored. Still, he made no move to stop her. His control goaded her on, making her push him into a confrontation, to either deny or accept what she offered.

His shirt fell open, exposing his chest limned by moonlight, dotted with sweat in the cool mountain air. He turned slowly, finally facing her.

His golden eyes, steeped in darkness, pierced hers. He lifted his hands and she saw that they shook. Carefully, gently, he encircled her wrists, weakly tugging her hands away from him, as though all of his strength had been given over to maintaining his quiescent stance and he had none left with which to defend himself against her touch.

"I beg you, don't," he said.

She barely heard his words. She had never before consciously touched a man's bare chest. Deliberately, she placed her hands on him.

He closed his eyes. The veins corded in his neck.

Her breath escaped in a low rush. Noble's skin was smooth, so very smooth, a thin, silken layer of flesh covering hard, straining muscle.

And he was warm. Who would have guessed

his body would be so warm and dense? So silky and clean and so hard and unyielding. The contrasting textures were exotic, stimulating.

She touched the flat, pebbled surface of a copper-colored nipple. He flinched, bowing at the waist as though he'd been hit in the belly. She snatched her hand back, alarmed. His eyes flew open, searching for hers.

She'd never seen anything quite so dangerous looking. Or fascinating. Her mouth went unaccountably dry. She wet her lips with her tongue and Noble groaned.

"I don't know why you're doing this. Are you making up for Trevor's actions? You don't owe me anything, Venice." He sounded desperate.

"I owe this to myself," she replied quietly. "I owe it to myself to lie with the man I love."

"No."

"Yes."

Her fingers skittered hungrily over him, reaching the base of his neck and pulling his head down to meet hers.

Noble's self-restraint, tested beyond endurance, broke. One of his broad hands enveloped the back of her delicately shaped skull. Her hair spilled over the back of his hand and he seized a fistful of inky locks, forcing her head back. His other arm coiled around her waist, snatching her close, clamping her hips between his legs. He challenged her with eyes the color of molten gold.

"Do you want *me*, then? The Irish cook's boy?" His voice was tortured, raw. There was a full measure of pain in his hopeless defiance.

"No."

He bared his teeth, anguished.

"I'm not a little girl in need of a friend. I'm a woman in love with a man. One man. I want you, Noble McCaneaghy."

"My God," Noble whispered. "Do you know what you're asking? I have nothing. No family. No fortune."

She understood then. *She* was his forbidden fruit, forbidden because he'd been taught the harsh lesson not to want what you can't have. And Noble thought he couldn't have her.

"You have me."

"I have you," he repeated in a hushed whisper. "So it is."

She forgot all else, all words, everything but the feel of his lips on hers, his mouth open over hers, his fingers pressing into her jaw, gently forcing her lips farther apart. Then his tongue was in her mouth, stroking the slick lining of her cheeks, probing deep.

His hands loosened. He held her transfixed by the sensuality of his kiss. Catching her hips in his big palms, he pulled her against his loins, against the hardness between his legs.

He bent farther over her, angling a leg behind her knee and pulling her closer still, surrounding her with his body. And now the center of pleasure warred between her mouth and the press of unmistakable maleness at the juncture of her own legs, a center flooded with raw nerve endings, taunting her with the promise of a culmination to this incredible stimulation.

"Please!"

She clutched at his shoulders, certain she would fall.

She should have known; Noble would never let her fall. Effortlessly, he swung her up in his arms.

The wind racing across the mountains did not cool him. He trembled, holding her high against his chest, all self-imposed constraints on the verge of breaking.

"Venice."

He carried her to the tent, shivering when her cheek rubbed luxuriously over his chest. He kicked the tent flap back and looked inside. It was too dark. He needed to see her.

With one hand, he grabbed the canvas flap and pulled. The tent fluttered loose from its stakes and collapsed. Impatiently he kicked it away. Carefully, he set her atop the soft pine bough mattress. Following her down, he braced his forearms on either side of her, imprisoning her between his arms, holding her captive, afraid she'd come to her senses and deny him what he'd spent a decade wishing for.

Afraid she wouldn't.

"Venice." She reached up, spearing her fingers through his hair.

She was touching him. He shifted his weight down against her, cradling himself between her soft thighs, giving her yet another chance to refuse him.

She didn't.

"Venice, I'll not repent of a single thing that goes on between us. But be sure, lass. I could not stand to have you regret this night."

"I won't regret it." She smiled into his kiss. "I love you."

"I love you, too, lass. But you don't have to prove it with the gift of your body. There's no going back from where we're heading."

"I know. I love you, Noble. I want you. I want all of you, everything that love can mean. Please."

"God, don't ask," he whispered against her lips. "Don't ever ask. Take."

Ineffectually, she tugged at her own clothes. Muttering a curse, Noble pulled her shirt over her head, snapped the leather band free of belt loops, dragged the denim pants from her hips.

She rose up on her elbows. His gaze fell to her

breasts, pale in the moonlight. Delicately, he traced the soft, curving fullness, brushing gently back and forth until he reached the rosy crest. He stroked her nipple and instinctively she arched her back into the light touch, wanting more.

His mouth closed hotly over her. A cry broke from her at the first deep pull on her breast. His tongue lathed her nipple. She panted, holding his head to her.

With a sudden growl, he swept her arms from beneath her, laying her flat on her back. Reaching between them, he fumbled with his trousers, his knuckles rubbing against the unexpected center of pleasure. Her hips jerked with fundamental knowledge, moving to deepen the contact.

He stilled and rose above her, his upper body braced on his muscular forearms, his biceps trembling, his lower body pressed tightly against her.

His hair hung in golden ropes, shielding his expression from her. She could only feel his breath laboring in and out, sluicing over her hot cheeks. With terrible gentleness, he traced her lower lip with two fingertips. A feather's touch, insubstantial as a butterfly's wing. Too insubstantial. She turned her head, licking the finger nearest her mouth, nipping its end.

He stroked the satiny curve of her waist, followed her hip bone, brushed aside the pitifully inadequate safeguard of her boy's pants until he felt the silky tangle of curls between her legs. Carefully, he slid his fingers along the moist cleft. She gasped, her back bowing off the woolen blankets. He petted her there, stroking her, moving one leg over both of hers to keep her still, finally easing his finger into her. Wet, hot velvet.

His head fell against her shoulder, as though he was exhausted. In pleasuring her, he would certainly lose control of his own body. Fighting for time to teach her as much of this incredible pleasure as he himself was learning, he forced himself to go slowly. His muscles ached with the effort of containing his passion.

Her hips bucked again and he gave in to the silent, instinctive plea, moving his fingers in and out, establishing a rhythm that another part of his body wanted to maintain. She snatched at his shoulders, searching his face.

"Please!"

"Yes, love. Venice, yes. Quiet, now. Easy. Yes," he coaxed until he could stand it no longer.

Jerking his pants away from himself, he rolled into the cradle of her hips. Reaching between them, he replaced his finger with his member, stroking her silky center with its head. She shuddered. Then the abrupt, instinctive lunge of her hips took him just within her body.

Discipline vanished. A harsh moan erupted from deep within his throat. With a monumental effort at control, he pushed deeply into her, past the flimsy barrier of her maidenhead. His hips ground against hers, the pleasure of that single thrust making his head spin with ecstasy.

She felt the discomfort, but it was soon lost amidst other sensations: his body, big and strong as he held himself buried, motionless and straining, above her; the sharp tang of pine mingling with the rich, musky scent of his flesh; the rush of blood singing in her body.

The need to move became overwhelming, yet his weight held her pinned beneath him. Her hands, clutching at him, did not make any impression on the dark muscles of his arms. She had only words to make him understand, to make him give her what she wanted.

"I can't ... Please!"

A sound, desperate and filled with anguish,

rasped between his grated teeth. "God help me, Venice. I'm sorry."

"Please. You have to—!" Frantically, she tried to make him understand.

"Don't move!" he thundered. "A minute, a second. I can't leave your body. Not quite yet! Not now!"

"Don't," she sobbed. It sounded as though he echoed her sob. "Don't stop. Please! I want you! Please."

She wanted him.

He had no great experience with making love and none at all with virgins and that she wanted this, wanted his body in hers, was a stimulant more potent than any physical sensation he'd ever known.

Cupping her hips, he slowly buried himself in her warm, tight body. He forced himself to curb the need for a deeper stroke, teaching her the cadence of bodies mating. Slow mind-numbing thrust, slow excruciating withdrawal.

He was going mad.

Venice whimpered.

Her fingernails delicately scored Noble's back with each shuddering, deliberate movement. A pinnacle of pleasure danced just beyond her reach. She lifted her hips to meet his thrust with her own. He groaned. She drove up, wrapping her legs about his flanks, making the contact deeper, harder.

She met each thrust with her own unbridled passion, each coming together fiercer, more elemental.

And then, with exquisite timing, Noble ground his hips against hers, pushing her to a culmination, delivering her to the zenith.

She threw back her head, her heels riding his hard buttocks, her mouth open in a gasp of ecstasy

that joined Noble's hoarse cry of fulfillment before
she collapsed, sweat-sheened and shivering beneath his big body.

And Noble, watching her lashes flutter against
her pale cheeks, hearing her ragged breath come
from between swollen lips, feeling her heart
pound in her breast, threw back his head as high
above, the silent stars fell down.

Making love with Venice had been just that:
love. It was something Noble had never experienced before and it was both shattering and fulfil-
ling.

Raising himself on one elbow the next morning,
he leaned over her, casting a deeper shadow
across the pale slopes and curves of her body. She
signed, burrowing beneath the blankets. Her
breathing had quieted, drawn between petal-soft
lips.

Venice's declaration of love had devastated him,
destroyed each defense he'd built, each sound, log-
ical reason why he should keep his distance, both
physically and emotionally. Her words had fanned
into flames all the hopes and desires that he'd kept
so carefully suppressed.

He had thought Venice Leiland was as beyond
his scope as the bloody stars that had beguiled
him last night. She had spent her life vying for the
love and approval of her father, a man who'd
hated Noble so much that he'd used all of his political influence to ensure that Noble was drafted
to the front lines of the war.

Noble raked his hair from his face. What could
he offer Venice?

He sighed. She was no fool. For whatever reason, she loved him. She'd chosen him over the life
of grace and privilege Noble had glimpsed beyond

Trevor's kitchen doors. God, he hoped he didn't live to see the day when she rued her choice.

With a groan, Noble flopped onto his back.

The sound roused Venice. Her whole body felt drained, languid, as though she'd just run five miles, soaked in a hot bath, drank cream, and was now wrapped in the most luxurious cashmere. Cream? No, chocolate. Hot, steaming, chocolate. Venice purred and stretched.

Yes, there was definitely chocolate mixed up with all the other sensual impressions. She felt sated, spent, complete. Because of Noble.

With a start, Venice opened her eyes.

Noble lay on his back beside her, a forearm flung across his eyes. Creeping closer, she pulled the blanket over her shoulders.

She had never known that two people could be joined so closely, so deeply, as they had been last night. Their union was just a part of a greater union, the overwhelming pleasure just the beginning. She made a soft sound of contentment.

Noble lowered his arm.

He looked over at her. Silvery eyes stared back at him from above a thick blanket. She was a hand's space from touching him, her fingers wadding the blanket beneath her chin, black hair framing her face.

Her eyes held a quiet, watchful intensity. Hesitantly, she extended her hand, touching one of his ribs.

His breath hissed from between his teeth. He covered her hand with his, flattening her palm against his stomach.

She gave him a tentative smile and then, as if she had needed his consent to touch him, as if he wouldn't pretty much swear to walk naked across the desert at high noon for that luxury, she looked askance before gently combing her nails through the coarse, dark hair that disappeared beneath the blanket riding low on his hips.

His breath caught in his throat. She looked up, a guarded expression on her face. And then he realized: she was shy! She was as uncertain of his reception as a pauper at a banquet. Apparently, his body was the banquet. The thought was stimulating, amusing, provocative.

He locked his fingers around her wrists, urging her to explore his body. Willingly, she followed his direction. He sighed with gratification. Venice's hand dipped beneath the blanket and Noble's belly instantly knotted with tension.

Venice felt the spasm. Her hand flew out to safer ground. "I'm sorry," she muttered, her cheeks scarlet.

She was as loath to be presumptive as a girl wanting a second helping of cake at a birthday party. Well, thought Noble, good manners oughta be carried only so far.

"Venice," he said softly, "you can touch me."

He twisted his mouth with self-disgust. He made it sound as if he was offering the ultimate boon to womanhood. It was a wonder she didn't slap his face.

"I mean, I really like it when you touch me. Really." Better and better. Talk about damning with faint praise! Her eyes were darkening to the color of ancient pewter. It was impossible to interpret their expression.

"Look, Venice . . ." Whatever words Noble had been about to say died on his lips as he stared into her eyes. Mesmerized, he reached out a fingertip and gently swept the thick sable lashes framing her eyes. He traced her dark brows, touched her lips, skimmed down her throat, and paused at the pulse fluttering there.

"I don't have the words, Venice. I'd give them to

you if I did. I'd give you anything in my power just to feel your hands upon me, have you love me. What can I do? What can I say? Tell me."

She parted her lips to answer, but he was too quick, too hungry. Dipping his head, he covered her lips with his. She opened for him and he filled her mouth, his tongue lapping at hers. Her taste filled his mouth. The fragrance of crushed pines and lovemaking surrounded them.

Desire erupted. Her ardor enflamed his own passion to the point of conflagration.

"Make love to me, Noble. Make it happen again."

He needed no further encouragement.

Noble hauled on his trousers and lingered a minute, committing each of Venice's delicate, sleeping features to memory. He would let her sleep. She must be nearly exhausted. But it was hard not to touch her and so, loath to disturb her, he finally left.

He followed the path to the edge of the gorge. Far below, still shrouded in darkness, black water boiled. He sank down, resting on his heels. With unseeing eyes, he stared over the deep chasm, the questions that had hounded him from sleep yet to be answered.

"Noble?"

She was a small graceful shadow materializing from the early morning mist. She was hugging the blanket close under her chin, her black hair cascading over her shoulders.

"I woke and you were gone."

"I'm sorry."

"I just ... I didn't ..." Venice searched for some way to explain. She'd awoken and he'd been gone. The frightful sense of abandonment, which always seemed to be waiting with jeering certainty, poured through her. "I didn't like it."

He smiled. "I'll be there whenever you wake up, from now on."

"If only I could make myself believe that."

"Believe it. That's where a husband wakes up, isn't it? Next to his wife."

"A husband?" She was staring at him oddly.

"Yes," he said softly. "Not very well done of me, is it?" He took the few steps to her side and slowly sank to his knees in front of her. He caught her hand, refusing to let her pull it from his grip. He hadn't said any of the pretty words she deserved. He hadn't courted her properly and he'd taken her maidenhead before he'd had her vows. This, at least, he would do right.

"I love you, Venice. I guess in one way or another, I've loved you most all my life. Marry me. Please."

Her eyes were enormous in her pale face. She was tugging her hands from his.

"Marry me, lass."

She looked away from him, wildly scanning the sky and the mountains and the chasm as though searching for some answer.

"Venice?" Something was wrong. Terribly wrong.

She took a deep breath and looked him directly in the eye. Her own were glistening with unshed tears.

"Noble." Her throat worked convulsively. "While I am fully cognizant of the honor you do me, I am afraid I must decline your flattering offer."

"What?!"

"I won't marry you, Noble."

Chapter 20

"**W**hat do you mean, you won't marry me? Or do you mean you can't?" Noble demanded, vaulting to his feet. His face was set in grim, determined lines and Venice found herself backing away from his anger. "If it's because of your father, Venice, I'll deal with him. I promise," he said.

"No. It's not just him—"

"Not *just* him? What, then?" His angry expression turned grim. "Are you betrothed to someone else? Because I assure you that after last night, my claim far exceeds that of any other beau's, whether you've had the damned banns published or not!"

"No. There's no one else. I'm not engaged."

"Then what the bloody hell do you mean?" He raked his hand through his hair, obviously making an effort to stay calm. He wasn't doing a very good job of it.

She should have known he'd react like this. Noble was ... noble.

"I just can't. It wouldn't be fair to either of us."

He strode one step closer, his head lowered belligerently.

"You're not going to look me in the eye and tell me there's been someone before me, because even though I might not be an expert regarding the ways of a man and a woman, I sure as hell know enough about female anatomy to know there hasn't been anyone else."

"Of course not!" she gasped and found that she had taken a step forward. Still, some buried part of her could not help but be pleased that Noble did not have a lot of experience with other women.

"Then why the bloody hell won't you marry me?" he demanded. They were standing nearly toe to toe.

Her gaze fell before his. "I . . . couldn't handle it."

"Handle *what?*" His golden eyes narrowed as an idea occurred to him. "Regrets so soon, Venice?" he asked bitterly. "What happened to 'I love you'? Or did you get lust all mixed up with love?"

"You big, dumb oaf! I *do* love you!"

"Right." There was a mountain of disbelief in the single sharp word.

"I do," she said simply, lifting her chin. "And you know it."

He stared at her for a moment, confusion warring with anguish until at last, with an oath, he grabbed hold of her shoulder and gave her a little shake.

"You're right. I *do* know it. And that's why this doesn't make any sense. Why won't you marry me?"

Taking hold of his shirt collar, she gave him her own shake. "Don't you see?" And now it was her voice that spilled over with anguish. "We'd just end up hating each other."

"Hating each other?" he echoed in disbelief. "Why would we—Does this have anything to do with me being the cook's son and you being a rich man's daughter?"

"No," she said. "Yes."

"Which one is it, Venice?"

"You'd end up despising me, Noble. I couldn't stand that."

He wrapped his arms around her, pulling her close and tucking the top of her head beneath his chin. She smelled musty and pine tarry and altogether wonderful.

"Honey, you're not making sense. I love you."

"It wouldn't last."

"It's already lasted. More than a decade."

"Only because you haven't had to live with me, live as a Leiland, feel the burden of Leiland duty."

"Leiland duty? I have no intention of living as a Leiland, Venice. I have every intention of living pretty much as I have for the past seven years. I sorta thought you found that appealing."

"Oh, I do. I wish I could."

"No reason you can't."

"There's every reason," she said sadly.

"I assume the damn foundation is what you mean by 'Leiland duty.' Venice, your daddy lives to run that little empire. He doesn't need you."

"I know. But he won't live forever."

"I wouldn't be too sure of that," Noble said sardonically, lifting a strand of her hair and fingering the fine texture.

"Eventually," Venice continued, "I will inherit certain obligations and duties."

"Listen, if you're worried about ole Trev thinking I married you for his money, frankly Venice, I wouldn't touch another red cent of the Leiland estate. The price first time around was a mite high."

She pushed herself away from him. "That's just it, Noble," she said. "The foundation, the power, the wealth, that's who I am. It's useless to try and change what you are. It only leads to heartbreak. I don't want to spend each day loving you, only to have it all fall apart."

He was confused and angry. "It's not going to fall apart."

"I couldn't stand to lose you then. And I won't. You can't ask me to!" Her voice broke.

He gritted his teeth, trying to find words to make her believe in him, believe in their love.

"Venice, I *am* asking you and I'll keep on asking you until you say yes. I know we don't come from the same background, but we want the same things out of life. We're both adventurers, remember? We'll have a grand old time, even without your father's blessing, money, or duty."

"I want to believe there's a happily ever after—"

"Believe it."

"I can't," she cried.

"You won't!"

"I won't," she admitted, her head hanging.

He let loose an oath and, closing his right hand into a fist, punched his open palm with it. Venice stared at him in dismay.

"Wait a minute," he said suddenly, impaling her with a glare. "Wait just a minute here. You mean you *never* had any intention of marrying me? You made love with me without any idea of making a commitment?"

"You didn't ask me what my future intentions were when you—"

"You led me on!" he thundered.

"I did not!" she answered with a mortified gasp. "I didn't realize that you'd assume that because we . . . just because I—"

"You didn't think that just because we shared our bodies in the most intimate way human beings can, just because we are both of age and unwed, just because we said we loved each other, I would make this enormous assumption that we would marry. Well, I am sorry I was so bloody impertinent," he ground out, "but you, m'dear, shouldn't have ever made love with me if you had no intention of honoring our unspoken commitment."

"I'm sorry."

"I don't want you to be sorry!" he shouted. "I want you to marry me!"

"Don't you see? It's history repeating itself."

"What the hell are you talking about?" he asked, throwing his hands up in despair.

"We're just like my father and—"

"Yoo-hoo! Yoo-hoo!" The sudden call echoed through the small canyon, resounding with cheerfulness and goodwill.

"Venice! There you are! My dear!"

Venice started. With a frustrated growl, Noble spun around. A small, dapper figure came trotting across the meadow on a diminutive burro. Milton Leiland, Venice's uncle, to the rescue.

A damned twelve hours too late!

Milton lifted his beaver skin top hat from his balding pate as he jostled forth. Gaily he waved it over his head while cupping a hand around his mouth and hollering over his shoulder. "They're in the vale, Carter! Just as you supposed, old man!"

"Uncle Milton!" Venice called, bolting from Noble's grip and running to meet her uncle. "Thank heavens, you're all right!"

He trotted up to her and hastily clambered off the burro's back, catching Venice in a tight embrace. "I'm all right? Of course, I'm all right!" he said. He pushed her gently from his embrace, holding her at arm's length, his grin broadening. "Until two days ago, I had no idea you were even here, in the territory. What a delightful surprise! Just like old times, eh? Have you come to burn every pot in my camp again?"

He patted Venice on the top of the head, beaming happily. Venice blushed.

"Must say, you had us a bit concerned for a

while there. Trees-Too-High and Crooked Hand
said you were traveling with some hairy chap and
only a half day's ride behind them."

"Trees-Too-High is with you?" Venice asked.

"Not any more, he delivered the merchandise—
and thank you for the fossilized nautilus shells,
Noble. Quite nice examples of their sort—told me
about you and this chap, and then he and Crooked
Hand left."

"When I get my hands on that—"

"He couldn't have been talking about Noble,
here?" Milton asked incredulously, giving Noble a
reproachful look.

"Oh, for God's sake, Milton, you know me better than that!" Noble said, disgusted.

Venice turned and fixed him with an equally reproachful look. "You didn't tell me you and Uncle
Milton knew each other well."

"Didn't think to mention it," he said.

"Who was the bounder?"

"Which one?" Venice asked narrowly.

Milton took Venice's question seriously, which
didn't make Noble feel too happy. "This hairy fel-
low Trees-Too-High mentioned."

"Cassius Thornton Reed," Noble ground out.

"And where is this man? I admit I was slightly
nonplused when I heard that some chap had sent
Trees-Too-High and Crooked Hand away, but then
I didn't know Noble was with you, too, Venice.
Thought the Reed chappie might be something of
an opportunist."

"Oh, he is that," Venice said tightly.

"Eh?"

"It's a long story, dear." Venice smiled wanly
and touched her uncle's cheek. "So, you aren't a
welcoming committee but rather a search party."

"Well, when you didn't arrive and didn't arrive,
I thought it best we have a look see." Milton's

canny gaze, so similar to Trevor's in its intelligence, passed over Venice and rested on Noble. "Of course, as I've said, had I known you were safely with Noble, I wouldn't have bothered leaving the excavation site at all!"

"Safely with Noble!" Noble cursed loudly. Milton cheerfully disregarded his outburst and stood back, gripping Venice's shoulder and studying her up and down. He took in her bloodstained shirt, dirty jacket, and tangled hair, then Noble's bare chest, strapped ribs, and plastered cuts.

"How glad I am to see," he finally said with absolute sincerity, "that everything is just fine."

" . . . a magnificent discovery! Nothing like this has ever seen the light of day. You will be spellbound, Venice. Spellbound." Milton paused in the middle of his excited recitation, dabbing at a small piece of the omelet aux herbes that clung to the corner of his mouth.

Templeton, Milton's long-suffering valet, scurried over and placed a plate of delicate lemon meringues in front of Venice. "And would madame care for more tea?"

"No, thank you, Templeton," Venice said in her grandest tones, hoping to impress upon Noble how sophisticated she was.

She should have known he'd propose marriage. While she did not doubt that he loved her, she doubted even less that his proposal came from his lifelong drive to protect her, even from the consequences of her own foolish heart . . . and body.

Noble was simply "doing the right thing" and it was up to her to make him see that she was a worldly, sophisticated woman who didn't require wedlock from her sexual partners.

She stole a look at him. He was shoveling paté and watercress sandwiches into his mouth.

Carter Makepeace, Milton's companion and colleague, made vague motions with his fork at the desserts. "May I?"

Caught dipping her hands into a crystal finger bowl, Venice hastily wiped her fingers dry on her linen napkin before passing the silver platter to Carter. With a look of satisfaction, he slid three of the airy pastries onto his china plate.

She still had a hard time believing she was in the middle of the wilderness eating a meal worthy of the Savoy. A scant six hours after Milton had ridden into their campsite, he'd had Noble and her packed, escorted them to the excavation site, and settled them down to lunch.

They were sitting beneath a pennant-topped, open-sided tent. The sweet, rain-washed breeze ruffled the skirts of the Irish linen tablecloth and the lazy drone of bees provided a lulling musical backdrop to their conversation.

It was relaxing, sumptuous, as exotic as any Indian bazaar or African safari. Except Venice wasn't enjoying it. She couldn't enjoy anything with Noble McCaneaghy's hard amber eyes watching her from across the table.

" . . . I can hardly wait to show you," Milton was saying, spooning sugar into his teacup.

Carter bobbed his head vigorously in agreement. "Shan't see the like of it again should I live to be a hundred."

Venice forced herself to smile at the two older men as they sat grinning at each other.

"Where is it?" Noble asked, sounding only vaguely interested as he folded his napkin.

"In a narrow chasm," Carter said.

Milton nodded. "When we scouted here a few years ago it was no more than a crack a few inches wide. I hypothesize that each spring it has filled with water. And each winter the water has frozen and the resultant ice expanded, acting as a wedge, forcing the rock apart. Over the past few seasons, the crack has grown into a good-sized fissure."

"And the ancient sediment it cleaves," Carter said portentously, "has held our find trapped in a rocky crypt. Until now."

"That's quite a theory," said Noble.

"Thank you," said Milton before continuing in a soft, dreamy voice. "Now it waits, entombed in ice and rock, on the threshold of breaking free from the very earth that has shielded it for countless generations."

"What is it?" Noble asked, settling back and balancing on the back two legs of his chair. He shot Venice another glance, *another* one filled with dark promise.

Milton blinked, clapping his hand against his thigh. "Don't know," he said. "Certainly it is some type of prehistoric creature."

"An ancient animal?" Venice asked, her interest finally awakening. *A fossil that could grant Salvage a reprieve from the closing of the spur line?*

"Is it remarkable enough to warrant a long-term investigation? Do you think Father will agree to further funding?" Venice asked.

Milton furrowed his brow. "Oh, I don't doubt that. As for that financing coming from the Leiland Foundation ... we'll just have to see what they're willing to offer."

Carter popped another meringue in his mouth. "They shall have to be very, very generous."

"Why's that?" Noble asked, the front legs of his chair coming to earth with a thump.

"I expect we shall have half a dozen societies and foundations scurrying about begging to give us financial backing," Milton said.

Noble shook his head. "Trev ain't gonna like that kinda attitude in you, boy!" His beautifully molded lips were set in a tight line.

Venice tensed, reading his bitterness. How could he want *anything* to do with his enemy's daughter, anything to do with the man who'd offered him to the Union Army as cannon fodder?

Lord, Noble had even saved Cassius's miserable life. "Heroic" was just part and parcel of the man, as instinctive for him as breathing!

With a little start, Venice realized she had been staring at him. He was returning her regard steadily, watching her as the murmur of academic conversation flowed back and forth between Milton and Carter.

"I always thought you two got on rather well," Milton said, his words shocking Venice from her private absorption. "And yet, ever since we've been here, you two haven't traded a word."

"What?" Venice blushed.

"You and Noble," Milton said insistently. "You used to trail after him like a puppy when he lived with you at the Park Avenue address. Poor lad, couldn't turn around without running into you."

"Yeah." With a determined movement, Noble pushed his chair back from the table and stood up. "That brings up something I've been meaning to tell you, Milton. Venice and I have a little announcement—"

She bolted to her feet, upending her own chair.

"Yes! We . . . we are—" she gulped. She couldn't let him do this. He was scowling at her fiercely.

"Yes?" Carter asked with interest.

"We are delighted you've found something that can insure the future of Salvage," Venice said.

Milton and Carter traded confused looks and Noble made a sound of disgust.

"Of all the ridicul—" he started to say.

"Ridiculous?" she asked icily.

"Did you two have a fight?"

"I don't know what you are talking about," Venice said, trying to escape the conversation.

"Yes, you do," Milton insisted. "It used to be 'Slats this' and 'Slats that,' 'I have to find Slats,' and 'Slats says.' I remember feeling quite jealous when I visited. I was used to being the center of attention and then suddenly this young lad appeared and quite stole your affection away." Milton smiled.

"I don't remember," Venice murmured faintly. *How well she remembered.*

"Certainly, you do," Milton said.

"You must," Carter seconded.

"*You* weren't there!" Immediately, she was embarrassed by her rudeness to Carter. He, however, didn't seem to mind.

"I heard all about it," he said, nodding sagely. "Feel quite a member of the family. Milton's told me everything. *Everything*. And really, Miss Venice, you do remember. Whyever would you say you don't?"

"Maybe she did follow me about," Noble broke in. "I was handy enough for a time. Then she got interested in other things. Probably bugs." The grin he flashed didn't reach his eyes. "End of story. There's no reason on God's green earth why Trevor's daughter should remember much about a brat from belowstairs."

A muscle balled in his lean, hard jaw. His gaze was fixed and flat. Venice doubted whether anyone other than herself saw the dull, red flush on the bronzed skin of his strong throat.

Lord, he must be very hurt to say something like this.

She'd never meant to hurt him.

"Noble," Milton said kindly, "I think you underestimate your place in Venice's heart."

"Do I?" He stared at her, waiting for her reply.

She took a deep breath. "Enough of this trip down memory lane," she said faintly. "Let's get on with it. Sooner done, sooner over."

"On with what?" Carter asked.

"Let's examine your find, gentlemen," she said, forcing a businesslike tone. "There are people in Salvage whose livelihoods may well depend on it."

Milton frowned. "But, my dear, you can't examine it. It's impossible."

"But why not? Why is it impossible?"

Milton rose from the table. "It's rather difficult to explain. I'd better take you there and show you. With one look you'll understand."

Chapter 21

"That* is why you can't make a hands-on examination, Venice," Milton said, pointing. "The logistics, m'dear, preclude it."

They were looking into a fissure located on a flat shelf of land near the foot of an enormous rock wall. The thirty-foot-long chasm was ten feet across at its widest point, a few feet across at either end. Even in the warmth of midday cold air rose from the deep gash, chilling them.

Noble watched Venice pace the perimeter of the chasm, staying as far away from him as possible.

It would have been amusing, if it weren't so damn exasperating. She was as determined that they would not spend a moment alone as he was determined that they would. And she absolutely refused to be drawn into anything resembling a conversation.

By the end of the disastrous lunch, Milton had been reduced to muttering calming platitudes as he tried to diffuse some of the tension between them. He'd impatiently waved away Templeton's suggestion of tea, and had managed to get them all over here. Now Venice was flitting about, trying to avoid making eye contact with him. Fine. There would be plenty of contact later, if he had his way. He could afford to grant her a few hours reprieve.

It just wasn't fair, he thought ruefully. He had

been sincere in his attempt to do right by Venice. He'd fought the good fight and lost—okay, *won*—and now, damn it, he wanted his just desserts! He wanted Venice!

It had never occurred to him that she might say no because—if he understood her anguished, odd, and perfectly ridiculous explanation—she *loved* him too much!

At least she loved him. He let his breath out in a harsh hiss. He'd bide his time.

Seeing Venice's eyes widen as she looked into the chasm, Noble craned his neck over the edge. Fifteen feet down from the opening, the chasm was filled with dark, cloudy ice.

Carter uncoiled the length of rope he had brought with him and tied one end to a sturdy ship's lantern.

"Imagine the problems proper excavation will entail," Milton said, as Carter lit the wick and snapped the brass top down.

"Will people be able to see it displayed in situ?" Venice asked.

"No. Far too dangerous. It will take years to excavate this properly," Milton said.

The prospect, Noble noticed, didn't seem in the least discouraging to either of the older men. They fairly twinkled with satisfaction.

Carefully, Carter lowered the lantern into the darkness. The flame cast a spectral glow, shimmering off the icy surface below. Coming around from the other side, Venice edged closer to where Noble stood, her curiosity apparently overcoming her aversion to him. Flopping onto her stomach, she leaned well into the opening, trying to get a better look.

Without a word, Noble took the few steps to her side and knelt, grabbing her belt in a tight grip.

He'd bet she didn't even notice someone was holding onto her, she was so intent on the view.

The bobbing lantern finally settled on the glassy surface. All Noble could see was a gleaming darkness streaked with gray marbling.

"More to the left," Milton suggested.

Carter nodded and, hopping over the narrowest point of the rift, gingerly slid the lantern over the ice.

Venice gasped. Instinctively, Noble's hand tightened, pulling her back from the edge. She scrambled even farther into the draw. Scooting forward on his knees, Noble looked, interested in seeing for himself what held her so absorbed.

He jerked back, startled, and then immediately spread himself flat, next to Venice.

A huge—jawbone? snout?—tilted up toward them, emerging from the side of the fissure as though pushing through the very rock in an attempt to free itself. It floated eerily behind the cloudy darkness of its icy tomb. The lantern cast a glinting light off something that could only be a fang, a sharp angling curve some four inches in length.

"Can we get down in there?" Venice asked in an awed whisper. Noble scrambled back to his knees beside her, still holding tightly to her belt.

"We have," Milton answered slowly.

"Can we go in now?" Venice asked, her upper body wiggling still farther into the fissure.

Without a word, Noble straddled her thighs, guaranteeing she couldn't accidentally upend herself and plunge headfirst into the chasm. Again, she didn't appear to notice.

"I don't think that would be a wise idea, Venice," Carter said.

"Why?" Her voice bounced off the ice surface below her.

"It's unstable. We were hoping to extract the entire block as a piece but that will be impossible."

"Damn," muttered Venice.

"Our initial attempts at building a working platform have been unsuccessful. The surrounding rock is too brittle. All we've managed to do is mine a half ton of granite." Milton pointed at a heap of rocks piled nearby.

Venice turned at the waist, frowning, her hair hanging forward over her face. Impatiently, she caught the rippling length with one hand and held it out of her eyes. She looked subdued but still determined. "This is wonderful, Uncle Milton. Truly extraordinary."

"I know." Milton clasped his hands together, rocking back and forth on the balls of his feet, his eyes glowing like a zealot's. "When we finally disinter it, think, Venice! When we can bring it out, what an accomplishment! Every museum in the country—nay, the world—will be begging for a chance to display it."

Venice was silent. Noble could almost see her quick mind studying, with lightning speed, the possible uses of Milton's find.

"Venice is trying to figure if she can build a museum right in Salvage," Noble drawled.

She started at his voice and began to clamber back, but, since Noble was still sitting on the back of her legs, it was impossible. She twisted around to see what was holding her and her eyes settled on him with undisguised horror.

Noble ginned. Welcome back, he thought.

"Get off me!"

"Sure thing." He swung his leg over her and rose, lifting her by the back of the belt as he stood up. For a few seconds, she dangled helplessly, arms wheeling frantically, legs trying ineffectively to kick his shins. Then he had her well clear of the edge. He lifted her to chest level, hooked an arm around her waist, and lightly set her on her feet.

Angrily, she swatted his arm from around her waist. Immediately, he dropped it and she stumbled away from him.

He followed her. Each step she made in retreat, he mirrored with an advancing one.

Her slender back was stiff, her chin held at an imperious angle.

"I want to find some way for Salvage to survive. If that means building a museum there, so be it. Period."

"Are you sure you don't want to find something that'll stonewall the Yellowstone Park bill so your daddy has time to rally the troops for the expansionist cause?" Noble asked sarcastically.

"I didn't even know about your bloody bill. My concern is Salvage."

Noble snorted. "Honey, saving one lice-plagued, no-account town in the middle of nowhere isn't going to impress Trevor Leiland. No returns: political, economic, or personal. Salvage can't afford to erect a monument to Trev."

Her teeth clicked together. "Have you ever considered the possibility that I am doing this for me?"

"No."

"And why not?"

"Because you're already determined to build the rest of your life, *our* lives, around what Trevor wants. Why should this be any different?"

She was oblivious to their gape-mouthed audience. Her dirty, nail-torn hands clenched into fists at her side.

"I have already explained that."

"You haven't explained anything. Not to my satisfaction."

"Ahem."

"I hadn't realized *your* satisfaction was the only one that mattered."

"If you weren't such a spoiled—"

"Ahem!"

Both Noble and Venice wheeled around, glaring at Milton. Immediately, Venice blushed when she saw the rapt expression of interest on Carter's round face.

"Noble and I, we, ah, we disagree on a, ah, certain matter," she mumbled.

"So it would appear," Milton said, wide-eyed.

"I'm sorry we subjected you to that unfortunate scene. It won't happen again."

"Ha!" Noble said.

Without another word, she broke off the contest of wills, sidestepping over to her uncle. Snatching up one of the chunks of rock, she angrily bounced it in the air, catching it and gripping it so tightly that her knuckles showed white against the dark surface. Noble had the uneasy suspicion that only a supreme act of will kept her from hurling it at him.

"What do you suggest we do next?" she asked Milton.

"About?" If Milton's brows rose any higher, they'd disappear under his hairline.

"About the creature there!" Noble wouldn't have thought it would be possible for Venice to turn a more brilliant scarlet. He was wrong.

"Oh! The creature!"

"Of course!" Carter nodded vigorously.

"Well," said Milton, "first we need to find some reliable workmen. Salvage is populated with many skilled miners who have been out of work since the gold mines played out. That shouldn't pose too much of a problem. Then we have to send east for equipment. I'd like to get Eddings from the Smithsonian involved, too. Perhaps Cartucci."

"Definitely, Cartucci. Man's a genius," Carter said.

"When do you propose to start?" Noble asked.

"Tomorrow," Milton said firmly. "Since Trees-Too-High and Crooked Hand have gone, I was hoping you would guide us to Salvage, Noble. These spring floods have washed out all the trails that I am familiar with, and I don't want to waste time getting turned about."

"Tomorrow?" Venice and Noble asked in unison.

"Milton, really!" Carter said. "We are being incredibly selfish. Your niece and Mr. McCaneaghy have just endured an arduous, dangerous journey up the mountains. We should let them rest."

"Oh. Of course." Milton tapped his nose, obviously not happy at the delay but just as obviously flustered by his thoughtlessness. "Unforgivable of me. Perhaps in a few days?"

"We can go tomorrow," Noble drawled laconically. "Makes no never mind to me."

"Spare us more of your salt-of-the-earth cant," Venice said. "You're in no shape to make a trip back out of the mountains. You'll stay here. I can find our way well enough."

"Don't be a fool," Noble heard himself say and winced. Oh, she was going to *love* that.

"I am *not* a fool. I am a seasoned traveler! You yourself commended me on how competent I am."

"You are competent. But competent ain't gonna cut it."

"I hate it when you refuse to use proper English." She delivered the non sequitur through stiff lips. "And why won't competent cut it?"

"I *ain't* a proper *kinda feller*. And the reason why you can't go alone is simple: you don't know these mountains. You don't know which draws are most likely to wash out, what areas are safest to camp in, whether a pass will be open or closed, if a mountain could come tumbling down on your head in an avalanche of snow. And *you* don't have a *map!*"

She strode up to him, planting her hands on her hips. "Maybe I haven't made myself clear, Mr. Mc-Caneaghy. I don't need you."

"No, you made that real clear," he growled. "But, honey, you got me!"

She actually stomped one scufffy, booted foot, she was so angry.

"Even if you don't have a care for your own lovely neck, me darlin'," Noble continued in a thick Irish accent, "there's the question of a few more people you should be concerning yerself with. Like yer uncle, Mr. Makepeace, and Templeton over there. Would you be willing to risk them for the sake of your own wrongheaded pride?"

Her fine, dark brows drew together in consternation. "Of course not," she murmured. "I never meant to put anyone in danger. I guess we'll all go, then."

Defeated in her attempt to rid herself of his company, she turned the rock she held over in her hand, rubbing the sharp ridges along her thumb, studying it pensively, before dropping it into the cold, dark hole yawning at her feet.

Venice succeeded in avoiding Noble for the rest of the day. It was for the best, she thought again miserably as she fetched a tape measure. He'd get over his hurt. Just as she'd get over hers.

She *had* to believe that.

Above all else she had to believe that she'd get over Noble McCaneaghy. If just one night in his arms, loving and being loved by him, could result in this much pain, just think of what a year or two or even three years of sharing his life and then having to watch him leave would do.

She blinked back threatening tears and made her way to the crevice. She had some measurements to take.

With that thought, she staked one end of the tape measure and started pacing the length of the gash. At the sound of running feet, her head snapped up. Noble. He saw her at the same moment and skidded to a stop. For a second he just stared at her, his face tight and angry.

It dawned on her. He'd been running to see that she was *safe*. And he wasn't in the least happy about it.

The thought made her smile. "You can go back, Noble," she said. "I'm fine."

"Yeah." He didn't leave. His expression became one of patent self-disgust as he rounded the end of the crevice, walked over to the rock wall, and settled his shoulders against it.

"Over the past decade, I have managed to take care of myself very well without you," she said tartly.

He didn't answer, just plucked a blade of tall grass, shoved it in his mouth, and began gnawing on it as though it was a nail.

She shrugged. Let him suit himself. She had work to do. Carefully, she took measurements of the rift; length, various widths, the depth to the ice floe surface. She was nearly finished when she heard Noble ask, "Why are you doing that?"

She glanced in his direction. He hadn't moved but he'd spat the mangled grass from his mouth and the anger had faded from his expression, leaving curiosity in its stead.

"I'm taking these measurements to give to an engineer."

"I don't think Milt's going to like you handing this project over to any other paleontologist."

"Oh, I'm not going to. This is for a viewing platform."

He lifted a dark brow questioningly.

"If we could erect a viewing platform that could be used while the crews actually work on the excavation, it might be quite a tourist draw."

"Think so?"

"Hey, if people are willing to drive out of their way to see the site where Wingo Clemens indulged in his disgusting dining practices, just think of how they would flock to see a real dinosaur!"

"I have to admit, I've thought the same thing myself."

"You have?"

He nodded and came toward her. "Sure. The National Park bill is dependent on tourism, the idea that this land—and everything it holds—has an intrinsic value for everyone, not just the few who can pry some gold from it."

They smiled at each other in unexpected accord.

"That," she said, "along with the experts who will surely be sent by the various geologic societies, will all but assure Salvage's future."

"I didn't hear you mention the foundation," Noble said.

She looked up from the numbers she was scribbling on a folded piece of paper. "Well, the Leiland Foundation might not be the best backer for this enterprise."

"You mean you might actually be able to do something without the blessing of the Leiland Foundation?" he asked mockingly.

So much for their accord, she thought. "You don't have to be so mean."

"I'm not trying to be mean. I'm trying to make you cut the apron strings, Venice!"

"Apron strings! Just because I take my responsibilities seriously! Just because I won't throw everything over for the pleasure of a few nights in your arms—"

"A few nights! Lady, I'm asking you to marry me!"

Marriage? What was marriage? Vows made to be broken. She went on as though he hadn't spoken. "Please understand, Noble. If I try very hard, and work even harder, I might eventually have a vote on the Leiland Foundation board. I'll have a chance to do something good, something real."

"Bull," Noble spat. "You can do *good* and *real* things without a fortune or a board of trustees. You're just using the foundation as an excuse. What's the real reason you won't marry me, Venice?" he demanded furiously.

"What's the real reason you *want* to marry me, Noble?" she countered, just as angrily. "You didn't want to marry me at all until we'd made love!"

"Sh!" He looked around, his mouth tight.

"Why? Afraid someone might hear? That's why you want to marry me. Your conscience is telling you that we sinned. That's why you're proposing and nothing more!"

"That's not true."

"Convince me," she challenged him. "I didn't hear any suggestions about 'the rest of our lives' until *after* we made love. You're just trying to do the right thing, Noble. And that's the most wrong thing you can do."

"Venice," he said, "until the other night, I didn't know you loved me. I never dreamt that you could feel for me half of what I feel for you. Just the thought of you loving me nearly brings me to my knees in awe, it's that wondrous a gift."

His face was stark with the need to make her understand the extent of his love. "That's why I didn't ask you before. I was afraid to. I didn't think I stood a chance. But now I know you love me. I don't want to spend my life without you. I won't. And I won't let the foundation keep you from marrying me. *That* would be a sin."

His gaze was steady, his sincerity unquestionable.

If only she could believe the promise in his words.

She turned and fled.

Chapter 22

Crooked Hand and Trees-Too-High strode into Mil-Ton's camp and dumped the antelope carcass near the fire. There were only the two old men sitting there, Mil-Ton smoking a pipe, Carter reading from a little book.

Trees-Too-High's eyes flickered about the area, disappointment obvious in the thinning of his lips. Templeton—the little English valet it was so much fun to torment—was not in sight.

"Fare you well, Mil-Ton Leiland," Trees-Too-High said. "We bought you this meat as you paid us to do."

"Well, thank you—"

"Trees-Too-High! Crooked Hand!" a voice hailed them. Noble McCaneaghy slipped from a stand of young fir, a brace of rabbits in his hand.

"Where is Templeton?" Trees-Too-High asked.

Crooked Hand scowled at him. He was being badly influenced by the ill manners of these whites.

"Templeton and Venice have gone to see if there are any berries around."

"This Venice is the same woman we led up here with the man with hair under his nose? The woman you watch so hungrily?"

"Venice is here, all right."

Crooked Hand could feel Trees-Too-High's interest awaken. As far as he, or any man of the Ute nation knew, white women were good for only one thing: harassing. Still, what with Templeton and a white woman ... the potential for amusement was increasing.

"We will stay," Crooked Hand said.

"Of course you must stay, my dear chaps," Mil-Ton said. "Remiss of me to keep you standing there. Might I get you something? A spot of tea?"

Crooked Hand managed to keep his expression sublime. Tea! He had drunk a shaman's stomach purge that had tasted better than tea!

"No," he said. "I will sit."

Trees-Too-High had just begun investigating the tents, starting with Templeton's, when the little man himself bellowed, *"Please!* Remove yourself from my tent, sir!"

Trees-Too-High straightened, his eyes dancing with delight. "Ah, Templeton, my friend!" he shouted, approaching the stocky figure. The slight, black-haired woman trailed behind.

Templeton snatched the silk cravat that Trees-Too-High was holding. "Kindly refrain from touching my personal belongings, sir."

Trees-Too-High clapped Templeton on the back. "We have brought food. Now, while the woman cooks it, we will tell each other stories."

"Miss Leiland will *not* cook," said Templeton, aghast.

Crooked Hand and Trees-Too-High exchanged bewildered looks and turned to consider Venice.

"We don't treat our women the same way your people do, Trees-Too-High," Mil-Ton said. "Miss Leiland has other things to do."

"What?"

"Miss Leiland is a philanthropist, a ... a scholar," Carter said.

"What is 'scholar'?"

"A wise woman," Mil-Ton said.

"You are a shaman?" Crooked Hand asked.

She looked up. Her eyes were as he remembered, the color of a wolf's pelt, soft and gray, ticked with silver.

"No," she said.

"What is this 'scholar'?"

"I have studied things at a university," she said, struggling for the right words. Crooked Hand could commiserate. English was so limiting. "Mostly old, old things. Things like books, even— like Uncle Mil-Ton—the earth. These things . . . tell me stories."

Ah! The Ute nation knew well that the earth told stories. But Crooked Hand had never heard any white people tell these stories. His mother had once said she suspected the whites' ears had been stopped for some grievous crime they had committed. It was thought-provoking to learn that this white woman heard the earth's tales.

The woman had piqued Trees-Too-High's interest, too. "Where is your man?" he asked suddenly. "The man with hair beneath his nose."

"My *man*?" Venice exclaimed. "Is that what that overweening, self-deluding, paean to male vanity implied?"

"What does she mean?" Crooked Hand demanded.

"She says she's not married to Reed," McCaneaghy said.

Crooked Hand nodded. It was as he suspected. "This Reed tried to steal her from you, yes?" he asked McCaneaghy.

"I'm not *his* to steal *from!*" Venice said fiercely, pointing at Noble. "I am not married. Nor will I be married!"

"Why not?" Crooked Hand turned to McCaneaghy, repeating the question in the mother tongue.

"She is having no man who cannot . . . bring ponies to her father." Crooked Hand wished McCaneaghy would not insist on speaking in the tongue. He hadn't any idea what McCaneaghy meant with his babbling about ponies.

"You want her," Crooked Hand said.

"More than the breath of my enemies." That, at least, was succinct enough, Crooked Hand thought.

Even Trees-Too-High looked impressed.

"What did you say?" asked the woman.

"I said you were too nasty-tempered to take on." Noble grinned. The woman almost answered his smile with her own. Crooked Hand could see it forming on her lips. He turned. There were better things to do than watch McCaneaghy and this woman.

"Templeton!" Crooked Hand hailed the little man who was darting about on the fringes of the camp.

"Sir?" Templeton said.

"I have new stories for you."

"Really, sir, don't put yourself out on my account."

"I am not out, Templeton," Crooked Hand said. "You like."

"I don't really care to—"

"I'd like to hear the stories," the white woman said.

Crooked Hand stopped where he was. His back was to her. Every man in the camp could see his eyes gleaming with anticipation. Smiling broadly, he swung around and strode back to Venice.

"Sit." He pointed to the ground.

Carter covered his face with his hands. Mil-Ton sputtered worriedly and Templeton went rigid with shock. McCaneaghy, on the other hand, sat down, propped his back against a nearby tree,

crossed his long arms behind his head, and
stretched out his legs in an attitude of utter relax-
ation. He was smiling.

"Really, Trees-Too-High," Mil-Ton said. "I don't—"

"It's all right, Uncle Mil-Ton." Venice waved
away his protest. "I'm sure I've heard—or read—
worse."

"Don't be at all sure of that, Miss Venice,"
warned Templeton, edging his way backward out
of camp. "I think I'll see if . . ." He disappeared.

Venice slid gracefully to the ground, crossing
her legs and looking expectantly at Crooked
Hand. With a shrug, he sat down across from her.
This wasn't going to be nearly as much fun as
baiting little Templeton. It was a well-known fact
that white women didn't have a shred of humor.
She would be scared away before he'd finished his
first sentence.

"This story is about old Bear, who was very
proud because his member was the longest of any
animal's in the forest . . ."

Mil-Ton and Carter choked. McCaneaghy laughed
and Trees-Too-High smiled. The white woman did
not respond for a minute. She scowled.

"Did I hear you right?" she demanded.

Crooked Hand nodded happily.

"I thought so," she said. "Forgive my interrup-
tion. I had always heard this story with *Coyote* as
the animal with the longest member," she said.
She leaned back on her elbows. "Do go on."

". . . she rode that bull until he shriveled up and
vanished!" Venice finished with a flourish of hand
movements.

Noble wiped the tears from his cheeks, struggling for breath. The inimitable and impassive
Trees-Too-High had given up his composure about
half an hour ago and was slapping his thighs right

alongside Crooked Hand. Venice beamed with delight, her laughter rippling through her words.

She'd even forgotten her anger at Noble long enough to wink at him. It was hard for Noble not to jump up there and kiss the saucy lass.

Gray eyes sparkling, Venice had regaled the two Utes with every bawdy piece of Greek mythology Noble had ever heard. After her store of those had been depleted, she'd switched to German and Celtic fables and then to Egyptian tales.

There was no doubt about it, Venice Leiland had a way with a dirty story.

Carter and Milton had stopped looking as if their eyes were going to pop out of their heads, even relaxing enough to add a few embellishments of their own. Only Templeton, having returned from "berry hunting," had continued to look as if he was sucking a lemon.

"Wherever did you hear such, er . . . colorful tales, Miss Leiland?" Carter asked.

She dimpled. "At Uncle Milton's knee." Milton immediately blazed with color and started making sputtering sounds of protest. "Rather," she hurried on, a gleam of devilment in her eye, "at his camp. He used to send me to bed just after dinner. But I would lie awake and listen to his crew trade stories. The local workmen were invariably inventive."

"Well, I never—" Milton said.

"This woman might have some value after all," Trees-Too-High said to Noble. "She would be . . . entertaining during long winter nights," he continued slyly, punching Noble in the ribs. He winced.

"Ribs broken up pretty bad?" asked Crooked Hand.

"Nah, they're okay," Noble replied.

"Look like a pretty good ride you take down the

river. Surprised you are not dead," Crooked Hand said.

"You saw it?" Noble asked.

"Yes. We were at top of—what is this?—cliff? Saw that Reed kick until you fell."

"What?" Venice said, her eyes riveted on Crooked Hand. "Cassius *deliberately* kicked Noble loose?"

Crooked Hand nodded. "Yup. Kicked until Mc-Caneaghy fell. We watched McCaneaghy try to swim to shore until we saw he got hung up on that bunch of logs."

"Why didn't you help him?" Venice asked.

Crooked Hand shrugged. "Had things to do. We come back later, but he's already gone. McCaneaghy's tough . . . for a white man. Lived through that knife fight with that loco man."

"Even the bear didn't kill him," Trees-Too-High added casually.

"The bear? Knife fight?!"

Ah, shit, thought Noble.

"There was this loco white man. He was a wound in the Shining Mountains. It is good McCaneaghy killed him."

"What?!"

"Now listen, I didn't *kill* anyone, he fell on his knife—" protested Noble.

Venice rounded on him, eyes flashing. "*You* be quiet. Crooked Hand, what happened? Tell me the story."

Happily, Crooked Hand obliged. "The loco man was a long time here. Like a outlaw wolf that feeds off the dead of his own kind, the loco man tracks in the mountain. Only whites, though. He was loco but not stupid.

"He was made sick by wanting gold. He sees McCaneaghy and thinks McCaneaghy's bags hold the yellow rock. He attacks him at night. They fight. Noble gets cut up pretty bad. The loco man dies."

Venice's eyes had darkened to the color of tarnished steel.

"Gee, thanks for relating that, Trees-Too-High," Noble said, knowing his sarcasm was pointless.

"And the bear?" Venice asked.

"The bear was McCaneaghy's own damn fault." Trees-Too-High shrugged. "He should have seen tracks. Lucky for him she was an old sow. Still plenty of teeth though, eh, McCaneaghy?" He grinned at Noble as though the whole thing was an enormous joke.

"Do you get some sort of titillation from courting death?" Venice demanded, rounding on Noble. "Running around getting knifed, bit, clawed, falling into raging torrents, and . . . and . . ."

She loved him. It couldn't be clearer. And come hell or high water, he was going to convince her that they belonged together.

"Don't you have anything to say?" she demanded, her booted foot tapping the ground.

"Yeah." Noble bent over and blew the soft, raven hair from her temples. "You better stick around and make sure I don't get into any more trouble."

Her lips pressed together in a tight line. "Aha," she said after a few seconds, "I see. Blackmail."

"Huh?" Noble, Mil-Ton, and Carter asked in unison.

"*Blackmail.* If I don't"—she flashed a quick glance at the other men—"if I don't do what you want me to do, you'll put your life at risk."

"What a gift you have for words, Venice!" Noble shouted, his face burning. He jumped up and stood over her. "Just how do you think that sounds to Milton and Carter? 'If I don't do what you want . . .'!"

"Ahem." Milton cleared his throat, casting a grave look in Noble's direction. "Just what *does* Noble want you to do, Venice?"

"Oh!" Venice said, color flooding her throat and cheeks. "Not *that!*"

"Not *what?*" Carter asked in confusion. Trees-Too-High and Crooked Hand looked bored.

"Tell them, Venice," Noble urged in low, melo-dramatic accents. "Tell them about the dark and unnatural thing I'm asking you to do."

"*You* are pathetic."

"You don't have to tell me. I'm the one who wants a crazy woman to marry me!"

"Crazy?" Venice asked in a deadly calm voice.

"Marry?" asked Milton.

"Yes, *crazy*," Noble said. "Only a crazy woman would think I was trying to blackmail her into marriage. Of all the fool, self-absorbed ... Believe it or not, Venice, I like my hide whole. And you'll agree to marry me without blackmail!"

"I wouldn't hold my breath!"

"*Marry?*" Milton asked again.

"This isn't any of your business, Milt," Noble said. "No offense intended."

"None taken."

Templeton appeared from the woods with a pail of berries in his hand, his face alight with the suc-cess of his hunt. "Would anyone like some cob-bler?"

"I would!" Venice sprang to her feet. She stomped over to Templeton and grabbed the bucket from his hand. "There should be *something* palatable around here!"

"You had an exemplary service record," Milton said the next day. He had appeared beside Noble as he started packing the mules for their trip down the mountain.

"So? And how would you know anything about that?" With a grunt, Noble jerked the leather straps tightly around his bedroll.

"Oh, I've been kept apprised of your movements ever since you were drafted. I felt it was rather a family obligation," Milton returned easily.

On his knees beside his gear, Noble sat back on his heels and squinted up into Milton's tranquil face. "That why you looked me up when I first came out here? Family obligation?" Noble grunted. "Keeping track of the people Trevor used and discarded must amount to a full-time occupation."

"No. I looked you up because I remembered you as a bright, mature lad and I liked you."

That was the thing about Milton, Noble thought. He was as direct as Trevor was devious. "Why the devil are you standing here discussing my army record? I thought we were trying to break camp before noon."

"Oh, yes," Milton said vaguely. "Noon."

"How come you're not all in a lather to get to Salvage? I'd have thought Venice would have you and Carter mounted on ponies and trotting down the trail by now. She sure isn't going to like your wasting time chatting about the war when she wants to get away from me."

Milton gazed thoughtfully at him. "Answer me this, Noble: do you love Venice?"

Hell! How'd he get drawn into this?

"Yeah," he snapped. "I love her."

"Then why are you both so miserable?"

"Listen, Milt," Noble said, "I asked her to marry me. But when it came to a choice between her father and me, Daddy won and I lost. That's all there is to it." There, he'd said it and it hurt like hell.

"I can't believe Venice chose Trevor over you.

It's been a long time since she was his adoring little girl."

"Yeah, then why is it still so damn important for her to win Trevor's respect?"

"She *needs* Trevor's respect if she's ever to have any say in the administration of the Leiland Foundation."

Noble sighed, releasing some of the hostility that had been building all day. He suddenly felt old and defeated. Tiredly he draped an arm across the mule's back. "You know, Milt," he said, "it isn't doing a whole lot for my pride to have you tell me that my rival for Venice's affection isn't her father, but a foundation. Wanta tell me why that damn foundation is so important to her?"

"Venice sees the foundation as the only permanent thing of value in her life. But it's not only something she can be sure of, it's something that just might garner her, if not *affection*, at least the *regard* of the people she wants to help."

Noble scowled at Milton.

"Oh, I know it sounds absurd and I'm sure Venice would be aghast to learn that I'd ever suggested such a thing to you. But I've thought about it, Noble. And I believe it's true."

Milton leaned forward, his elbows on his knees, his hands clasped tightly together. "Ever since she was a little girl, she's held the gift of her love out for anyone, *anyone* to accept. And each and every time, the people she loved left her. The nurses, the governesses, the maids. Me. You. Her parents. Is it any wonder she wants something permanent in her life? Something that has always been there and always will be there? Something she can devote herself to without fear of being abandoned?"

"Come on, Milton. Her father was there."

"Trevor might have been there in body, but not in any meaningful way."

"Why?" Noble asked.

Milton shook his head. "Everytime he looks at Venice, I imagine he sees Juliette. Venice's mother."

"He loved her that much?" Noble asked, certain that if her mother had been so like Venice, he must have loved her greatly. Still, that was no reason to make a little girl suffer.

"Trevor hated Juliette. That's why he divorced her."

"What?" Noble straightened and looked down at the older man in disbelief. "I thought Venice's mother was dead. That she died when Venice was a baby."

"That's what everyone was supposed to think. That's what Trevor made Venice tell everyone."

"Why?"

"A man of Trevor's rank? With his position in society to consider? *Divorced?*" Milton asked with uncharacteristic bitterness. "Think of the stigma. If it were discovered that he was divorced, he would never be allowed in polite society again. His career would be ruined, his political future dashed. Society has only a few sacrosanct rules, Noble. Marriage unto death is one of them."

"Then Venice's mother is alive?"

Milton shook his head sadly. "Not anymore. She died when Venice was sixteen."

"Did Venice ever visit her?"

"No. Trevor refused to allow Juliette to see her daughter. After the divorce, Juliette returned to France, where Trevor first met her."

"How could a mother abandon her own child?" Noble demanded.

"Venice asked me that once," Milton said softly. "It surprised me. She was always so careful, even as a child, to keep her hurt to herself. In order to reveal herself like that, she must have been desperate for an answer."

"What did you tell her?"

"I told her the truth, that a divorced woman has no rights. None."

"She didn't *have* to get divorced," Noble protested.

"Trevor had made his mind up. Juliette was to be dispensed with and dispensed with she was."

Noble nodded. He had firsthand experience with Trevor's expedience. "But divorce," he said. "With all the potential for scandal, why would Trevor go to such lengths? Why not just send Venice's mother away? Buy her off?"

"Trevor did not want Juliette to have any legal hold on him or Venice whatsoever. He didn't want to run the risk that she might suddenly appear at some future point and disrupt his life."

"Could she do that?"

"No. And she wouldn't have even if she'd had the power. But Trevor sees in others what are really flaws in himself. He was sure that given the power, Juliette would try to destroy him."

"Why did he marry her in the first place?"

"Marrying Juliette was probably the only impulsive act Trevor ever took," Milton said flatly. "And even then, I suspect it wasn't all motivated by passion. I believe it was a gamble gone bad. Juliette was beautiful, you see. Every bit as beautiful as Venice. And quixotic and appealing. And poor."

"Poor?"

"Yes. Her family worked for one of the great vineyards in Champagne. Trevor met her on a wine-buying junket. I imagine he was enthralled by Juliette and I also imagine, having known Juliette, that she would have none of Trevor's propositions except one that involved a ring."

"But he *must* have loved her, to have proposed marriage."

Milton shrugged. "As much as Trevor can love,

perhaps. I think he saw Juliette as a valuable commodity, an exotic addition to his Park Avenue mansion. Someone the other men would covet and the drab New York City hostesses would emulate.

"It didn't work out that way. Juliette withered in the city. She was offended by the advances of Trevor's male friends and disapproved of by society matrons. She didn't have any notion of how to become a successful political hostess and, worse, she didn't want to. She loathed New York, Trevor's friends, and Trevor's way of life, and she made no secret of it."

Noble nodded. He could easily understand the fury such behavior would have incited in someone as proud as Trevor.

"Trevor divorced her within a year of her arrival here. He told everyone that she died while on holiday in Italy. I don't even think Venice knew her mother was alive until she was seven or eight. And by that time Trevor had worked on Venice's sense of loyalty to him to the point where he trusted her not to reveal his secret."

"She never even told me," Noble said.

"She wouldn't have seen it as her secret to share."

"But it was her mother!"

Milton didn't reply.

"How did Trevor explain the divorce to Venice?" Noble asked, though he thought he already knew.

"He told her that Juliette's background made her incapable of living in the city. That it had been a terrible, terrible mistake to try and mix their two worlds, but that neither of them should have had to spend the rest of their lives regretting their mutual error."

"That doesn't sound like Trevor."

Milton's mouth flattened into a hard line. "I told Trevor that if he told Venice anything different, I would make sure the world heard about his divorce."

Noble was quiet, replaying in his mind Venice's words to him the morning Milton had arrived. Clearly, she thought they were on the verge of repeating the same disastrous pattern as her parents. Milton's well-intentioned explanation of her parents' divorce had built a mountain of self-doubt and fear of being hurt between Venice and him.

But, hell, he scaled mountains for a living.

Milton was regarding Noble closely. "Venice loves you, Noble. Don't let her turn her back on love now, when she's finally so close to finding it."

"I got some courting to do," Noble said softly. "And I promise, nothing's going to make me give up trying . . . not even if it takes me the rest of my life."

Chapter 23

T hey weren't hurrying to Salvage, Venice thought, they were sauntering.

Somewhere, somehow, in the past twenty-four hours the impelling need for haste had been lost and their trip had become a tour.

They had strolled along the trail this morning. Carter had stopped to examine every bit of fauna. Milton had lagged behind to study some odd geologic structure, and Templeton had constantly dived into the underbrush after early spring berries. The Utes had disappeared and reappeared at odd moments, their expressions noncommittal. And Noble had decided to make camp after only four hours in the saddle."Why?" she demanded. "And why are we going so slowly?"

"Honey." He *tch*ed. "You have to make allowances for your uncle and Carter's advanced years. They aren't used to riding for any length of time.

Milton and Carter nodded owlishly.

"Besides," he continued, "who could be unhappy about spending a bit more time in such beautiful surroundings?"

When she didn't answer, he just shrugged in what she was sure was feigned apology.

She wasn't in a very appreciative mood at dinner, in spite of the delicious trout and wild greens Templeton somehow conjured. She retired soon after eating and spent the rest of the evening listening to the murmured conversation of the men.

The next morning, looking about the campsite, Venice had to agree with Noble. How could anyone want to hurry through *this?*

The mountain air was so clean and clear, it made her light-headed. The sun, beaming down benevolently, had swollen the tree buds until they had finally, overnight, burst open. Butterflies flitted like brilliant confetti strewn by a capricious hand.

Having risen early, Venice made coffee and went for a short walk around the campsite long before anyone else was stirring. She delighted in the rich, loamy smell of rain-scented earth, the early morning cacophony of migrating song birds, and the fresh, bright pigments of spring. With a sigh of regret at having to abandon her walk, she retraced her footsteps back to camp.

Coming around the corner of her tent, she stopped short. Noble stood a dozen feet away ... shaving. They'd been on the trail a scant day now and it seemed as if he had spent half of that time bare-chested.

Here he was again, *sans* shirt. He was standing sideways to her, peering into a square of polished tin he'd propped on one of the lower branches of a tree, lathering his face. The muscles on the back of his left arm and across his shoulder rippled smoothly beneath golden skin. A few white plaster strips still covered the cuts on his long, sleek body. The bandage she'd tied around his ribs hung loosely.

He had the widest shoulders, the flattest belly. All she could think about was how warm and alive and strong he had felt pressed naked against her. Even his spine was provocative: a shallow, muscle-flanked line that disappeared beneath the soft, worn denim of his pants. His long, thick hair, tied back in a single tail of streaked gold, lay between his shoulder blades.

As Venice watched, Noble plucked his razor from the branch. Opening the blade, he reached out and pulled tight a leather strip he'd tied waist level to the tree trunk. Carefully, he started stropping the blade.

She was mesmerized by the razor's hypnotic movement over the leather strap. He held the blade precisely, angling the sharp surface just so, smoothly pushing the razor away from him in a sensual, sweeping motion and then turning it over and gliding it back toward him.

As though he felt her watching him, Noble lifted his gaze without moving his head. His gaze locked with hers in the mirror. A knowing smile stretched the white lather on his face.

Lazily, he closed his eyes and Venice knew he was *feeling* her watch him. He looked like a big, half-tamed puma about to purr. Tilting his head back, he angled his chin high and she saw his eyes had opened again and he was studying her in the mirror.

Carefully, he laid the razor against his throat. Even from where she stood, Venice heard the rasp of the blade against his skin. A long, burnished line of smooth skin was exposed by the swath he shaved. His throat looked strong, supple, masculine.

Venice wet her lips with the tip of her tongue. Noble's eyes narrowed. Carefully, he wiped the razor clean on a towel hanging overhead.

"Honey," he drawled, "if you stand there watching me like that, you're likely to have my death on your conscience. 'Cause I surely will cut my throat, the way you're makin' my hand shake."

She couldn't help but laugh. She knew it wasn't

fair to encourage Noble, but she couldn't help being drawn into his game when he teased her like this. He was too appealing.

"Oh, I don't think you're in too grave a danger."

He straightened, placing his hand over his heart and swore, "You take my breath away. I can't think straight, talk straight—hell, Venice I can't even *walk* straight when you're around."

"Then it sounds as though I'd better ride well behind you or we'll end up back at the excavation sight," she retorted.

"Don't do that! I'd spend so much time swinging my head around just to get a glimpse of you that I'd probably lead us all straight off a cliff!"

"Humph."

"It'll be better for everyone if you just stay close to me . . . forever." He was still smiling, but his eyes shone with sincerity.

"Noble—"

"When are you gonna have pity on me and marry me?"

"I'm not." She left him before he could get his shirt on, hastening away from his seductive words.

Drat and blast the man! she thought. She should be concentrating on what ramifications Milton's find would have on Salvage. Salvage, she reminded herself sternly, where people were depending on her. She didn't have time to waste wishing for what couldn't be.

And why couldn't it be? an inner voice urged. Because she loved Noble far too much to marry him and end up as her parents had, hating and resenting each other.

Oh, he made it sound so easy. "Give up the foundation. Let others run it."

But she'd spent her life wanting to accomplish something worthwhile and as a member of the foundation's board, she'd be able to do just that.

She couldn't give that up; not for love. Love was too capricious. Time after time, example after example, it had been demonstrated to her that love didn't last.

Her father, her cousin, her social acquaintances, even Cayuse Katie—they all testified to the same thing: don't build your life around someone else; you'll only end up alone and embittered.

"Venice."

She tried darting away, but Noble caught her wrist in a gentle, unbreakable clasp, staying her. "Venice, don't run away." He put a hand on her other shoulder, turning her to face him.

He'd put on a clean shirt and the brilliant white cotton contrasted tantalizingly with his tanned skin. Immediately self-conscious, she started tucking in the loose tail of her own sweat-stained, grubby garment.

"I'm not running away," she said gruffly. Liar, she told herself.

"Good." He grinned. "Because there's something I want to show you." He paused a second, taking in her suspicious expression, and suddenly burst out laughing. "Nothing like that! I swear! My, you have a dirty mind, Venice Leiland."

Her cheeks and throat burned. "I don't know what you're talking about."

"Right," he said, still chuckling. "Though if you really want—"

"I don't!" she burst out.

"I thought you didn't know what I was talking about."

"I don't," she said haughtily. "But knowing you, I deduced what sort of lascivious suggestion *you* were likely to insinuate."

He leaned forward. "You're right. Where you're concerned, I'm capable of a whole book full of lascivious suggestions."

"I see."

"But not this time. I just found something I want to share with you." The teasing tone dropped from his voice and he held out his hand, so confidently that before she realized what she was doing, she took it.

"I don't suppose it would be a bathtub?" she asked wistfully.

"I'm afraid I can't help you there. Besides, you look beautiful."

"Sure," she said sardonically, holding back. "I'm a veritable wood nymph, one that's so covered in dirt she's about to send out shoots."

He laughed and pulled her forward. Delight lighting his handsome face, he led her by the hand up a narrow trail. They picked their way a quarter mile along the eastern face of the mountain until they came to a huge rock outcropping, rising hard against a stand of lodge pole pines.

"Wait here," Noble said. He walked under one of the taller trees and, grabbing hold of the lower branch, swung himself easily into the lower boughs. He climbed effortlessly to the top and, while Venice held her breath, leapt from the top of the tree to the top of the boulder.

"Was that necessary?" Venice shouted.

"No, but this way we save an hour of hard climbing," he returned, uncoiling the rope he'd looped over his arm. He dropped the end to her.

"Tie this around your waist and then lean back against the rope while—"

"While I walk up the side of the boulder and you pull," she said, doing as he'd told her and positioning herself at the base of the huge outcropping.

"You've done this before." He took up the slack.

"Twice before. I thought it was exhilarating."

"Then prepare to be exhilarated for a third time, Venice," he said, and started pulling her up.

It went smoothly. She scrambled up, hand over hand, leaning against the taut rope. In a few minutes she reached the top. Noble grabbed hold of her jacket collar and lifted her up beside him.

Together they stood on top of the boulder, grinning at each other and panting.

"Okay," she said, pleasure and excitement warring for precedence. "What next? Where do we go from here?"

Wordlessly, Noble placed his hands gently on her shoulders and turned her around.

Beneath them, a meadow was being born.

Amongst the black, charred remains of a burnt-out forest, green grass spread out like a bolt of the finest cloth. A delicate interweaving of tender, long grasses and mountain flowers rippled in a gentle breeze.

"It's fantastic," Venice murmured.

Noble nodded. "It always strikes me that way, too. It's nearly magic the way the earth reclaims what it loses."

"How long ago was the fire?"

"Three years."

"You're teasing me! It would all be burnt earth if the fire were that recent."

"I know it's hard to believe, but it's true. I was worried I wasn't going to make it out of this particular fire's path."

"You were here?"

"Not *right* here." He chuckled. "About two miles southeast. I saw the smoke. Let's go down there."

He lowered her down the side of the boulder and quickly descended after her. Upon reaching the ground, he once more took her hand and led her into the field. The thick grass cushioned their steps as they made their way amongst the oddly dignified spires of charred tree trunks that lent the meadow a cathedrallike quality.

"I feed as though I should whisper," she said.

"Me, too." He stopped and released her hand and pointed to a fluttering movement in a low bush. "It won't have this solemn atmosphere for much longer. Already the birds are back and from the amount of berries around I wouldn't be surprised if the bears were back, too."

"Bears?" Venice asked.

He reached for her, his brows arching wickedly. "Don't worry, Venice. I'll protect you from the big, bad bears."

"Ha," she said, swatting his hands away. "I'm not *worried* about the bears. I'm *interested*. I've never seen a grizzly bear. If I were worried about needing protection from anything, it would be from *you*."

He bent closer. "Wise woman," he said, his tone playful.

"Yeah? If I'm so wise, what am I doing out here with you?" The words were out before she could stop them.

Immediately, Noble became sober. "Because you love me and you want to be with me, just as I love you and want to be with you."

"Love isn't enough, Noble," she said sadly.

"Why? Because it wasn't enough for your father and mother?"

She stared at him, trying to discern whether there was aversion in his expression. She saw only compassion.

"Milton told you about their divorce," she guessed.

"Yes. But why didn't *you* tell me, Venice?"

"It wasn't for me to tell," she said simply. "And by the time you had come to live with us, I had all but convinced myself that my mother really was dead. And, too, I thought that you, being Catholic and all, would despise me if you knew my parents were divorced."

He shook his head. "Tell me about her, Venice."

"About my mother?"

"Why do you sound so surprised?"

"I don't know," she said truthfully. "I . . . I've never talked about her before."

"*Never?*"

"Only a few times with Uncle Milton. No one was allowed to mention her name. It became a habit I just sort of kept."

"What do you remember about her?"

"Nothing. No, don't look so skeptical. Really. She and my father were divorced when I was barely two." He looked so sad and concerned, she raked her memory for something to offer him. "I think she used to dance with me. I remember being spun around and around in circles and giggling."

"Go on."

"There's nothing more to go on about," she said uncomfortably. "I don't even recall what her voice was like."

"What about letters?"

"There were no letters," she said flatly. "I don't even know whether she could write."

"Oh, Venice surely—"

"I'm sorry, Noble. All I know about my mother came from Milton or the occasional comment from my father. Both were adamant about one thing—my father and mother should never have wed." Maybe she could make him understand. "Uncle Milton said they were like oil and water, that Juliette needed freedom like some people need air."

"And Trevor?"

"Father only said that if he had no affection left

for me, I should blame it on my mother since she destroyed his ability to love."

"And you believed him?" Noble asked incredulously.

Venice threw up her hands, exasperated by the same questions that had hounded her youth. "I don't know what to believe. I used to think that I'd see her one day," she went on in a wistful voice, "but after some years, I realized she wasn't coming back. And then, she died. Uncle Milton told me.

"He came to the house for Christmas one year. I was sixteen. One evening, when father was out, he took the opportunity to express his condolences. I hadn't any idea what he was talking about. He was so uncomfortable, so upset. Poor Uncle Milton. My mother, he explained, had died six months previously."

"Lord, Venice." Noble reached out and she stepped easily into his embrace.

"I sound so self-pitying," she said against his shirt. His arms were warm and strong, and she sighed deeply.

"No, you don't."

She looked up at him, a note of surprise in her voice. "I should have told you. It all seems rather silly now. You wouldn't have thought any the less of me, would you?"

"There are a lot of things that would seem silly if you gave them ample thought. Like your reasons for not marrying me."

"Please, Noble. I've just tried—" she stepped back.

" 'Please, Noble' what? 'Please, Noble, love me'? 'Please, Noble, spend your life with me'? I shall."

He curved a finger beneath her chin, pulling her face up to meet his gaze.

"Venice." He caressed her throat with the back

of his fingers, moving his knuckles lightly across her sensitive skin, his gentleness overpowering her where strength would have failed.

Angling his head, he brought his mouth close to her throat. She closed her eyes. She heard him inhale, deeply, felt the soft swoosh of his breath on her neck.

"Exotic and innocent, rare and familiar," he murmured. His lips grazed her throat. "Want me, Venice." It was a demand, a plea.

She looked up into his golden eyes. The dark fire smoldering in his eyes leapt to life, burning with pure desire. She recognized it easily. It was kindred to her own. His mouth was so near. Lord, she wanted to taste him again, to feel his lips moving over hers, to stroke his tongue with hers.

"Lord, how I dream of you touching me," he murmured. "Let me taste you, hold you."

She should close her ears to the siren images he wove, the erotic memory of their one night together, the memory that was always waiting just beneath the surface, catching her unawares, stunning her with the intensity of the desire it aroused.

"But it's not just the physical pleasuring, the heat and scent and dark velvet of your embrace. I want *you*, Venice. After the burning, after the physical need is satisfied. It's not just your body—though, God knows, just standing here breathing your scent, almost kissing you, swells me to the point of pain."

She had to make him stop. He was too seductive, too sure. And she was suddenly not sure. Not at all. And she'd thought she was so determined to refuse him.

Is this how her mother had felt? Knowing she was moving inexorably along a path toward heartbreak but unable to stop?

She was torn, part of her wanting him regardless of what the future offered, regardless of the terms. But part of her couldn't barter her heart any further. Part of her was terrified.

The terrified part won. She pulled away from him, her breath jumping in her throat, her heart hammering madly in her chest, and stared at the crushed grass beneath her feet.

"Take me back. Please. I want to go back."

"Venice—"

"Please, Noble. Do you want me to beg?" she asked. He must have heard the desperation in her voice.

"No, Venice. I never want you to plead with me for anything. Everything I have, I gladly give you. Everything I am is yours. I'll take you back, Venice. But I'm not going to give up. I'm never going to give up."

And with no further words spoken between them, he did.

Chapter 24

"Venice! Why don't you ride up here?" Noble called out. In answer, Venice, trailing fifty yards behind him on the narrow path, dropped back another ten feet.

Dammit, thought Noble. They were only a day or so out of Salvage and, though he'd paced their trip as slowly as possible, unless they crawled on their hands and knees, they would arrive before sundown the next day.

Despite what he'd told Venice, their snail's pace wasn't because of his saintly concern for the comfort of the two old scholars. Every day's unhurried, leisurely trek was for one reason alone: Noble wanted time. Time to court Venice and convince her that together they could overcome any obstacles. But time was running out and he was getting desperate.

"I know of a clearing just ahead. We'll camp there," he called to the others.

"You are getting to be an old woman, McCaneaghy," Trees-Too-High said, reining up alongside Noble. "There is many, many hours of sun left."

"Yup."

Disgusted, Trees-Too-High and Crooked Hand turned the pack mules they'd commandeered. "We go and see if the trout are spawning in the waters up ahead."

"Great," Noble said. "Don't let me slow you

321

down. Take your time. See ya later. And best watch out. I saw some bear scat a ways back."

Crooked Hand's expression spoke volumes about Noble's well-intentioned warning. "You are making a joke, yes?"

"Ah, yeah."

Noble looked over his shoulder to where Venice plodded along on her mule. Each day the mauve stains beneath her eyes looked a bit darker, she ate less, and she grew quieter.

And she wouldn't let him near her at all.

At the clearing where he planned to camp, Noble slipped from the saddle and went to help first Milton and then Carter dismount. By the time he was done, Templeton and Venice were already starting to set up camp.

Though the morning air had been so cold that he could see his breath, the afternoon sun beat down fiercely. Hefting the packs from the mules and then setting up the tents, Noble felt sweat trickle down his back. An evil notion tempted him. What the hell? he thought.

The only way he'd been able to tease any reaction from Venice at all was with the method he'd tumbled on the morning when she'd watched him shave.

Venice, Noble thought, *liked* his body and he was more than willing to shamelessly put it to use. Casually—well, he hoped it looked casual—he unbuttoned his shirt and yanked it off, tossing it over a granite rock. He felt her watching him.

Unfortunately, in tormenting Venice, he had to torture himself, too. It was enough to make a man go absolutely mad, knowing she was watching. She tried so hard to be nonchalant. Venice, who told the bawdiest stories without a hint of embarrassment, couldn't look at his naked chest without getting all breathy and agitated.

Within five minutes, she disappeared around the back of the tents. Worried she was heading into the woods—a disconcerting habit he'd discovered she had—and concerned about the bear sign, Noble followed.

He rounded the corner of her tent just as she came out.

He couldn't help his big, fat grin. She had donned a thick wool jacket over her corduroy shirt and union suit, as if sweating under three layers of cloth somehow made up for the fact that he was bare-chested. She did it every time Noble took his shirt off. It was fascinating phenomenon.

"You're going to catch a cold," Venice said.

"Darlin', it's hot out here under the sun. You're going to get overheated wrapped up in those heavy things. Here, let me help you out of that." He'd love the opportunity to take off each one of those layers, real slow.

He reached out to take her jacket from her shoulders and she darted back, her eyes gleaming. She was perspiring, the sheen of her pale skin reminding him of when they'd . . . God, in heaven. This was *worse* than torture.

"Listen, Venice," he said, dropping all kidding, "we *are* going to talk. You can keep running away, catch a train to New York, visit friends in Munich, sail for Egypt. But, I swear to God, I'll be one step behind you. There are some things you just can't stop, run from, or buy your way out of and I, lass, am one of them."

Surprisingly, Venice smiled. "You sound so threatening, Mr. McCaneaghy."

"Threatening? I feel threatening. Every time you call me 'Mr. McCaneaghy,' I want to wring your lovely little neck. I want to hear the names you called me when you lay beneath me, *cluricaune*."

"*Cluricaune.* You used to call me that all the time." Venice's hand fluttered to her throat.

"Past and present, Venice. They're bound up together so tightly you'll never be able to separate them."

"How very true," said Carter, rounding the corner of the tent. He paused, scowled into the bowl of the pipe he was carrying, and banged it against his open palm. He looked up at them, as though surprised to find them there. "That's what makes the past so fascinating to study."

Noble stared at the dapper little man.

"Was I interrupting something?" Carter asked, suddenly self-conscious.

"No," Venice said.

"Yes," Noble growled.

"No," Venice said more forcefully. She glared at Noble. "Now, what were you saying about the study of artifacts, Mr. Makepeace?"

"Oh." Carter popped the pipe into his mouth, biting the mouthpiece and making a sweeping gesture with his hands. "Not just artifacts, m'dear. Any study of the past is worthwhile. And necessary."

"Necessary?" Venice asked politely.

"Of course. The study of the past will ultimately be our salvation. Only by contemplating past errors can we hope to avoid future ones."

Venice shot Noble a telling look.

"We can't live our lives looking behind us," Noble said urgently.

"History," Carter said portentously, "repeats itself."

"So I've been told," Venice said. There was no triumph in her voice.

"Venice. He's talking about political events, not individual lives—"

"Indeed, I am," said Carter cheerfully. "Look

back in history and you'll see that the errors in judgment that plagued the ancients are the same ones to which modern man so often succumbs."

"Carter," Noble said. Carter looked over at him, all bright inquisitiveness. "Would you do us the kind favor of shut—"

"Noble!" Venice broke in, sounding terribly shocked and just a little amused. It was this last that gave Noble hope. She hadn't wanted to hear Carter's assertion any more than he did. And that meant that she wanted to believe in their future together.

"Carter! Venice! Noble!" Milton's voice echoed in the camp. "Come here! Quickly!"

"We have to see this," Milton said as he bustled about the campsite, collecting tape measures and calipers and folding spades. "Noble, please saddle mounts for yourself and Venice. I have already seen to mine and Carter's."

It was impossible for Venice to tell if he was excited or worried. He just sounded flustered.

"See what?" Noble asked, obligingly throwing a saddle on his pony.

"Trees-Too-High and Crooked Hand just told me there is another dig site being excavated!"

"What?" gasped Carter.

"That's right, old man." Milton paused in his packing and shook his head morosely. "And apparently it is the site of a *prehistoric being*."

"No!"

"Yes. They were quite clear on the matter. No more than a few hours down this trail, not half a day's ride out of Salvage itself, there are some men excavating."

"Crooked Hand actually saw this prehistoric being?" Noble asked suspiciously. Having finished saddling his pony, he'd thrown a saddle over Venice's mule and was tightening the cinch.

"No. Not quite. But he spoke to one of the townspeople who had and apparently it is quite a sight. It is being maintained in situ."

"What are the townspeople doing there?" Venice asked.

"Apparently, whoever is heading the team is not above a bit of gross commercialism. Already they are charging a fee to view the being."

"Where is Crooked Hand?" Noble asked slowly. "I'd like a chance to talk to him myself."

"They've left. Didn't want to get any closer to Salvage," Milton said, struggling up onto his mule. "Come along, come along. Daylight is wasting."

"But our things—" Venice started to protest. Carter was already pulling himself into his saddle.

"Templeton will stay here with them. We'll return to camp for tonight."

"What's the hurry?" Noble asked.

"The hurry? We are scientists, dear boy. We owe it to the scientific community to ascertain whether this . . . find is being properly excavated."

He kicked his little mule forward and set off at a trot, Carter close behind him.

Noble raised an eyebrow at Venice, who shrugged and mounted her own mule. Noble followed suit.

Soon they caught up to Milton and Carter and settled into a bone-bruising trot. They jostled along on the backs of the pack mules for nearly three hours, most of which Milton spent muttering to himself. "I can't quite believe it's true.

"Trees-Too-High is so reliable though," he continued. "I wish he had agreed to stay. We may well have two teams of paleontologists working out of Salvage this summer. Both camps will need to be provided with fresh game."

"You won't see those two for a while," Noble said.

"Why not?" asked Carter.

Noble shrugged. "They don't need the money and thanks to a certain member of our party, they've gathered enough dirty stories to last them through the next five winters." He could see the bare outline of Venice's profile. It looked like she was biting her lip to keep from smiling.

"Just think, Carter," Milton said, ignoring Noble. "These fellows might have found the actual remains of a prehistoric man."

"I wouldn't be all too sure of that, Milton," Noble said. "You said Trees-Too-High never got a look."

"That's right." Milton bobbed his head. "Trees-Too-High said there were twenty to twenty-five people gathered 'round the place, all paying what was apparently admission to the site."

Noble frowned. "What the hell are twenty-five people doing a half day's ride out of Salvage? Something's not right."

"Apparently news of this find has already spread. If people will cross oceans to see a poorly engineered building—"

"Pisa." Carter kindly offered Noble an explanation.

"Thank you."

"—they will certainly ride a few hours to see a prehistoric man!" Milton finished. "Probably brought picnic baskets! And as for paying, men will invariably pay money for the privilege of viewing an oddity or a rare specimen. Museums, my lad, are nothing more than permanent medicine shows. Just think of it! And I was so close!"

"I agree with Noble, Uncle Milton," Venice said. "Let's wait until we are there before we get ex-

cited. So many times appearances are deceptive."
She shot a deliberate look at Noble.

"Ouch," he said.

She started to laugh. That was her biggest problem. She found Noble's straightforwardness, damn-
to-all-obstacles, and ability to laugh at himself
absolutely captivating.

She frowned.

"Uh-uh," Noble said.

He must have been watching her. Well, he was
always watching her. She should be used to it by
now.

"No frowning allowed," he said. "Save your
scowls for the suspect fossil. We're almost there."

"There!" Carter shouted from a little distance
ahead. Kneeing their mules into a faster trot, the
group broke through a stand of aspens into a
basin-shaped meadow. At the far end of the field,
hard against the forest, huge boulders jutted out of
the ground. Poles strung with Chinese lanterns
formed a semicircular enclosure around the small-
est boulder.

A couple of boards, painted with red barn paint,
were nailed between two trees near the entrance of
the enclosure.

ANCHENT OLD DEAD MAN.
25¢ A LOOK.
REEL OLD AND UGLIE

Venice slowed her mule as Milton and Carter
charged past her across the meadow, jiggling vio-
lently atop the trotting mules. Venice's teeth felt
jarred just watching. Wordlessly, Noble fell into
pace by her side.

Her uncle and Carter were waiting when they
pulled their ponies to a stop. So was Harry Grundy.
He had tipped his beaver top hat back on his red

hair and was regarding her uncle with a flat expression.

"Mr. Grundy." Venice nodded a greeting. "I didn't know you were interested in archaeological sciences."

"Yup," Harry said. "Yup, I am."

"And you are the happy discoverer of this unique find?"

"Me and my brother, ma'am. We found this here wondrous thing a week ago whilst we was, ah, panning fer gold. Been out here ever since."

Venice looked around for any sign of a creek bed. There wasn't one. She studied Harry who was innocently blinking at her.

"But where were you—"

"Have you a dollar, Venice?" Milton broke in breathlessly.

"What for?" Noble asked.

"Everyone who wants to see the Fossil Man gots to pay. No exceptions," Harry said.

"Why, you miserable, tight-fisted, bloodsucking—!" Noble swung out of the saddle and started forward.

"Anton!" Harry squeaked.

Anton Grundy, all three hundred pounds of him, appeared from behind the boulder. His head, unusually small as it was, was covered with an oversized bowler. The brim folded the tips of his ears down. He was red. An awful, ungodly, angry red. As if he'd been staked out in the sun for hours. And he was scowling.

Anton in one of his most felicitous moods was no treat. Anton scowling and looking like a broiled salmon wasn't something Noble wanted to tangle with, particularly with his bruised ribs. Contenting himself with a curse, Noble dug in his pocket and flipped a two-dollar gold piece at

Harry. Snapping it out of the air, Harry dropped it into a bulging coin purse.

"Take the folks back, Anton."

Sullenly, Anton motioned them to follow. Carter and Milton stepped eagerly forward, craning their necks as they trailed Anton around to the back of the boulder. A big, pink blanket with purple nosegays, which Noble recognized as having come from the Grundy's back room, covered an area at the base of the rock.

In a high, singsong voice, Anton recited, "We found this find when we were out lookin' to find gold. Imagine our surprise when we found this here instead of gold. It were a big surprise."

"Not much in the way of delivery," Noble whispered to Venice.

She bit her lip. If he made her giggle, Anton would probably hit him.

"So here is our find," Anton said, flipping back the blanket. "Voo-lah."

Venice, Milton, and Carter all leaned over the edge of the shallow excavation.

Venice squeezed her eyes shut. Her shoulders started shaking and in a few seconds she was snorting through her fingers. She gave up abruptly, doubling over, holding her stomach, and laughing uproariously.

Milton was next and then Carter. They collapsed into each other's arms, sobbing with hysteria. Curiously, Noble angled his head, looking over Venice's shoulder to see what was so funny.

A replica of Anton Grundy was lying in the grave. Or as reasonable an approximation as concrete, plaster of Paris, shoe black, and mule dung could fashion.

It was a complete body cast of Anton Grundy. Complete even to the texture of the long underwear Anton must have been wearing when Harry made the mold. The face perfectly captured Anton's sullen grimace.

Apparently, Noble noticed, feeling his mouth spreading into a huge grin, Anton Grundy owned an unexpected streak of bashfulness. He'd been cast with his hands modestly covering certain private parts of his anatomy.

How anyone could mistake this thing for a fossil was beyond Noble. Why there were even little tufts of hair . . .

"Anton," Noble said, trying to keep a straight face, "I don't remember you ever being partial to hats."

Venice had herself under control. Sort of. She was staring at Anton with round eyes, tears gleaming as she strove to keep a neutral expression on her face. Anton looked as if he wanted to kill someone. Venice blinked furiously.

"What, McCaneaghy?" Anton growled. "Why are y'all laughing fer?"

"Anton, will you take off your hat?"

"No, I won't take off my hat!"

"I think there is a big, black spider on the brim," Noble said.

"What?!" The bowler sailed off his head.

What was left of Anton's hair stuck out in little tufts all over a bright red, baby-smooth scalp. Plaster clung to the pathetic remnants of a once-fine head of hair.

Just thinking of washing off all that concrete and plaster made Noble wince. Geez, it looked like Harry had let it dry too hard and taken a wire brush to Anton's hide to get it off. Anton had probably never been so clean.

"God," Noble whispered in awe, "that musta hurt!"

"You ain't sayin' shit!" Anton thundered.

Harry appeared from the other side of the boulder, his vigilance in keeping unpaying spectators away from the fossil interrupted by Anton's bellow.

"What the hell is going on?" he demanded.

"This isn't fooling anyone," Noble said.

"I don't know what yore talkin' about," Harry said. "We done made a sci-in-tif-ic discovery and now Miss Leiland and her uncle will just hang around Salvage lookin' fer more of the same."

There was a note of desperation in the sullen assertion.

"Why," Venice said incredulously, "why, *you're* the one who sent me that coyote!"

"Nope," said Harry, looking everywhere but at Venice's face.

"And the bird thing. That was you, too!"

"Nah-uh!"

Hurt ribs be damned, thought Noble. He was going to find out why these two oafs had been terrorizing Venice. Striding over to Anton, Noble gripped a fistful of shirt and jerked him forward. It was like trying to jerk an ox, but anger lent Noble strength.

"Why the hell are you trying to scare Venice?" he growled into Anton's face.

"Scare her?" There was so much honest confusion in Harry's voice that Noble dropped his hold on Anton and swung around to confront the brother.

"We wasn't tryin' to scare her!" Harry protested. "We was trying to—"

"Shit, jes' tell em, Harry. McCaneaghy looks ready to piss bullets," Anton mumbled, rubbing his throat.

"We was just tryin' to make her and her ditsy old coot of an uncle think there was some of them fossils they's lookin' fer around here."

"Why?"

" 'Cause if there ain't, she's gonna talk her uncle into pulling out of Salvage. And that means no spur line and that means—"

"No Grundy Mercantile," Anton burst in pitiably. "And that means *Dubuque!*"

"Geez," muttered Noble, shaking his head. He looked over to see how Venice was taking this news.

She was staring down at the "fossil man." She turned back to them, eyes shining, lips quivering. "Gentlemen, who am I to keep a discovery of this magnitude from the world?"

"What's she mean?" Harry demanded.

"She's not going to tell on you," Noble said.

The Grundys' hoots of happiness echoed down the canyon.

Chapter 25

"Poor Grundys," said Milton, stirring the campfire. It was late. Hours ago, they'd finished the dinner Templeton had had waiting for them.

" 'Poor Grundys,' nothing," Noble said. "They're already turning that thing into a gold mine."

"Yes." Milton smiled. "I must admit to feeling a bit of one-upmanship. Not that it won't be years before we're able to put *our* find before the public eye ..."

Noble half-listened as Carter added his speculations about how long it would take to excavate the jawbone. His gaze rested on Venice.

She'd taken herself to the far side of the campfire, wrapping up in a thick blanket. Her dark hair fell in a cloud about her smooth, ivory face, making her look like some lovely night spirit come to play at a mortal's fire, beguiling a poor man with her unnatural beauty and fine-boned grace.

And if ever a man was beguiled, Noble had to admit, it was he.

She kept casting him tentative glances, too, as if that same spirit were intrigued by a mortal man and feeling threatened by the attraction.

Threatened? Fine. Why should he be the only one who was so vulnerable, so exposed? If loving him was threatening, then yes, and yes, and yes, he'd like her damn near terrified.

He shook his head, tired and worn down by the prospect of beating down the wall Venice had built between them.

"I'd think you'd be heartened, m'boy." Milton's voice penetrated Noble's thoughts. "Why do you shake your head?"

"Hm?"

"The tourists who will flock to see the dig site will certainly benefit your own purposes," Milton said.

"Of course," Noble agreed, trying to work up some enthusiasm.

"How's that?" Venice asked, curious.

Noble looked up eagerly. "Remember our earlier discussion?"

She nodded.

"Well, the prospect of tourism on a large scale might be the incentive Congress needs to set aside large portions of land as a *national* resource."

Seeing her interest, he continued. "If the Yellowstone River area becomes a national park, we'll be able to draw public attention to the undeveloped areas of the country. It might awaken interest on the subject of unregulated territorial expansion."

She regarded him thoughtfully. "The dinosaur, the wildlife, the scenery . . . they're a perfect argument for a national trust," she said pensively. "None of these have any monetary value. All of their worth is of an academic or sports nature. Their appeal is to the wealthy: scientists who can afford the luxury of study, the privileged enthusiast, the wealthy game hunter. In other words, the people who have Congress's ear."

"That's right," Noble said.

"And if this area becomes a *national* park," Venice said, "it will be safeguarded from private interests."

"Yes," Noble said.

"Safe from men like my father."

"He's one of them ... yes. But this isn't a private vendetta against Trevor, Venice."

"I know," she said quietly. "But business always finds a way. It'll find a way around your bill."

"So, I'm a die-hard optimist."

Venice smiled at him. "Oh? Then let a die-hard *realist* look for the holes in your logic."

She was into the spirit of the debate, now. She moved from the other side of the fire and sat down, Milton between them. She leaned forward. Noble leaned forward. After a second's hesitation, Milton leaned back.

"What of your tourists?" Venice asked, settling her chin in her hand. "Aren't you afraid your precious Yellowstone River park is going to be overrun with them?"

"Not on the scope that's being proposed," Noble said. "We're not talking about a few square miles, a Central Park in the midst of these mountains. The bill that will create the Yellowstone park is designed to encompass *thousands* of square miles."

Venice paused, her gaze focused, a sharp gleam of excitement in the silvery depths. "But will the bill pass?"

"Noble's been working on it for ages, Venice," Milton said. "He was amongst the military men the government sent to explore the northern parts of the territory a few years back. His recommendations have been instrumental in getting this bill written. He hasn't said as much, but *he* is one of those powers that be."

Venice flung Noble a startled look.

" 'Powers' is overstating it by a long stretch, Milton," he said uncomfortably.

"No, it isn't," Carter piped up. "Noble has worked with Lieutenant Wheeler, Mr. Powell, and he even knows Clarence King. You know, of the Fortieth Parallel fame? I hear he's writing a book."

"On how to be a specious ass," Noble mumbled.

Carter continued blithely on. "And our young friend here has penned a number of erudite studies for various geological periodicals and other learned tomes."

"My, my. You've been busy, haven't you?" Venice said. Her voice sounded odd, not quite amused, not quite condemning.

"Influence can be achieved in more ways than through wealth, Venice."

"Apparently."

"And while I don't think Noble could be called a *rich* man, I doubt he's a pauper," Milton said.

"Indeed, no," Noble said with mock pride. "I own two, count 'em, two suits."

Venice's look of surprise caused Noble to smile. He remembered her earlier offer to buy him a new shirt, certain he couldn't afford one himself. She must be remembering too, because suddenly she turned bright pink.

"I expect you'll be going to Washington for the fall session, Noble?" Carter asked.

"Unless it's unavoidable, no, I won't."

"Do you hate leaving the mountains so very much?" Venice asked.

It was Noble's turn to be surprised. "No. I'm planning on it. I just don't want to go to Washington. It's hot and muggy. Besides my presence at the hearings would be redundant. They already have all my reports. They don't need me. I'd rather spend the time traveling. There's a place that I've always wanted to explore. I was hoping to get there this autumn."

"Traveling." Venice smiled dreamily, staring into the flames. The group fell silent, caught in their own musings until a sudden, unhappy braying broke their reverie.

Noble stood up and dusted off his pants' legs. "I'd best water and feed the mules," he said, and strode off toward the increasing racket.

Milton, too, got up, grimacing as he rose to his full height. "Old, stiff bones. I'd better stretch them out a bit or I won't be able to rise in the morning. Would you care to join me in an evening stroll, m'dear?" he asked Venice.

"Certainly," she said, getting up and taking his arm.

"Carter?" Milton asked politely.

"No, you two go on. I'll stay here and keep Templeton company."

Milton led Venice beyond the edges of the firelight and out under the star-blanketed sky. She looked up and shivered.

"Yes," Milton said in response, drawing her closer. "I fear it's going to be cold tomorrow. But, thankfully, we shouldn't have to camp out tomorrow night. We should be safely tucked into our own little beds in Salvage."

"Yes."

"The prospect doesn't seem inordinately cheering to you, m'dear."

"Oh, it is," she said, trying to sound excited. "I am eager to wire the various institutes about your dinosaur. Really. I have no doubt it will be the making of Salvage. Alongside the Grundys' prehistoric man."

"Oh, yes,"Milton murmured. "Salvage. You're quite concerned about that little hamlet, aren't you?"

Venice shrugged, slowing her pace to match her uncle's. "I feel Salvage is our responsibility. The Leiland Foundation made Salvage and I can't let it unmake Salvage. It doesn't seem fair."

"Sometimes life isn't fair. Oh, Lord. I just realized what I must sound like. The patronizing old uncle handing down pearls of wisdom from his exalted heights. I wonder you don't trip me."

She laughed. "I appreciate your wisdom," she said and kissed his cheek.

"I'm not worthy of your affection."

"Don't say that."

"It's true, Venice. I know you think of Trevor and I as being opposites. He as a cold, dogmatic, and rigid man and me as a sweet, loving, and lenient uncle. I wish I did have those qualities." He sighed. "But I don't. In truth, we're very much alike, your father and I. Both selfish, self-absorbed, and determined. Your father's mistake was that for a short time he allowed another person to affect his happiness."

"My mother."

Milton nodded. "And when she failed to make him happy, he banished her. I, on the other hand," Milton continued, "was wiser. I never allowed another human that power over me. If I had, I don't doubt that it would have ended similarly."

"That's not true," Venice protested. "You have always been a loving and devoted uncle to me."

He stopped and patted her hand. "I am not proud of this, Venice, but I am capable of a few sacrifices and your good opinion must be one of them." His tone was self-mocking. "Think, my dear. I was devoted and loving at *my* discretion. At *my* convenience. Never yours.

"I could have come to New York when I heard your mother had died, but I was too busy in Egypt." His voice had lowered, roughened. She couldn't see his face. "I could have taken you away and put you in private school wherever I was digging. Trevor wouldn't have protested. But I didn't. It would have been inconvenient."

"Why are you saying this?" Venice asked. "Why are you hurting us both like this?"

"Because I want you to see the truth, Venice. Your father and I are the same. Don't judge all men against our measure. It wouldn't be fair. There are men who know how to love. Who know how to give. Don't make the mistake of believing that convenience is all you deserve. You're a loving woman, Venice. Just like your mother was."

"My mother?" Venice sniffed and dashed a tear from her cheek. "My mother divorced my father."

"Don't judge her too harshly, Venice. The reason she agreed to divorce your father was because she couldn't live as his wife without his love. Their divorce was his failing, Venice. Not hers."

She was quiet, staring at the sky above.

"Do you understand what I'm saying, Venice?" he asked softly.

"Yes." She looked down into his shadowed face. "But how do you know that I'm like my mother? What if I'm just like Trevor? Or . . . you? Incapable of a lasting love."

She was startled by his laugh.

"Oh, Venice. You? Incapable of a lasting love? Open your eyes, my dear," he said.

"What do you mean?"

He just shook his head and, tucking her hand back into the crook of his arm, led her back to the camp.

She had been lying flat on her back, staring up at the black roof of her tent for an hour. Milton and Carter were still sitting about the campfire with Noble. Tomorrow she'd be in Salvage. Tomorrow she would say good-bye to Noble. Maybe, this time, forever.

She rolled onto her stomach and punched the

pillow. Milton's words had confused her. And she was already confused enough.

Obviously Milton believed there was a future for her and Noble. But Carter had reminded her that history repeats itself.

She and Noble were echoes of her parents. They came from different backgrounds, with different expectations, and against all reason, they had fallen in love. Just like her parents.

Love? Her mother may have loved her father, but love hadn't stopped her from leaving him. Love hadn't stopped Cayuse Katie's husband from running away from her, and love certainly hadn't kept their spouses from abandoning the hundreds of women who crowded the Leiland Foundation's bread lines.

She was doing the right thing, she told herself. She was saving them both from making a disastrous mistake.

She pulled her legs into a tight ball, protecting herself against the coming cold, protecting herself against the darkness.

Chapter 26

"Venice."

She rolled over and pushed herself up on her forearms, blinking. "Noble?"

"Shh. You'll wake everyone up. Come on out."

"Just a minute!" she whispered back. She didn't stop to consider what she was doing; she simply wanted to be alone with Noble. Maybe for the last time.

She kicked off the blankets and scrambled upright, pushing her shirttails into her skirt. Her nose wrinkled. She smelled awful. But what could she expect? She'd been wearing the same clothes for more than a week. From what Noble told her, Cassius Thornton Reed's mule had scattered every bit of her clothing across the continental divide.

She thrust her fingers through her hair, wincing as she tried to untangle the worst of the snarls. Lord, an animal could nest in her hair!

"Come on, Venice!" Noble called softly. She crawled under the tent flap. Her eyes widened.

It was snowing.

Small white flakes drifted and twirled, dancing across the green grass and melting on larkspur and columbine in the soft pre-dawn light. She lifted her face to the dove-gray sky above. Snow fell from above, catching on her lips and eyelashes and melting on her sleep-warmed cheeks. It was entrancing, whimsical, and breathtakingly beautiful.

"But it's June!" she whispered in delight.

"I know. I've seen it a dozen times and it never ceases to enchant me."

She shivered and Noble placed a blanket over her shoulders.

"Fool woman," he muttered, wrapping her close. "Spends days warm enough to melt butter all wrapped up and comes gallivanting out here in the middle of a snowstorm without a coat!"

She giggled at his severe tone. He grabbed her hat from the tree branch she'd hung it on last night and plunked it on her head.

"Do you want a bath?" he asked.

"A bath?"

"Yeah."

"Sure," she said, joining in his nonsense. "But only if I can have lavender soap. And I'd like some clean clothes and a set of tortoiseshell combs and, well, what the heck, throw in a *masseuse*."

"What's that?"

"Someone who manipulates the various muscles of your neck and back and arms and, er, nether regions to relieve strain and aches associated with athleticism."

" 'Someone'?" Noble scowled.

Venice laughed. "A woman."

"Oh. And where did you hear of this *masseuse?*"

"In France. I had just gotten back from a rather strenuous exploration of the Alps when my friend introduced me to this delightful woman!" She sighed in fond memory. "It was wonderful!"

"Sorta like rubbing down a horse."

She loved it when he teased her. He tried so hard to look serious and his eyes, flashing with those wicked coppery lights, gave him away so easily.

She nodded solemnly. "A thoroughbred."

He broke into a full, rich laugh and she hushed him, looking guiltily around at the other tents. It was still early, very early, and it would be their last day together. She wanted every moment alone with him that she could get.

"Well, I don't know what I can do about tortoiseshell combs, but I think I might accommodate your other demands."

"Demands? You are the one who woke me from a sound and blameless slumber—"

"Shh! You want a bath or not?"

She didn't hesitate. "Sure."

He took her hand. His fingers felt warm and strong and sure as he wrapped them around hers and guided her over to where a mule and his pony stood, saddled and waiting.

"Are we abandoning them?" Venice asked, looking back at the tents.

Noble snorted. "They'll probably still be sleeping when we get back. We aren't going in to Salvage, Venice."

Without asking her permission, he lifted her into the saddle and mounted his pony.

As they traveled south, angling away from the Grundys' "Reel Old Man," the snow showed no sign of letting up. Indeed, the flakes grew bigger and drifted more lazily, as though winter was starting all over again.

They had gone about five miles when Noble stopped. He dropped to the ground and came round to her side, holding his hands out. She put her hands on his broad shoulders and slid into his embrace, standing for a second, her eyes closed, enjoying the feeling of him, so big and strong and loving.

"Come on, Stinky," he said, turning her around and giving her a little push.

"Stinky!"

"You wouldn't like my other nicknames for you."

She felt her cheeks heat. He laughed and grabbed her hand and pulled her as she vehemently protested that she didn't want to inflict her "odorous person on his fragrant self." They came around a stand of pines and he stopped and pushed her in front of him.

She gasped. Ten feet beyond her was the promised bathtub, one nature had created. An irregular-shaped pool, twenty feet long and roughly eight feet wide, sent delicate tendrils of steam into the cold air.

A hot spring.

She sighed with pleasure. Tossing off the blanket and kicking at her boots, she clawed at her belt, finally freeing it and pushing her pants to her knees.

"Hey!" Noble protested, laughing. "What happened to modesty?"

"Modesty be damned. I'm going to have a bath!" She said the last word on an ecstatic sigh.

Frantically, she worked the buttons of her shirt, finally giving up and pulling the stiff, filthy fabric over her head. She hopped on one foot and then the other, pulling off the gray socks as she closed the ten-foot span between her and the spring, naked now except for the red union suit.

She didn't bother to peel that off. She simply jumped in, feet first.

The water closed over her head and she sank deep before spreading her arms and pushing back to the top. She broke the surface and laughed with pure pleasure.

The water was hot. Not just warm, hot. Wonderfully, bone-seeping, body-draining hot.

She looked at Noble, who stood smiling at the

water's edge. He was as happy for her pleasure as he would be for his own. Lord, she loved him.

"This," she called to him, "is heaven."

"Looks mighty inviting."

She didn't hesitate. "Come on in."

His brows rose. "Really?"

"I couldn't be so selfish as to keep all this wonderful *hot* water to myself!" she answered, noting that he was already sitting on the ground and pulling off his boots.

It took him about a minute to strip down to his union suit. When he didn't take that off, too, she realized how disappointed she was. She had seen his bare chest a half dozen times, but she had never seen his entire body naked. Suddenly that seemed like a grave, grave oversight.

She didn't have time to say anything. He jumped in, making a huge splash and, surfacing immediately, shook his long hair out of his face, spraying her with water. He leaned the back of his head into the water and paddled closer, shaking his head again. The third time, she realized he was doing it on purpose.

She dove under the water and caught him about the waist, dragging him beneath the surface. She put her hands on his shoulders and pushed him down as deep as she could, laughing as she burst to the top.

She didn't laugh too long. From under the water he grabbed hold of her ankle. She shrieked, kicking at him. His hand closed around her calf.

The more she fought, the higher up her legs he grabbed. She couldn't believe he could hold his breath so long. She wiggled and twisted. He had her knee. She squirmed frantically. Finally catching her about her waist, he pulled her down to meet him beneath the surface of the hot, dark water.

His mouth closed over hers.

He was weightless and sinewy, long and hard, pressed to her chest, his thighs riding between her own.

They burst to the surface, mouths still open hungrily on each other, arms holding each other tightly, fiercely.

"Venice?" Her name was a question.

Her only answer was that she wanted this, wanted to make love to him, wanted to stay in this fantasy world of snow and heat and spring flowers and winter storms.

She pushed the sodden union suit from his broad shoulders, peeling it from his upper torso. As soon as she was done, he swam her to the edge of the pool. Bracing his arms on either side of her, he clutched the hard, lichen-studded rock in a white knuckled grip while she clung to his neck.

He stared at her, motionless, forcing himself to wait. She had to want this as much as he did.

Her gaze locked with his; she reached up and fumbled with the buttons of her union suit. A drop of water clung to her lower lip. He couldn't resist. He leaned forward and licked the drop away. She made a sound like a whimper deep in her throat, shrugging the suit off and kicking her legs free.

His breath caught. The upper swells of her breasts rose above the water. Her hair, drifting languidly in a dark sheath about the pale crests, was no less provocative than a silken veil coyly revealing a seductress's charms. He threaded the fingers of one hand through the dark, streaming tresses. Soft and heavy and lush.

His fingertips, hidden in her floating hair, brushed against her nipple. She arched into his unintentional touch, tipping her chin up, baring her throat. Boldly, he traced the coral-colored tip, delicately fingering the swollen bud until it puckered, even here, in this heated pool, with excitement.

He dipped his head, his mouth opening under the water on her nipple. Languidly he stroked it with his tongue. She shuddered, her hands closing on his shoulders.

"Make love to me," she said. There was something in her tone that made him wary.

He raised his head and grasped her legs behind her knees, lifting them and settling them around his waist.

"This isn't a good-bye," he swore. "This isn't once more, for the memory. No matter what you think." He moved his lower body, pressing his swollen shaft intimately against the soft juncture of her thighs. It was a deliberately sexual contact and she answered its primitive demand.

He rocked against her and she leaned back, arching into the feel of him between her legs, squirming down, wanting to feel his hard length inside her. He felt so good, so solid, so *male.*

She could never love another man as she loved Noble.

"This isn't good-bye," he said again, bringing one hand down under her buttocks and lifting her, settling her on him. He pushed, his belly muscles rippling, and she inhaled sharply, her eyes widening as he thrust deeply into her.

She panted. A sudden gust of wind blew across the hot spring, and thick white billows of steam rose in answer. He was a merman come to woo a foolish maid, Venice thought, gleaming and mist-wreathed and passionate. She touched his smooth cheek with near reverence.

"Don't look at me like that," he growled, thrusting hard into her, pushing her against the moss-slick side of the pool. The fragile banners of steam were torn by his movement.

"Like what?" she gasped, clutching tightly to him.

"As if you're memorizing my face," he rasped.

He would make her stop, make her live this moment and this moment alone. Make her forget about leaving him and last times and final good-byes.

Abruptly, he withdrew from her and she clutched at him, a sound of distress rang from her lips. Her eyes, lustrous gray jewels, shone with reproach. He turned her around and, settling his back against the rim of the pool, hooked his elbows up on the pool's rocky rim.

She treaded water in front of him. "What are you doing?" she asked uncertainly.

His feet must have found some purchase beneath the water, because his chest, water streaming down the tanned contours, rose partially above the surface. The soft, silent snow dissolved against his heated skin. "Waiting."

"For what?"

"For you to make love to me," he said flatly.

"I . . . I don't understand."

"I don't want to make love knowing that you're saying good-bye, knowing you're committing to memory each little detail, each flick of my tongue, each thrust of my hip, just so you can relegate it to some musty little corner of your memory."

"It's not like that!"

"It's *just* like that. And I won't be used that way. If you want to make love, make love. No spectators allowed at this sport. Not even those with the best intentions," he ground out.

She stared at him for a moment and then, almost shyly, she swam forward. She draped her arms around his neck and her eyelids drifted shut.

She rubbed her body against his, a sinuous gliding movement. He rested the back of his head against the rock.

"All right," she whispered against his throat, nibbling her way to his lower lip. "Just now. Just here. Just us. But you promise, too. No past. No future. Just now."

Once before he'd said his body was at her disposal. She wasn't at all shy about his gift. She wanted to give him back some of the intense pleasure he had introduced her to.

She lifted herself higher, her breasts dragging across the water-slick surface of his chest, heavy and warm. Slowly, deliberately, she wrapped her legs around his hips, her hands stroking his chest, her breath warm in his ear, her teeth nipping at the rough angle of his jaw.

"Do you love me?" she whispered.

"God, yes."

"I love you, too." Her hands traveled low on his body and his stomach clenched tightly as her fingernails gently raked his belly, moving lower until her hand found and closed around his thick, rigid staff.

He groaned. His lips jerked forward in response to her hand's movement. Experimentally, Venice moved her hand again. He clenched his teeth. She grasped the velvet hardness more firmly and stroked its satiny length, trying to mimic the rhythm of their lovemaking.

He arched his throat, the air hissing in a sharp in-drawn breath. His eyes flew open and he grabbed her wrist beneath the water.

"I'd rather your body sheathe me than your hand, lass," he said and, in one motion, pulled her up and pushed himself deep inside her.

She found the elusive rhythm, using the broad span of his shoulders to brace herself as she moved up and down on his tensile length. His hands stroked her buttocks. His voice, harsh and urgent, rasped appeals for his sanity. His tongue stroked and tasted her shivering breasts, her straining arms, her lips, her mouth.

Still she moved, meeting each powerful thrust with the tilt of her hips and driving back against his force, seeking a deeper union.

She heard his hoarse cry and felt the deepest and most elemental of shudders move through his big frame just as she felt her own pleasure crest and swell and spin liquid pleasure throughout her own body.

She collapsed, panting in his embrace, feeling his own harsh breath on her shoulder as he bent forward. For a long time they stayed like that. She felt limp and exhausted and wonderful.

"Venice?" There was a question in his voice and she didn't have an answer.

"You promised."

"Aye. I promised. And you already have scant reason to believe my promises, right?" he whispered sadly in her ear.

"Noble," she said, moving out of his embrace. She touched his lips with a fingertip. "I don't blame you for the past. Truly."

"Then let me say this to you. I won't badger you or threaten to leave you here or do anything more than talk. But please, listen to me."

She nodded.

"I know you've been taught to think that you should get married to provide a proper little heir for an empire. Don't believe it. The Leiland Foundation isn't the last chance you'll have to do something worthwhile with your life, Venice. It's not the only chance. It's *a* chance."

"I know," she said quietly.

"Good." He swallowed. "The first step's taken,

then. Now, take the second. I know you don't trust promises of forever. Why should you? Your mother abandoned you, your father neglected you. The maids, the nannies, me ... we all left you. But Venice, I was seventeen years old! I was young and furious and mortified by your father's suggestion of something unnatural between you and me."

He gripped her shoulders, squeezing tightly. "But I'm not seventeen anymore and there is nothing, *nothing* that is going to send me away from you this time. The only one with that power is you. This"—he lifted her hand and pressed her palm over his heart—"love, Venice, it's your responsibility."

She blinked and spread her hand over the steady beat of his heart. Warm, vital ... real.

"I can't promise you tomorrow, Venice. No one can. There are lightning bolts and runaway trains." He smiled teasingly. "Even flash floods."

Her breath caught in her throat.

He kissed her lightly on the forehead. "But I *can* promise that I'll never willingly leave you. Ever."

He stared into her eyes. "I won't hound you any longer. Just promise me you'll think about what I've said." He turned and effortlessly hoisted himself up onto the bank, unselfconsciously walking over to the mule's saddle pack.

She watched him. Broad shoulders tapering to narrow hips and tight buttocks; long-muscled thighs and calves, oddly pale in contrast to his bronzed upper torso and water-dark hair laying in slick ropes on his strong neck.

"Here you go," he said, turning and tossing her something palm-sized, hard, and cream-colored. She caught it.

"Soap!" she breathed. "Lavender soap! Wherever did you get it?"

"Templeton found a piece in the mess kit yesterday. He uses it for the bed linen at your uncle's camp."

"Bless Templeton."

"Double bless Templeton. He also had a comb."

"Oh," Venice purred in pleasure, starting to soap her arms. "I shall truly love combing my hair. Next you'll tell me you have a masseuse in there."

In answer, he paused in his rummaging and turned his head, flashing her a wolfish smile. "I'm a quick study."

He was tempting and tantalizing and she was a weak, weak woman. She cleared her throat, chasing away the erotic images he inspired. "I don't suppose you have anything I could wear in there?" she asked doubtfully.

"Yup. You owe Templeton again. He also gave up some of his clothes for your sake."

"*His* clothes?" Venice asked, her eyes widening.

"I have here a clean white shirt, compliments of your Uncle Milton, a pair of wool trousers—black, of course—from Templeton, and from my own cache of things never to be without, a pair of fresh socks."

She dunked under the water, coming up already working a thick lather of soap into her hair, to find him laughing.

His humor was irresistible.

"Thank you, Noble," she said softly.

His smile crinkled the corners of his eyes. He opened his mouth as if to say something and must have thought better of it. "Anything for love," he said flippantly and left her to finish her bath alone.

"How much longer, m'boy?" Carter asked as they plodded along on their mounts.

Soon, thought Venice. The terrain looked familiar

and the scents of coal, grease, and baking refuse—
Salvage's own unique perfume—danced past them
on the wind.

"Just down the next draw," Noble said. He
sounded distracted and he looked tired. His big
body drooped in the saddle as if he'd been up all
night wrestling demons. She watched as he
stretched in the saddle, twisting this way and that.

True to Noble's word, they rode into town
twenty minutes later. Salvage was just as appealing a little hamlet as she remembered. The only
discernible difference was that the deep ruts in the
hard-baked surface of the main street held a thin
scum of stagnant water, and there were a few
more men than usual leaning against the sides of
the buildings, enjoying the afternoon sun. On further consideration, Venice decided there were simply a few more men than usual sleeping off a
drunk.

A few curious faces turned toward them as they
made their way down the street. The curiosity
quickly turned into expressions of incredulity and
then bewilderment, and finally shock.

Venice was uncomfortably aware of her pur-
loined valet's outfit. Still, this seemed an extreme
reaction to a woman dressing in black trousers and
a white bib shirt. At least *she* didn't smell bad.

"She's *alive!*" a miner hollered through cupped
hands. "Venice Leiland's alive!"

Venice scowled. *What the devil?*

"She's *alive!*" The call bounced from man to
man, shouted from doorway to window, traveling
twenty yards ahead of the small bewildered troop.

On reaching the far end of town and the Gold
Dust Emporium, Venice dropped lightly from her
saddle to the ground. Immediately, she was surrounded by a group of men.

"You're not dead," said one of the rougher-looking fellows, wiping a tear from his creased cheeks.

"No," Venice agreed.

"What the hell is—" Noble began. His words were abruptly cut off as someone elbowed her way past him, hitting him in the ribs in her hurry. It was Katie.

She pushed through the milling group until she was within reach of Venice. Her lower lip trembled, threatening a display of emotion Noble was willing to bet Katie hadn't indulged in for decades.

"You ain't *dead!*" she sniffed and pulled Venice into a back-thumping embrace.

"No, no. But I might be if you don't loosen up your grip! Geez, Miss Jones! I can't breathe!" protested Venice.

"*Geez?*" Katie laughed, releasing her. "We'll turn you into a western gal, yet!"

She stepped back but not before reaching out and patting Venice's face as though she were a favored child and Katie a fond parent. Venice gave the blonde saloonkeeper a baffled smile.

"You call me Katie, hon."

Venice blinked in confusion. "Thank you . . . Katie."

Tim Gilpin emerged from the crowd. "Miss Leiland!"

"Mr. Gilpin."

"I am so happy—that is, I am so pleased to see—"

"Well, look who's here to welcome the corpse! The undertaker what took the gold fillings," Katie drawled. Tim flushed.

"What's going on?" Milton demanded.

"*Mr.* Gilpin here wrote your obituary," Katie explained to Venice. "Sold it to the New York newspaper on the telegraph and made hisself a pretty penny doing it, too."

"My obituary? Why would you sell my obituary to the newspapers, Mr. Gilpin?"

Noble couldn't help hearing the hurt in her voice. He *hated* hearing Venice sound hurt. He took a step forward.

"Why would anyone think that Miss Leiland was, er, dead?" asked Carter.

"Who's that?" Katie asked, jerking her head at Carter, who was fastidiously retucking the tails of his shirt.

"Mr. Makepeace, an associate and great friend of my uncle's," explained Venice. "And please, Miss Jones, *Katie*, why *is* everyone surprised to see me alive?"

Katie's brows dropped in a thunderous line over her eyes. Her fists leapt to her hips and she straddled the ground. "Why?" she said. "*Why?* 'Cause that pissant piece of toad-sucking crap said you were dead!"

"Which pissant piece of—ah, whatever might that be?" asked Milton.

"Who's that?" Katie pointed at Milton.

"My uncle, Milton Leiland."

"Oh." Katie nodded. She gave scant attention to Milton, one of the richest men in the territory, her anger apparently robbing her of her usual financial acumen. "I'm talking about Mr. Cassius Thornton Reed, who has spent the past five nights getting drunk in my saloon and wailing about how he tried to save you from a flood up in the mountains but couldn't 'cause his rescue was botched by Noble McCaneaghy!"

"What?!"

"That's right, Venice. He told how Noble—having an animal lust fer you—stalked after you and stole you away from the camp one night. The

Utes disappeared and ole Thorny lit out after you, only to find the both of you clinging to a tree in the middle of a flooding river. He swam out after you, but Noble here in a panic flung himself on Thorny and they was both swept away. When he waked up he was lying on the river bank and you and Noble was dead!"

Venice's eyes narrowed. "*Noble's* cowardice got us killed?"

"Yup."

"And he tried to *save* us?"

"You got it. The yellow-bellied son of a bitch has been wallowing in it ever since he dragged his sorry ass down out of the mountains. And Mr. Gilpin here hammered out a telegram, a grandiose piece of cake about Venice Leiland's Last Great Adventure. Made me sick!"

"Miss Leiland. I . . ." The editor obviously didn't know what to say. His distress was as acute as it was apparent.

One look at Venice's face and Noble found he wasn't feeling particularly merciful. "You just had to use her," he accused Gilpin. "Just like every other rag. Must be a great passion you have . . . for a buck."

"Grand passion?" Venice said bemused. "I don't understand. The obituary doesn't matter, Noble."

Noble promised himself he was going to have a little talk with Tim Gilpin—after the one he had with Cassius Reed. "So ole Thorny knew Venice was alive," he murmured in a dangerous voice. "Thought I was dead and still he left Venice up there, alone."

Noble started pushing his way through the crowd.

"Where are you going?" Venice demanded, following him. He just kept pushing his big shoulders through the crowd.

"Noble!" She caught up with him and seized his wrist in both hands, digging in her heels and making him drag her a few feet before he realized she was holding on to him. He looked down at her and frowned, obviously annoyed.

"Noble," she said, trying to sound calm, reasonable, but still refusing to relinquish his wrist.

"What?"

"Might I ask where you are off to?"

"No."

"Well, I shall just have to restrain you until you are more forthcoming with your answers."

A corner of his mouth quirked up.

"Really?" he said.

"Yes, really. Now, I reiterate, where are you going?"

"I thought I'd have me a little drink."

" 'Have me a little drink.' Every time you are on the cusp of doing something hideously reckless and extravagantly *masculine*, you fall into these atrocious speech patterns. Where do you intend to have you a little drink?"

"Wherever Cassius Reed is. There. Is that what you wanted to know?"

"Really, dear boy, I'd leave it," said Milton, who'd hurried over to them. "You'll only end up in jail."

"Don't go," Venice pleaded.

Noble smiled, not a pleasant smile, and shook his head. "Lass, you are something else again. The man left you, fully expecting you to die. In fact, he was so sure you were going to die that he gave the story out that you *were* dead. And you expect me to do nothing about it?"

She was enraptured by the love she read in his eyes. There was nothing of himself he would keep from her. Noble McCaneaghy would always offer himself as a friend, a protector, a lover, a mentor, a companion, whatever she had need of.

She released her grip on his wrist.

"Stay with me, Noble."

"What?"

"Stay with me."

"Where?"

"She-et," Katie said softly, her eyes growing wide. She cleared her throat. "Okay, ain't all you gawking jerkwater, no-accounts got nuthin' better to do than ogle a lady in need of ... of a ... bath? Go on, all of you. Get on! Drinks are on the house!"

As a single entity, the crowd wheeled away from Venice and Noble and stampeded for the doors of the Gold Dust. Within three minutes, the street was empty except for the Leiland party and Katie. Katie wiped her heavy satin skirts with her palms.

"Ah, Venice?" she said.

Venice ignored her. She was still lost in the love she read in Noble's eyes.

"Venice, about your room. Well, I never did get around to changing nuthin' and none of the other girls wanted to sleep where a dead—What I'm trying to say is that all your things is still there. All the things you told me to keep till you came back for them."

"Venice will be staying with me, ma'am," Milton said.

" 'Fraid not, Milty," Katie said. "Your house has been reoccupied by the skunks."

"What?"

"Skunks, Uncle Milton," Venice murmured. "We can't stay there."

"Well, this is a fine pickle," Milton said. "Might you have rooms to let, Miss Jones?"

Katie pondered a minute. To her credit it didn't

take much more time than that to decide Venice needed her privacy more than Katie needed Milton's money. She must be going soft in the head.

"Uh-uh. Sorry, Milty. You might try the Pay Dirt, though," she suggested. Her mind racing to come up with a way to extort a finder's fee from the Pay Dirt's owner, she wandered into the Gold Dust.

"Oh," Milton said. "Oh, well. I suppose we'd best be getting along. Carter. Templeton." He looked as if he was going to add Noble's name to the list, but after a quick glance, he turned and got back up on the pony Templeton had been patiently holding.

"We'll see you for dinner, Venice?" Milton said over his shoulder, plodding down the street, Carter and Templeton trailing behind him.

Venice nodded, waggling her fingers in farewell. Her eyes never left Noble's face.

He was not happy. A thunderous scowl marred his lean, handsome face. She had offered him a horrible dilemma: go and enjoy beating the living hell out of Cassius Reed, the man who'd blind-sided him, almost gotten him killed, and—by far the most grievous sin—left Venice alone in the mountains. Or stay with Venice.

He wanted to stay with Venice.

She took a deep breath. She needed to talk to Noble, and she didn't want any interruptions. Besides, it was way too late for a chaperone.

"Noble."

"Lass?" She let go of him, suddenly shy, and looked down. The movement drew her attention to her sweat-stained shirt and boys' trousers. Her hand flew to the ratty old red felt hat crammed atop her snarled locks. She made an attempt at discreetly hoisting up her trousers. Noble began to smile. This would never do.

"I would like to invite you to have ..." Have what? Her mind raced. " ... tea with me this afternoon."

His gentlemanly facade cracked. *"Tea?"*

"Yes. Shall we say three o'clock? In my room?"

A wolfish, altogether charming smile bent Noble's lips.

He'd be able to have his cake and eat it too. "My pleasure, Miss Leiland," he said, tipping two fingers to a nonexistent hat and bowing forward at the waist.

"At three, then?"

"Aye."

She started to turn around and then, thinking better of it, stopped.

"And, Noble, should I hear you have been engaged in any 'discussions' with Mr. Reed, you needn't bother showing up ... *ever*."

"Now, Venice, that's—"

"Those are the terms, Mr. McCaneaghy," Venice said. She wasn't going to have the daft man getting killed. Not now. Not ever.

"Agreed?"

Silence.

"Agreed?"

"Yes, goddammit, agreed," Noble ground out.

Chapter 27

Venice dragged a brush through her hair for the third time. The long black strands crackled and snapped, clinging to her hand in a static sheet, falling over her face and flying about her head.

Drat! Hauling her hair back, she ruthlessly twisted the thick mass into a long coil, tugging it into a heavy loop on the crown of her head. She glanced in the mirror and waved a dismissive hand at her reflection. The curls were already springing free and sticking to her forehead. She'd deal with her hair later.

Slipping into a white petticoat, Venice tied the satin waistband over her delicately edged camisole.

"Which dress, which dress . . ." she muttered, rifling through the armoire packed with clothes. She scrunched her nose at a primrose muslin, puffed distraught cheeks as she considered a lilac print dress with velvet piping, dismissed an organdy gown of deep emerald green. She ran her hands through her hair, vaguely conscious of the loop falling askew at the side of her head. Her gaze lit on the periwinkle dress.

Perfect.

She snatched it from the closet and tossed it on the bed. Digging through the bureau's top drawer, she pulled out a pair of sheer silk stockings, cream-colored with pale green ribbons at the top. She sat down on the edge of the bed and flipped up her petticoats.

The door opened. Noble walked in, his eyes widening for a second before he gulped and glued his gaze a foot over Venice's head.

"Damn it, Venice," he said. "Get dressed!"

Get dressed? Now, where had she gotten the notion that he'd been spending the past week trying to get her *undressed?* He was wearing his priest-at-the-pulpit look of worried censure again.

Reaching for a sheet to pull over herself, Venice was surprised to realize she wasn't the least bit disconcerted to have Noble see her half-clad. Which only made sense. He had, after all, seen her naked. The thought didn't make her feel awkward or shy. It was right, natural.

She'd known what she wanted from the moment she'd seen Noble beneath her balcony: strong, tall, beautiful. And when he'd started making those breathtaking contortions, her heart had recognized what her eyes had not—the self-deprecating humor and wit of "Slats." She loved Noble. How *could* she be embarrassed?

Venice smiled. Noble flushed. Poor Noble. He seemed very disconcerted, one might even say nonplussed.

"You're early," Venice said, languidly extending a leg and slipping her foot into the stocking.

"Yeah," Noble returned tightly.

"You didn't knock."

He let himself look at her. Her stocking was unrolled halfway up a smooth, shapely calf, creeping toward a smooth, shapely thigh. Sweat popped out on his forehead. He forced himself to look at the lampshade behind Venice's bed.

"I knocked. You must not have heard."

"Oh."

She was fussing around with the top of that damned stocking. From the corner of his eye, he could see her long legs emerging from a flurry of white lace and frothy ruffles, a ribbon of white satin shining around her waist, her skin glowing pink and clean above the low neckline of the camisole.

"Maybe I should come back later."

"No," she said calmly. "It's okay. Did you know that in the previous century it was customary to have several gentlemen attend a lady's toilette to advise her on her choices."

"This isn't the previous century."

"No," Venice agreed. "But think of it this way: if I were attending a ball, I would certainly have on less than I am currently wearing."

"The hell you say!" Noble ground out and immediately felt like a fool. God, he hoped Venice didn't think he was possessive. He hated possessive people. But there were certain matters of decency . . .

He gave up the argument. He *was* possessive. He didn't want men ogling Venice. He was too straight-laced, too proprietal, and too old-fashioned. His mother would be proud.

He looked around for something else to occupy his attention. Seeing a folded newspaper on a table, he snatched it up and read. It was Venice's obituary, two entire columns of copy, nearly half a page.

Old Tim had had a field day with the Venice Leiland legend, all right. It was the rankest collection of half-truths, sentimental slop, and occasional gleanings of honest feeling Noble had ever read. Angrily, he tossed it away.

"The hypocritical son-of-a—"

"Don't be too hard on him." Venice stood up, having finished trying the dainty little bow at the top of her stockings. "Tim was simply doing his job."

How could she be so understanding? She must be so accustomed to being judged and used. It made the muscles in his biceps bunch in a painfully familiar way.

He took a deep breath. "Yup, Tim went all the way, the whole 'scatterbrained heiress in search of a party' thing ... like I did."

Venice paused in the middle of lacing her soft kid boots. She didn't lift her head, but he heard her words clearly.

"You don't have to explain yourself to me, Noble. Now or ever."

But Noble vowed that there wouldn't be any unspoken questions shadowing their future.

"Yes, Venice," he said. "I do."

She sat back on the bed and folded her hands in her lap, regarding him with clear, gray eyes.

"When I saw you, for the first time after all those years, you were more beautiful then I had imagined a woman could be. And then, later, I found out it was you who'd lured me to her window and it seemed to confirm what I'd spent ten years telling myself, that you had become a thrill-seeking, indiscriminate coquette."

"I know," Venice said. "I sort of liked it."

Noble raked his fingers through his hair. She would forever keep him off balance. "Whatever for?"

"It was sort of novel to be accused of something I'd actually *done*. And I really had whistled at you." She was serious. She leaned forward, her voice earnest. "You reacted to me like any stiff-necked, proud man might react to any forward woman. Being with you has always been so easy; easy as breathing, natural as a heartbeat. Even flirting with you comes naturally."

"God, Venice." Noble lifted his hands.

"There, you know the horrible truth. I'd rather be correctly accused of being a tease than unjustly accused of wearing human bones." She laughed.

"Venice," Noble said, his voice strained and urgent. "I loved you when you were just a kid. How was I supposed to keep from loving you as a woman? You're passionate, intelligent, and so damn valiant. I still can't believe what you did for me in the mountains. How was I to protect myself against *you*? You're everything I've wanted: friend, lover, even opponent."

"I know," she said softly.

"I shouldn't ask you to choose between your father and the foundation and me. Your father and I, well, we aren't ever going to be friends. I thought I'd be honorable and chivalrous by walking away. But that was just an excuse. The real reason I wanted to walk away was because I didn't think I was good enough for you."

"Noble, *I* never thought that."

"I know, but *I* did. I thought maybe your father was right, I wasn't worth the trouble. I was scared, Venice, a plain old run-of-the-mill coward." He lifted his hands, palms out at his side. The gesture mirrored the simple honesty of his words, exposing him, putting his heart clearly in her hands. No one had ever trusted her so completely.

"I was a coward like you're being." There, he'd said it.

"I can't keep away from you either," Venice said softly. He took an involuntary step toward her and stopped.

"You gotta understand, though. I can't let you be a coward. There's more to think of now than just ourselves."

"Huh?" she asked, puzzled.

He started pacing around the room, poking a

finger in a jar of powder, shoving his fists into his trouser pockets, taking them out, raking a hand through his hair. He was nervous.

"Yeah. You have to marry me now. You haven't any choice."

"*Have* to? No choice?" she parroted.

"Yeah." He stopped in the middle of the room, pressing his lips together and nodding emphatically. "Yup." He looked her directly in the eye. "You're pregnant."

"What?"

He nodded again, lips set. "That's right. I hate to break it like this, but it's true. Well, it's most likely true."

She stared at him.

"I know. You're shocked. But we just have to look at it as God's way of making His will known. It's going to be for the best. Really."

"And how," she asked, "were you able to determine my interesting condition?"

"You don't have to sound so angry." Noble frowned. "I admit, I don't have a lot of experience with women."

Again her betraying heart gave that odd little flip-flop that bespoke approval.

"But I know a helluva—I mean, a great deal more about reproduction than a virginal young girl from the Upper East Side of New York City," he pronounced, and added under his breath so that she could barely hear, "I hope.

"And I know that when you make love twice in the same week, the woman gets pregnant. Almost always."

"I see," Venice said blandly.

He flashed his most charming smile. She almost returned it. He shrugged, lifting his hands in a gesture of defeat. He didn't look unhappy in the least.

"What can I say?" he asked. "That's that. We gotta get married. We should do it now. Today. Before all these people—like that Katie woman—get hold of you and tell you ... er... to occupy your time. The spur line's in town. We could take the train to Denver and be married before midnight. Okay." He clapped his hand on his leg. "Let's go."

"I have something to say first."

"Sure. Shoot."

"I believe the exact words are: Though I might not be an expert regarding the ways of a man and a woman, I sure as hell know enough about female anatomy to know that making love twice in a week does not necessarily result in a baby. And that you definitely wouldn't be able to tell if I were pregnant so soon. I was a virgin, Noble, not an idiot."

"Oh."

"Yes."

"Damn. Well, you *could* be pregnant."

She shook her head. "I could be, but I am very, very doubtful about the possibility. The, er, timing is all off."

"Damn."

"Would you kindly stop using that language?"

"Sorry."

"Besides, I am not ready for motherhood yet. Not for a long time."

He crossed the room to her and sank down on his knees beside her, grasping her shoulders in a hard grip and turning her to face him. "Venice, when you *are* ready for motherhood, I'm the one who should be the father. I'm the only one."

She touched his cheek in a tender gesture. "I know."

He went utterly still. "What do you mean?"

"You were right about one thing. I was a coward. I don't want to be a coward anymore. I want

you." She stood up. "What you said back there at
the spring—I haven't been able to think of anything else. You're right. I have been hiding behind
the Leiland Foundation, using it as an excuse. It
was a pretty good one, too." She smiled. "All the
power I could wield, all the potential good I could
do, if only I could prove myself to my father. But
I'm not ever going to be good enough for him, am
I?"

Noble gave a small, sad shake of his head.

"And if I want to do something worthwhile, I
don't need to be the richest woman in America to
do it. You illustrate that point rather well. Don't
protest, you do. So where does that leave me?"

"You tell me." His voice was tense, urgent.

"It leaves me worrying about whether we
would end up like my parents. I *wanted* to believe
that we would. I even tried to convince myself, cit-
ing the similarities."

"Why?" Noble asked, frowning.

"It was safe to believe that. It was comfortable
in a weird way. I didn't need to wonder what the
future held, I already knew. I didn't have to take
any chances."

"Venice, we aren't like your parents."

"I know," she said softly. "We love each other.
I'm not sure my parents ever did."

"What changed your mind?"

"It was when you said no one was promised tomorrow, that we might die next week. I thought
about how close I had come to losing you in that
flash flood. It overwhelmed me.

She went on. "I had always thought of you being there. Somewhere, even if I wasn't with you.
As long as you and I were alive, there was the
possibility of our love finding a way. But you
made me see that it's no good knowing you're out
there somewhere if I never have the courage to do

something about it. I don't want to be a coward anymore."

"You're sure?" Noble said grimly.

She laughed. "This from the man who was just trying to hoodwink me into matrimony?"

"I'd do anything for your love."

"As would I," Venice replied, her breath taken away by the sincerity of his expression.

"Even marry me?"

"Yes. Even marry you."

Noble didn't twitch a muscle, but a smile was shaping up in his golden eyes. "Trevor's gonna be furious."

"And I'll be sorry he's furious. But *nothing* else."

If he kept looking into her silver eyes, they were not going to get out of this room anytime soon, thought Noble. She was moving toward him, the sway of her hips making the deep ruffles flutter as she walked. The rise and fall of her breasts shivered the delicate tatting on the very edges of her camisole. The fabric was so sheer he could see a dark bloom of rose at the tips of her breasts.

He cleared his throat and cast about for something to keep his mind off her body, the scent of pine and flowers teasing his nostrils.

"Well, Salvage is going to want another party," he said.

"Yes, our wedding party."

"Yes. Well."

She recognized the hint of uncertainty in his voice, the struggle not to get carried away, the battle he fought pitting his desire against what he saw as her welfare. Even if it meant denying himself. He would have to learn that she didn't need protection. She needed him.

Close to him now—bold, adventurous coquette that she was—she reached up and encircled his neck, dimpling at him.

"You know, Noble, I've always loved you."

"*Loved?*" Noble's hands slid of their own volition to her trim waist, drawing her closer. His head bent to meet the invitation of her warm lips. She opened them slightly and he inhaled the sweet fragrance of her breath, lifted his callused hands to touch the sheen of her smooth, pale skin.

"*Love*. And I always will. Promise."

"Venice—" he began, closing the few inches between their lips.

Abruptly, she twisted in his arms, turning her back to him, still within the circle of his embrace. She lifted the heavy length of her hair over her shoulder and glanced at him from beneath the dense fringe of her black lashes, fluttering them audaciously.

Noble bent forward, nuzzling the silky, fragrant hair on the nape of her neck, his mouth touching her throat gently, his hands finding the jut of her hip bones and clamping firmly, pulling her back, hard, against him.

"Please, would you tie my hair back up?" She asked in a throaty whisper.

Shameless hussy. Noble's mouth curved upward, captivated by the roguish gleam in her eyes. He complied, lifting the black rope and twining it slowly into one thick coil. She leaned against him, tilting her head back onto his shoulder to expose the creamy column of her throat.

His fingers barely shook at all.

Lightly clasping her shoulders, he turned her around to face him.

She looked disappointed. He grinned.

"What? You didn't think I could touch you without hauling you into my arms and having my wicked way with you?" he asked in amusement, his brogue husky, seductive.

The look she gave him was sultry, piquant, intoxicating. She splayed her hand wide against his chest. His heart hammered beneath her palm, racing nearly out of control.

"A girl can only hope . . ." she mourned softly.

Noble hauled her into his arms.

Epilogue

The public bar at the Gold Dust Emporium was overflowing with people waiting for a chance to get a glimpse of the resurrected Miss Leiland, so Noble sent a note requesting that Milton and Carter meet them at the Pay Dirt. Noble swung down from the balcony and caught Venice in a tight and prolonged embrace as she dropped into his arms from above.

The moon was rising in a velvet blanket of deepening blue. Streaks of brilliant, fantastical purple and rose limned the western range. Evening bird song drifted from the pine forest, a telling counterpoint to the din of human voices rising from Salvage's fifteen saloons.

"Tonight," Noble was saying as they made their way down the boardwalk.

"We can't just present this to my Uncle Milton as a fait accompli," Venice said.

"Tonight," Noble insisted. "I have me immortal soul on the line here, Venice. I know you pagans don't put much store in the hallowed state, but now that you've had your wicked way with me ..."

Venice laughed. "Well, as long as it's for a good cause."

"Me immortal soul," Noble said solemnly, picking up her hand and placing it over his heart. For a few seconds they simply stood, reading the love in each other's eyes.

"All right." Venice said softly. She was just bending forward to kiss him when she heard a familar voice hail her.

"Miss Leiland!"

She turned to find Blaine Farley approaching her, his arm linked close to a supremely satisfied-looking Suzanne Gates.

"Why, Mr. Farley," she said. "I didn't realize you were in town."

"Yeah," Noble concurred sardonically. "I woulda thought you'd be one of the first people to greet Venice."

Blaine's mouth opened, but before he could speak Suzanne scooted in front of him, tugging his arm closer still as she said, "There's only one woman that Blaine Farley's gonna be greeting from now on and that's me!"

"Really?" Venice asked interestedly.

"Yup. We're getting married," she said, and with that final bit of information she dragged a bewildered, but not unhappy-looking Blaine after her down the boardwalk.

Noble chuckled after the retreating pair and turned back to Venice.

"Now what?" she asked, a hint of excitement entering her voice. The world, hitherto an interesting place, had suddenly expanded into a rich and spectacular feast awaiting her pleasure.

He tilted her chin up. "There's an expedition being planned along the Amazon that I've been asked to take part in. I am sure we will need someone to coordinate the provisions."

"And you think I could do it?" Venice asked.

"As long as you don't neglect your wardrobe," he answered. "But those people will need to come up with some financing quickly if they're to get the expedition under way before the coming rainy season."

"I could back them," Venice offered.

"With what money?" Noble asked sardonically. "Once Trevor hears about me he'll more than likely disown you."

Venice bit her lip. "Perhaps."

"Does that bother you?"

"No."

"What are you thinking about, then? You look like you're plotting something."

"I was wondering how I could convince Uncle Milton to make me his heir. Lavender soap is expensive."

Noble shouted with laughter.

"Are there any other alternatives to the Amazon expedition?" she asked.

"Well," he said slowly, "I have been in touch with a gentleman regarding making an assessment of resources in a rather large section of unexplored land . . ."

"Really? Where?"

"Alaska."

"You're teasing me."

"No. Mr. Seward has been badgering me to do an exploration of the southern coastline. I haven't had the time so far."

"Will you do it?"

"You mean will *we* do it?"

She nodded happily.

"If you think it sounds like fun."

"Oh, I do," she breathed.

Noble laughed. "Save your avowals for the priest later—"

"Tonight," Venice finished for him and leaned against his arm. She was just in the process of pulling his handsome face down for another kiss, reveling in the fact that she could have kisses on demand, when a voice caught her attention.

"You!"

She looked up.

Cassius Thornton Reed stood fifty yards down the boardwalk. He was white-faced and bleary-eyed and wobbling. It was obvious he had just staggered through the still-swinging doors of one of the seedier saloons, and he was staring at Venice in absolute horror.

"They said you weren't dead. I didn't believe them. I still don't. You're a ghost!"

His bloodshot eyes flickered to Noble. "And you! You're dead. I saw you go under after I kicked you off—"

Noble heard Venice growl. There was no other word for it. And then she was running down the walkway, her skirts flapping around her knees as she launched herself at Cassius, who was transfixed with dread, riveted by the sight of her.

Noble raced after her, managing to catch hold of her just before she reached Cassius. Lord, the woman could run! He swung an arm around her waist, scooped her up and held her tightly against his side. She struggled wildly in his embrace. Grunting, Noble shifted her weight so she dangled from the waist, arms and legs, windmilling wildly, mouth sputtering furiously.

"Let me down!" she cried. "Let—me—down! You heard what Crooked Hand said. He kicked you into the river—on purpose! He coulda *killed* you! Lemme go!"

"Now, Venice," Noble said soothingly as he struggled to hold on to her.

"Don't let her go, McCaneaghy." Apparently, Cassius had decided that Venice wasn't a ghost after all. He was groping his way backward, his face twitching with various emotions, mostly fear.

Looking down at the hissing, arm-swinging, leg-thrashing woman at his side, Noble could almost sympathize.

Suddenly one of Venice's boots made contact with Noble's shin. Bellowing, he loosened his grip. Immediately, she took advantage, scrambling free and dropping to her hands and knees on the sidewalk. Her hair, having tumbled loose during her struggle, streamed over her face. She crouched for a second, feral and intent, like a she-cat about to spring.

Cassius took one look at the enraged thing in front of him and jumped back. Too late. Venice uncoiled, hurling herself at him.

"Don't you ever, *ever* try to hurt Noble again!" she shouted, and swung straight from the shoulder in a magnificent roundhouse punch. Her fist slammed into Cassius's face. For a second he teetered, a comical expression of incredulity stamped on his face. Then he collapsed.

Immediately, Venice started dancing around, frantically shaking her hand and yipping, "Ow! Ow! Ow!"

"Satisfied?" Noble asked.

Grimacing, Venice looked down at the unconscious man at her feet. She nudged Cassius's body with her toe. It didn't look like she was being too gentle about it, either. She looked up and, without the least trace of sheepishness, grinned at Noble. "Only if his jaw's broken," she declared unrepentantly.

She was completely irresistible. In an instant, Noble was before her, pulling her into his arms. Lifting her high against his chest, he held her in a tight embrace and bent close, smiling. His lips were a hair breadth from hers and closing fast when she heard him whisper, laughter threading his voice, "My hero!"

Author's Note

Much of the enjoyment I get from writing romances come from weaving fact into fiction. While researching *Anything for Love*, I read anecdotes, diaries, and various accounts of daily life that were often as entertaining and outlandish as anything I could invent. So I used them. While Reverend Niss and the Grundys are fictional characters, the "revival meeting" and "prehistoric man" have their basis in fact. Were I to follow history further, the Grundys would end up displaying their "fossil" at the Centennial Exposition in Philadelphia in 1876 and Reverend Niss would be jailed in Chicago shortly thereafter.

Dinosaur bones were not actually discovered in Colorado until 1878, and then they were found far west of the site where I place Milton and Carter. But perhaps there are others still waiting in some deep rock fold . . .

And finally, the Yellowstone National Park was created by an Act of Congress in 1873 upon the recommendation of people committed to ensuring future generations a part of our natural heritage.